PRAISE FOR DEAN R KOONTZ
THE No. 1 BESTSELLING AUTHOR

THE BAD PLACE
'He combines rich, evocative prose, some of the
warmest — and also some of the most despicable —
characters to be found in fiction, technical speculations
that seem to come directly from today's headlines and
a sense of on-the-edge-of-the-seat pacing to create
thrillers that are not just convincing, but thought-
provoking as well'   *Mystery Scene*

MIDNIGHT
'A triumph'   *New York Times*

LIGHTNING
'[It] sizzles . . . Wow! It's a mix to tingle any reader's
fancy'   *New York Daily News*

WATCHERS
'His best story yet. A tightly woven plot . . . this is the
sort of thoroughly frightening and entertaining tale that
has its readers listening for noises in the night'
                                      Publishers Weekly

THE MASK
'A master of sheer fright!'   *Florida Times-Union*

THE FACE OF FEAR
'Super suspenseful with a double-take finish'
Observer

TWILIGHT EYES
'A spine-chilling adventure . . . will keep you turning
pages to the very end!'   *Rave Reviews*

STRANGERS
'The best novel he has written'   Stephen King

PHANTOMS
'A grabber. You will read with nail-biting compulsion!'
Bestsellers

WHISPERS
'Pulls out all the stops . . . an incredible, terrifying tale'
Publishers Weekly

NIGHT CHILLS
'Will send chills down your back!' *New York Times*

SHATTERED
'A chilling tale . . . sleek as a bullet' *Publishers Weekly*

THE VISION
'Kept me glued to my chair . . . sinister and spine-
tingling. Page-turning excitement'   *Spectator*

THE VOICE OF THE NIGHT
'A fearsome tour of an adolescent's tortured psyche.
Terrifying, knee-knocking suspense'
Chicago Sun Times

CHASE
'This superb book is more than a novel of suspense. It
is a brutally realistic portrait of the role of violence in
our society'   *Saturday Review*

Also by Dean R Koontz from Headline

The Bad Place
Midnight
Lightning
Watchers
The Mask
The Face of Fear
Twilight Eyes
Strangers
Phantoms
Whispers
Night Chills
Shattered
The Vision
The Voice of the Night
Chase
Darkness Comes

The Servants of Twilight

Dean R Koontz

Previously published as
The Servants of Twilight
by Leigh Nichols

Previously published as THE SERVANTS OF TWILIGHT under
the pseudonym Leigh Nichols

The author gratefully acknowledges permission to quote from
Something Wicked This Way Comes © 1962 by Ray Bradbury,
permission granted by Simon & Schuster, Inc., 130 Avenue of the
Americas, New York, New York 10020.

First published in Great Britain in 1985 by Fontana Paperbacks,
a division of William Collins Sons & Co

Reprinted in this edition in 1991
by HEADLINE BOOK PUBLISHING PLC

A HEADLINE FEATURE paperback

10 9 8 7 6 5 4 3 2

ISBN 0 7472 3638 0

Typeset by Medcalf Type Ltd, Bicester, Oxon
Printed and bound by Collins Manufacturing, Glasgow

HEADLINE BOOK PUBLISHING PLC
Headline House, 79 Great Titchfield Street, London W1P 7FN

This book is dedicated to very special people, George and Jane Smith — and to their lovely offspring, Diana Summers, and to their cats. May they have all the success and happiness they so well deserve. (I mean, of course, George and Jane and Diana, not the cats.) And may they have much fun catching mice and singing on backyard fences. (That is, the *cats*, not George, Jane and Diana.)

PART ONE
The Hag

An' all us other children, when
  the supper things is done,
We sit around the kitchen fire
  an' has the mostest fun
A-list-nin' to the witch-tales
  that Annie tells about,
An' the Gobble'uns that gits you
If you
    Don't
      Watch
        Out!

— *Little Orphant Annie*,
James Whitcomb Riley

*. . . the Dust Witch came, mumbling. A moment later,
looking up, Will saw her. Not dead! he thought. Carried
off, bruised, fallen, yes, but now back, and mad! Lord,
yes, mad, looking especially for me!*

— *Something Wicked This Way Comes*,
Ray Bradbury

1

It began in sunshine, not on a dark and stormy night.

She wasn't prepared for what happened, wasn't on guard. Who would have expected trouble on a lovely Sunday afternoon like that?

The sky was clear and blue. It was surprisingly warm, for the end of February, even in southern California. The breeze was gentle and scented with winter flowers. It was one of those days when everyone seemed destined to live forever.

Christine Scavello had gone to South Coast Plaza in Costa Mesa to do some shopping, and she had taken Joey with her. He liked the big mall. He was fascinated by the stream that splashed through one wing of the building, down the middle of the public promenade and over a gentle waterfall. He was also intrigued by the hundreds of trees and plants that thrived indoors, and he was a born people-watcher. But most of all he liked the carousel in the center courtyard. In return for one ride on the carousel, he would tag along happily and quietly while Christine spent two or three hours shopping.

Joey was a good kid, the best. He never whined, never threw tantrums or complained. Trapped in the house on a long, rainy day, he could entertain himself for hour after hour and not once grow bored or restless or crabby the way most kids would.

To Christine, Joey sometimes seemed to be a little old

3

man in a six-year-old boy's small body. Occasionally he said the most amazingly grown-up things, and he usually had the patience of an adult, and he was often wiser than his years.

But at other times, especially when he asked where his daddy was or why his daddy had gone away — or even when he *didn't* ask but just stood there with the question shimmering in his eyes — he looked so innocent, fragile, heartbreakingly vulnerable that she just had to grab him and hug him.

Sometimes the hugging wasn't merely an expression of her love for him, but also evasion of the issue that he had raised. She had never found a way to tell him about his father, and it was a subject she wished he would just drop until *she* was ready to bring it up. He was too young to understand the truth, and she didn't want to lie to him — not *too* blatantly, anyway — or resort to cutesy euphemisms.

He had asked about his father just a couple of hours ago, on the way to the mall. She had said, 'Honey, your daddy just wasn't ready for the responsibility of a family.'

'Didn't he like me?'

'He never even *knew* you, so how could he not like you? He was gone before you were born.'

'Oh, yeah? How could I have been borned if he wasn't here?' the boy asked sceptically.

'That's something you'll learn in sex education class at school,' she had said, amused.

'When?'

'Oh, in about six or seven more years, I guess.'

'That's a long time to wait.' He had sighed. 'I'll bet he didn't like me and that's why he went away.'

Frowning, she had said, 'You put that thought right out of your mind, sugar. It was *me* your daddy didn't like.'

'You? He didn't like you?'

4

'That's right.'

Joey had been silent for a block or two, but finally he had said, 'Boy, if he didn't like you, he musta been just plain *dumb*.'

Then, apparently sensing that the subject made her uneasy, he had changed it. A little old man in a six-year-old boy's small body.

The fact was that Joey was the result of a brief, passionate, reckless, and *stupid* affair. Sometimes, looking back on it, she couldn't believe that she had been so naive . . . or so desperate to prove her womanhood and independence. It was the only relationship in Christine's life that qualified as a 'fling,' the only time she had ever been swept away. For that man, for no other man before or since, for *that* man alone, she had put aside her morals and principles and common sense, heeding only the urgent desires of her flesh. She had told herself that it was Romance with a capital R, not just love but the Big Love, even Love At First Sight. Actually she had just been weak, vulnerable, and eager to make a fool of herself. Later, when she realized that Mr. Wonderful had lied to her and used her with cold, cynical disregard for her feelings, when she discovered that she had given herself to a man who was utterly without respect for her and who lacked even a minimal sense of responsibility, she had been deeply ashamed. Eventually she realized there was a point at which shame and remorse became self-indulgent and nearly as lamentable as the sin that had occasioned those emotions, so she put the shabby episode behind her and vowed to forget it.

Except that Joey kept asking who his father was, where his father was, why his father had gone away. And how did you tell a six-year-old about your libidinous urges, the treachery of your own heart, and your regrettable capacity for occasionally making a complete fool of yourself? If it could be done, she hadn't seen the way. She was just going to have to wait until he was grown up enough to understand that adults could sometimes be just as dumb and confused as little kids. Until then, she stalled him with vague answers and evasions that satisfied neither of them.

She only wished he wouldn't look quite so lost, quite so small and vulnerable when he asked about his father. It made her want to cry.

She was haunted by the vulnerability she perceived in him. He was never ill, an extremely healthy child, and she was grateful for that. Nevertheless, she was always reading magazine and newspaper articles about childhood diseases, not merely polio and measles and whooping cough — he had been immunized for those and more — but horrible, crippling, incurable illnesses, often rare although no less frightening for their rarity. She memorized the early-warning signs of a hundred exotic maladies and was always on the watch for those symptoms in Joey. Of course, like any active boy, he suffered his share of cuts and bruises, and the sight of his blood always scared the hell out of her, even if it was only one drop from a shallow scratch. Her concern about Joey's health was almost an obsession, but she never quite allowed it to actually *become* an obsession, for she was aware of the psychological problems that could develop in a child with an overly protective mother.

That Sunday afternoon in February, when death suddenly stepped up and grinned at Joey, it wasn't in the form of the viruses and bacteria about which Christine worried. It was just an old woman with stringy gray hair, a pallid face, and gray eyes the shade of dirty ice.

When Christine and Joey left the mall by way of Bullock's Department Store, it was five minutes past three. Sun glinted off automobile chrome and windshield glass from one end of the broad parking lot to the other. Their

6

silver-gray Pontiac Firebird was in the row directly in front of Bullock's doors, the twelfth car in the line, and they were almost to it when the old woman appeared.

She stepped out from between the Firebird and a white Ford van, directly into their path.

She didn't seem threatening at first. She was a bit odd, sure, but nothing worse than that. Her shoulder-length mane of thick gray hair looked windblown, although only a mild breeze washed across the lot. She was in her sixties, perhaps even early seventies, forty years older than Christine, but her face wasn't deeply lined, and her skin was baby-smooth; she had the unnatural puffiness that was often associated with cortisone injections. Pointed nose. Small mouth, thick lips. A round, dimpled chin. She was wearing a simple turquoise necklace, a long-sleeved green blouse, green skirt, green shoes. On her plump hands were eight rings, all green: turquoise, malachite, emeralds. The unrelieved green suggested a uniform of some kind.

She blinked at Joey, grinned, and said, 'My heavens, aren't you a handsome young man?'

Christine smiled. Unsolicited compliments from strangers were nothing new to Joey. With his dark hair, intense blue eyes, and well-related features, he was a strikingly good-looking child.

'Yes, sir, a regular little movie star,' the old woman said.

'Thank you,' Joey said, blushing.

Christine got a closer look at the stranger and had to revise her initial impression of grandmotherliness. There were specks of lint on the old woman's badly wrinkled skirt, two small food stains on her blouse, and a sprinkling of dandruff on her shoulder. Her stockings bagged at the knees, and the left one had a run in it. She was holding a smouldering cigarette, and the fingers of her right hand were yellow with nicotine. She was one of those people from whom kids should never accept candy or cookies or any other treat — not because she seemed the type to poison or molest children (which she did not), but because she seemed the type to keep a dirty kitchen. Even on close inspection, she didn't appear dangerous, just unkempt.

Leaning toward Joey, grinning down at him, paying no attention whatever to Christine, she said, 'What's your name, young man? Can you tell me your name?'

'Joey,' he said shyly.

'How old are you, Joey?'

'Six.'

'Only six and already pretty enough to make the ladies swoon!'

Joey fidgeted with embarrassment and clearly wished he could bolt for the car. But he stayed where he was and behaved courteously, the way his mother had taught him.

The old woman said, 'I'll bet a dollar to a doughnut that I know your birthday.'

'I don't have a doughnut,' Joey said, taking the bet literally, solemnly warning her that he wouldn't be able to pay off if he lost.

'Isn't that cute?' the old woman said to him. 'So perfectly, wonderfully cute. But I *know*. You were born on Christmas Eve.'

'Nope,' Joey said. 'Febroonary second.'

'February second? Oh, now, don't joke around with me,' she said, still ignoring Christine, still grinning broadly at Joey, wagging one nicotine-yellowed finger at him. 'Sure as shootin', you were born December twenty-fourth.'

Christine wondered what the old woman was leading up to.

Joey said, 'Mom, you tell her. Febroonary second. Does she owe me a dollar?'

'No, she doesn't owe you anything, honey,' Christine said. 'It wasn't a real bet.'

'Well,' he said, 'if I'd lost, I couldn't've given her any doughnut anyway, so I guess it's okay if she don't give me a dollar.'

Finally the old woman raised her head and looked at Christine.

Christine started to smile but stopped when she saw the stranger's eyes. They were hard, cold, angry. They were neither the eyes of a grandmother nor those of a harmless old bag lady. There was power in them − and stubbornness and flinty resolve. The woman wasn't smiling any more, either.

What's going on here?

Before Christine could speak, the woman said, 'He was born on Christmas Eve, wasn't he? Hmmm? Wasn't he?' She spoke with such urgency, with such force that she sprayed spittle at Christine. She didn't wait for an answer, either, but hurried on: 'You're lying about February second. You're just trying to hide, both of you, but I know the truth. I know. You can't fool me. Not *me*.'

Suddenly she seemed dangerous, after all.

Christine put a hand on Joey's shoulder and urged him around the crone, toward the car.

But the woman stepped sideways, blocking them. She waved her cigarette at Joey, glared at him, and said, 'I know who you are. I know *what* you are, everything about you, everything. Better believe it. Oh, yes, yes, I know, yes.'

A nut, Christine thought, and her stomach twisted. Jesus. A crazy old lady, the kind who might be capable of anything. God, please let her be harmless.

Looking bewildered, Joey backed away from the woman, grabbed his mother's hand and squeezed tight.

'Please get out of our way,' Christine said, trying to maintain a calm and reasonable tone of voice, wanting very much not to antagonize.

The old woman refused to move. She brought the cigarette to her lips. Her hand was shaking.

Holding Joey's hand, Christine tried to go around the stranger.

But again the woman blocked them. She puffed nervously on her cigarette and blew smoke out her nostrils. She never took her eyes off Joey.

Christine looked around the parking lot. A few people were getting out of a car two rows away, and two young men were at the end of this row, heading in the other direction, but no one was near enough to help if the crazy woman became violent.

Throwing down her cigarette, hyperventilating, eyes bulging, looking like a big malicious toad, the woman said, 'Oh, yeah, I know your ugly, vicious, hateful secrets, you little fraud.'

Christine's heart began to hammer.

'Get out of our way,' she said sharply, no longer trying to remain − or even *able* to remain − calm.

'You can't fool me with your play-acting−'

Joey began to cry.

'− and your phoney cuteness. Tears won't help, either.'

For the third time, Christine tried to go around the woman − and was blocked again.

The harridan's face hardened in anger. 'I know exactly what you are, you little monster.'

Christine shoved, and the old woman stumbled backwards.

Pulling Joey with her, Christine hurried to the car, feeling as if she were in a nightmare, running in slow-motion.

The car door was locked. She was a compulsive door-locker.

She wished that, for once, she had been careless.

The old woman scuttled in behind them, shouting

something that Christine couldn't hear because her ears were filled with the frantic pounding of her heart and with Joey's crying.

'Mom!'

Joey was almost jerked out of her grasp. The old woman had her talons hooked in his shirt.

'Let go of him, damn you!' Christine said.

'Admit it!' the old woman shrieked at him. 'Admit what you are!'

Christine shoved again.

The woman wouldn't let go.

Christine struck her, open-handed, first on the shoulder, then across the face.

The old woman tottered backwards, and Joey twisted away from her, and his shirt tore.

Somehow, even with shaking hands, Christine fitted the key into the lock, opened the car door, pushed Joey inside. He scrambled across to the passenger's seat, and she got behind the wheel and pulled the door shut with immense relief. Locked it.

The old woman peered in the driver's-side window. 'Listen to me!' she shouted. 'Listen!'

Christine jammed the key in the ignition, switched it on, pumped the accelerator. The engine roared.

With one milk-white fist, the crazy woman thumped the roof of the car. Again. And again.

Christine put the Firebird in gear and backed out of the parking space, moving slowly, not wanting to hurt the old woman, just wanting to get the hell away from her.

The lunatic followed, shuffling along, bent over, holding on to the door handle, glaring at Christine. 'He's got to die. He's got to die.'

Sobbing, Joey said, 'Mom, don't let her get me!'

'She won't get you, honey,' Christine said, her mouth so dry that she was barely able to get the words out.

The boy huddled against his locked door, eyes streaming tears but open wide and fixed on the contorted face of the stringy-haired harpy at his mother's window.

Still in reverse, Christine accelerated a bit, turned the wheel, and nearly backed into another car that was coming slowly down the row. The other driver blew his horn, and Christine stopped just in time, with a harsh bark of brakes.

'*He's got to die!*' the old woman screamed. She slammed the side of one pale fist into the window almost hard enough to break the glass.

This can't be happening, Christine thought. Not on a sunny Sunday. Not in peaceful Costa Mesa.

The old woman struck the window again.

'*He's got to die!*'

Spittle sprayed the glass.

Christine had the car in gear and was moving away, but the old woman held on. Christine accelerated. Still, the woman kept a grip on the door handle, slid and ran and stumbled along with the car, ten feet, twenty, thirty feet, faster, faster still. Christ, was she human? Where did such an old woman find the strength and tenacity to hold on like this? She leered in through the side window, and there was such ferocity in her eyes that it wouldn't have surprised Christine if, in spite of her size and age, the hag had torn the door off. But at last she let go with a howl of anger and frustration.

At the end of the row, Christine turned right. She drove too fast through the parking lot, and in less than a minute they were away from the mall, on Bristol Street, heading north.

Joey was still crying, though more softly than before.

'It's all right, sweetheart. It's okay now. She's gone.'

She drove to MacArthur Boulevard, turned right, went three blocks, repeatedly glancing in the rearview mirror to see if they were being followed, even though she knew there wasn't much chance of that. Finally she pulled over to the curb and stopped.

She was shaking. She hoped Joey wouldn't notice.

Pulling a Kleenex from the small box on the console, she said, 'Here you are, honey. Dry your eyes, blow your nose, and be brave for Mommy. Okay?'

'Okay,' he said, accepting the tissue. Shortly, he was composed.

'Feeling better?' she asked.

'Yeah. Sorta.'

'Scared?'

'I was.'

'But not now?'

He shook his head.

'You know,' Christine said, 'she really didn't mean all those nasty things she said to you.'

He looked at her, puzzled. His lower lip trembled, but his voice was steady. 'Then why'd she say it if she didn't mean it?'

'Well, she couldn't help herself. She was a sick lady.'

'You mean . . . like sick with the flu?'

'No, honey. I mean . . . mentally ill . . . disturbed.'

'She was a real Looney Tune, huh?'

He had gotten that expression from Val Gardner, Christine's business partner. This was the first time she'd heard him use it, and she wondered what other, less socially acceptable words he might have picked up from the same source.

'Was she a real Looney Tune, Mom? Was she crazy?'

'Mentally disturbed, yes.'

He frowned.

She said, 'That doesn't make it any easier to understand, huh?'

'Nope. 'Cause what does crazy really mean, anyway, if it doesn't mean being locked up in a rubber room? And

13

even if she was a crazy old lady, why was she so mad at me? Huh? I never even saw her before.'

'Well . . .'

How do you explain psychotic behaviour to a six-year-old? She could think of no way to do it without being ridiculously simplistic; however, in this case, a simplistic answer was better than none.

'Maybe she once had a little boy of her own, a little boy she loved very much, but maybe he wasn't a good little boy like you. Maybe he grew up to be very bad and did a lot of terrible things that broke his mother's heart. Something like that could . . . unbalance her a little.'

'So now maybe she hates *all* little boys, whether she knows them or not,' he said.

'Yes, perhaps.'

'Because they remind her of her own little boy? Is that it?'

'That's right.'

He thought about it for a moment, then nodded. 'Yeah. I can sorta see how that could be.'

She smiled at him and mussed his hair. 'Hey, I'll tell you what — let's stop at Baskin-Robbins and get an ice cream cone. I think their flavour of the month is peanut butter and chocolate. That's one of your favorites, isn't it?'

He was obviously surprised. She didn't approve of too much fat in his diet, and she planned his meals carefully. Ice cream wasn't a frequent indulgence. He seized the moment and said, 'Could I have one scoop of that and one scoop of lemon custard?'

'*Two* scoops?'

'It's Sunday,' he said.

'Last time I looked, Sunday wasn't so all fired special. There's one of them every week. Or has that changed while I wasn't paying attention?'

'Well . . . but . . . see, I've just had . . .' He screwed

14

up his face, thinking hard. He worked his mouth as if chewing on a piece of taffy, then said, 'I've just had a . . . a traumamatatic experience.'

'Traumatic experience?'

'Yeah. That's it.'

She blinked at him. 'Where'd you get a big word like that? Oh. Of course. Never mind. Val.'

According to Valerie Gardner, who was given to theatrics, just getting up in the morning was a traumatic experience. Val had about half a dozen traumatic experiences every day – and thrived on them.

'So it's Sunday, and I had this traumatic experience,' Joey said, 'and I think maybe what I better do is, I better have two scoops of ice cream to make up for it. You know?'

'I know I'd better not hear about *another* traumatic experience for at least ten years.'

'What about the ice cream?'

She looked at his torn shirt. 'Two scoops,' she agreed.

'Wow! This is some terrific day, isn't it? A real Looney Tune and a double-dip ice cream!'

Christine never ceased to be amazed by the resiliency of children, especially the resiliency of this child. Already, in his mind, he had transmuted the encounter with the old woman, had changed it from a moment of terror to an adventure that was not quite – but almost – as good as a visit to an ice cream parlour.

'You're some kid,' she said.

'You're some mom.'

He turned on the radio and hummed along happily with the music, all the way to Baskin-Robbins.

Christine kept checking the rearview mirror. No one was following them. She was sure of that. But she kept checking anyway.

2

After a light dinner at the kitchen table with Joey, Christine went to her desk in the den to catch up on paperwork. She and Val Gardner owned a gourmet shop called Wine & Dine in Newport Beach, where they sold fine wines, specialty foods from all over the world, high quality cooking utensils, and slightly exotic appliances like pasta-makers and espresso machines. The store was in its sixth year of operation and was solidly established; in fact, it was returning considerably more profit than either Christine or Val had ever dared hope when they'd first opened their doors for business. Now, they were planning to open a second outlet this summer, then a third store in West Los Angeles sometime next year. Their success was exciting and gratifying, but the business demanded an ever-increasing amount of their time. This wasn't the first weekend evening that she had spent catching up on paperwork.

She wasn't complaining. Before Wine & Dine, she had worked as a waitress, six days a week, holding down two jobs at the same time: a four-hour lunch shift in a diner and a six-hour dinner shift at a moderately expensive French restaurant, Chez Lavelle. Because she was a polite and attentive waitress who hustled her butt off, the tips had been good at the diner and excellent at Chez Lavelle, but after a few years the work numbed and aged her: the sixty-hour weeks; the busboys who often came to work so high on drugs that she had to cover for them and do two jobs instead of one; the lecherous guys who ate lunch at the diner and who could be gross and obnoxious and frighteningly persistent, but who had to be turned down with coquettish good humor for the sake of business. She spent so many hours on her feet that, on her day off, she did nothing but sit with her aching legs raised on an ottoman while she read the Sunday papers with special attention to the financial section, dreaming of one day owning her *own* business.

But because of the tips and because she lived frugally – even doing without a car for two years – she had eventually managed to put enough aside to pay for a one-week cruise to Mexico aboard a luxury liner, the *Aztec Princess*, and had accumulated a nest egg large enough to provide half the cash with which she and Val had launched their gourmet shop. Both the cruise and the shop had radically changed her life.

And if spending too many evenings doing paperwork was better than working as a waitress, it was immeasurably better than the two years of her life that had preceded her jobs at the diner and Chez Lavelle. The Lost Years. That was how she thought of that time, now far in the past: the bleak, miserable, sad and stupid Lost Years.

Compared to *that* period of her life, paperwork was a pleasure, a delight, a veritable *carnival* of fun . . .

She had been at her desk more than an hour when she realized that Joey had been exceptionally quiet ever since she'd come into the den. Of course, he was never a noisy child. Often he played by himself for hours, hardly making a sound. But after the unnerving encounter with the old woman this afternoon, Christine was still a little jumpy, and even this perfectly ordinary silence suddenly seemed strange and threatening. She wasn't exactly frightened. Just anxious. If anything happened to Joey . . .

She put down her pen and switched off the softly humming adding machine. She listened.

Nothing.

In an echo chamber of memory, she could hear the old woman's voice: *He's got to die, he's got to die . . .*

17

She rose, left the den, quickly crossed the living room, went down the hall to the boy's bedroom.

The door was open, the light on, and he was there, safe, playing on the floor with their dog, Brandy, a sweet-faced and infinitely patient golden retriever.

'Hey, Mom, wanna play *Star Wars* with us? I'm Han Solo, and Brandy's my buddy, Chewbacca the Wookie. You could be the princess if you want.'

Brandy was sitting in the middle of the floor, between the bed and the sliding closet doors. He was wearing a baseball cap emblazoned with the words RETURN OF THE JEDI, and his long fur ears hung out from the sides of it. Joey had also strapped a bandoleer of plastic bullets around the pooch, plus a holster containing a futuristic-looking plastic gun. Panting, eyes bright, Brandy was taking it all in stride; he even seemed to be smiling.

'He makes a great Wookie,' Christine said.

'Wanna play?'

'Sorry, Skipper, but I've got an awful lot of work to do. I just stopped by to see if . . . if you were okay.'

'Well, what happened is that we almost got vaporized by an empire battle cruiser,' Joey said. 'But we're okay now.'

Brandy snuffled in agreement.

She smiled at Joey. 'Watch out for Darth Vader.'

'Oh, yeah, sure, *always*. We're being super careful 'cause we know he's in this part of the galaxy somewhere.'

'See you in a little while.'

She took only one step toward the door before Joey said, 'Mom? Are you afraid that crazy old lady's going to show up again?'

Christine turned to him. 'No, no,' she said, although that was precisely what had been in her mind. 'She can't possibly know who we are or where we live.'

Joey's eyes were even a more brilliant shade of blue than

18

usual; they met her own eyes unwaveringly, and there was disquiet in them. 'I told her my name, Mom. Remember? She asked me, and I told her my name.'

'Only your first name.'

He frowned. 'Did I?'

'You just said, "Joey." '

'Yeah that's right.'

'Don't worry honey. You'll never see her again. That's all over and done with. She was just a sad old woman who — '

'What about our license plate?'

'What about it?'

'Well, see, if she got the number, maybe there's some way she can use it. To find out who we are. Like they sometimes do on those detective shows on TV.'

That possibility disconcerted her, but she said, 'I doubt it. I think only policemen can track down a car's owner from the license number.'

'But just maybe,' the boy said worriedly.

'We pulled away from her so fast she didn't have time to memorize the number. Besides, she was hysterical. She wasn't thinking clearly enough to study the license plate. Like I told you, it's all over and done with. Really. Okay?'

He hesitated a moment, then said, 'Okay. But, Mom, I been thinking . . .'

'What?'

'That crazy old lady . . . could she've been . . . a witch?'

Christine almost laughed, but she saw that he was serious. She suppressed all evidence of her amusement, put on a sober expression that matched the grave look on his face, and said, 'Oh, I'm sure she wasn't a witch.'

'I don't mean like Broom Hilda. I mean a *real* witch. A real witch wouldn't need our license number, you know? She wouldn't need anything. She'd sniff us out. There's no place in the whole universe where you can hide when there's a witch after you. Witches have magic powers.'

He was either already certain that the old woman was a witch or was rapidly convincing himself of it. Either way, he was scaring himself unnecessarily because, after all, they really never would see her again.

Christine remembered the way that strange woman had clung to the car, jerking at the handle of the locked door, keeping pace with them as they pulled away, screeching crazy accusations at them. Her eyes and face had radiated both fury and a disturbing power that made it seem as if she might really be able to stop the Firebird with her bare hands. A witch? That a child might think she had supernatural powers was certainly understandable.

'A real witch,' Joey repeated, a tremor in his voice.

Christine was aware that she had to snip this line of thought right away, before he became obsessed with witches. Last year, for almost two months, he had been certain that a magical white snake — like one he'd seen in a movie — was hiding in his room, waiting for him to go to sleep, so that it could slither out and bite him. She'd had to sit with him each evening until he'd fallen asleep. Frequently, when he awakened in the middle of the night, she had to take him into her own bed in order to settle him down. He'd gotten over the snake thing the same day that she'd made up her mind to take him to a child psychologist; later, she'd cancelled the appointment. After a few weeks had passed, when she'd been sure that mentioning the snake wouldn't get him started on it again, she asked what had happened to it. He looked embarrassed and said, 'It was only 'magination, Mom. I sure was acting like a dumb little kid, huh?' He'd never mentioned the white snake again. He possessed a healthy, rampaging imagination, and it was up to her to rein it in when it got out of control. Like now.

Although she had to put an end to this witch stuff, she couldn't just tell him there was no such thing. If she tried that approach, he would think she was just babying him. She would have to go along with his assumption that witches were real, then use the logic of a child to make him see that the old woman in the parking lot couldn't possibly have been a witch.

She said, 'Well, I can understand how you might wonder about her being a witch. Whew! I mean, she did look a little bit like a witch is supposed to look, didn't she?'

'More than a little bit.'

'No, no, just a little bit. Let's be fair to the poor old lady.'

'She looked *exactly* like a mean witch,' he said. 'Exactly. Didn't she, Brandy?'

The dog snorted as if he understood the question and was in full agreement with his young master.

Christine squatted, scratched the dog behind the ears, and said, 'What do you know about it, fur-face? You weren't even there.'

Brandy yawned.

To Joey, Christine said, 'If you really think about it, she didn't look all that much like a witch.'

'Her eyes were creepy,' the boy insisted, 'bugging out of her head like they did. You saw them, sort of wild, Jeez, and her frizzy hair just like a witch's hair.'

'But she didn't have a big crooked nose with a wart on the tip of it, did she?'

'No,' Joey admitted.

'And she wasn't dressed in black, was she?'

'No. But all in *green*,' Joey said, and from his tone of voice it was clear that the old woman's outfit had seemed as odd to him as it had to Christine.

'Witches don't wear green. She wasn't wearing a tall, pointed black hat, either.'

He shrugged.

'And she didn't have a cat with her,' Christine said.

'So?'

'A witch never goes anywhere without her cat.'

'She doesn't?'

'No. It's her familiar.'

'What's that mean?'

'The witch's familiar is her contact with the devil. It's through the familiar, through the cat, that the devil gives her magic powers. Without the cat, she's just an ugly old woman.'

'You mean like the cat watches her and makes sure she doesn't do something the devil wouldn't like?'

'That's right.'

'I didn't see any cat,' Joey said, frowning.

'There wasn't a cat because she wasn't a witch. You've got nothing to worry about, honey.'

His face brightened. 'Boy, that's a relief! If she'd been a witch, she might've turned me into a toad or something.'

'Well, life as a toad might not be so bad,' she teased. 'You'd get to sit on a lily pad all day, just taking it easy.'

'Toads eat flies,' he said, grimacing, 'and I can't even stand to eat *veal*.'

She laughed, leaned forward, and kissed his cheek.

'Even if she was a witch,' he said, 'I'd probably be okay because I've got Brandy, and Brandy wouldn't let any old cat get anywhere near.'

'You can rely on Brandy,' Christine agreed. She looked at the clown-faced dog and said, 'You're the nemesis of all cats and witches, aren't you, fur-face?'

To her surprise, Brandy thrust his muzzle forward and licked her under the chin.

'Yuck,' she said. 'No offense, fur-face, but I'm not sure whether kissing you is any better than eating flies.'

Joey giggled and hugged the dog. Christine returned to

22

the den. The mound of paperwork seemed to have grown taller while she was gone.

She had no sooner settled into the chair behind the desk than the telephone rang. She picked it up.

'Hello?'

No one answered.

'Hello?' she said again.

'Wrong number,' a woman said softly and hung up.

Christine put the receiver down and went back to work. She didn't give the call a second thought.

3

She was awakened by Brandy's barking, which was unusual because Brandy hardly ever barked. Then she heard Joey's voice.

'Mom! Come quick! *Mommy!*'

He wasn't merely calling her; he was *screaming* for her.

As she threw back the covers and got out of bed, she saw the glowing red numbers on the digital alarm clock. It was 1:20 A.M.

She plunged across the room, through the open door, into the hall, headed toward Joey's room, flipping up light switches as she went.

Joey was sitting in bed, pressing back against the headboard as if he were trying to pass through it and slip magically into the wall behind it, where he could hide. His hands were filled with twisted lumps of sheet and blanket. His face was pale.

Brandy was at the window, forepaws up on the sill. He was barking at something in the night beyond the glass.

When Christine entered the room, the dog stopped barking, padded to the bed, and looked inquiringly at Joey, as if seeking guidance.

'Someone was out there,' the boy said. 'Looking in. It was that crazy old lady.'

Christine went to the window. There wasn't much light. The yellowish glow of the streetlamp at the corner didn't reach quite this far. Although a moon ornamented the sky, it wasn't a full moon, and it cast only a weak, milky light that frosted the sidewalks, silvered the cars parked along the street, but revealed few of the night's secrets. For the most part, the lawn and shrubbery lay in deep darkness.

'Is she still out there?' Joey asked.

'No,' Christine said.

She turned away from the window, went to him, sat on the edge of his bed.

He was still pale. Shaking.

She said, 'Honey, are you sure —'

'She was there!'

'Exactly what did you see?'

'Her face.'

'The old woman?'

'Yeah.'

'You're sure it was her, not somebody else?'

He nodded. 'Her.'

'It's so dark out there. How could you see well enough to —'

'I saw somebody at the window, just sort of a shadow in the moonlight, and then what I did was I turned on the light, and it was her. I could see. It was *her*.'

'But, honey, I just don't think there's any way she could have followed us. I know she didn't. And there's no way she could've learned where we live. Not this soon, anyway.'

He said nothing. He just stared down at his fisted hands

and slowly let go of the sheet and blanket. His palms were sweaty.

Christine said, 'Maybe you were dreaming, huh?'

He shook his head vigorously.

She said, 'Sometimes, when you wake up from a nightmare, just a few seconds, you can be sort of confused about what's real and what's just part of the dream. You know? It's all right. It happens to everybody now and then.'

He met her eyes. 'It wasn't like that, Mom. Brandy started barking, and then I woke up, and there was the crazy old lady at the window. If it was just a dream . . . then what was Brandy barking at? He don't bark just to hear himself. Never does. You know how he is.'

She stared at Brandy, who had plopped down on the floor beside the bed, and she began to feel uneasy again. Finally she got up and went to the window.

Out in the night, there were a lot of places where the grip of darkness was firm, places where a prowler could hide and wait.

'Mom?'

She looked at him.

He said, 'This isn't like before.'

'What do you mean?'

'This isn't a 'maginary white snake under my bed. This is *real* stuff. Cross my heart and hope to die.'

A sudden gust of wind soughed through the eaves and rattled a loose rain gutter.

'Come on,' she said, holding out a hand to him.

He scrambled out of bed, and she took him into the kitchen.

Brandy followed. He stood in the doorway for a moment, his bushy tail thumping against both jambs, then came in and curled up in the corner.

Joey sat at the table in his blue pajamas with the words

SATURN PATROL, in red, streaking across his chest. He looked anxiously at the windows over the sink, while Christine telephoned the police.

The two police officers stood on the porch and listened politely while Christine, in the open front door with Joey at her side, told them her story — what little there was to tell. The younger of the two men, Officer Statler, was dubious and quick to conclude that the prowler was merely a phantom of Joey's imagination, but the older man, Officer Templeton, gave them the benefit of the doubt. At Templeton's insistence, he and Statler spent ten minutes searching the property with their long-handled flashlights, probing the shrubbery, circling the house, checking out the garage, even looking in the neighbors' yards. They didn't find anyone.

Returning to the front door where Christine and Joey waited, Templeton seemed somewhat less willing to believe their story than he had been a few minutes ago. 'Well, Mrs. Scavello, if that old woman was around here, she's gone now. Either she wasn't up to much of anything . . . or maybe she was scared away when she saw the patrol car. Maybe both. She's probably harmless.'

'Harmless? She sure didn't seem harmless this afternoon at South Coast Plaza,' Christine said. 'She seemed dangerous enough to me.'

'Well . . .' He shrugged. 'You know how it is. An old lady . . . maybe a little senile . . . saying things she really didn't mean.'

'I don't think that's the case.'

Templeton didn't meet her eyes. 'So . . . if you see her again or if you have any other trouble, be sure to give us a call.'

'You're leaving?'

'Yes, ma'am.'

'You're not going to do anything else?'

He scratched his head. 'Don't see what else we *can* do. You said you don't know this woman's name or where she lives, so we can't go have a chat with her. Like I said, if she shows up again, you call us soon as you spot her, and we'll come back.'

With a nod of his head, he turned away and went down the walk, toward the street, where his partner waited.

A minute later, as Christine and Joey stood at the living room windows, watching the patrol car drive away, the boy said, 'She was out there, Mom. Really, really. This isn't like the snake.'

She believed him. What he had seen at the window could have been a figment of his imagination or an image left over from a nightmare — but it hadn't been that. He had seen what he thought he'd seen: the old woman herself, in the flesh. Christine didn't know why she was so sure of that, but she was. Dead sure.

She gave him the option of spending the rest of the night in her room, but he was determined to be brave.

'I'll sleep in my bed,' he said. 'Brandy'll be there. Brandy'll smell that old witch coming a mile away. But . . . could we sorta leave a lamp on?'

'Sure,' she said, though she had only recently weaned him away from the need for a night light.

In his room she closed the draperies tight, leaving not even a narrow crack through which someone might be able to see him. She tucked him in, kissed him goodnight, and left him in Brandy's care.

Back in her own bed once more, with the lights out, she stared at the tenebrous ceiling. She was unable to sleep. She kept expecting a sudden sound — glass shattering, a door being forced — but the night remained peaceful.

Only the February wind, with an occasional violent gust, marred the nocturnal stillness.

*   *   *

In his room Joey switched off the lamp that his mother had left on for him. The darkness was absolute.

Brandy jumped onto the bed, where he was never supposed to be (one of Mom's rules: no dog in bed), but Joey didn't push him off. Brandy settled down and was welcome.

Joey listened to the night wind sniffing and licking at the house, and it sounded like a living thing. He pulled the blanket all the way up to his nose, as if it were a shield that would protect him from all harm.

After a while he said, 'She's still out there somewhere.'

The dog lifted his square head.

'She's waiting, Brandy.'

The dog raised one ear.

'She'll be back.'

The dog growled in the back of his throat.

Joey put one hand on his furry companion. 'You know it, too, don't you, boy? You know she's out there, don't you?'

Brandy woofed softly.

The wind moaned.

The boy listened.

The night ticked toward dawn.

4

In the middle of the night, unable to sleep, Christine went downstairs to Joey's room to look in on him. The lamp she had left burning was off now, and the bedroom was tomb-black. For a moment fear pinched off her breath.

But when she snapped on the light, she saw that Joey was in bed, asleep, safe.

Brandy was comfortably ensconced in the bed, too, but he woke when she turned on the light. He yawned and licked his chops, and gave her a look that was rich with canine guilt.

'You know the rules, fuzzy-butt,' she whispered. 'On the floor.'

Brandy got off the bed without waking Joey, slunk to the nearest corner, and curled up on the floor. He looked at her sheepishly.

'Good dog,' she whispered.

He wagged his tail, sweeping the carpet around him.

She switched off the light and started back toward her own room. She had gone only a step or two when she heard movement in the boy's room, and she knew it was Bandy returning to the bed. Tonight, however, she just didn't care all that much whether he got dog hairs on the sheets and blankets. Tonight, the only thing that seemed to matter was that Joey was safe.

She returned to her bed and dozed fitfully, tossing and turning, murmuring in her sleep as night crept toward dawn. She dreamed of an old woman with a green face, green hair, and long green fingernails that hooked wickedly into sharp claws.

Monday morning came at last, and it was sunny. Too damned sunny. She woke early, and light spread through her bedroom windows, making her wince. Her eyes were grainy, sensitive, bloodshot.

She took a long, hot shower, steaming away some of her weariness, then dressed for work in a maroon blouse, simple gray skirt, and gray pumps.

Stepping to the full-length mirror on the bathroom door, she examined herself critically, although staring at her reflection always embarrassed her. There was no mystery about her shyness; she knew her embarrassment was a result of the things she had been taught during the Lost Years, between her eighteenth and twentieth birthdays. During that period she had struggled to throw off all vanity and a large measure of her individuality because gray-faced uniformity was what had been demanded of her back then. They had expected her to be humble, self-effacing, and plain. Any concern for her appearance, any slightest pride in her looks, would have brought swift disciplinary action from her superiors. Although she had put those grim lonely years and events behind her, they still had a lingering effect on her that she could not deny.

Now, almost as a test of how completely she had triumphed over the Lost Years, she fought her embarrassment and resolutely studied her mirror image with as much vanity as she could summon from a soul half-purged of it. Her figure was good, though she didn't have the kind of body that, displayed in a bikini, would ever sell a million pin-up posters. Her legs were slender and well shaped. Her hips flared just right, and she was almost too small in the waist, though that smallness made her bustline – which was only average – seem larger than it was. She sometimes wished she were as busty as Val, but Val said that very large breasts were more of a curse than a blessing, that it was like carrying around a pair of saddlebags, and that some evenings her shoulders ached with the strain of that burden. Even if what Val said was true and not just a white lie told out of sympathy for those less amply endowed, Christine nevertheless wished she had big boobs, and she knew that this desire, this hopeless vanity, was a blatant reaction to – and rejection of – all that she had been taught in that gray and dreary place where she had lived between the ages of eighteen and twenty.

By now, her face was flushed, but she forced herself to remain in front of the mirror a minute more, until she had determined that her hair was properly combed and that her makeup was evenly applied. She knew she was pretty. Not gorgeous. But she had a good complexion, a delicate chin and jawline, a good nose. Her eyes were her best feature, large and dark and clear. Her hair was dark, too, almost black. Val said she would trade her big boobs for hair like that any day, but Christine *knew* that was only talk. Sure, her hair looked good when the weather was right, but as soon as the humidity rose past a certain point, it got either lank and flat or frizzy and curly, and then she looked like either Vampira or Gene Shalit.

At last, blushing furiously but feeling that she had triumphed over the excessive self-effacement that had been hammered into her years ago, she turned away from the mirror.

She went to the kitchen to make coffee and toast, and found Joey already at the breakfast table. He wasn't eating, just sitting there, face turned away from her, staring out the window at the sun-splashed rear lawn.

Taking a paper filter from a box and fitting it into the basket of the dripolator, Christine said, 'What can I get for you for breakfast, Skipper?'

He didn't answer.

Spooning coffee into the filter, she said, 'How about cereal and peanut butter toast? English muffins? Maybe you even feel like an egg.'

He still didn't answer. Sometimes – not often – he could be cranky in the morning, but he always could be teased into a better mood. By nature, he was too mild-mannered to remain sullen for long.

Switching on the dripolator and pouring water into the top of it, she said, 'Okay, so if you don't want cereal or toast or an egg, maybe I could fix some spinach, brussel sprouts, and broccoli. They're all your favorites, aren't they?'

He didn't rise to the bait. Just stared out the window. Unmoving. Silent.

'Or I could put one of your old shoes in the microwave and cook it up nice and tender for you. How about that? Nothing's quite as tasty as an old shoe for breakfast. Mmmmmmmm! Really sticks to your ribs.'

He said nothing.

She got the toaster out of the cupboard, put it on the counter, plugged it in — then suddenly realized that the boy wasn't merely being cranky. Something was wrong.

Staring at the back of his head, she said, 'Honey?'

He made a wretched, stifled little sound.

'Honey, what's wrong?'

At last he turned away from the window and looked at her. His tousled hair hung down in his eyes, which were possessed by a haunted look, a bleak expression so stark for a six-year-old that it made Christine's heart beat faster. Bright tears glistened on his cheeks.

She quickly went to him and took his hand. It was cold.

'Sweetheart, what is it? Tell me.'

He wiped at his reddened eyes with his free hand. His nose was runny, and he blotted it on his sleeve.

He was so *pale*.

Whatever was wrong, it wasn't simply a standard complaint, no ordinary childhood trauma. She sensed that much and her mouth went dry with fear.

He tried to speak, couldn't get out even one word, pointed to the kitchen door, took a deep shuddery breath, began to shake, and finally said, 'The p-p-porch.'

'What about the porch?'

He wasn't able to tell her.

Frowning, she went to the door, hesitated, opened it. She gasped, rocked by the sight that awaited her.

Brandy. His furry, golden body lay at the edge of the

porch, near the steps. But his head was immediately in front of the door, at her feet. The dog had been decapitated.

5

Christine and Joey sat on the beige sofa in the living room. The boy was no longer crying, but he still looked stunned.

The policeman filling out the report, Officer Wilford, sat on one of the Queen Anne armchairs. He was tall and husky, with rough features, bushy eyebrows, an air of rugged self-sufficiency: the kind of man who probably felt at home only outdoors and especially in the woods and mountains, hunting and fishing. He perched on the very edge of the chair and held his notebook on his knees, an amusingly prim posture for a man his size; apparently he was concerned about rumpling or soiling the furniture.

'But who let the dog out?' he inquired, after having asked every other question he could think of.

'Nobody,' Christine said. 'He let himself out. There's a pet portal in the bottom of the kitchen door.'

'I saw it,' Wilford said. 'Not big enough for a dog that size.'

'I know. It was here when we bought the house. Brandy hardly ever used it, but if he wanted out badly enough, and if there wasn't anyone around to let him out, he could put his head down, wriggle on his belly, and squeeze through that little door. I kept meaning to have it closed up because I was afraid he might get stuck. If only I *had* closed it up, he might still be alive.'

'The witch got him,' Joey said softly.

33

Christine put an arm around her son.

Wilford said, 'So you think maybe they used meat or dog biscuits to lure him outside?'

'No,' said Joey adamantly, answering for his mother, clearly offended by the suggestion that a gluttonous impulse had led to the dog's death. 'Brandy went out there to protect me. He knew the old witch was still hanging around, and went to get her, but what happened was . . . she got him first.'

Christine was aware that Wilford's suggestion was probably the correct explanation, but she also knew that Joey would find it easier to accept Brandy's death if he could believe that his dog had died in a noble cause. She said, 'He was a very brave dog, very brave, and we're proud of him.'

Wilford nodded. 'Yes, I'm sure you've got every reason to be proud. It's a darned shame. A golden retriever's such a handsome breed. Such a gentle face and sweet disposition.'

'The witch got him,' Joey repeated, as if numbed by that terrible realization.

'Maybe not,' Wilford said. 'Maybe it wasn't the old woman.'

Christine frowned at him. 'Well, of course it was.'

'I understand how upsetting the incident was at South Coast Plaza yesterday,' Wilford said. 'I understand how you'd be inclined to link the old woman to this thing with the dog. But there's no solid proof, no real reason to think they *are* linked. It might be a mistake to assume they are.'

'But the old woman was at Joey's window last night,' Christine said exasperatedly. 'I told you that. I told the officers who were here last night, too. Doesn't anyone listen? She was at Joey's window, looking in at him, and Brandy was barking at her.'

'But she was gone when you got there,' Wilford said.

'Yes,' Christine said. 'But – '

Smiling down at Joey, Wilford said, 'Son, are you absolutely, positively sure it was the old lady there at your window?'

Joey nodded vigorously. 'Yeah. The witch.'

'Because, see, when you looked up and noticed someone at the window, it would have been perfectly natural for you to figure it was the old woman. After all, she'd already given you one bad scare earlier in the day, so she was on your mind. Then, when you switched the light on and got a glimpse of who it was there at the window, maybe you had the old woman's face so firmly fixed in your mind that you would've seen her no matter who it *really* was.'

Joey blinked, unable to follow the policeman's reasoning. He just stubbornly repeated himself: 'It was her. The witch.'

To Christine, Officer Wilford said, 'I'd be inclined to think the prowler was the one who later killed the dog – but that it wasn't the old woman who was the prowler. You see, most always, when a dog's been poisoned – and it happens more often than you think – it's not the work of some total stranger. It's someone within a block of the house where the dog lived. A neighbor. What I figure is, some neighbor was prowling around, looking for the dog, not looking for your little boy at all, when Joey saw them at the window. Later they found the dog and did what they'd come to do.'

'That's ridiculous,' Christine said. 'We've got good neighbors here. None of them would kill our dog.'

'Happens all the time,' Wilford said.

'Not in *this* neighborhood.'

'Any neighborhood,' Wilford insisted. 'Barking dogs, day after day, night after night . . . they drive some people a little nuts.'

'Brandy hardly ever barked.'

'Well, now, "hardly ever" to you might seem like "all the time" to one of your neighbors.'

'Besides, Brandy wasn't poisoned. It was a hell of a lot more violent than that. You saw. Crazy-violent. Not something any neighbor would do.'

'You'd be surprised what neighbors will do,' Wilford said. 'Sometimes they even kill each other. Not unusual at all. It's a strange world we're living in.'

'You're wrong,' she said hotly. 'It was the old woman. The dog and the face at the window — they were both connected with that old woman.'

He sighed. 'You may be right.'

'I *am* right.'

'I was only suggesting that we keep our minds open,' he said.

'Good idea,' she said pointedly.

He closed his notebook. 'Well, I guess I've got all the details I need.'

Christine got up as the officer rose from his chair. She said, 'What now?'

'We'll file a report, of course, including your statement, and we'll give you an open case number.'

'What's an open case number?'

'If anything else should happen, if this old woman should show up again, you give the case number when you call us, and the officers answering your call will know the story before they get here; they'll know what to look for on the way, so if maybe the woman leaves before they arrive, they'll spot her in passing and be able to stop her.'

'Why didn't they give us a case number after what happened last night?'

'Oh, they wouldn't open a file just for one report of a prowler,' Wilford explained. 'Last night, you see, no crime had been committed — at least so far as we could tell. No evidence of any sort of crime. But this is . . . a little worse.'

'A *little* worse?' she said, remembering Brandy's severed head, the dead glassy eyes gazing up at her.

'An unfortunate choice of words,' he said. 'I'm sorry. It's just that, compared to a lot of other things we see on this job, a dead dog isn't so —'

'Okay, okay,' Christine said, increasingly unable to conceal her anger and impatience. 'You'll call us and give us an open case number. But what else are you going to do?'

Wilford looked uncomfortable. He rolled his broad shoulders and scratched at his thick neck. 'The description you've given us is the only thing we've got to go on, and that's not much. We'll run it through the computer and try to work backwards to a name. The machine'll spit out the name of anyone who's been in trouble with us before and who fits at least seven of the ten major points of standard physical comparison. Then we'll pull mug shots of whatever other photos we have in the files. Maybe the computer'll give us several names, and we'll have photos of more than one old woman. Then we'll bring all the pictures over here for you to study. As soon as you tell us we've found her . . . well, then we can go have a talk with her and find out what this is all about. You see, it really isn't hopeless, Mrs. Scavello.'

'What if she hasn't been in trouble with you before and you don't *have* a file on her?'

Moving to the front door, Wilford said, 'We have data-sharing arrangements with every police agency in Orange, San Diego, Riverside, and Los Angeles Counties. We can reach their computers through our own. Instant access. Datalink, they call it. If she's in any of their files, we'll find her just as quickly as if she were in our own.'

'Yeah, sure, but what if she's never been in trouble anywhere?' Christine asked anxiously.

Opening the front door, Wilford said, 'Oh, don't worry, we'll probably turn up something. We almost always do.'

'That's not good enough,' she said, and she would have said it even if she had believed him, which she didn't. They wouldn't turn up anything.

'I'm sorry, Mrs. Scavello, but it's the best we can do.'

'Shit.'

He scowled. 'I understand your frustration, and I want to assure you we won't file this away and forget about it. But we can't work miracles.'

'Shit.'

His scowl deepened. His bushy eyebrows drew together in a single thick bar. 'Lady, it's none of my business, but I don't think you should use words like that in front of your little boy.'

She stared at him, astonished. Astonishment turned to anger. 'Yeah? And what're you — a born-again Christian?'

'In fact, I am, yes. And I believe it's extremely important for us to set good examples for our young ones, so they'll grow up in God's image. We've got to —'

'I don't *believe* this,' Christine said. 'You're telling me that I'm setting a bad example because I used a four-letter word, a harmless word —'

'Words aren't harmless. The devil beguiles and persuades with words. Words are the —'

'What about the example *you're* setting for my son? Huh? By your every act, you're teaching him that the police really can't protect anyone, that they really can't help anyone, that they can't do much more than come around afterwards and pick up the pieces.'

'I wish you didn't see it that way,' Wilford said.

'How the hell else am I supposed to see it?'

He sighed. 'We'll call you with the case number.' Then he turned away from the door, away from her and Joey, and moved stiffly down the walkway.

After a moment, she hurried in his wake, caught up with him, put a hand on his shoulder. 'Please.'

He stopped, turned to her. His face was hard, his eyes cold.

She said, 'I'm sorry. I really am. I'm just distraught. I don't know what to think. All of a sudden I don't know where to turn.'

'I understand,' he said, as he had said a couple of times before, but there was no understanding in his granite face.

Glancing back to make sure Joey was still in the doorway, still too far away to hear, she said, 'I'm sorry I flew off the handle at you. And I guess you're right about watching my language around Joey. Most of the time I do watch it, believe me, but today I'm not thinking straight. That crazy woman told me that my little boy had to die. That's what she said. *He's got to die*, she said. And now the dog's dead, poor old fur-face. *God*, I liked that mutt a lot. He's dead and gone, and Joey saw a face at the window in the middle of the night, and all of a sudden the world's turned upside-down, and I'm scared, really scared, because I think somehow that crazy woman followed us, and I think she's going to do it, or at least *try* to do it, try to kill my little boy. I don't know why. There can't *be* a reason. Not a reason that makes any sense. But that doesn't make any difference, does it? Not these days. These days, the newspapers are full of stories about punks and child molesters and lunatics of all kinds who don't *need* a reason to do what they do.'

Wilford said, 'Mrs. Scavello, please, you've got to keep control of yourself. You're being melodramatic. I won't say hysterical, but definitely melodramatic. It's not as bad as you're making out. We'll get to work on this, just like I told you. Meanwhile, you put your trust in God, and you'll be all right, you and your boy.'

She couldn't reach this man. Not ever. Not in a million

years. She couldn't make him feel her terror, couldn't make him understand what it would mean to her if she lost Joey. It was hopeless, after all.

She could barely remain on her feet. All the strength went out of her.

He said, 'I sure am glad, though, to hear you say you'll watch your language around the boy. The last couple generations in this country, we've been raising anti-social, know-it-all snots who have no respect for anything. If we're ever going to have us a good, peaceful, God-loving and God-fearing society, then we got to raise 'em up by the right example.'

She said nothing. She felt as if she were standing here with someone from another country — maybe even from another planet — who not only didn't speak her language but who had no capacity to learn. There was no way he could ever grasp her problems, appreciate her concerns. In every way that counted, they were thousands of miles apart, and there was no road between them.

Wilford's flinty eyes sparked with the passion of a true believer as he said: 'And I also recommend you don't go around without a bra in front of the boy, the way you are now. A woman built like you, even wearing a loose blouse like that, certain ways you turn or stretch . . . it's bound to be . . . arousing.'

She stared at him in disbelief. Several cutting remarks came to mind, any one of which would have stopped him dead, but for some reason she couldn't seem to summon the words to her lips. Of course, her reticence was in part the result of having had a mother who would have made General George Patton look soft-hearted, a mother who had insisted on good manners and unfailing politeness. There were also the lessons of the Church, deeply ingrained in her, which said you were supposed to turn the other cheek. She told herself she had broken loose from all of that, had left it far behind, but now her inability to put Wilford in his place was indisputable proof that, to her dismay, she was still to some degree a prisoner of her past.

Wilford went right on babbling, oblivious of her fury. 'Maybe the boy doesn't even notice now, but in a couple of years he'll notice for sure, and a boy shouldn't be having those kinds of thoughts about his own mother. You'd be leading him in the way of the devil.'

If she hadn't been so weak, if she hadn't been weighed down by the terrible awareness of her and Joey's helplessness, Christine would have laughed in his face. But right now there was no laughter in her.

Wilford said, 'Well, okay then. I'll be talking to you. Trust in God, Mrs. Scavello. Trust in God.'

She wondered what he'd say if she told him it wasn't *Mrs.* Scavello. What would he do if she told him Joey had been born out of wedlock, a bastard child? Would he work on the case a little less eagerly? Would he be at all concerned about preserving the life of an illegitimate little boy?

God damn all hypocrites.

She wanted to hit Wilford, kick him and hit him and take out her frustration on him, but she only watched as he got into the patrol car where his partner waited for him. He looked back at her, raised one hand, and gave her a curt little wave through the window.

She returned to the front door.

Joey was waiting for her.

She wanted to say something reassuring to him. He looked as if he needed that. But even if she'd been able to find the words, she wouldn't have been able to deceive him by speaking them. Right now, until they knew what the hell was happening, it was probably better to be scared. If he was frightened, he would be careful, watchful.

41

She felt disaster coming.

Was she being melodramatic?

No.

Joey felt it coming, too. She could see a dreadful anticipation in his eyes.

6

She stepped into the house, closed the door, locked it.

She ruffled Joey's hair. 'You okay, honey?'

'I'm gonna miss Brandy,' he said in a shaky voice, trying to be a brave little man but not quite succeeding.

'Me too,' Christine said, remembering how funny Brandy had looked in the role of Chewbacca the Wookie.

Joey said, 'I thought . . .'

'What?'

'Maybe it would be a good idea . . .'

'Yeah?'

'. . . a good idea to get another dog soon.'

She hunkered down to his level. 'You know, that's a very mature idea. Very wise, I think.'

'I don't mean I want to forget Brandy.'

'Of course not.'

'I couldn't ever forget him.'

'We'll always remember Brandy. He'll always have a special place in our hearts,' she said. 'And I'm sure he'd understand about us getting another dog right away. In fact, I'm sure that's what he'd want us to do.'

'So I'll still be protected,' Joey said.

'That's right. Brandy would want you to be protected.'

In the kitchen, the telephone rang.

42

'Tell you what,' she said, 'I'll just answer the phone, and then we'll make arrangements for burying Brandy.'

The phone rang again.

'We'll find a nice pet cemetery or something, and we'll lay Brandy to rest with all the right honors.'

'I'd like that,' he said.

The phone rang a third time.

Heading toward the kitchen, she said, 'Then later we'll look for a puppy.' She picked up the phone just as it completed a fifth ring. 'Hello?'

A woman said, 'Are you part of it?'

'Excuse me?'

'Are you part of it — or don't you know what's happening?' the woman asked.

Although the voice was vaguely familiar, Christine said, 'I think you've got the wrong number.'

'You *are* Miss Scavello, aren't you?'

'Yes. Who's this?'

'I've got to know if you're part of it. Are you one of *them*? Or are you an innocent? I've got to know.'

Suddenly Christine recognized the voice, and a chill crept up her spine.

The old woman said, 'Do you know what your son really is? Do you know the evil in him? Do you know why he's got to die?'

Christine slammed the phone down.

Joey had followed her into the kitchen. He was standing just this side of the door to the dining room, chewing on a thumbnail. In his striped shirt and jeans and somewhat tattered sneakers, he looked pathetically small, defenseless.

The phone began to ring again.

Ignoring it, Christine said, 'Come on, Skipper. Stay with me. Stay close to me.'

She led him out of the kitchen, through the dining room and living room, upstairs to the master bedroom.

He didn't ask what was wrong. From the look on his face, she thought he probably knew.

The phone kept ringing.

In the bedroom she pulled the top drawer out of the highboy, rummaged under a stack of folded sweaters, and came up with a wicked-looking pistol, a selective double-action Astra Constable .32 automatic with a snub-nosed barrel. She had purchased it years ago, before Joey was born, when she'd begun living alone, and she had learned how to use it. The gun had given her a much-needed sense of security — as it did now, once again.

The phone rang and rang.

When Joey had come into her life, especially when he had begun to walk, she'd been afraid that, in his ceaseless curiosity, he would find the weapon and play with it. Protection against burglars had to be weighed against the more likely — and more frightening — possibility that Joey would hurt himself. She had unloaded the gun, had put the empty magazine in a dresser drawer, and had buried the gun itself beneath the sweaters in the highboy, and fortunately had never needed it since then.

Until now.

The shrill ringing of the telephone became louder and more irritating by the moment.

Pistol in hand, Christine went to the dresser and located the empty magazine. She hurried to the closet where she kept a box of ammunition on the top shelf, all the way at the back. With trembling and clumsy fingers, she pushed cartridges into the magazine until it was full, then slapped it into the butt of the pistol hard enough to lock it in place.

Joey watched in wide-eyed fascination.

At last the telephone stopped ringing.

The sudden silence had the force of a blow. It briefly stunned Christine.

Joey was the first to speak. Still chewing on a thumbnail, he said, 'Was it the witch on the phone?'

There was no point in hiding it from him and no point in telling him the old woman wasn't really a witch. 'Yeah. It was her.'

'Mommy . . . I'm scared.'

For the past several months, ever since he had overcome his fear of the imaginary white snake that had disturbed his sleep, he had called her 'Mom' instead of 'Mommy' because he was trying to be more grown-up. His reversion to 'Mommy' was an indication of just how badly frightened he was.

'It'll be all right. I'm not going to let anything happen to either of us. If we're just careful, we'll be okay.'

She kept expecting to hear a knock at the door or see a face at the window. Where had the old woman been calling from? How long would it take her to get here now that the cops were gone, now that she had a clear shot at Joey?

'What're we gonna do?' he asked.

She put the loaded gun on top of the six-drawer highboy and dragged two suitcases from the back of the closet. 'I'm going to pack a bag for each of us and then we're getting out of here.'

'Where're we going?'

She threw one of the suitcases onto her bed and opened it. 'I don't know for sure, sweetheart. Anywhere. To a hotel, probably. We'll go someplace where that crazy old hag won't be able to find us no matter how hard she looks.'

'Then what?'

As she folded clothes into the open suitcase, she said, 'Then we'll find someone who can help us . . . *really* help us.'

'Not like the cops?'

'Not like the cops.'

45

'Who?'

'I'm not sure. Maybe . . . a private detective.'

'Like Magnum on TV?'

'Maybe not exactly like Magnum,' Christine said.

'Like who, then?'

'We need a big firm that can provide us with bodyguards and everything while they're tracking down that old woman. A first-rate organization.'

'Like in them old movies?'

'What old movies are those?'

'You know. Where they're in real bad trouble, and they say, "We'll hire Pinkelton." '

'Pinkerton,' she corrected. 'Yeah. Something like Pinkerton. I can afford to hire people like that and, by God, I'm going to hire them. We're not just going to be a couple of sitting ducks the way the cops would have us.'

'I'd feel a whole bunch safer if we just went and hired Magnum,' Joey said.

She didn't have time to explain to a six-year-old that Magnum wasn't a real private eye. She said, 'Well, maybe you're right. Maybe we will hire Magnum.'

'Yeah?'

'Yeah.'

'He'll do a good job,' Joey said soberly. 'He always does.'

At her direction, Joey took the empty suitcase and headed toward his room. She followed, carrying the suitcase that she had already packed – and the pistol.

She decided they wouldn't go to a hotel first. They'd go straight to a detective agency and not waste any time dealing with this.

Her mouth was sandpaper-dry. Her heart thudded. She was breathing hard and fast.

In her mind a terrible vision rose, an image of a bloody

and decapitated body sprawled on the back porch. But in the vision, it wasn't Brandy she saw in gory ruin. It was Joey.

7

Charlie Harrison was proud of his accomplishments. He had started with nothing, just a poor kid from the shabby side of Indianapolis. Now, at thirty-six, he was owner of a thriving business — full owner since the retirement of the company's founder, Harvey Klemet — and was living the good life in southern California. If he wasn't exactly on top of the world yet, he was at least eighty percent of the way there, and the view from his current elevation was quite satisfying.

The offices of Klemet-Harrison were not remotely like the seedy quarters of private investigators in novels and films. These rooms, on the fifth floor of a five-story building on a quiet street in Costa Mesa, were comfortably and tastefully decorated.

The reception lounge made a good first impression on new clients. It was plushly carpeted, and the walls were covered with a subtle grass cloth. The furniture was new — and not from the low end of the manufacturer's line, either. The walls weren't adorned only with cheap prints; there were three Eyvind Earle serigraphs worth more than fifteen hundred dollars apiece.

Charlie's private office was even somewhat plusher than the reception area, yet it avoided the ponderous and solemn look favored by attorneys and many other professionals. Bleached wood paneling reached halfway up the walls.

There were bleached-wood shutters on the windows, a contemporary desk by Henredon, armchairs covered in an airy green print from Brunschwig & Fils. On the walls were two large, light-filled paintings by Martin Green, undersea scenes of ethereal plant life fluttering gracefully in mysterious currents and tides. A few large plants, mostly ferns and pothos, hung from the ceiling or rested on rosewood stands. The effect was almost subtropical yet cool and rich.

But when Christine Scavello walked through the door, Charlie suddenly felt that the room was woefully inadequate. Yes, it was light and well balanced and expensive and truly exquisite; nevertheless, it seemed hopelessly heavy, clunky, and even garish when compared to this striking woman.

Coming out from behind his desk, he said, 'Ms. Scavello, I'm Charlie Harrison. I'm so pleased to meet you.'

She accepted his hand and said she was pleased to meet him, too.

Her hair was thick, shiny, dark-dark brown, almost black. He wanted to run his fingers through it. He wanted to put his face in her hair and smell it.

Unaccustomed to having such a strong and immediate reaction to anyone, Charlie reined himself in. He looked at her more closely, as dispassionately as possible. He told himself that she wasn't perfect, certainly not breathtakingly beautiful. Pretty, yes, but not a total knockout. Her brow was somewhat too high, and her cheekbones seemed a little heavy, and her nose was slightly pinched.

Nevertheless, with a breathless and ingratiating manner that wasn't like him, he said, 'I apologize for the condition of the office,' and was surprised and dismayed to hear himself make such a statement.

She looked puzzled. 'Why should you apologize? It's lovely.'

He blinked. 'You really think so?'

'Absolutely. It's unexpected. Not at all what I thought a private detective's office would look like. But that just makes it even more interesting, appealing.'

Her eyes were huge and dark. Clear, direct eyes. Each time he met them, his breath caught for an instant.

'Did it myself,' he said, deciding the room didn't look so bad, after all. 'Didn't use an interior decorator.'

'You've got a real flair for it.'

He showed her to a chair and noticed, as she sat down, that she had lovely legs and perfectly shaped ankles.

But I've seen other legs as lovely, other ankles as well shaped, he thought with some bafflement, and I haven't ever before been swept away by this adolescent longing, haven't felt this ridiculously sudden surge in hormone levels.

Either he was hornier than he thought, or he was reacting to more than her appearance.

Perhaps her appeal was as much in the way she walked and shook hands and carried herself (with an easy, graceful minimum of movement), and in her voice (soft, earthy, feminine, yet unaffected, with a note of strength), and in the way she met his eyes (forthrightly), as it was in the way she looked. In spite of the circumstances in which he was meeting her, in spite of the fact that she had a serious problem about which she must be worried, she possessed an uncommon inner tranquility that intrigued him.

That doesn't quite explain it either, he thought. Since when have I ever wanted to jump into bed with a woman because of her uncommon inner tranquility?

All right, so he wasn't going to be able to analyze this feeling, not yet. He would just have to go with it and try to understand it later.

Stepping behind his desk, sitting down, he said, 'Maybe I shouldn't have told you I'm interested in interior design. Maybe that's really the wrong image for a private detective.'

'On the contrary,' she said, 'what it tells me is that you're observant, perceptive, probably quite sensitive, and you have an excellent eye for details. Those are the qualities I'd hope for in any man in your line of work.'

'Right! Exactly,' he said, beaming at her, delighted by her approval.

He was stricken by an almost irresistible urge to kiss her brow, her eyes, the bridge of her nose, the tip of her nose, her cheeks, her chin, and last of all her sculpted lips.

But all he did was say, 'Well, Ms. Scavello, what can I do for you?'

She told him about the old woman.

He was shocked, intrigued, and sympathetic, but he was also uneasy because you never knew what to expect from flaky types like this old woman. Anything might happen, and it probably would. Furthermore, he knew how difficult it was to track down and deal with any perpetrator of this type of irrational harassment. He much preferred people with clear, understandable motivations. Understandable motivations were what made his line of work possible: greed, lust, envy, jealousy, revenge, love, hate — they were the raw materials of his industry. Thank God for the weaknesses and imperfections of mankind, for otherwise he would have been without work. He was so uneasy because he was afraid he might fail Christine Scavello, and if he failed her, she would walk out of his life forever. And if she walked out of his life forever, he would have to be satisfied with only dreams of her, and he was just too damn old for dreams of that kind.

When Christine finished recounting the events of this

morning – the murder of the dog, the call from the old woman – Charlie said, 'Where's your son now?'

'Out in your waiting room.'

'All right. He's safe there.'

'I'm not sure he's safe anywhere.'

'Relax. It's not the end of the world. It's really not.'

He smiled at her to show her that it wasn't the end of the world. He wanted to make her smile back at him because he was certain that her smile would make her lovely face even lovelier, but she didn't seem to have a smile in her.

He said, 'All right, about this old woman . . . You've given me a pretty detailed description of her.' He had made notes as she talked. Now he glanced at them. 'But is there anything else about her that might help us make an identification?'

'I've told you everything I remember.'

'What about scars? Did she have any scars?'

'No.'

'Did she wear glasses?'

'No.'

'You said she was in her late sixties or early seventies –'

'Yes.'

' – yet her face was hardly lined.'

'That's right.'

'Unnaturally smooth, somewhat puffy, you said.'

'Her skin, yes. I had an aunt who took cortisone injections for arthritis. Her face was like the woman's face.'

'So you think she's being treated for some form of arthritis?'

Christine shrugged. 'I don't know. Could be.'

'Was she wearing a copper bracelet or any copper rings?'

'Copper?'

'It's only a wives' tale, of course, but a lot of people

think copper jewelry helps arthritis. I had an aunt with arthritis, too, and she wore a copper necklace, two copper bracelets on each wrist, a couple of copper rings, and even a copper ankle bracelet. She was a thin little bird of a woman, weighed down with crummy-looking jewelry, and she swore by it, said it did her a world of good, but she never moved any easier and never had any relief from the pain.'

'This woman didn't have any copper jewelry. Lots of other jewelry, like I said, but nothing copper.'

He stared at his notes. Then: 'She didn't tell you her name —'

'No.'

' — but was she wearing a monogram, like maybe on her blouse —'

'No.'

' — or were her initials spelled out on one of her rings?'

'I don't think so. If they were, I didn't notice.'

'And you didn't see where she came from?'

'No.'

'If we knew what kind of car she got out of —'

'I've no idea. We were almost to our car, and she just stepped out from beside it.'

'What kind of car was parked next to yours?'

She frowned, trying to remember.

While she thought, Charlie studied her face, looking for imperfections. Nothing in this world was free of imperfections. Everything had at least one flaw. Even a bottle of Lafite Rothschild could have a bad cork or too much tannic acid. Not even a Rolls Royce had an unblemished paint job. Reese's Peanut Butter Cups were unquestionably delicious — but they made you fat. However, no matter how carefully he studied Christine Scavello's face, he could find nothing whatsoever wrong with it. Oh, yes, well, the pinched nose, and the heavy cheekbones, and the too-high brow, but in her case those didn't strike him as imperfections; they were merely . . . well, deviations from the ordinary definition of beauty, minor deviations that gave her character, a look of her own —

And what the hell is wrong with me? he wondered. I've got to stop mooning over her as if I were a lovesick schoolboy.

On one hand, he liked the way he felt; it was a fresh, exhilarating feeling. On the other hand, he *didn't* like it because he didn't understand it, and it was his nature to want to understand everything. That was why he'd become a detective — to find answers, to *understand*.

She blinked, looked up at him. 'I remember. It wasn't a car parked next to us. It was a van.'

'A paneled van? What kind?'

'White.'

'I mean, what make?'

She frowned again, trying to recall.

'Old or new?' he asked.

'New. Clean, sparkling.'

'Did you notice any dents, scrapes?'

'No. And it was a Ford.'

'Good. Very good. Do you know what year?'

'No.'

'A recreational vehicle, was it? With one of those round windows on the side or maybe a painted mural?'

'No. Very utilitarian. Like a van somebody would use for work.'

'Was there a company name on the side?'

'No.'

'Any message at all painted on it?'

'No. It was just plain white.'

'What about the license plate?'

'I didn't see it.'

'You passed by the back of the van. You noticed it was a Ford. The license plate would've been right there.'

'I guess. But I didn't look at it.'

'If it becomes necessary, we can probably get it out of you with hypnosis. At least now we have a little something to start with.'

'*If* she got out of the van.'

'For starters, we'll assume she did.'

'And that's probably a mistake.'

'And maybe it isn't.'

'She could've come from anywhere in the parking lot.'

'But since we have to start somewhere, we might as well begin with the van,' he said patiently.

'She might've come from another row of cars altogether. We might just be wasting time. I don't want to waste time. *She* isn't wasting time. I have an awful feeling we don't *have* much time.'

Her nervous, fidgety movements escalated into uncontrollable shivers that shook her entire body. Charlie realized that she had been maintaining her composure only with considerable effort.

'Easy,' he said. 'Easy now. Everything'll work out fine. We won't let anything happen to Joey.'

She was pale. Her voice quavered when she spoke: 'He's so sweet. He's such a sweet little boy. He's the center of my life . . . the center of everything. If anything happened to him . . .'

'Nothing's going to happen to him. I guarantee you that.'

She began to cry. She didn't sob or wail or get hysterical. She just took deep, shuddery breaths, and her eyes grew watery, and tears slipped down her cheeks.

Pushing his chair back from the desk, getting up, wanting to comfort her, feeling awkward and inadequate, Charlie said, 'I think you need a drink.'

She shook her head.

'It'll help,' he said.

'I don't drink much,' she said shakily, and the tears poured from her even more copiously than before.

'Just one drink.'

'Too early,' she said.

'It's past eleven-thirty. Almost lunchtime. Besides, this is medicinal.'

He went to the bar that stood in the corner by one of the two big windows. He opened the lower doors, took out a bottle of Chivas Regal and one glass, put them on the marble-topped counter, poured two ounces of Scotch.

As he was capping the bottle, he happened to look out the window beside him — and froze. A white Ford van, clean and sparkling, with no advertising on it, was parked across the street. Looking over the tops of the uppermost fronds of an enormous date palm that rose almost to his fifth-floor window, Charlie saw a man in dark clothing leaning against the side of the van.

Coincidence.

The man seemed to be eating. Just a workman stopped on a quiet sidestreet to grab an early lunch. That's all. Surely, it couldn't be anything more than that.

Coincidence.

Or maybe not. The man down there also seemed to be watching the front of this building. He appeared to be having a bite of lunch and running a stakeout at the same time. Charlie had been involved in dozens of stakeouts over the years. He knew what a stakeout looked like, and this sure as hell looked like one, although it was a bit obvious and amateurish.

Behind him, Christine said, 'Is something wrong?'

He was surprised by her perspicacity, by how sharply attuned to him she was, especially since she was still highly agitated, still crying.

He said, 'I hope you like Scotch.'

He turned away from the window and took the drink to her. She accepted it without further protestations. She held the glass in both hands but still couldn't keep it from shaking. She sipped rather daintily at the whiskey.

Charlie said, 'Drink it straight down. Two swallows. Get it inside you where it can do some good.'

She did as he said, and he could tell that she really didn't drink much because she grimaced at the bitterness of the Scotch, even though Chivas was about the smoothest stuff ever to come out of a distillery.

He took the empty glass from her, carried it back to the bar, rinsed it out in the small sink, and set it on the drainboard.

He looked out the window again.

The white truck was still there.

So was the man in the dark pants and shirt, eating his lunch with studied casualness.

Returning to Christine, Charlie said, 'Feel better?'

Some color had crept back into her face. She nodded. 'I'm sorry for coming apart on you like that.'

He sat half on the edge of his desk, keeping one foot on the floor. He smiled at her. 'You have nothing to apologize for. Most people, if they'd had the scare you've had, would've come through the door blubbering incoherently, and they'd *still* be blubbering incoherently. You're holding up quite well.'

'I don't *feel* as if I'm holding up.' She took a handkerchief from her purse and blew her nose. 'But I guess you're right. One crazy old lady isn't the end of the world.'

'Exactly.'

'One crazy old lady can't be *that* hard to deal with.'

'That's the spirit,' he said.

But he thought: One crazy old lady? Then who's the guy with the white truck?

8

Grace Spivey sat on a hard oak chair, her ice-gray eyes shining in the gloom.

Today was a red day in the spirit world, one of the reddest days she had ever known, and she was dressed entirely in red in order to be in harmony with it, just as she had dressed entirely in green yesterday, when the spirit world had been going through a green phase. Most people weren't aware that the spirit world around them changed color from day to day; of course, most people couldn't see the supernatural realm as clearly as Grace could see it when she really tried; in fact, most of them couldn't see it at all, so there was no way they could possibly understand Grace's manner of dress. But for Grace, who was a psychic and a medium, it was essential to be in harmony with the color of the spirit world, for then she could more easily receive clairvoyant visions of both the past and future. These visions were sent to her by benign spirits and were transmitted on brilliantly colored beams of energy, beams that, today, were all shades of red.

If she had tried to explain this to most people, they would have thought her insane. A few years ago her own daughter had committed Grace to a hospital for psychiatric evaluation; but Grace had slipped out of that trap, had disowned her daughter, and had been more cautious ever since.

Today she wore dark red shoes, a dark red skirt, and a lighter red, two-tone, striped blouse. All her jewelry was red: a double strand of crimson beads and matching bracelets on each wrist; a porcelain brooch as bright as fire; two ruby rings; one ring with four dazzling ovals of highly polished carnelian; four other rings with cheap red glass, vermilion enamel, and scarlet porcelain. Whether precious, semi-precious, or fake, all the stones in her rings glinted and sparkled in the flickering candlelight.

The quivering flames, adance upon the points of the wicks, caused strange shadows to writhe over the basement walls. The room was large, but it seemed small because the candles were grouped at one end of it, and three-quarters of the chamber lay beyond the reach of their inconstant amber light. There were eleven candles in all, each fat and white, each fitted in a brass holder with an ornate drip guard, and each brass candlestick was gripped firmly by one of Grace's followers, all of whom were waiting eagerly for her to speak. Of the eleven, six were men and five were women. Some were young, some middle-aged, some old. They sat on the floor, forming a semicircle around the chair on which Grace sat, their faces gleaming and queerly distorted in the fluttering, shimmering, eldritch glow.

These eleven did not constitute the entire body of her followers. More than fifty others were in the room overhead, waiting anxiously to hear what transpired during this session. And more than a thousand others were elsewhere, in a hundred different places, engaged upon work that Grace had assigned to them.

However, these eleven at her feet were her most trusted, valued, and capable lieutenants. They were the ones she most cherished.

She even knew and remembered their names, although it wasn't easy for her to remember names (or much of anything else) these days, not as easy as it had been before the Gift had been given to her. The Gift filled her, filled her mind, and crowded out so many things that she had once taken for granted — such as the ability to remember names and faces. And the ability to keep track of time.

She never knew what time it was any more; even when she looked at a clock, it frequently had no meaning for her. Seconds, minutes, hours, and days now seemed like ridiculously arbitrary measurements of time; perhaps they were still useful to ordinary men and women, but she was beyond the need of them. Sometimes, when she thought only a day had passed, she discovered that an entire week was missing. It was scary but also curiously exhilarating, for it made her constantly aware that she was special, that she was Chosen. The Gift had also crowded out sleep. Some nights she didn't sleep at all. Most nights she slept one hour, never more than two, but she didn't seem to *need* sleep any more, so it didn't matter how little she got. The Gift crowded out everything that might interfere with the great and sacred work she must accomplish.

Nevertheless, she remembered the names of these eleven people because they were the purest members of her flock. They were the best of the best, largely untainted souls who were the most worthy of carrying out the demanding tasks ahead of them.

One other man was in the basement. His name was Kyle Barlowe. He was thirty-two, but he looked older — older, somber, mean, and dangerous. He had lank brown hair, thick but without luster. His high forehead ended in a heavy shelf of bone under which his deeply set brown eyes were watchful and shrewd. He had a large nose, but it wasn't regal or proud; it had been broken more than once and was lumpy. His cheekbones and jawbone were heavy, crudely formed, like the plate of bone from which his forehead had been carved. Although his features were for the most part over-sized and graceless, his lips were thin, and they were so bloodless and pale that they seemed even thinner than they actually were; as a result, his mouth appeared to be nothing more than a slash in his face. He was an extraordinarily big man, six-eleven, with a bull neck, slab shoulders, well-muscled chest and arms. He looked as if he could break a man in half — and as if he frequently did exactly that, strictly for the fun of it.

In fact, for the past three years, since Kyle had become one of Grace's followers and then a member of her inner circle and then her most trusted assistant, he hadn't raised a hand against anyone. Before Grace had found and saved him, he had been a moody, violent, and brutal man. But those days were gone. Grace had been able to see beyond Kyle Barlowe's forbidding exterior, had glimpsed the good soul that lay beneath. He had gone astray, yes, but he had been eager (even if he hadn't realized it himself) to return to the good and righteous path. All he needed was someone to show him the way. Grace had shown him, and he had followed. Now, his huge, powerful arms and his marble-hard fists would harm no virtuous man or woman but would smite only those who were the enemies of God and, even then, only when Grace *told* him to smite them.

Grace knew the enemies of God when she saw them. The ability to recognize a hopelessly corrupt soul in the first instant upon encountering it — that was but one small part of the Gift that God had bestowed upon her. One split second of eye contact was usually all Grace needed in order to determine if a person was habitually sinful and beyond redemption. She had the Gift. No one else. Just her, the Chosen. She heard evil in the voices of the wicked; she saw evil in their eyes. There was no hiding from her.

Some people, given the Gift, would have doubted it, would have wondered if they were wrong or even crazy. But Grace never doubted herself or questioned her sanity. Never. She knew she was special, and she knew she was always right in these matters because God had told her that she was right.

The day was rapidly coming when she would finally call upon Kyle (and upon some of the others) to strike down many of those disciples of Satan. She would point to the evil ones, and Kyle would destroy them. He would be the hammer of God. How wonderful that day would be! Sitting in the basement of her church, on the hard oak chair, in front of her innermost circle of believers, Grace shivered with anticipatory pleasure. It would be so fine, so satisfying to watch the big man's hard muscles bunch and flex and bunch again as he brought the wrath of God to the infidels and Satanists.

Soon. The time was coming. The Twilight.

Now, the candlelight flickered, and Kyle said softly, 'Are you ready, Mother Grace?'

'Yes,' she said.

She closed her eyes. For a moment she saw nothing, only darkness, but then she quickly established contact with the spirit world, and lights appeared behind her eyes, bursts and squiggles and fountains and spots and shifting-heaving-writhing shapes of light, some brilliant and some dim, all shades of red, naturally, because they were spirits and spectral energies, and this was a red day in their plane of existence. It was the reddest day Grace had ever known.

The spirits swarmed on all sides of her, and she moved off among them as if she were drifting away into a world that was painted on the backs of her own eyelids. At first she drifted slowly. She felt her mind and spirit separating from her body, gradually leaving the flesh behind. She was still aware of the temporal plane in which her body existed – the odor of burning candles, the hard oak chair beneath her, an occasional rustle or murmur from one of her disciples – but eventually all that faded. She accelerated until she was rushing, then flying, then rocketing through the light-spotted void, faster and faster, with exhilarating, now sickening, now terrifying speed –

Sudden stillness.

She was deep in the spirit world, hanging motionless,

as if she were an asteroid suspended in a distant corner of space. She was no longer able to see, hear, smell, or feel the world she had left behind. Across an infinite night, red-hued spirits of all descriptions moved in every direction, some fast and some slow, some purposefully and some erratically, on adventures and holy errands that Grace could not begin to comprehend.

Grace thought about the boy, Joey Scavello. She knew what he really was, and she knew he had to die. But she didn't know if the time had come to dispose of him. She had made this journey into the spirit world for the sole purpose of inquiring as to when and how she should deal with the boy.

She hoped she would be told to kill him. She wanted so much to kill him.

9

The double shot of Chivas Regal seemed to have calmed Christine Scavello, although not entirely. She finally leaned back in her chair, and her hands were no longer knotted together, but she was still tense and noticeably shaky.

Charlie continued to sit on the edge of his desk with one foot on the floor. 'At least until we know who this old woman is and what kind of person we're dealing with, I think we should put two armed bodyguards with Joey around the clock.'

'All right. Do it.'

'Does the boy go to school?'

'Pre-school. He starts regular school next fall.'

'We'll keep him out of pre-school until this blows over.'

'It won't just blow over,' she said edgily.

'Well, of course, I didn't mean we were just going to wait it out. I meant to say that we'll keep him out of pre-school until we put a stop to this thing.'

'Will two bodyguards be enough?'

'Actually, it'll be six. Three pairs working in eight-hour shifts.'

'Still, it'll only be two men during any one shift, and I —'

'Two can handle it. They're well trained. However, this can all get pretty expensive. If —'

'I can afford it,' she said.

'My secretary can give you a fee sheet —'

'Whatever's needed. I can pay.'

'What about your husband?'

'What about him?'

'Well, what's he think about all this?'

'I don't have a husband.'

'Oh. I'm sorry if —'

'No need for sympathy. I'm not a widow, and I wasn't divorced, either.' Here was the forthrightness he had seen in her; this refusal to be evasive was refreshing. 'I've never been married.'

'Ah,' he said.

Although Charlie was sure his voice contained not the slightest note of disapproval, Christine stiffened as if he had insulted her. With a sudden, irrational, quiet yet steel-hard anger that startled him, she said, 'What're you trying to tell me? That you've got to approve of your client's morality before you accept a case?'

He gaped at her, astonished and confused by her abrupt change of attitude. 'Well of course not! I only —'

'Because I'm not about to sit here like a criminal on trial —'

'Wait, wait, wait. What's wrong? Huh? What'd I say?

Good heavens, why should I care if you've been married or not?'

'Fine. Glad you feel that way. Now, how are you going to track down that old woman?'

Anger, like a smouldering fire, remained in her eyes and voice.

Charlie couldn't understand why she was so sensitive and defensive about her son's lack of a legal father. It was unfortunate, yes, and she probably wished the situation were otherwise. But it really wasn't a terrible social stigma these days. She acted as if she were living in the 1940s instead of the '80s.

'I really mean it,' he said. 'I don't care.'

'Terrific. Congratulations on your open-mindedness. If it was up to me, you'd get a Nobel Prize for humanitarianism. Now can we drop the subject?'

What the hell is wrong with her? he wondered. He was *glad* there was no husband. Couldn't she sense his interest in her? Couldn't she see through his tissue-thin professional demeanor? Couldn't she see how she got to him? Most women had a sixth sense for that sort of thing.

He said, 'If I rub you the wrong way or something, I can turn this case over to one of my junior men — '

'No, I — '

'They're all quite reliable, capable. But I assure you I didn't mean to disparage or ridicule you — or whatever the heck you think I did. I'm not like that cop this morning, the one who chewed you out about using four-letter words.'

'Officer Wilford.'

'I'm not like Wilford. I'm easy. Okay? Truce?'

She hesitated, then nodded. The stiffness left her. The anger faded and was replaced by embarrassment.

She said, 'Sorry I snapped at you, Mr. Harrison — '

'Call me Charlie. And you can snap at me anytime.' He

smiled. 'But we have to talk about Joey's father because maybe he's connected with this.'

'With the old woman?'

'Maybe.'

'Oh, I doubt it.'

'Maybe he wants custody of his son.'

'Then why not just come and ask?'

Charlie shrugged. 'People don't always approach a problem from a logical point of view.'

She shook her head. 'No. It's not Joey's . . . father. As far as I know, he isn't even aware that Joey exists. Besides, that old woman was saying Joey had to *die*.'

'I still think we have to consider the possibility and talk about his father, even if that's painful for you. We can't leave any possibility unexplored.'

She nodded. 'It's just that . . . when I got pregnant with Joey, it nearly destroyed Evelyn . . . my mother. She had expected so much of me . . . She made me feel terribly guilty, made me wallow in guilt.' She sighed. 'I guess, because of the way my mother treated me, I'm still overly sensitive about Joey's illegitimacy.'

'I understand.'

'No. You don't. You can't.'

He waited and listened. He was a good and patient listener. It was part of his job.

She said, 'Evelyn . . . Mother . . . doesn't like Joey much. Won't have much to do with him. She blames *him* for his illegitimacy. She sometimes even treats him as if . . . as if he's wicked or evil or something. It's wrong, it's sick, it doesn't make sense, but it's so much like Mother to blame *him* because *my* life didn't turn out exactly the way she planned it for me.'

'If she actively dislikes Joey, is it possible that your mother might be behind this thing with the old woman?' he asked.

That thought clearly startled her. But she shook her head. 'No. Surely not. It isn't Evelyn's style. She's direct. She tells you what she thinks, even if she knows she's going to hurt you, even if she knows every word she speaks is going to be like a nail going into you. She wouldn't be asking her friends to harass my boy. That's ludicrous.'

'She might not be involved directly. But maybe she's talked about you and Joey to other people, and maybe this old woman at the mall was one of those people. Maybe your mother said intemperate things about the boy, not realizing this old woman was unbalanced, not realizing the old woman would take what your mother said the wrong way, take it too literally and actually act upon it.'

Scowling, Christine said, 'Maybe . . .'

'I know it's far-fetched, but it is possible.'

'Okay. Yeah. I suppose so.'

'So tell me about your mother.'

'I assure you, she couldn't be involved with this.'

'Tell me anyway,' he coaxed.

She sighed and said, 'She's a dragon lady, my mother. You can't understand, and I can't really make you understand, because you had to live with her to know what she's like. She kept me under her thumb . . . intimidated . . . browbeaten all those years . . .'

. . . all those years.

Her mind drifted back, against her will, and she became aware of a pressure on her chest and began to have some difficulty drawing her breath, for the predominant feeling associated with her childhood was one of suffocation.

She saw the rambling Victorian house in Pomona that had been passed from her Grandma Giavetti to Evelyn, where they had lived from the time Christine was a year old, where Evelyn still lived, and the memory of it was an unwelcome weight. Although she knew it to be a white house with pale yellow trim and awnings, with charming gingerbread ornamentation and many windows to admit the sun, in her mind's eye she always saw it crouched in shadows, with Halloween-bare trees crowding close to it, beneath a threatening gray-black sky. She could hear the grandfather clock ticking monotonously in the parlor, an ever-present sound that in those days had seemed always to be mocking her with its constant reminder that the misery of her childhood stretched almost to eternity and would be counted out in millions and millions of leaden seconds. She could see again, in every room, heavy over-stuffed pieces of furniture pressed too close to one another, and she supposed that her memory made the ticking clock louder and more maddeningly intrusive than it had actually been, and that in reality the furniture hadn't been quite so large and clunky and ugly and dark as it was in recollection.

Her father, Vincent Scavello, had found that house, that life, as oppressive as it was in Christine's memory, and he had left them when she was four and her brother, Tony, was eleven. He never came back, and she never saw him again. He was a weak man with an inferiority complex, and Evelyn made him feel even more inadequate because she set such high standards for everyone. Nothing he did could satisfy her. Nothing *anyone* did — especially not Christine or Tony — was half as good as Evelyn expected of them. Because he couldn't measure up to her expectations, Vincent developed a drinking problem, and that only made her nag him more, and finally he just left. Two years later, he was dead. In a way he committed suicide, though not with a gun — nothing so dramatic as that; it was just a case of drunken driving; he ran head-on into a bridge abutment at seventy miles an hour.

Evelyn went to work the day after Vincent walked out, not only supported her family but did a good job of it, living up to her own high standards. That made things even worse for Christine and Tony. 'You've got to be the best at what you do, and if you aren't the best there's no use doing it at all,' Evelyn said — at least a thousand times.

Christine had one especially clear memory of an entire, tense evening spent at the kitchen table, after Tony brought home a report card with a D in math, a failure that, in Evelyn's eyes, was in no way mitigated by the fact that he had received an A in every other subject. This would have been bad enough, but that same day he had been mildly reprimanded by the school principal for smoking in the boys' washroom. It was the first time he tried a cigarette, and he didn't like it and didn't intend to smoke again; it was just an experiment, hardly unusual for a fourteen-year-old boy, but Evelyn was furious. That night the lecture had gone on for almost three hours, with Evelyn alternately pacing, sitting at the table with her head in her hands, shouting, weeping, pleading, pounding the table. 'You're a Giavetti, Tony, more of a Giavetti than a Scavello. You might carry your father's name, but by God, there's more of *my* blood in you; there must be. I couldn't bear to think half your blood is poor weak Vincent's, because if that was true, God knows what would become of you. I won't have it! I won't! I work my fingers to the bone to give you every chance, every opportunity, and I won't have you spitting in my face, which is what this is, goofing off in school, goofing off in math class — it's just the same as spitting in my face!' The anger gave way to tears, and she got up from the table, pulled a handful of Kleenex from the box on the kitchen counter, noisily blew her nose. 'What good does it do for me to worry about you, to care what happens to you? *You* don't care. There's that few drops of your father's blood in you, that loafer's blood, and it only takes a few drops to contaminate you. Like a disease. Scavello Disease. But you're also a Giavetti, and Giavettis always work harder and study harder, which is only right, only fitting, because God didn't intend for us to loaf and drink our lives away, like some I could mention. You've got to get As in school, and even if you don't like math, you've got to just work harder until you're perfect in it, because you *need* math in this world, and your father, God pity him, was lousy with figures, and I won't have you being like poor weak Vincent; that scares me. I don't want my son being a bum, and I'm afraid I see a bum in you, just like your father, weakness in you. Now, you're also a *Giavetti*, and don't you forget it. Giavettis always do their best, and their best is always as good as anyone could do, and don't you tell me that you're already spending most of your time studying, and don't tell me about your weekend job at the grocery store. Work is good for you. I got you that job because you show me a teenage boy who doesn't have a part-time job and I'll show you a future bum. Why, even with your job and your studying and the things you do around here, you should still have plenty of free time, too much, way too much. You should maybe even be working a night or two during the week at the market. There's *always* more time if you want to find it; God made the whole world in six days, and don't tell me you aren't God because if you listened to your catechism lessons you'd know you were made in His image, and remember you're a Giavetti, which means you were made in His image just a little more than some other people I could name, like Vincent Scavello, but I won't. Look at *me*! I work all day, but I cook good meals for you, too, and with Christine I keep this big house immaculate, absolutely immaculate, God as my witness, and though I may be tired sometimes and feel like I just can't go on, I do go on, for you, for you I go on, and your clothes are always nicely pressed − Aren't they? − and your socks are always mended − Tell me *once* you ever had to wear a sock with a hole in it! − so if I do all this and not drop dead and not even *complain*, then you can be the kind of son to make me proud, and by God you're *going* to be! And as for you, Christine . . .'

Evelyn never ceased lecturing them. Always, every day, holidays, birthdays − there was no day free of her lectures. Christine and Tony sat captive, not daring to answer back because that brought the most withering scorn and the worst punishment − and encouraged even *more* lecturing. She pushed them relentlessly, demanded the greatest possible accomplishments in everything they did, which wasn't necessarily a bad thing; it might even have been good for them. However, when they *did* achieve the best grade possible, win the highest award being given, move up to the first seats in their sections of the school orchestra, when they did all that and more, much more, it never satisfied their mother. The best wasn't good enough for Evelyn. When they achieved the best, reached the pinnacle, she chastised them for not having gotten there sooner, set new goals for them, and suggested they were trying her patience and running out of time in which to make her proud of them.

When she felt lecturing wasn't sufficient, she used her ultimate weapon − tears. She wept and blamed herself for their failures. 'Both of you are going to come to a bad end, and it'll be my fault, all my fault, because I didn't know how to reach you, how to make you see what was important. I didn't do enough for you, I didn't know how to help you overcome the Scavello blood that's in you, and I should have known, should have done better. What good am I as a mother? No good, no mother at all.'

. . . all those years ago . . .

But it seemed like yesterday.

Christine couldn't tell Charlie Harrison everything about her mother and that claustrophobic childhood of shadowy rooms and heavy Victorian furniture and heavy Victorian guilt, for she would have needed hours to explain. Besides, she wasn't looking for pity, and she was not by nature the kind of person given to sharing the intimate details of her life with others — not even with friends, let alone strangers like this man, nice as he might be. She only alluded to her past with a few sentences, but from his expression, she thought he sensed and understood more than she told him; perhaps the pain of it was in her eyes and face, more easily read than she supposed.

'Those years were worse for Tony than for me,' she told the detective. 'Mainly because, on top of everything else that Evelyn expected of him, she also wanted him to be a priest. The Giavettis had produced two priests in her generation, and they were the most revered members of the family.'

In addition to the Giavettis' tradition of service to the Church, Evelyn was a religious woman, and even without that family history, she would have pushed Tony toward the priesthood. She pushed successfully, too, for he went straight from parochial school into the seminary. He had no choice. By the time he was twelve, Evelyn had him brainwashed, and it was impossible for him to imagine being anything *but* a priest.

'Evelyn expected Tony to be a parish priest,' Christine told Charlie Harrison. 'Maybe eventually a monsignor, perhaps even a bishop. Like I said, she had high standards. But when Tony took his vows, he asked to be assigned to missionary work, and he was — in Africa. Mother was so upset! See, in the Church, like in government, the way you usually move up through the hierarchy is largely through astute politicking. But you can't be a constant, visible presence in the corridors of power when you're stuck in some remote African mission. Mother was furious.'

71

The detective said, 'Did he choose missionary work because he knew she'd be against it?'

'No. The problem was Mother saw the priesthood as a way for Tony to bring honor to her and the family. But to Tony, the priesthood was an opportunity to serve. He took his vows seriously.'

'Is he still in Africa?'

'He's dead.'

Startled, Charlie Harrison said, 'Oh. I'm sorry. I –'

'It's not a recent loss,' she assured him. 'Eleven years ago, when I was a high school senior, Tony was killed by terrorists, African revolutionaries. For a while Mother was inconsolable, but gradually her grief gave way to a . . . sick anger. She was actually angry with Tony for getting himself killed – as if he'd run away like my father before him. She made me feel I ought to make up for how Daddy and Tony had failed her. In my own grief and confusion and guilt . . . I said I wanted to become a nun, and Evelyn . . . Mother leaped at the idea. So, after high school, at her urging, I entered the convent . . . and it was a disaster . . .'

So much time had passed, yet she could still vividly remember the way the novice's habit had felt when she'd first worn it: the unexpected weight of it; the surprisingly coarse texture of the black fabric; the way she had continually caught the flowing skirts on doorknobs, furniture, and everything else that she passed, unaccustomed as she was to such voluminous clothes. Being trapped within that venerable uniform, sleeping within a narrow stone cubicle on a simple cot, day after day spent within the dreary and ascetically furnished confines of the convent – it all stayed with her in spite of her efforts to forget. Those Lost Years had been so similar to the suffocating life in the Victorian house in Pomona that, like thoughts of childhood, any recollection of her convent days was apt to put pressure on her chest and make breathing difficult.

'A nun?' Charlie Harrison said, unable to conceal his astonishment.

'A nun,' she said.

Charlie tried to picture this vibrant, sensuous woman in a nun's habit. He simply couldn't do it. His imagination rebelled.

At least he understood why she projected an uncommon inner tranquility. Two years in a nunnery, two years of long daily sessions of meditation and prayer, two years isolated from the turbulent currents of everyday life were bound to have a lasting effect.

But none of this explained why she exerted such an instant, powerful attraction on him, or why he felt like a randy teenager in her company. That was still a mystery — a pleasant mystery, but a mystery nonetheless.

She said, 'I hung on for two years, trying to convince myself I had a vocation in the sisterhood. No good. When I left the convent, Evelyn was crushed. Her entire family had failed her. Then, a couple of years later, when I got pregnant with Joey, Evelyn was horrified. Her only daughter, who might've been a nun, instead turned out to be a loose woman, an unwed mother. She piled the guilt on me, smothered me in it.'

She looked down, paused for a moment to compose herself.

Charlie waited. He was as good at waiting as he was at listening.

Finally she said, 'By that time, I was a fallen-away Catholic. I'd pretty much lost my religion . . . or been driven away from it. Didn't go to Mass any more. But I was still enough of a Catholic to abhor the idea of abortion. I kept Joey, and I've never regretted it.'

'Your mother's never had a change of heart?'

'No. We speak to each other, but there's a vast gulf between us. And she won't have much to do with Joey.'

'That's too bad.'

'Ironically, almost from the day I got pregnant, my life turned around. Everything's gotten better and better since then. I was still carrying Joey when I went into business with Val Gardner and started Wine & Dine. By the time Joey was a year old, I was supporting my mother. I've had a lot of success, and it doesn't matter at all to her; it isn't good enough for her, not when I *could* have been a nun, and not when I *am* an unwed mother. She still heaps guilt on me each time I see her.'

'Well, now I can understand why you're sensitive about it.'

'So sensitive that . . . when all this started with the old woman yesterday . . . well, in the back of my mind I sort of wondered if maybe it was meant to be.'

'What do you mean?'

'Maybe I'm meant to lose Joey. Maybe it's inevitable. Even . . . predestined.'

'I don't follow you.'

She fidgeted, managed to look angry and dispirited and frightened and embarrassed all at the same time. She cleared her throat and took a deep breath and said, 'Well, uh, maybe . . . just maybe it's God's way of punishing me for failing as a nun, for breaking my mother's heart, for drifting away from the Church after once having been so close to it.'

'But that's . . .'

'Ridiculous?' she suggested.

'Well, yes.'

She nodded. 'I know.'

'God isn't spiteful.'

'I know,' she said sheepishly. 'It's silly. Illogical. Just

plain dumb. Yet . . . it gnaws at me. Silly things can be true sometimes.' She sighed and shook her head. 'I'm proud of Joey, fiercely proud, but I'm not proud of being an unwed mother.'

'You were going to tell me about the father . . . in case he might have something to do with this. What was his name?'

'He told me his name was Luke — actually Lucius — Under.'

'Under what?'

'That was his last name. Under. Lucius Under, but he told me to call him Luke.'

'Under. It's an unusual name.'

'It's a *phony* name. He was probably thinking about getting me out of my underwear when he made it up,' she said angrily, and then she blushed. Clearly, she was embarrassed by these personal revelations, but she forged ahead. 'It happened aboard a cruise ship to Mexico, one of those Love Boat-type excursions.' She laughed without humor when she spoke of love in this context. 'After I left the sisterhood and spent a few years working as a waitress, that trip was the first treat I gave myself. I met a man only a few hours out of LA. Very handsome . . . charming. Said his name was Luke. One thing led to another. He must have seen how vulnerable I was because he moved in like a shark. I was so different then, you see, so timid, very much the little ex-nun, a virgin, utterly inexperienced. We spent five days together on that ship, and I think most of it was in my cabin . . . in bed. A few weeks later, when I learned I was pregnant, I tried to contact him. I wasn't after support, you understand. I just thought he had a right to know about his son.' Another sour laugh. 'He'd given me an address and phone number, but they were phony. I considered tracking him down through the cruise line, but it would've been so . . . humiliating.' She smiled ruefully. 'Believe me, I've led a tame life ever since. Even before I knew I was pregnant, I felt . . . *soiled* by this man, that tawdry shipboard affair. I didn't want to feel like that again, so I've been well, not exactly a sexual recluse but . . . cautious. Maybe that's the ex-nun in me. And it's definitely the ex-nun in me that feels I need to be punished, that maybe God will punish me through Joey.'

He didn't know what to tell her. He was accustomed to providing physical, emotional, and mental comfort for his clients, but spiritual comfort wasn't something he knew how to supply.

'I'm a little crazy on the subject,' she said. 'And I'll probably drive *you* a little crazy with all my worrying. I'm always scared that Joey'll get sick or be hurt in an accident. I'm not just talking about ordinary motherly concern. Sometimes I'm almost *obsessed* with worry about him. And then yesterday this old crone shows up and tells me that my little boy is evil, says he's got to die, comes prowling around the house in the middle of the night, kills our dog . . . Well, God, I mean, she seems so relentless, so inevitable.'

'She's not,' Charlie said.

'So now that you know a little something about Evelyn . . . my mother . . . do you still think she could be involved in this?'

'Not really. But it's still possible the old woman heard your mother talking about you, talking about Joey, and that's how she fixated on you.'

'I think it was probably just pure chance. We were in the wrong place at the wrong time. If we hadn't been at the mall yesterday, if it had been some other woman with her little boy, that old hag would have fixated on them instead.'

'I imagine you're right,' he said.

He got up from the desk.

'But don't you worry about this crazy person,' he said. 'We'll find her.'

He went to the window.

'We'll put a stop to this harassment,' he said. 'You'll see.'

He looked out, over the top of the date palm. The white van was still parked across the street. The man in dark clothes was still leaning against the front fender, but he was no longer eating lunch. He was just waiting there, arms folded on his chest, ankles crossed, watching the front entrance of the building.

'Come here a minute,' Charlie said.

Christine came to the window.

'Could that be the van that was parked beside your car at the mall?'

'Yeah. One like that.'

'But could this be the *same* one?'

'You think I was followed this morning?'

'Would you have noticed if you had been?'

She frowned. 'I was in such a state . . . so nervous, upset . . . I might not have realized I was being tailed, not if it was done with at least some circumspection.'

'Then it could be the same van.'

'Or just a coincidence.'

'I don't believe in coincidences.'

'But if it's the same van, if I *was* followed, then who's the man leaning against it?'

They were too far above the stranger to get a good look at his face. They could tell very little about him from this distance. He might have been old or young or middle-aged.

'Maybe he's the old woman's husband. Or her son,' Charlie said.

'But if he's following me, he'd have to be as crazy as she is.'

'Probably.'

'The whole family can't be nuts.'

'No law against it,' he said.

He went to his desk and placed an in-house telephone call to Henry Rankin, one of his best men. He told Rankin about the van across the street. 'I want you to walk past it, get the license number, and take a look at that guy over there, so you'll recognize him later. Glom anything else you can without being conspicuous about it. Be sure to come and go by the back entrance, and circle all the way around the block, so he won't have any idea where you came from.'

'No sweat,' Rankin said.

'Once you've got the number, get on the line to the DMV and find out who holds the registration.'

'Yes, sir.'

'Then you report to me.'

'I'm leaving now.'

Charlie hung up. He went to the window again.

Christine said, 'Let's hope it's just a coincidence.'

'On the contrary — let's hope it's the same van. It's the best lead we could've asked for.'

'But if it is the same van, and if that guy's with it —'

'He's with it all right.'

'— then it's not just the old woman who's a threat to Joey. There're *two* of them.'

'Or more.'

'Huh?'

'Might be another one or two we don't know about.'

A bird swooped past the window.

The palm fronds stirred in the unseasonably warm breeze.

Sunshine silvered the windows of the cars parked along the street.

At the van, the stranger waited.

Christine said, 'What the *hell* is going on?'

78

10

In the windowless basement, eleven candles held the insistent shadows at bay.

The only noise was Mother Grace Spivey's increasingly labored breathing as she settled deeper into a trance. The eleven disciples made no sound whatsoever.

Kyle Barlowe was silent, too, and perfectly still even though he was uncomfortable. The oak chair on which he sat was too small for him. That wasn't the fault of the chair, which would have provided adequate seating for anyone else in the room. But Barlowe was so big that, to him, most furniture seemed to have been designed and constructed for use by dwarves. He liked deep-seated, over-stuffed easy chairs and old-fashioned wing-backed armchairs but only if the wings were angled wide enough to accommodate his broad shoulders. He liked king-sized beds, Lay-Z-Boy recliners, and ancient claw-foot bathtubs that were so large they didn't force him to sit with his legs drawn up as if he were a baby taking a bath in a basin. His apartment in Santa Ana was furnished to his dimensions, but when he wasn't at home he was usually uncomfortable to one degree or another.

However, as Mother Grace slipped deeper into her trance, Barlowe became increasingly eager to hear what message she would bring from the spirit world, and gradually he ceased to notice that he seemed to be perched on a child's playroom chair.

He adored Mother Grace. She had told him about the coming of Twilight, and he had believed every word. Twilight. Yes, it made sense. The world was long overdue for Twilight. By warning him that it was coming, by soliciting his help to prepare mankind for it, Mother Grace had given him an opportunity to redeem himself before it was too late. She had saved him, body and soul.

Until he met her, he had spent most of his twenty-nine years in the single-minded pursuit of self-destruction. He'd been a drunkard, a barroom brawler, a dope addict, a rapist, even a murderer. He'd been promiscuous, bedding at least one new woman every week, most of them junkies or prostitutes or both. He'd contracted gonorrhea seven or eight times, syphilis twice, and it was amazing he hadn't gotten both diseases more often than that.

On rare occasions, he had been sober and clear-headed enough to be disgusted or even frightened by his lifestyle. But he had rationalized his behavior by telling himself that self-loathing and anti-social violence were simply the natural responses to the thoughtless — and sometimes intentional — cruelty with which most people treated him.

To the world at large, he was a freak, a lumbering giant with a Neanderthaloid face that would scare off a grizzly bear. Little children were usually frightened of him. People of all ages stared, some openly and some surreptitiously. A few even laughed at him when they thought he wasn't looking, joked about him behind his back. He usually pretended not to be aware of it — unless he was in a mood to break arms and kick ass. But he was *always* aware, and it hurt. Certain teenagers were the worst, especially certain girls, who giggled and laughed openly at him; now and then, when they were at a safe distance, they even taunted him. He had never been anything but an outsider, shunned and alone.

For many years, his violent and self-destructive life had been easy to justify to himself. Bitterness, hatred, and rage had seemed to be essential armor against society's cruelty. Without his reckless disregard for personal well-being and without his diligently nurtured lust for revenge, he would have felt defenseless. The world insisted on making an outcast of him, insisted on seeing him as either a seven-foot buffoon with a monkey's face or a threatening monster. Well, he wasn't a buffoon, but he didn't mind playing the monster for them; he didn't mind showing them just how viciously, shockingly monstrous he could be when he really put his mind to it. *They* had made him what he was. He wasn't responsible for his crimes. He was bad because they had *made* him bad. For most of his life, that's what he had told himself.

Until he met Mother Grace Spivey.

She showed him what a self-pitying wretch he was. She made him see that his justifications for sinful and self-indulgent behavior were pitifully flimsy. She taught him that an outcast could gain strength, courage, and even pride from his condition. She helped him see Satan within himself and helped him throw the devil out.

She helped him understand that his great strength and his singular talent for destruction were to be used only to bring terror and punishment to the enemies of God.

Now, sitting in front of Mother Grace as she drifted in a trance, Kyle Barlowe regarded her with unqualified adoration. He didn't see that her untrimmed mane of gray hair was frizzy, knotted, and slightly greasy; to him, in the flickering golden light, her shining hair was a holy nimbus framing her face, a halo. He didn't see that her clothes were badly wrinkled; he didn't notice the threads and lint and dandruff and food stains that decorated her. He saw only what he wanted to see, and he wanted to see salvation.

She groaned. Her eyelids fluttered but did not open.

Still sitting on the floor and holding their candles steady, the eleven disciples of the inner council became tense, but none of them spoke or made any sound that might break the fragile spell.

'Oh God,' Mother Grace said as if she had just seen something awesome or perhaps terrifying. 'Oh God oh God oh *God*!'

She winced. She shuddered. She licked her lips nervously.

Sweat broke out on her brow.

She was breathing harder than before. She gasped, open-mouthed, as if she were drowning. Then she drew breath through clenched teeth, with a cold hissing sound.

Barlowe waited patiently.

Mother Grace raised her hands, grabbed at the empty air. Her rings gleamed in the candlelight. Then her hands fell back into her lap, fluttered briefly like dying birds, and were still.

At last she spoke in a weak, strained, tremulous voice that was barely recognizable as her own. 'Kill him.'

'Who?' Barlowe asked.

'The boy.'

The eleven disciples stirred, looked at one another meaningfully, and the movement of their candles caused shadows to twist and flap and shift all over the room.

'You mean Joey Scavello?' Barlowe asked.

'Yes. Kill him,' Mother Grace said from a great distance. '*Now*.'

For reasons that neither Barlowe nor Mother Grace understood, he was the only person who could communicate with her when she was in a trance. If others spoke to her, she wouldn't hear them. She was the only contact they had with the spirit world, the sole conduit for all messages from the other side, but it was Barlowe, through his careful and patient questioning, who made certain that those messages were always clear and fully detailed. More than anything else, it was this function, this precious gift that convinced him he was one of God's chosen people, just as Mother Grace said he was.

'Kill him . . . kill him,' she chanted softly in a raspy voice.

'You're sure this boy is the one?' Barlowe asked.

'Yes.'

'There's no doubt?'

'None.'

'How can he be killed?'

Mother Grace's face was slack now. Lines had appeared in her usually creaseless skin. Her pale flesh hung like wrinkled, lifeless cloth.

'How can we destroy him?' Barlowe inquired again.

Her mouth hung open wide. Breath rattled in her throat. Saliva glistened at one corner of her lips, welled up, and drooled slowly onto her chin.

'Mother Grace?' Barlowe prodded.

Her voice was even fainter than before: 'Kill him . . . any way you choose.'

'With a gun, a knife? Fire?'

'Any weapon . . . will succeed . . . but only if . . . you act soon.'

'How soon?'

'Time is running out. Day by day . . . he becomes . . . more powerful . . . less vulnerable.'

'When we kill him, is there a ritual we must follow?' Barlowe asked.

'Only that . . . once dead . . . his heart . . .'

'What about his heart?'

'Must be . . . cut *out*,' she said, her voice becoming somewhat stronger, sharper.

'And then?'

'It will be black.'

'His heart will be black?'

'As coal. And rotten. And you will see . . .'

She sat up straighter in her chair. The sweat from her brow was trickling down her face. Tiny beads of perspiration had popped out of her upper lip. Like a pair of stricken moths, her white hands fluttered in her lap. Color returned to her face, although her eyes remained closed. She was no longer drooling, but spittle still shone on her chin.

'What will we see when we cut his heart out?' Barlowe asked.

'Worms,' she said with disgust.

'In the boy's heart?'

'Yes. And beetles. Squirming.'

A few of the disciples murmured to one another. It didn't matter. Nothing could disturb Mother Grace's trance now. She was thoroughly caught up in it, swept away by her visions.

Leaning forward in his chair, his big hands clamped on his meaty thighs, Barlowe said, 'What must we do with the heart once we've cut it out of him?'

She chewed on her lip so he was afraid she would draw blood. She raised her spastic hands again and worked them in the empty air as if she could wring the answer from the ether.

Then: 'Plunge the heart into . . .'

'Into what?' Barlowe asked.

'A bowl of holy water.'

'From a church?'

'Yes. The water will remain cool . . . but the heart . . . will boil, turn to dark steam . . . and evaporate.'

'And then we can be certain the boy is dead?'

'Yes. Dead. Forever dead. Unable to return through another incarnation.'

'Then there's hope?' Barlowe asked, hardly daring to believe that it was so.

'Yes,' she said thickly. 'Hope.'

'Praise God,' Barlowe said.

'Praise God,' the disciples said.

Mother Grace opened her eyes. She yawned, sighed, blinked, and looked around in confusion. 'Where's this? What's wrong? I feel all clammy. Did I miss the six o'clock news? I mustn't miss the six o'clock news. I've got to know what Lucifer's people have been up to.'

'It's only a few minutes till noon,' Barlowe said. 'The six o'clock news is hours away.'

She stared at him with that familiar, blurry-eyed, muddle-headed look that always marked her return from a deep trance. 'Who're you? Do I know you? I don't think I do.'

'I'm Kyle, Mother Grace.'

'Kyle?' she said as if she'd never heard of him. A suspicious glint entered her eyes.

'Just relax,' he said. 'Relax and think about it. You've had a vision. You'll remember it in a moment. It'll come back to you.'

He held out both of his large, calloused hands. Sometimes, when she came out of a trance, she was so frightened and lost that she needed friendly contact. Usually, when she gripped his hands, she drew from his great reservoir of physical strength and soon regained her senses, as if he were a battery that she was tapping.

But today she pulled away from him. She frowned. She wiped at her spittle-damp chin. She looked around at the candles, at the disciples, clearly baffled by them. 'God, I'm so thirsty,' she said.

One of the disciples hurried to get her a drink.

She looked at Kyle. 'What do you want from me? Why'd you bring me here?'

'It'll all come back to you,' he said patiently, smiling reassuringly.

'I don't like this place,' she said, her voice thin and querulous.

'It's your church.'

'Church?'

'The basement of your church.'

'It's dark,' she whined.

'You're safe here.'

She pouted as if she were a child, then scowled, then said, 'I don't like the dark. I'm afraid of the dark.' She hugged herself. 'What've you got me here in the dark for?'

One of the disciples got up and turned on the lights. The others blew out the candles.

'Church?' Mother Grace said again, looking at the paneled basement walls and at the exposed ceiling beams. She was trying hard to get a handle on her situation, but she was still disoriented.

There was nothing Barlowe could do to help her. Sometimes, she needed as long as ten minutes to shake off the confusion that always followed a journey into the spirit world.

She stood up.

Barlowe stood, too, towering over her.

She said, 'I gotta pee real bad. *Real* bad.' She grimaced and put one hand on her abdomen. 'Isn't there anywhere to pee in this place? Huh? I got to *pee*.'

Barlowe motioned to Edna Vanoff, a short stout woman who was a member of the inner council, and Edna led Mother Grace to the lavatory at the far end of the basement. The old woman was unsteady; she leaned against Edna as she walked, and she continued to look around in bewilderment.

In a loud voice that carried the length of the room, Mother Grace said, 'Oh, boy, I gotta pee so bad I think I'm gonna bust.'

Barlowe sighed wearily and sat down on the too-small, too-hard wooden chair.

The most difficult thing for him — and for the other disciples — to understand and accept was Mother Grace's bizarre behavior after a vision. At times like this she didn't seem at all like a great spiritual leader. Instead, she seemed as if she were nothing more than a befuddled, crazy old woman. In ten minutes, at most, she would have regained her wits, as she always did; soon she would be the same intense, sharp-minded, clear-eyed woman who had converted him from a life of sin. Then no one would doubt her insight, power, and holiness; no one would question the truth of her exalted mission. However, just for these few disconcerting minutes, even though he had seen her in this dismaying condition many times before and knew it wouldn't last, Barlowe nevertheless felt uneasy, sick with uncertainty.

He doubted her.

And hated himself for doubting.

He supposed that God put Mother Grace through these sorry, undignified spells of disorientation for the very purpose of testing the faith of her followers. It was God's way of making certain that only Mother Grace's most devoted disciples remained with her, thereby insuring a strong church during the difficult days ahead. Yet, every time she was like this, Barlowe was badly shaken by the way she looked and acted.

He glanced at the members of the inner council, who were still sitting on the floor. All of them looked troubled, and all of them were praying. He figured they were praying for the strength not to doubt Mother Grace the way he was doubting her. He closed his eyes and began to pray, too.

They were going to need all the strength, faith, and confidence they could find within themselves, for killing the boy wasn't going to be easy. He wasn't an ordinary child. Mother Grace had adamantly made that clear. He would possess awesome powers of his own, and perhaps he would even be able to destroy them the moment they dared lift a hand against him. But for the sake of all mankind, they had to try to kill him.

Barlowe hoped Mother Grace would permit him to strike the mortal blow. Even if it meant his own death, he wanted to be the one who actually drew the boy's blood because whoever killed the boy (or died in the attempt) was assured of a place in Heaven, close to the throne of God. Barlowe was convinced that this was true. If he used his tremendous physical strength and his pent-up rage to strike out at this evil child, he would be making amends for all the times he had harmed the innocent in the days before Mother Grace had converted him.

Sitting on the hard oak chair, eyes closed, praying, he slowly curled his big hands into fists. He began to breathe faster. Eagerness was apparent in the hunch of his shoulders and in the bunching of muscles in his neck and jaws. Tremors passed through him. He was impatient to do God's work.

11

Less than twenty minutes after he had left, Henry Rankin returned to Charlie Harrison's office with the Department of Motor Vehicles' report on the white van's license number.

Rankin was a small man, five-three, slender, with an athletic grace and bearing. Christine wondered if he had ever been a jockey. He was well dressed in a pair of black Bally loafers, a light gray suit, white shirt, and a blue knit tie, with a blue display handkerchief carefully folded in the breast pocket of his jacket. He didn't look anything like Christine's conception of a private investigator.

After Rankin was introduced to Christine, he handed Charlie a sheet of paper and said, 'According to the DMV, the van belongs to a printing company called The True Word.'

Come to think of it, Charlie Harrison didn't look much like a private investigator, either. She expected a PI to be tall. Charlie wasn't short like Henry Rankin, but he was only about five-ten or five-eleven. She expected a PI to be built like a truck, to look as if he could ram through a brick wall. Charlie was lean, and although he looked as if he could take care of himself well enough, he would never ram through a wall, brick or otherwise. She expected a PI to seem at least a little bit dangerous, with a violent aspect to his eyes and perhaps a tight-lipped, cruel mouth. Charlie appeared to be intelligent, efficient, capable – but not dangerous. He had an unremarkable, though generally handsome face framed by thick blond hair that was neatly combed. His eyes were his best features, gray-green, clear, direct; they were warm, friendly eyes, but there was no violence in them, at least none that she could detect.

In spite of the fact that neither Charlie nor Rankin looked like Magnum or Sam Spade or Philip Marlowe, Christine sensed she had come to the right place. Charlie Harrison was friendly, self-possessed, plain-spoken. He walked, turned, and performed every task with an unusual economy of motion, and his gestures, too, were neat and precise. He projected an aura of competence and trustworthiness. She suspected that he seldom, if ever, failed to do his job well. He made her feel secure.

Few people had that effect on her. Damned few. Especially men. In the past, when she had relied upon men, her faith had not always – or even usually – been well placed. However, instinct told her that Charlie Harrison was different from most other men and that she would not regret placing her trust in him.

Charlie looked up from the paper Rankin had given him. 'The True Word, huh? Anything on it in our files?'

'Nothing.'

Charlie looked at Christine. 'You ever hear of them?'

'No.'

'You ever have any brochures or stationery or anything printed for that gourmet shop of yours?'

'Sure. But that's not the printer we use.'

'Okay,' Charlie said, 'we'll have to find out who owns the company, try to get a list of their employees, start checking everyone out.'

'Can do,' Henry Rankin said.

To Christine, Charlie said, 'You might have to talk with your mother about this, Ms. Scavello.'

'I'd rather not,' she said. 'Not unless it becomes absolutely necessary.'

'Well . . . all right. But it probably *will* become necessary. For now . . . you might as well go on to work. It'll take us a while to dig into this.'

'What about Joey?'

'He can stay here with me this afternoon,' Charlie said. 'I want to see what'll happen if you leave without the boy. Will the guy in the van follow you — or will he wait for Joey to come out? Which of you is he most interested in?'

He'll wait for Joey, Christie thought grimly. Because it's Joey he wants to kill.

Sherry Ordway, the receptionist at Klemet-Harrison, wondered if she and Ted, her husband, had made a mistake. Six years ago, after three years of marriage, they had decided they didn't really want children, and Ted had had a vasectomy. With no children, they could afford a better house and better furniture and a nicer car, and they were free to travel, and the evenings were always peaceful and perfect for curling up with a book – or with each other. Most of their friends were tied down with families, and every time Sherry and Ted saw someone else's child being rude or downright malevolent, they congratulated themselves on the wisdom of avoiding parenthood. They relished their freedom, and Sherry never regretted remaining childless. Until now. As she answered the telephone and typed letters and did filing, she watched Joey Scavello, and she began to wish (just a little) that he was hers.

He was such a good kid. He sat in one of the armchairs in the waiting area, dwarfed by it, his feet off the floor. He spoke when spoken to, but he didn't interrupt anyone or call attention to himself. He leafed through some of the magazines, looking at pictures, and he hummed softly to himself, and he was just about the cutest thing she'd ever seen.

She had just finished typing a letter and had been surreptitiously watching the boy as, with much frowning and tongue-biting, he checked the knots in the laces of his sneakers and retied one of them. She was about to ask him if he would like another of her butterscotch Life Savers when the telephone rang.

'Klemet-Harrison,' Sherry said.

A woman said, 'Is Joey Scavello there? He's just a little boy, six years old. You can't miss him if he's there; he's such a charmer.'

Surprised that anyone would be calling the boy, Sherry hesitated.

'This is his grandmother,' the woman said. 'Christine told me she was bringing Joey to your office.'

'Oh. His grandmother. Why, yes, of course, they're here right now. Mrs. Scavello is in Mr. Harrison's office at the moment. She's not available, but I'm sure –'

'Well, it's Joey I really want to talk to. Is he in with Mr. Harrison, too?'

'No. He's right here with me.'

'Do you think I could speak to him for a moment?' the woman said. 'If it's not too much trouble.'

'Oh, it's no trouble — '

'I won't tie up your line for long.'

'Sure. Just a minute,' Sherry said. She held the phone away from her face and said, 'Joey? It's for you. Your grandmother.'

'Grandma?' he said, and seemed to be amazed.

He came to the desk. Sherry gave him the phone, and he said hello, but didn't say anything else. He went stiff, his small hand clenching the handset so tightly that his knuckles looked as if they would pierce the skin that sheathed them. He stood there, wide-eyed, listening. The blood drained out of his face. His eyes filled with tears. Suddenly, with a gasp and shudder, he slammed the phone down.

Sherry jumped in surprise. 'Joey? What's wrong?'

His mouth became soft and tremulous.

'Joey?'

'It was . . . h-her.'

'Your grandmother.'

'No. The w-witch.'

'Witch?'

'She said . . . she's gonna . . . c-c-cut my heart out.'

Charlie sent Joey into his office with Christine, closed the door after them, and remained in the lounge to question Sherry.

She looked distraught. 'I shouldn't have let her talk to him. I didn't realize — '

'It wasn't your fault,' Henry Rankin said.

'Of course it wasn't,' Charlie told her.

'What sort of woman – '

'That's what we're trying to find out,' Charlie said. 'I want you to think about the call and answer a few questions.'

'There wasn't much said.'

'She claimed to be his grandmother?'

'Yes.'

'She said she was Mrs. Scavello?'

'Well . . . no. She didn't give her name. But she knew he was here with his mother, and I never suspected . . . I mean, well, she *sounded* like a grandmother.'

'Exactly what did she sound like?' Henry asked.

'God, I don't know . . . a very pleasant voice,' Sherry said.

'She speak with an accent?' Charlie asked.

'No.'

'Doesn't have to have been a real obvious accent to be of help to us,' Henry said. 'Almost everyone speaks with at least a mild accent of some kind.'

'Well, if it was there, I didn't notice it,' Sherry said.

'Did you hear anything in the background?' Charlie asked.

'Like what?'

'Any noise of any kind?'

'No.'

'If she was calling from an outdoor pay phone, for instance, there would've been traffic noises, street noises of some kind.'

'There wasn't anything like that.'

'Any noises that might help us figure the kind of place she was calling from?'

'No. Just her voice,' Sherry said. 'She sounded so *nice*.'

12

After her vision, Mother Grace dismissed all her disciples except Kyle Barlowe and Edna Vanoff. Then, using the phone in the church basement, she placed a call to the detective agency where Joey Scavello and his mother had gone, and she spoke briefly with the boy. Kyle wasn't sure he saw the sense of it, but Mother Grace was pleased.

'Killing him isn't sufficient,' she said. 'We must terrify and demoralize him, too. Through the boy, we'll bring fear and despair to Satan himself. We'll make the devil understand, at last, that the Good Lord will never permit him to rule the earth, and then he'll finally abandon his schemes and hopes of glory.'

Kyle loved to hear her talk like that. When he listened to Mother Grace, he knew that he was a vital part of the most important events in the history of the world. Awe and humility made his knees weak.

Grace led Kyle and Edna to the far end of the basement, where a wood-paneled wall contained a cleverly concealed door. Beyond the door lay a room measuring twenty by twenty-six feet. It was full of guns.

Early in her mission, Mother Grace had received a vision in which she had been warned that, when Twilight came, she must be prepared to defend herself with more than just prayer. She had taken the vision very seriously indeed. This was not the church's only armory.

Kyle had been here many times before. He enjoyed the coolness of the room, the vague scent of gun oil. Most of all he took pleasure from the realization that terrible destruction waited quietly on these shelves, like a malevolent genie in a bottle, needing only a hand to pull the cork.

Kyle liked guns. He liked to turn a gun over and over in his enormous hands, sensing the power in it the way a blind man senses the meaning in lines of Braille.

Sometimes, when his sleep was particularly deep and dark, he dreamed about holding a large gun in both hands and pointing it at people. It was a .357 Magnum, with a bore that seemed as big as a cannon's, and when it roared it was like the voice of a dragon. Each time it bucked in his hands, it gave him a jolt of intense pleasure.

For a while he had worried about these night-fantasies because he had thought it meant the devil hadn't been driven out of him, after all. But he came to see that the people in the dreams were God's enemies and that it was good for him to fantasize their destruction. Kyle was destined to be an instrument of divine justice. Grace had told him so.

Now, in the armory, Mother Grace went to the shelves along the wall to the left of the door. She took down a box, opened it, removed the plastic-wrapped revolver that lay within, and put the weapon on a work table. The gun she had chosen was a Smith & Wesson .38 Chiefs Special, a snub-barreled piece that packed a lot of wallop. She took another one from the shelf, removed it from its box, and placed it beside the first.

Edna Vanoff removed the weapons from their plastic wrappings.

Before the day was done, the boy would be dead, and it might be one of these two weapons that destroyed him.

Mother Grace removed a Remington 20-gauge shotgun from one of the shelves and brought it to the work table.

Kyle's excitement grew.

13

Joey sat in Charlie's chair, behind the big desk, sipping Coca-Cola that Charlie had poured for him.

Christine was in the client's chair once more. She was shaken. A couple of times, Charlie saw her put her fingernail between her teeth and almost bite it before she realized she'd be biting acrylic.

He was upset that they had been reached and disturbed *here*, in his offices. They had come to him for help, for protection, and now both of them were frightened again.

Sitting on the edge of his desk, looking at Joey, he said, 'If you don't want to talk about the phone call, I'll understand. But I'd really like to ask you some questions.'

To his mother, Joey said, 'I thought we were going to hire Magnum.'

Christine said, 'Honey, you've forgotten that Magnum's in Hawaii.'

'Oh, yeah. Jeez, that's right,' the boy said. He looked troubled. 'Magnum would've been the best one to help us.'

For a moment Charlie didn't know what the boy was talking about, and then he remembered the television show, and he smiled.

Joey took a long drink of his Coke, studying Charlie over the rim of the glass. Finally he said, 'I guess you'll be okay.'

Charlie almost laughed. 'You won't be sorry you came to us, Joey. Now . . . what did the woman on the phone say to you?'

'She said . . . "You can't hide from me." '

Charlie heard fear ooze into the boy's voice, and he quickly said, 'Well, she's wrong about that. If we have to

96

hide you from her, we can. Don't you worry about that. What else did she say?'

'She said she knew what I was.'

'What do you think she meant by that?'

The boy looked baffled. 'I don't know.'

'What else did she say?'

'She said . . . she'd cut my heart out.'

A strangled sound came from Christine. She stood, nervously clutching her purse. 'I think I ought to take Joey . . . away somewhere.'

'Maybe eventually,' Charlie said soothingly. 'But not just yet.'

'I think now's the time. Before . . . anything happens. We could go to San Francisco. Or farther. I've never been to the Caribbean. This is a good time of the year for the Caribbean, isn't it?'

'Give me at least twenty-four hours,' Charlie said.

'Yeah? Twenty-four hours? And what if that hag catches up with us? No. We should leave today.'

'And how long do you intend to stay away?' Charlie asked. 'A week? A month? A year?'

'Two weeks should be long enough. You'll find her in two weeks.'

'Not necessarily.'

'Then how long?'

Understanding and sympathizing with Christine's concern, wanting to be gentle with her, knowing that he had to be blunt instead, Charlie said, 'Clearly, she's got some sort of fixation on Joey, some sort of obsession about him. It's Joey that keeps her motor running, so to speak. Without him around, she might pull in her horns. She might evaporate on us. We might never find her if Joey isn't here to bring her out. Do you intend to go on vacation *forever*?'

'Are you saying you intend to use my son as *bait*?'

'No. Not exactly. We'd never put him right in the jaws of a trap. We'll use him more as a lure.'

'That's outrageous!'

'But it's the only way we'll get her. If he's not around, there'll be no reason for her to show herself.' He went to Christine and put a hand on her shoulder. 'He'll be guarded at all times. He'll be safe.'

'Like hell he will.'

'I swear to you –'

'You've already got the van's license number,' she said.

'That might not be enough. It might not lead anywhere.'

'You've got the name of the company that owns it. The True Word.'

'That might not be enough, either. And if it's not enough, if it doesn't lead us anywhere, then Joey has to be around so the old woman has a reason to risk exposing herself.'

'Seems like *we're* the ones taking the risks.'

'Trust me,' he said softly.

She met his eyes.

He said, 'Sit down. Come on. Give me a chance. Later, if I see any indication – the *slightest* indication – that we might not able to handle the situation, I'll send you and Joey out of town for a while. But please . . . not just yet.'

She looked past him at her son, who had put down his glass of Coke and was sitting on the edge of Charlie's big chair. She seemed to realize that her fear was directly transmitted to the boy, and she sat down and composed herself as Charlie requested.

He sat on the edge of his desk again. 'Joey, don't worry about the witch. I know just how to deal with witches. Leave the worrying to me. Now . . . you were on the phone, and she said she wanted to cut . . . cut you. What did she say after that?'

The boy screwed up his face, trying to remember. 'Not much . . . just something about some judges.'

'Judges?'

'Yeah. She said something like . . . God wants her to bring some judge men to me.'

'Judgment?' Charlie asked.

'Yeah,' the boy said. 'She said she was bringing these judge men to see me. She said God wasn't gonna let me escape from her.' He looked at his mother. 'Why does God want that old witch to get me?'

'He doesn't want her to get you, honey. She was lying. She's crazy. God has nothing to do with this.'

Frowning, Charlie said, 'Maybe, in a roundabout way, He does. When Henry said the van was owned by a printing company called The True Word, I wondered if maybe it was a religious printing company. "The True Word" — meaning the holy word, scripture, the *Bible*. Maybe what we've got on our hands here is a religious fanatic.'

'Or two,' she said, glancing at the window, obviously remembering the man with the white van.

Or more than two, Charlie thought uneasily.

During the past couple of decades, when it had become fashionable to distrust and disparage all of society's institutions (as if there had been no wisdom at all in the creation of them), a lot of religious cults had sprung up, eager to fill the power vacuum. Some of them were honest, earnest off-shoots of long-established religions, and some were crackpot organizations established for the benefit of their founders, to enrich them, or to spread their gospels of madness and violence and bigotry. California was more tolerant of unusual and controversial views than any other state in the union; therefore, California was home to more cults, both good and bad, than anywhere else. It wouldn't be surprising if, for some bizarre reason, one of these cults had gone looking for scapegoats or sacrifices and had settled on an innocent six-year-old boy. Crazy, yes, but not particularly surprising.

Charlie hoped that wasn't the explanation for what had happened to the Scavellos. No one was harder to deal with than a religious fanatic on a holy mission.

Then, as Charlie turned away from Christine, as he looked back at the boy, something odd happened. Something frightening.

For a moment the boy's smooth young skin seemed to become translucent, then almost entirely transparent. Incredibly, the skull was visible beneath the skin. Charlie could see hollow dark eye sockets staring at him. Worms writhing deep in those calcimine pits. A bony smile. Gaping black holes where the nose should have been. Joey's face was still there, though it was like a vague photograph superimposed over the skeletal countenance. A presentiment of death.

Shocked, Charlie stood and coughed.

The brief vision left him almost as soon as it came, shimmering before him for no more than a split second. And he told himself it was his imagination, though nothing like this had ever happened to him before.

An icy snake of fear uncoiled in his stomach.

Just imagination. Not a vision. There *weren't* such things as visions. Charlie didn't believe in the supernatural, in psychic phenomena or any of that claptrap. He was a *sensible* man and prided himself on his solid, dependable nature.

To cover his surprise and fear, but also to put the grisly sight out of mind, he said, 'Uh, okay then, I think now you should just go on to work, Christine. As much as you can, try to carry on as if this were an ordinary day. I know it won't be easy. But you've got to get on with your business and your life while we're sorting this out for you. Henry Rankin will go with you. I've already talked to him about it.'

'You mean . . . he'll come along as my bodyguard?'

'I know he's not a big man,' Charlie said, 'but he's a martial arts expert, and he carries a gun, and if I had to choose any man from among my staff to entrust with my own life, I think it would be Henry.'

'I'm sure he's competent. But I don't really need a bodyguard. I mean it's *Joey* the woman wants.'

'And getting at you is an indirect way of getting at him,' Charlie said. 'Henry goes with you.'

'What about me?' Joey said. 'Am I going to pre-school?' He looked at his Mickey Mouse watch. 'I'm already late.'

'No pre-school today,' Charlie said. 'You'll stay with me.'

'Yeah? Am I gonna help you do some investigating?'

Charlie smiled. 'Sure. I could use a bright young assistant.'

'Wow! You hear him, Mom? I'm gonna be like Magnum.'

Christine forced a smile, and even though it was false it made her face lovelier than ever. Charlie longed to see a real, warm, genuine smile take possession of her.

She kissed her son goodbye, and Charlie could see that it was difficult, even painful, for her to leave the boy under these circumstances.

He walked her to the door while, behind them, Joey picked up his Coke again.

She said, 'Should I come back here after I leave work?'

'No. We'll bring him to the store at . . . what . . . five o'clock?'

'That'll be fine.'

'Then you and Joey'll go home with bodyguards. They'll stay the night. Two of them in the house with you. And I'll probably have a man stationed out on the street, watching for people who don't belong in the neighborhood.'

Charlie opened the door between his office and the reception lounge, but suddenly Joey called out to his mother, and she turned back.

'What about the dog?' the boy said, getting up, coming out from around Charlie's desk.

'We'll look for one tomorrow, honey.'

During the past few minutes, the boy had not been visibly frightened. Now, he became tense and uneasy again. 'Today,' he said. 'You promised. You said we'd get another dog today.'

'Honey —'

'I got to have a dog today, before it gets dark,' the boy said plaintively. 'I just got to, Mom. I got to.'

'I can take him to buy a dog,' Charlie said.

'You have work to do,' she said.

'This is not a hole-in-the-wall operation, dear lady. I've got a staff to do the leg work. My job, for the time being, is to look after Joey, and if getting him a dog is part of looking after him, then I'll take him to get a dog. No problem. Is there any pet store you'd prefer?'

'We got Brandy at the pound,' Joey said. 'Rescued him from certain death.'

'Did you?' Charlie said, amused.

'Yeah. They was gonna put Brandy to sleep. Only it wasn't just sleep, see. What it was . . . well, it was sleep, yeah, but it was a whole lot worse than just sleep.'

'I can take him to the pound,' Charlie told Christine.

'We'll rescue another one!' Joey said.

'If it's not too much trouble,' Christine said.

'Sounds like fun,' Charlie said.

She looked at him with evident gratitude, and he winked at her, and she smiled a halfway *real* smile this time, and Charlie wanted to kiss her, but he didn't.

'Not a German shepherd,' Christine said. 'They sort of scare me. Not a boxer either.'

'What about a Great Dane?' Charlie asked, teasing her. 'Or maybe a St. Bernard or a Doberman?'

'Yeah!' Joey said excitedly. 'A Doberman!'

'How about a big, fierce Alsatian with three-inch-long teeth?' Charlie said.

'You're incorrigible,' Christine said, but she smiled again, and it was that smile he was trying so hard to elicit.

'We'll get a good dog,' Charlie said. 'Don't worry. Trust me.'

'Maybe I'll call him Pluto,' Joey said.

Charlie looked askance. 'Why would you want to call me Pluto?'

Joey giggled. 'Not *you*. The new dog.'

'Pluto,' Charlie said, mulling it over. 'Not bad.'

For that one shining moment, it seemed as if all was right with the world. It seemed there was no such thing as death. And for the first time, Charlie had the feeing that the three of them somehow belonged together, that their destinies were linked, that they had more of a future together than just their investigator-client relationship. It was a nice, warm feeling. Too bad it couldn't last.

14

Two revolvers and two shotguns lay on the work table in the armory. All four weapons had been loaded. Boxes of spare ammunition stood beside the firearms.

Mother Grace had sent Edna Vanoff on another errand. She and Kyle were alone.

Kyle picked up the shotgun. 'I'll lead the attack.'

'No,' Mother Grace said.

'No? But you've always told me I'd be allowed to –'

'The boy won't be easy to kill,' Mother Grace said.

'So?'

'He isn't fully human. Demonic blood flows in his veins.'

'He doesn't frighten me,' Kyle said.

'He should. His powers are great and growing every day.'

'But I've got the power of Almighty God behind me.'

'Nevertheless, this first attack will almost surely fail.'

'I'm prepared to die,' he said.

'I know, dear boy. I know. But I mustn't risk losing you at the very beginning of this battle. You're too valuable. You're my link between this world and the spirit realm.'

'I'm also the hammer,' he said petulantly.

'I'm aware of your strength.'

She took the shotgun away from him, returned it to the table.

He felt a terrible need to strike out at something – as long as he was striking out in the name of God, of course. He no longer needed to wreak pain and destruction on the innocent merely for the satisfaction of it. Those days were gone forever. But he longed to be a soldier for God. His chest tightened and his stomach twisted with his need.

He had been looking forward to the attack tonight. Anticipation had rubbed his nerves raw. 'The hammer of God,' he reminded her.

'And in time you'll be used,' she assured him.

'*When?*'

'When there's a real chance of destroying the child.'

'Huh? If there's no chance of destroying him tonight, then why go after the little bastard? Why not wait?'

'Because, if we're lucky, we might at least hurt him, wound him,' Mother Grace said. 'And that will shake his confidence. Right now, the little beast believes that we can never really cause him harm. If he begins to think he's vulnerable, then he'll *become* more vulnerable. We must first weaken his self-confidence. Do you see?'

Reluctantly, Kyle nodded.

'And if we're very fortunate,' Grace said, 'if God is with us and the devil is off guard, we might be able to kill the mother. Then the boy will be alone. The dog is already gone. If the mother is removed, as well, the boy will have no one, and his confidence will collapse, and he'll become extremely vulnerable.'

'Then let me kill the mother,' Kyle pleaded.

She smiled at him and shook her head. 'Dear boy, when God wants you to be His hammer, I'll tell you. Until then, you must be patient.'

Charlie stood at the window with a pair of high-power binoculars that doubled as a camera. He focused on the man standing by the white van on the street below. The stranger was about six feet tall, thin, pale, with a tightly compressed mouth, a narrow nose, and thick dark eyebrows that grew together in the center of his face. He was an intense looking man, and he couldn't keep his hands still. One hand tugged at his shirt collar. The other hand smoothed his hair, then pinched one ear lobe. Scratched his chin. Picked lint from his jacket. Smoothed his hair again. He would never pass for an ordinary workman taking a leisurely lunch break.

Charlie snapped several pictures of him.

When Christine Scavello and Henry drove away in the woman's gray Firebird, the watcher almost got in the van to follow them. But he hesitated, looked around, puzzled, and finally decided to stay where he was.

Joey stood beside Charlie. He was just tall enough to see out the window. 'He's waiting for me, huh?'

'Looks that way.'

'Why don't we go out there and shoot him?' Joey asked.

Charlie laughed. 'Can't go around shooting people. Not in California, anyway. Maybe if this was *New York* . . .'

'But you're a private eye,' Joey said. 'Don't you have a license to kill?'

'That's James Bond.'

'You know him, too?' Joey asked.

'Not really. But I know his brother,' Charlie said.

'Yeah? I never heard of his brother. What's his name?'

'Municipal Bond,' Charlie said.

'That's a weird name,' Joey said, not getting the joke.

He's only six, Charlie reminded himself. Sometimes the kid behaved as if he were a few years older, and he expressed himself with clarity that you didn't expect of a pre-schooler.

The boy looked out the window again. For a moment he was silent as Charlie snapped two final photographs of the man at the white van, and then he said, 'I don't see why we can't shoot him. He'd shoot me if he got the chance.'

'Oh, I don't think he'd really go that far,' Charlie said, trying to discourage the boy from frightening himself.

But with an equanimity and a steadiness of voice that, given the circumstances, were beyond his years, Joey said, 'Oh, yeah. He would. He'd shoot me if he could get away with it. He'd shoot me and cut my heart out, that's what he'd do.'

Five stories below, the watcher smoothed his hair with one pale, long-fingered hand.

PART TWO
The Attack

Is the end of the world a-coming?
Is that the Devil they hear humming?
Are those doomsday bells a-ringing?
Is that the Devil they hear singing?

Or are their dark fears exaggerated?
Are these doom-criers addlepated?

Those who fear the coming of all Hells
are those who should be feared themselves.

— *The Book of Counted Sorrows*

A fanatic does what he thinks the Lord
would do if He knew the facts of the case.

— *Finley Peter Dunne*

15

Wine & Dine was located in an attractive, upscale, brick-and-timber shopping center, half a block from Newport Beach's yacht harbor. Even on a Monday, the shop was busy, with a steady flow of customers through the imported foods section and almost as many in the wine department. At any one time there were at least two or three people browsing in the cookware department, inspecting the pots and pans, imported ice cream machines, food processors, and other kitchen tools. During the afternoon, in addition to food and wine and small culinary implements, Christine and Val and their clerk, Tammy, sold two top-of-the-line pasta makers, an expensive set of cutlery, one Cuisinart, a beautiful copper buffet warmer with three serving compartments, and an ornate copper and brass cappuccino machine that was priced at nine hundred dollars.

Although the shop had done uncannily well almost from the day they had opened the doors, and although it had actually become profitable in the third week of operation (an unheard-of situation for a new business), Christine was still surprised and delighted every day that the cash register kept ringing. Six and a half years of dependable profitability had still not made her blasé about success.

The hustle and bustle of Wine & Dine made Monday afternoon pass a lot faster than she had thought possible when, reluctantly, she had left Joey with Charlie Harrison. The crazy old woman was in the back of her mind, of course. Several times she thought of Brandy's decapitated corpse on the back porch, and she felt weak and dry-mouthed for a few minutes. And Henry Rankin was ever-present, helping bag purchases, putting price tags on some new merchandise, assisting them wherever he could, pretending to be an employee, but surreptitiously keeping an eye on the customers, prepared to tackle one of them if Christine appeared to be threatened. Nevertheless, in spite of the bloody images of the dog that haunted her, and in spite of the constant reminder of danger that Henry's presence provoked, the hours flitted past, and it was a relief to be kept busy.

Val Gardner was a help, too. With some misgivings, Christine had told her the situation, although she had expected Val to pester her with questions all day long and drive her half crazy by five o'clock. Val seemed to thrive on the smallest adversity, claiming to be 'traumatized' by even such minor setbacks as a leaky bathroom faucet or a run in her stockings. Val found drama and even tragedy in a head cold or a broken fingernail, but she was never really upset or depressed by any of the little twists of fate that brought on her histrionics; she just enjoyed being the heroine of her own soap opera, dramatizing her life, making it more colorful for herself. And if she was temporarily without a trauma to brighten her day, she could make do with the problems of her friends, taking them upon herself as if she were a combination of Dear Abby and Atlas with the world on her shoulders. But she was a well-meaning woman, with a good sense of humor, honest, hardworking. And now, somewhat to Christine's surprise, Val was sensitive enough to avoid dwelling on the crazy woman and the threats on Joey's life; she held her tongue even though she must have been eaten up by a thousand nibbling questions.

At five o'clock, Charlie Harrison showed up with Joey

and two guys who looked as if they were on their way to a casting call for a new Hercules movie. They were the bodyguards who would be on duty until another team replaced them at midnight.

The first was Pete Lockburn, who was six-three, with curly blond hair, a solemn face, and watchful eyes. The shoulders of his suit jacket looked as if they were padded out with a couple of railroad ties, but it was only Pete himself under there. The other was Frank Reuther, a black man, every bit as formidable as Lockburn, handsome, with the biggest hands Christine had ever seen. Both Lockburn and Reuther were neatly dressed in suits and ties, and both were soft-spoken and polite, yet you would somehow never mistake them for Baptist ministers or advertising account executives. They looked as if they wrestled grizzly bears and broke full-grown oak trees in half just to keep in shape.

Val stared at them, amazed, and a new look of concern took possession of her face when she turned to Christine. 'Oh, Chris, baby, listen, I guess maybe it didn't really hit me until your army here showed up. I mean, this is really *serious*, isn't it?'

'Really serious,' Christine agreed.

The two men Grace chose for the mission were Pat O'Hara and Kevin Baumberg. O'Hara was a twenty-four-year-old Irishman, husky, slightly overweight, a convert from Catholicism. Baumberg was a short, stocky man with a thick black beard. He had walked away from a lifetime of Judaism — as well as from a family and a prosperous jewelry store — to help Mother Grace prepare the world for Twilight, the coming of the Antichrist. She selected them for the assassination attempt because they symbolized two important things: the universal appeal of her message, and the brotherhood of all good men, which was the only power that had a chance of delaying or preventing the end of the world.

A few minutes after five o'clock, O'Hara and Baumberg carried a couple of laundry bags out of the church basement in Anaheim. They climbed a set of concrete steps into a macadam parking lot.

The early winter night, sailing across the sky like a vast black armada, had already driven most of the light toward the western horizon. A few threatening clouds had come in from the sea, and the air was cool and damp.

O'Hara and Baumberg put the laundry bags into the trunk of a white Chrysler sedan that belonged to the church. The bags contained two shotguns, two revolvers, and ammunition that had been blessed by Mother Grace.

Tense, frightened, preoccupied with thoughts of mortality, neither man felt like talking. In silence, they drove out of the parking lot and into the street, where a newborn wind suddenly stirred the curbside trees and blew dry leaves along the gutters.

16

As Tammy dealt with the last customer of the day, Charlie said to Christine, 'Any problems? Anybody cause any trouble?'

'No. It was peaceful.'

Henry Rankin said, 'What did you dig up on The True Word?'

'It'll take too long to tell you,' Charlie said. 'I want to take Christine and Joey home, make sure their house is secure, get them settled in for the night. But I brought your car. It's outside, and on the front seat there's a copy of the file to date. You can read it later and get caught up.'

'You need me any more tonight?' Henry asked.

'Nope,' Charlie said.'

And Joey said, 'Mom, come on. Come out to the car. I want to show you something really neat.'

'In a second, honey.'

Although both Lockburn and Reuther were, at least physically, the kind of men about whom most women fantasized, Val Gardner hardly gave either of them a second glance. She zeroed in on Charlie as soon as he was finished talking to Henry Rankin, and she turned up her charm until it was as hot as a gas flame.

'I've always wanted to meet a detective,' Val said breathlessly. 'It must be such an exciting life.'

'Actually, it's usually boring,' Charlie said. 'Most of our work is research or stakeout, hour after hour of boredom.'

'But once in while . . .' Val said teasingly.

'Well, sure, now and then there's some fireworks.'

'I'll bet those are the moments you live for,' Val said.

'No one looks forward to being shot at or punched in the face by the husband in a nasty divorce case.'

'You're just being modest,' Val said, shaking a finger at him, winking as cute as she knew how.

And she sure knows how, Christine thought. Val was an extremely attractive woman, with auburn hair, luminous green eyes, and a striking figure. Christine envied her lush good looks. Although a few men had told Christine that she was beautiful, she never really believed those who paid the compliment. She had never been attractive in her mother's eyes; in fact, her mother had referred to her as a 'plain' child, and although she knew her mother's standards were absurdly high and that her mother's opinions were not always rational or fair, Christine still had an image of herself as a *somewhat* pretty woman, in the most modest sense, more suited to being a nun than a siren. Sometimes, when Val was dressed in her finest and being coquettish, Christine felt like a boy beside her.

To Charlie, Val said, 'I'll bet you're the kind of man who needs a little danger in his life to spice it up, the kind of man who knows how to deal with danger.'

'You're romanticizing me, I'm afraid,' Charlie said.

But Christine could see that he enjoyed Val's attentions.

Joey said, 'Mom, please, come on. Come out to the car. We got a dog. A real beauty. Come see him.'

'From the pound?' Christine asked Charlie, cutting in on Val's game.

'Yeah,' he said. 'I tried to get Joey to go for a hundred-and-forty-pound mastiff named Killer, but he wouldn't listen to me.'

Christine grinned.

'Come on and see him, Mom,' Joey said. '*Please.*' He took her hand and pulled on it, urging her toward the door.

'Do you mind closing up by yourself, Val?' Christine asked.

'I'm not by myself. I've got Tammy,' Val said. 'You go on home.' She looked wistfully at Charlie, obviously wishing she had more time to work on him. Then, to Christine: 'And if you don't want to come in tomorrow, don't worry about it.'

'Oh,' Christine said, 'I'll be here. It'll help the day pass. I'd have gone crazy if I hadn't been able to work this afternoon.'

'Nice meeting you,' Charlie said to Val.

'Hope to see you again,' she said, giving him a hundred-kilowatt smile.

Pete Lockburn and Frank Reuther left the shop first, surveying the promenade in front of the rows of stores, suspiciously studying the parking lot. Christine was self-conscious in their company. She didn't think of herself as important enough to need bodyguards. The presence of these two hired guns made her feel awkward and strangely pretentious, as if she were putting on airs.

Outside, the sky to the east was black. Overhead, it was deep blue. To the west, over the ocean, there was a gaudy orange-yellow-red-maroon sunset back-lighting an ominous bank of advancing storm clouds. Although the day had been warm for February, the air was already chilly. Later, it would be downright cold. In California, a warm winter day was not an infrequent gift of nature, but nature's generosity seldom extended to the winter nights.

A dark green Chevrolet, a Klemet-Harrison company car, was parked next to Christine's Firebird. There was a dog in the back seat, peering out the window at them, and when Christine saw it her breath caught in her throat.

It was Brandy. For a second or two, she stood in shock, unable to believe her eyes. Then she realized it *wasn't* Brandy, of course, but another golden retriever virtually the same size and age and coloration as Brandy.

Joey ran ahead and pulled open the door, and the dog leaped out, emitting one short, deep, happy-sounding bark. He sniffed at the boy's legs and then jumped up, putting paws on his shoulders, almost knocking him to the ground.

Joey laughed, ruffled the dog's fur. 'Isn't he neat, Mom? Isn't he something?'

She looked at Charlie, whose grin was almost as big as Joey's. Still thirty feet away from the boy, out of his hearing, she spoke softly, with evident irritation: 'Don't you think some other breed would've been a better choice?'

Charlie seemed baffled by her accusatory tone. 'You mean it's too big? Joey told me it was the same as the dog . . . you lost.'

'Not only the same size. It's the same *dog*.'

'You mean Brandy was a golden retriever?'

'Didn't I tell you?'

115

'You never mentioned the breed.'

'Oh. Well, didn't Joey mention it?'

'He never said a word.'

'This dog's an exact double for Brandy,' Christine said worriedly. 'I don't know if that's such a good idea — psychologically, I mean.'

Turning to them, holding the retriever by its collar, Joey confirmed her intuition when he said, 'Mom, you know what I'm gonna call him? Brandy! Brandy the Second!'

'I see what you mean,' Charlie said to Christine.

'He's trying to deny that Brandy was ever killed,' she said, 'and that's not healthy.'

As the parking lot's sodium-vapor lamps came on, casting yellowish light into the deepening twilight, she went to her son and stooped beside him.

The dog snuffled at her, checking her out, cocked its head, looked at her as if it was trying to figure how she fit in, and finally put one paw on her leg, as if seeking her assurance that she would love it as much as its new young master did.

Sensing that she was already too late to take the dog back and get another breed, unhappily aware that Joey was already attached to the animal, she decided at least to stop him from calling the dog Brandy. 'Honey, I think it'd be a good idea to come up with another name.'

'I like Brandy,' he said.

'But using that name again . . . it's like an insult to the first Brandy.'

'It is?'

'Like you're trying to forget our Brandy.'

'*No!*' he said fiercely. 'I couldn't ever forget.' Tears came to his eyes again.

'This dog should have his own name,' she insisted gently.

'I really like the name Brandy.'

'Come on. Think of another name.'

'Well . . .'

'How about . . . Prince.'

'Yuck. But maybe . . . Randy.'

She frowned and shook her head. 'No, honey. Think of something else. Something totally different. How about something from *Star Wars*? Wouldn't it be neat to have a dog named Chewbacca?'

His face brightened. 'Yeah! Chewbacca! That'd be great.'

As if it had understood every word, as if voicing approval, the dog barked once and licked Christine's hand.

Charlie said, 'Okay, let's put Chewbacca in your Firebird. I want to get out of here. You and Joey and I will ride in the Chevy, and Frank will drive. Pete'll follow us in your car, with Chewbacca. And by the way, we still have company.'

Christine looked in the direction that Charlie indicated. The white van was at the far end of the parking lot, half in the yellowish light from the tall lampposts, half in shadow. The driver wasn't visible beyond the black windshield, but she knew he was in there, watching.

17

Night had fallen.

The storm clouds were still rolling in from the west. They were blacker than the night itself. They rapidly blotted out the stars.

In the white Chrysler, O'Hara and Baumberg cruised slowly, studying the well-maintained, expensive houses on both sides of the street. O'Hara was driving, and his hands kept slipping on the steering wheel because he was plagued by a cold sweat. He knew he was an agent of God in this matter because Mother Grace had told him so. He knew that what he was doing was good and right and absolutely necessary, but he still couldn't picture himself as an assassin, holy or otherwise. He knew that Baumberg felt the same way because the ex-jeweler was breathing too fast for a man who hadn't yet exerted himself. The few times that Baumberg had spoken, his voice had been shaky and higher-pitched than usual.

They weren't having doubts about their mission or about Mother Grace. Both of them had a deep and abiding faith in the old woman. Both of them would do what they were told. O'Hara knew the boy must die, and he knew why, and he believed in the reason. Murdering this particular child did not disturb him. He knew Baumberg felt the same way. They were sweat-damp and nervous merely because they were scared.

Along the tree-shrouded street, several houses were dark, and one of those might serve their purpose. But it was early in the evening, and a lot of people were still on their way back from work. O'Hara and Baumberg didn't want to select a house, break in, and then be discovered and perhaps trapped by some guy coming home with a briefcase in one hand and Chinese take-out in the other.

O'Hara was prepared to kill the boy and the boy's mother and any bodyguards hired to protect the boy, for all of them were in the service of Lucifer. Grace had convinced him of that. But O'Hara wasn't prepared to kill just any innocent bystander who happened to get in his way. Therefore, they would have to choose the house carefully.

What they were looking for was a place where a few days' worth of newspapers were piled up on the porch, or where the mailbox was overflowing, or where there was some other sign that the occupants were away from home. It had to be in this block, and they probably wouldn't find what they were looking for. In that case they'd have to shift to another plan of attack.

They had almost reached the north end of the block when Baumberg said, 'There. What about that place?'

It was a two-story Spanish house, light beige stucco with a tile roof, half hidden by large trees, banks of veronica, and rows of azaleas. The streetlight shone on a real estate company's sign that stood on the lawn, near the sidewalk. The house was for sale, and no lights glowed in any of its rooms.

'Maybe it's unoccupied,' Baumberg said.

'No such luck,' O'Hara said.

'It's worth taking a look.'

'I guess so.'

O'Hara drove to the next block and parked at the curb. Carrying an airline flight bag that he had packed at the church, he got out of the car, accompanied Baumberg to the Spanish house, hurried up a walkway bordered by flourishing begonias, and stopped at a gated atrium entrance. Here they were in deep shadow. O'Hara was confident they wouldn't be spotted from the street.

A cold wind soughed in the branches of the benjaminas and rustled the shiny-leafed veronicas, and it seemed to O'Hara that the night itself was watching them with hostile intent. Could it be that some demonic entity had followed them and was with them now, at home in these shadows, an emissary of Satan, waiting to catch them off guard and tear them to pieces?

Mother Grace had said Satan would do anything he could to wreck their mission. Grace saw these things. Grace knew. Grace spoke the truth. Grace was the truth.

His heart hammering, Pat O'Hara gazed blindly into the most impenetrable pockets of darkness, expecting to catch a glimpse of some lurking monstrosity. But he saw nothing out of the ordinary.

Baumberg stepped away from the wrought-iron atrium gate, onto the lawn, then into a planting bed filled with azaleas and dark-leafed begonias that, in the gloom, appeared to be utterly black. He peered in a window and said softly, 'No drapes and I don't think there's any furniture, either.'

O'Hara went to another window, put his face to the pane, squinted, and found the same signs of vacancy.

'Bingo,' Baumberg said.

They had found what they were looking for.

At the side of the house, the entrance to the rear lawn was also gated, but that gate wasn't locked. As Baumberg pushed it open, the wrought-iron barrier squealed on unoiled hinges.

'I'll go back to the car and get the laundry bags,' Baumberg said, and he slipped away through the night's black curtains.

O'Hara didn't think it was a good idea to split up, but Baumberg was gone before he could protest. Alone, it was more difficult to hold fear at bay, and fear was the food of the devil. Fear drew the Beast. O'Hara looked around at the throbbing darkness and told himself to remember that his faith was his armor. Nothing could harm him as long as he trusted the armor of his belief in Grace and God. But it wasn't easy.

Sometimes he longed for the days before his conversion, when he hadn't known about the approach of Twilight, when he hadn't realized that Satan was loose upon the earth and that the Antichrist had been born. He had been blissfully ignorant. The only things he had feared were cops, doing time in prison, and cancer because cancer had killed his old man. Now he was afraid of everything between sunset and dawn, for it was in the dark hours that evil was boldest. These days, his life was shaped by fear, and at times the burden of Mother Grace's truth was almost too much to bear.

Still carrying the airline flight bag, O'Hara continued to the rear of the house, deciding not to wait for Baumberg. He'd show the devil that he was not intimidated.

18

Joey wanted to ride up front with Pete Lockburn, to whom he chattered ceaselessly and enthusiastically all the way home.

Christine sat in back with Charlie, who occasionally turned to look through the rear window. Frank Reuther followed in Christine's Pontiac Firebird, and a few cars back of Reuther, the white van continued to trail them, easily identified even at night because one of its headlights was slightly brighter than the other.

Charlie said, 'I can't figure that guy out. Is he so dumb he thinks we don't notice him? Does he really think he's being discreet?'

'Maybe he doesn't care if we see him,' Christine said. 'They seem so . . . arrogant.'

Charlie turned away from the rear window and sighed. 'You're probably right.'

'What've you found out about the printing company — The True Word?' Christine asked.

'Like I suspected. The True Word prints religious material — booklets, pamphlets, tracts of all kinds. It's owned by the Church of the Twilight.'

'Never heard of them,' Christine said. 'Some crackpot cult?'

'As far as I'm concerned, yeah. Totally fruitcake.'

'Mustn't be a big group, or I'd probably have heard of them.'

'Not big, but rich,' Charlie said. 'Maybe a thousand of them.'

'Dangerous?'

'They haven't been involved in any big trouble. But the potential is there, the fanaticism. We've had a run-in with them on behalf of another client. About seven months ago. This guy's wife ran off, joined the cult, took their two kids with her — a three- and a four-year-old. These twilight weirdos wouldn't tell him where his wife was, wouldn't let him see his kids. The police weren't too much help. Never are in these cases. Everyone's so worried about treading on religious liberties. Besides, the kids hadn't been kidnapped; they were with their mother. A mother can take her kids anywhere she pleases, as long as she's not violating a custody agreement in a divorce situation, which wasn't the case here. Anyway, we found the kids, snatched them away, returned them to the father. We couldn't do anything about the wife. She was staying with the cult voluntarily.'

'They live communally? Like those people at Jonestown a few years ago?'

'Some of them do. Others have their own homes and apartments — but only if Mother Grace allows them that privilege.'

'Who's Mother Grace?'

He opened a briefcase, took an envelope and a penlight from it. He handed her the envelope, switched on the light, and said, 'Have a look.'

The envelope contained an eight-by-ten glossy. It was a picture of the old woman who had harassed them in the

122

parking lot. Even in a black-and-white photograph, even in two dimensions, the old woman's eyes were scary; there was a mad gleam in them. Christine shivered.

19

Along the back of the house were windows to the dining room, kitchen, breakfast nook, and family room. A pair of French doors led into the family room. O'Hara tried them, even though he was sure they'd be locked; they were.

The patio was bare. No flowerpots. No lawn furniture. The swimming pool had been drained, perhaps for repainting.

Standing by the French doors, O'Hara looked at the house to the north of this one. A six-foot cinder block wall separated this property from the next; therefore, he could see only the second story of that other house. It was dark. To the south, beyond another wall, the second story of another house was visible, but this one was filled with light. At least no one was looking out any of the windows.

The rear of the property was walled, also, but the house in that direction was evidently a single-story model, for it couldn't be seen from the patio on which O'Hara stood.

He took a flashlight from the airline flight bag and used it to examine the panes of glass in the French doors and in one of the windows. He moved quickly, afraid of being seen. He was looking for wires, conductive alarm tape, and photo-electric cells — anything that would indicate the house was equipped with a burglar alarm. It was the kind of neighborhood where about a third of the houses would be wired. He found no indication that this place was part of that one third.

He switched the flashlight off, fumbled in the flight bag, and withdrew a compact, battery-powered electronic device the size of a small transistor radio. An eighteen-inch length of wire extended from one end of it, terminating in a suction cup as large as the lid of a mayonnaise jar. He fixed the suction cup to a pane in one of the French doors.

Again, he had the creepy feeling that something dangerous was moving in on him, and a chill quivered down his spine as he turned to peer into the shadow-draped rear yard. The wind clattered through the thick, somewhat brittle leaves of a huge ficus, hissed in the fronds of two palms, and caused smaller shrubs to sway and flutter as if they were alive. But it was the empty swimming pool that drew O'Hara's attention and became the focus of his fear. He suddenly got the idea that something large and hideous was hiding in the pool, crouched down in that concrete pit, listening to him, waiting for the opportune moment in which to make its move. Something that had coalesced out of the darkness. Something that had risen up from the pits of Hell. Something sent to stop them from killing the boy. Underlying the myriad sounds produced by the wind, he thought he could hear a sinister, wet, slithering sound coming from the pool, and he was suddenly cold clear through to his bones.

Baumberg returned with the two laundry bags, startling O'Hara.

'Do you feel it, too?' Baumberg asked.

'Yes,' O'Hara said.

'It's out there. The Beast himself. Or one of his messengers.'

'In the pool,' O'Hara said.

Baumberg stared at the black pit in the center of the lawn. Finally he nodded. 'Yeah. I feel it. Down there in the pool.'

It can only hurt us if we begin to doubt Mother Grace's power to protect us, O'Hara told himself. It can only stop us if we lose our faith or if we let our fear of it overwhelm us.

That was what Mother Grace had told them.

Mother Grace was never wrong.

O'Hara turned to the French doors again. The suction cup was still firmly affixed to one of the panes. He switched on the small device to which the suction cup was connected, and a glass-covered dial lit up in the center of the instrument case. The device was a sonic-wave detector that would tell them if the house was equipped with a wireless alarm system that protected the premises by detecting motion. The lighted dial did not move, which meant there was no radio wave activity of any kind within the family room, beyond the French doors.

Before Mother Grace had converted him, O'Hara had been a busy and professional burglar, and he had been damned good at his trade. Because Grace had a propensity for seeking converts from among those who had fallen the furthest from God, the Church of the Twilight could tap a wealth of skills and knowledge not available to the average church whose members were from the law-abiding segments of the population. Sometimes that was a blessing.

He popped the suction cup off the glass, switched off the wave detector, and returned it to the flight bag. He withdrew a roll of strapping tape and a pair of scissors. He cut several strips of tape and applied them to the pane of glass nearest the door handle. When the glass was completely covered, he struck it hard with one fist. The pane shattered, but with little sound, and the fragments all stuck to the tape. He pulled the pieces out of the frame, put them aside, reached through, fumbled for the deadbolt, unlocked it, opened the door.

He was now pretty sure there was no alarm, but he had

one last thing to check for. He got down on his knees on the patio, reached across the threshold, and pulled up the carpet from the tack strip. There was no alarm mat under the carpet, just ordinary quilted padding.

He put the carpet back in place. He and Baumberg went into the house, taking the laundry bags and the flight bag with them.

O'Hara closed and locked the French doors.

He looked out at the rear lawn. It was peaceful now.

'It isn't out there any more,' Baumberg said.

'No,' O'Hara said.

Baumberg peered across the unlighted family room, into the breakfast area and the dark kitchen beyond. He said, 'Now it's inside with us.'

'Yes,' O'Hara said. He had felt the hostile presence within the house the moment they'd crossed the threshold.

'I wish we could turn on some lights,' Baumberg said uneasily.

'The house is supposed to be deserted. The neighbors would notice light and maybe call the cops.'

Overhead, from an upstairs room, a floorboard creaked.

Before converting to Mother Grace's faith, in the days when he had been a thief, stealing his way along the road to hell, O'Hara would have figured the creaking was merely a settling noise, one of the many meaningless sounds that an empty house produced as joints expanded and contracted in response to the humidity — or lack of it — in the air. But tonight he knew it was no settling sound.

O'Hara's old friends and some in his family said that he had become paranoid since joining the Church of the Twilight. They just didn't understand. His behavior seemed paranoid only because he had seen the truth as Mother Grace taught it, and his old friends and family had not been saved. His eyes had been opened; their eyes were still blind.

More creaking noise overhead.

'Our faith is a shield,' Baumberg said shakily. 'We don't dare doubt that.'

'Mother has provided us with armor,' O'Hara said.

Creeeeeaaak.

'We're doing God's work,' Baumberg said, challenging the darkness that filled the house.

O'Hara switched on the flashlight, shielding it with one hand to provide just enough light to guide them but not enough to be seen from outside.

Baumberg followed him to the stairs and up to the second floor.

20

'Her name's Grace Spivey,' Charlie said as their car moved through the increasingly blustery February night.

Christine couldn't keep her eyes from the photograph. The old woman's black-and-white gaze was strangely hypnotic, and a cold radiation seemed to emanate from it.

In the front seat, Joey was talking to Pete Lockburn about Steven Spielberg's *E.T.*, which Joey had seen four times and which Lockburn seemed to have seen more often than that. Her son's voice sounded far away, as if he were on a distant mountain, already lost to her.

Charlie switched off the penlight.

Christine was relieved when shadow fell across the photograph, breaking the uncanny hold it had on her. She put it in the envelope, returned the envelope to Charlie. 'She's head of this cult?'

'She *is* the cult. It's primarily a personality cult. Her religious message isn't anything special or unique; the whole thing's in the way she delivers it. If anything happened to Grace, her followers would drift away and the church would probably collapse.'

'How can a crazy old woman like that draw any followers? She sure didn't seem charismatic to me.'

'But she is,' Charlie said. 'I've never spoken to her myself, but Henry Rankin has. He handled that case I mentioned, the two little kids whose mother took them with her into the cult. And he told me Grace has a certain undeniable magnetism, a very forceful personality. And though her message isn't particularly new, it's dramatic and exciting, just the sort of thing that a certain type of person would respond to with enthusiasm.'

'What *is* her message?'

'She says we're living in the last days of the world.'

'Every religious crackpot from here to Maine has made that proclamation at one time or another.'

'Of course.'

'So there must be more to it. What else does she say?'

Charlie hesitated, and she sensed that he dreaded having to tell her the rest.

'Charlie?'

He sighed. 'Grace says the Antichrist has already been born.'

'I've heard that one, too. There's one cult around that says the Antichrist is the King of Spain.'

'That's a new one to me.'

'Others say the Antichrist will be the man who takes over the Russian government after the current Premier.'

'Sounds a bit more reasonable than laying it on the King of Spain.'

'I wouldn't be surprised if there's a cult somewhere that thinks Burt Reynolds or Stephen King or Rodney Dangerfield is the Antichrist.'

Charlie didn't smile at her little joke. 'We're living in weird times,' he said.

'We're approaching the end of a millennium,' Christine said. 'For some reason, that brings all the nuts out of the trees. They say that, last time, when the year 1000 was approaching, there were all sorts of bizarre cults, decadence, and violence associated with people's fears of the end of the world. I guess it's going to be that way as we approach 2000. Hell, it's already started.'

'It sure has,' he said softly.

She perceived that he still hadn't told her everything Grace Spivey professed to believe. Even in the dim light that came through the car windows, she could see that he was deeply disturbed.

'Well?' she prodded him.

'Grace says we're in the Twilight, that period just before the son of Satan takes power over the earth and rules for a thousand years. How well do you know the Bible — especially the prophecies?'

'I was very familiar with it at one time,' she said. 'But not any more. In fact, I can't remember much of anything.'

'Join the club. But from what I understand of Grace Spivey's preaching, the Bible says that the Antichrist will rule for a thousand years, bringing mankind indescribable suffering, after which the battle of Armageddon will transpire, and God will at last descend to destroy Satan forever. She says that God has given her one last chance to avoid the devil's thousand-year dominion. She says He's ordered her to try to save mankind by organizing a church of righteous people who will stop the Antichrist before he reaches a position of power.'

'If I didn't know there were people — fanatical and maybe *dangerous* people — who believed in this kind of nonsense, I'd find it amusing. And how do they think their little band of righteous people is going to combat the

129

DEAN R KOONTZ

awesome power of Satan — presuming you believe in the awesome power of Satan in the first place?'

'Which I don't. But as far as I'm aware, their battle plans are a secret known only to those who've become members of the church. But I suspect I know what they've got in mind.'

'And what's that?'

He hesitated. Then: 'They intend to kill him.'

'The Antichrist?'

'Yes.'

'Just like that?'

'I don't imagine they think it'll be easy.'

'I should say not!' Christine said, smiling in spite of the situation. 'What kind of devil would allow himself to be killed with ease? Anyway, the logic's inconsistent. The Antichrist would be a supernatural figure. Supernatural beings can't be killed.'

'I know that Roman Catholicism has a tradition of justifying points of doctrine through logical processes,' Charlie said. 'St. Thomas Aquinas and his writings, for instance. But these people we're dealing with are fringe types. Fanatics. Consistency of logic isn't something religious fanatics require of one another.' He sighed. 'Anyway, assuming that you believe in all this mythology as presented by the Bible — and as interpreted by Grace — maybe it isn't such lousy logic. After all, Jesus was supposed to have been a supernatural being, the son of God, yet He was killed by the Romans.'

'That's different,' she said. 'According to the Christ story, that was His mission, His purpose, His destiny — to allow Himself to be killed to save us from the worst consequences of our sins. Right? But I hardly think the Antichrist would be as altruistic.'

'You're thinking logically again. If you want to

130

understand Grace and the Church of the Twilight, you've got to put logic behind you.'

'Okay. So who does she say is the Antichrist?'

'When we pulled those two little kids out of the cult,' Charlie said, 'Grace still hadn't identified the Antichrist. She hadn't found him yet. But now I think perhaps she has.'

'So? Who?' Christine asked, but before Charlie could respond, the answer hit her with the force of a sledgehammer blow.

Up front, Joey was still talking with Pete Lockburn, oblivious of the conversation between his mother and Charlie Harrison.

Nevertheless, Christine lowered her voice to a whisper. 'Joey? My God, does that crazy woman think my little boy is the Antichrist?'

'I'd almost bet on it.'

Christine could hear the old woman's hate-filled voice rising from a dark pool of memory. *He's got to die; he's got to die.*

'But why him? Why Joey? Why didn't she fixate on some other child?'

'Maybe it's like you said: You were just at the wrong place at the wrong time,' Charlie said. 'If some other woman with another child had been in the South Coast Plaza parking lot at that same time last Sunday, Grace would now be after another little boy instead of Joey.'

Christine knew that he was probably right, but the thought dizzied her. It was a stupid, cruel, malignant lunacy. What kind of world were they living in if an innocent shopping trip to the mall made them eligible for martyrdom?

'But . . . how do we ever stop her?' Christine asked.

'If she actually resorts to violence, we deflect it. If we can't deflect it, then . . . well, we blow her people away before they touch Joey. There's no question of legal responsibility. You've hired us to protect you, and we have legal sanction to resort to violent force, if that's necessary and unavoidable, to fulfill our obligation.'

'No. I mean . . . how do we change her mind? How do we get her to admit that Joey's just a little boy? How do we get her to go away?'

'I don't know. I would imagine a fanatic like this is about as single-minded as anyone can be. I don't think it would be easy to make her change her mind about anything, let alone anything as important to her as this.'

'But you said she's got a thousand followers.'

'Maybe even a few more than that by now.'

'If she keeps sending them after Joey, we can't kill them all. Sooner or later, one of them will get through our defenses.'

'I'm not going to let this drag on,' he assured her. 'I'm not going to give them a lot of chances to hurt Joey. I'll make Grace change her mind, back off, go away.'

'How?'

'I don't know yet.'

An image of the harpy in the parking lot returned to Christine — the windblown hair, the bulging eyes, the lint-specked and food-stained clothes — and she felt despair clutching at her. 'There's no way to change her mind.'

'There's a way,' Charlie insisted. 'I'll find it.'

'She'll never stop.'

'I have an appointment with an excellent psychologist in the morning. Dr. Denton Boothe. He's especially interested in cult psychology. I'm going to discuss the case with him, give him our profile on Grace, ask him to work with us to find her weak spot.'

Christine didn't see much promise in that approach. But then she didn't see much promise in any approach.

Charlie took her hand as the car sped through the windy darkness. 'I won't let you down.'

But for the first time she wondered if his promises were empty.

21

On the second floor of the empty house, O'Hara and Baumberg stood by the windows in the large master bedroom.

They still felt the menacing presence of an evil entity watching over them. They tried to ignore it, holding steadfast to their faith and to their determination to complete the task Mother Grace had given them.

Outside, the rear yard lay in darkness, scoured by a rising wind. From up here they could see into the swimming pool. No beast crouched within that concrete concavity. Not now. Now it was in the house with them.

Beyond this property was another lawn and another house, a sprawling, one-story, ranch-style place with a shake-shingle roof and a swimming pool of its own. The pool held water and was lit from the bottom, a glimmering blue-green jewel in the shape of a kidney.

O'Hara had taken a pair of night binoculars from the flight bag at his feet. They made use of available light to produce an enhanced image of a dark landscape. Through them, he had a pretty good view of all the properties that butted up against the rear of the lots along this street. Those houses faced out onto another street, parallel to this one.

'Which is the Scavello place?' Baumberg asked.

O'Hara slowly turned to his right, looking farther north. 'Not the house behind this one. The next one, with the rectangular pool and the swings.'

'I don't see any swings,' Baumberg said.

O'Hara handed him the binoculars. 'To the left of the pool. A child's swing set and a jungle gym.'

'Just two doors away,' Baumberg said.

'Yeah.'

'No lights on.'

'They aren't home yet.'

'Maybe they won't come home.'

'They'll come,' O'Hara said.

'If they don't?'

'We'll go looking for them.'

'Where?'

'Wherever God sends us.'

Baumberg nodded.

O'Hara opened one of the laundry bags and withdrew a shotgun.

22

As they turned into Christine's block and came within sight of her house, Charlie said, 'See that camper?'

Across the street, a pickup truck was parked at the curb. A camper shell was attached to the bed of the truck. It was just an ordinary camper; she had noticed it but hadn't given it a second thought. Suddenly it seemed sinister.

'Is that them, too?' she asked.

'No. That's *us*,' Charlie said. 'I've got a man in there, keeping an eye on every vehicle that comes along the street.

He's got a camera with infrared film, so he can record license plate numbers even in the dark. He's also got a portable telephone, so he can call your place, the police, or get in touch with me in a hurry.'

Pete Lockburn parked the green Chevy in front of the Scavello house, while Frank Reuther pulled Christine's Firebird into the driveway.

The white Ford van, which had been following them, passed by. They watched it in silence as its driver took it into the next block, found a parking space, and switched off its lights.

'Amateurs,' Pete Lockburn said scornfully.

'Arrogant bastards,' Christine said.

Reuther climbed out of the Firebird, leaving the dog in it, and came to their car.

As Charlie put down the window to talk to Frank, he asked Christine for her house keys. When she produced them from her purse, he gave them to Frank. 'Check the place out. Make sure nobody's waiting in there.'

'Right,' Frank said, unbuttoning his suit jacket to provide quick access to the weapon in his shoulder holster. He headed up the walk to the front door.

Pete got out of the Chevy and stood beside it, surveying the night-shrouded street. He left his coat unbuttoned, too.

Joey said, 'Is this where the bad guys show up?'

'Let's hope not, honey.'

There were a lot of trees and not many streetlights, and Charlie began to feel uneasy about sitting here at the curb, so he got out of the Chevy too, warning Christine and Joey to stay where they were. He stood at his side of the car, his back toward Pete Lockburn, taking responsibility for the approaches in his direction.

Occasionally a car swung around the corner, entered the block, drove past or turned into the driveway of another house. Each time he saw a new pair of headlights, Charlie tensed and put his right hand under his coat, on the butt of the revolver in his shoulder holster.

He was cold. He wished he'd brought an overcoat.

Sheet lightning pulsed dully in the western sky. A far-off peal of thunder made him think of the freight trains that had rumbled past the shabby little house in which he'd grown up, back in Indiana, in what now seemed like another century.

For some reason, those trains had never been a symbol of freedom and escape, as they might have been to other boys in his situation. To young Charlie, lying in his narrow bed in his narrow room, trying to forget his father's latest outburst of drunken violence, the sound of those trains had always reminded him that he lived on the wrong side of the tracks. The clattering-growling wheels had been the voice of poverty, the sound of need and fear and desperation.

He was surprised that this low thunder could bring back, with such disturbing clarity, the rumbling of those train wheels. Equally surprising was that the memory of those trains could evoke childhood fears and recall to mind the feeling of being trapped that had been such an integral part of his youth.

In that regard, he had a lot in common with Christine. His childhood had been blighted by physical abuse, hers by psychological abuse. Both of them had lived under the fist, one literally, one figuratively, and as children they had felt trapped, claustrophobic.

He looked down at the side window of the Chevy, saw Joey peering out at him. He gave a thumbs-up sign. The boy returned it, grinning.

Having been a target of abuse as a boy, Charlie was especially sensitive to children who were victims of violence. Nothing made him angrier than adults who battered children. Crimes against defenseless children gave him a cold, greasy, sick feeling and filled him with a hatred and a bleak despair that nothing else could engender.

He would not let them harm Joey Scavello.

He would not fail the boy. He didn't *dare* fail because, having failed, he very likely wouldn't be able to live with himself.

It seemed quite a long time before Frank came back. He was still watchful but a bit more relaxed than when he'd gone inside.

'Clean, Mr. Harrison. I looked in the back yard, too. Nobody around.'

They took Christine and Joey and Chewbacca inside, surrounding the woman and the boy as they moved, allowing no clear line of fire.

Christine had said that she was successful, but Charlie didn't expect such a large, well-furnished house. The living room had a huge fireplace surrounded by a carved mantel and oak bookshelves extending to the corners. An enormous Chinese carpet provided focus for a pleasing mix of Oriental and European antiques and antique reproductions of high quality. Along one wall was an eight-panel, hand-carved rosewood screen with a double triptych depicting a waterfall and bridge and ancient Japanese village, all rendered in intricately fitted pieces of soapstone.

Joey wanted to go to his room and play a game with his new dog, and Frank Reuther went with him.

At Charlie's suggestion, Pete Lockburn went through the house, from bottom to top and back again, checking to be sure all doors and windows were locked, shutting all the draperies, so no one could see inside.

Christine said, 'I guess I'd better see what I can find for supper. Probably hot dogs. That's the only thing I have plenty of.'

'Don't bother,' Charlie said. 'I've got a man bringing a lot of takeout at seven o'clock.'

'You think of everything.'

'Let's hope so.'

23

O'Hara trained his binoculars on an upstairs window of the Scavello house, then on the next window, and the next, eventually scanning the first floor as well. Light shone in every room, but all the draperies were drawn tight.

'Maybe she came home but sent the boy somewhere else for the night,' Baumberg said.

'The boy's there,' O'Hara said.

'How do you know?'

'Can't you *feel* him over there?'

Baumberg squinted through the window.

'*Feel* him,' O'Hara said in a hushed and frightened voice.

Baumberg groped for the awareness that had terrified his partner.

'The darkness,' O'Hara said. 'Feel the special darkness of the boy, the terrible darkness that rolls off him like fog off the ocean.'

Baumberg strained his senses.

'The evil,' O'Hara said, his voice reduced to a hoarse whisper. 'Feel it.'

Baumberg placed his hands against the cool glass, pressed his forehead to it, stared intently at the Scavello house. After a while he did feel it, just like O'Hara said. The darkness. The evil. It poured forth from that house like atomic radiation from a block of plutonium. It streamed through the night, through the glass in front of Baumberg, contaminating him, a malignant energy that produced no heat or light, that was bleak and black and frigid.

O'Hara abruptly lowered his binoculars, turned away from the window, put his back toward the Scavello house, as if the evil energy pouring from it was more than he could bear.

'It's time,' Baumberg said, picking up a shotgun and a revolver.

'No,' O'Hara said. 'Let them settle in. Let them relax. Give them a chance to lower their guard.'

'When?'

'We'll leave here at . . . eight-thirty.'

24

6:45 P.M.

Christine watched as Charlie unplugged the telephone in her study and replaced it with a device that he had brought with him. It looked like a cross between a phone, an answering machine, and a briefcase-sized electronic calculator.

Charlie picked up the receiver, and Christine could hear the dial tone even though she was a few feet away.

Replacing the handset in the cradle, he said, 'If someone calls, we'll come in here to answer it.'

'That'll record the conversation?'

'Yeah. But it's primarily a tracer phone. It's like the equipment the police have when you call their emergency number.'

'911?'

'Yeah. When you call 911, they know what number and address you're calling from because, as soon as they pick up their receiver and establish a connection with you, that information prints out at their end.' He indicated what looked like a short, blank length of adding machine paper that was sticking out of a slot in the device he'd put on her desk. 'We'll have the same information about anyone who phones here.'

'So if this Grace Spivey calls, we'll not only have a recording of her voice, but we'll have proof the call was made on her phone — or one that belongs to her church.'

'Yep. It probably wouldn't be admissible as court evidence, but it ought to help get the police interested if we can prove she's making threats against Joey.'

7:00 P.M.

The take-out food arrived precisely on the hour, and Christine noticed that Charlie was quietly pleased by how prompt his man was.

The five of them ate at the dining room table — beef ribs, barbecued chicken, baked potatoes, and cole slaw — while Charlie told funny stories about cases his agency had handled. Joey listened, spellbound, even though he didn't always understand or appreciate the details of the anecdotes.

Christine watched her son watching Charlie. More poignantly than ever, she realized what the boy had been missing by not having a father or any other male authority figure to admire and from whom he could learn.

Chewbacca, the new dog, ate from a dish in the corner of the room, then stretched out and put his head down on his paws, waiting for Joey. Obviously, he had belonged to a family that had cared for him and had trained him well. He was going to fit in quickly and easily. Christine was still disconcerted by his resemblance to Brandy, but she was beginning to think it would work out anyway.

At 7:20, the intermittent, distant sound of thunder suddenly grew louder. A blast split the night sky, and the windows rattled.

Startled, Christine dropped her fork. For an instant she thought a bomb had gone off outside the house. When she realized it was only thunder, she felt silly, but a glance at the others told her that they, too, had been briefly startled and frightened by the noise.

A few fat raindrops struck the roof, the windows.

At 7:35, Frank Reuther finished eating and left the table to make a complete circuit of the house, re-examining all the doors and windows that Pete had checked earlier. A light but steady rain was falling.

At 7:47, finished eating, Joey challenged Pete Lockburn to a game of Old Maid, and Pete accepted. They went off to the boy's room, the dog padding friskily and eagerly behind them.

Frank pulled a chair up to one of the living room windows and studied the rain-swept street through a narrow chink in the draperies.

Charlie helped Christine gather up the paper plates and napkins, which they carried to the kitchen, where the sound of the rain was louder, booming off the patio cover at the back of the house.

'What now?' Christine asked, stuffing the plates into the garbage can.

'We get through the night.'

'Then?'

'If the old woman doesn't call tonight and give us something to use against her, then tomorrow I'll talk to

Dr. Boothe, the psychologist I mentioned. He has a special interest in religious neuroses and psychoses. He's developed some successful deprogramming procedures to rehabilitate people who've been brainwashed by some of these weird cults. He knows how these cult leaders think, so maybe he can help us find Grace Spivey's weak spot. I'm also going to try to talk to the woman herself, face to face.'

'How're you going to arrange that?'

'Call the Church of the Twilight and ask for an appointment with her.'

'You think she'll actually see you?'

He shrugged. 'The boldness of it might intrigue her.'

'Can't we go to the cops now?'

'With what?'

'You've got proof Joey and I are being followed.'

'Following someone isn't a crime.'

'That Spivey woman called your office and threatened Joey.'

'We haven't any proof it was Grace Spivey. And only Joey heard the threat.'

'Maybe if we explain to the cops how this madwoman thinks Joey is the Antichrist –'

'That's only a theory.'

'Well . . . maybe we could find someone who used to belong to the cult, someone who's left it, and then they could substantiate this Antichrist nonsense.'

'People don't leave the Church of the Twilight,' Charlie said.

'What do you mean?'

'When we were hired to pull those two little kids out of the cult, we first figured we'd dig up someone who'd been a follower of Grace Spivey's but wasn't any more, someone who'd become disillusioned and could tell us where the kids might be and how we might best be able to snatch them. But we couldn't find anybody who'd quit the church. Once they join up, they seem committed for life.'

'There're always going to be a few disgruntled, disillusioned – '

'Not with the Church of the Twilight.'

'What kind of hold does that crazy old woman have on them?'

'Hard as iron and tight as a vise,' Charlie said.

Lightning pulsed so brilliantly that it was visible through the tiny spaces between the slats of the Levolor blinds.

Thunder crashed, reverberating in the windows, and the rain came down harder than ever.

At 8:15, after giving some final instructions to Lockburn and Reuther, Charlie left.

He insisted that Christine lock the door behind him before he would even walk away from the front porch.

She pulled aside the curtain on the window next to the door and watched him hurry toward the green Chevy, splashing through dark puddles, buffeted by the wet wind, hurrying in and out of dense night shadows that appeared to flap and billow like black draperies.

Frank Reuther suggested she get away from the window, and she took his advice, though reluctantly. Somehow, as long as she could still see Charlie Harrison, she felt safe. But the moment she dropped the curtain and turned away from the window, a crushing awareness of Joey's vulnerability (and her own) settled over her.

She knew Pete and Frank were well trained, competent, and trustworthy, but neither of them gave her the feeling of security that she got from Charlie.

8.20.

She went to Joey's room. He and Pete were sitting on the floor, playing Old Maid.

'Hey, Mom, I'm winning,' Joey said.

'He's a real card shark,' Pete said. 'If this ever gets back to the guys in the office, I'll never live it down.'

Chewbacca lay in the corner, watching his master, tongue lolling.

Christine could almost believe that Chewbacca was actually Brandy, that there had never been a decapitation, that Pete and Frank were just a couple of family friends, that this was merely an ordinary, quiet evening at home. Almost. But not quite.

She went into her study and sat at her desk, looking at the two covered windows, listening to the rain. It sounded like thousands of people chanting so far away that you couldn't make out their words but could hear only the soft, blended roar of many ardent voices.

She tried to work but couldn't concentrate. She took a book from the shelves, a light novel, but she couldn't even keep her attention focused on that.

For a moment she considered calling her mother. She needed a shoulder to cry on. But of course Evelyn wouldn't provide the comfort and commiseration she needed.

She wished her brother were still alive. She wished she could call him and ask him to come be with her. But Tony was gone forever. Her father was gone forever, too, and although she had barely known him, she missed him now in a way she never had before.

If only Charlie were here . . .

In spite of Frank and Pete and the unnamed man watching the house from the camper outside, she felt terribly alone.

She stared at the tracer phone on her desk. She wished the crazy old woman would call and threaten Joey. At least they would have sufficient evidence to interest the police.

But the phone didn't ring.

The only sounds were those of the storm.

At 8:40, Frank Reuther came into the study, smiled at her, and said, 'Don't mind me. Just making the rounds.'

He went to the first window, held the drape aside, checked the lock, peered into the darkness for a second, then let the drape fall back into place.

Like Pete Lockburn, Frank had taken off his jacket and had rolled up his shirt sleeves. His shoulder holster hung under his left arm. The butt of his revolver caught the light for an instant and gleamed blackly.

For a moment Christine felt as if, through some inexplicable interchange of fantasy and reality, she was trapped in a '30s gangster movie.

Frank pulled aside the drape at the second window — and cried out in surprise.

The shotgun blast was louder than the clashing armies of the thunder storm.

The window exploded inward.

Christine leaped up as a shower of glass and blood cascaded over her.

Before he had time to reach for his own gun, Frank was lifted off his feet by the force of the blast and pitched backward.

Christine's chair fell over with a bang.

The bodyguard collapsed across the desk in front of her. His face was gone. The shotgun pellets had hammered his skull into bloody ruin.

Outside, the gunman fired again.

Stray pellets found the ceiling light, pulverizing it, bringing down more glass, some plaster, and darkness. The desk lamp already had been knocked to the floor when Frank Reuther had fallen against it. The room was in darkness except for what little light came through the open doorway from the hall.

The pellet-shredded draperies were seized by an intrusive gust of wind. Tattered fragments lashed at one another, fluttered and whirled in the air, like the rotted burial garments of an animated corpse in a carnival funhouse.

Christine heard someone screaming, thought it was Joey, realized it was a woman, then discovered it was her own voice.

A squall of rain burst through the ribboned drapes. But the rain wasn't the only thing trying to get inside. Frank Reuther's killer was also clambering through the shattered window.

Christine ran.

25

In an adrenaline-hot, fear-scorched, dreamlike fever, with the urgent yet weirdly slow-motion time sense of a nightmare, Christine ran from her study to the living room. The short journey required only a few seconds, but it *seemed* as if the distance from one end of her house to the other was a hundred miles and that hours passed during her panicky progress from one room to another. She knew she was awake, yet she felt as if she were asleep. This was reality yet unreal.

When she reached the living room, Pete Lockburn and Joey were just entering from the direction of the boy's bedroom. Lockburn's revolver was in his hand.

Chewbacca came behind them, ears flattened, tail down, barking loudly.

A shotgun blast tore the lock out of the front door. Even as the wood chips were still flying, a man burst into the house. He crouched in the foyer that opened into the living room, holding a shotgun in front of him, eyes wide, face white with anger or terror or both, an incongruously ordinary-looking man, short and husky, with a thick black beard jeweled with raindrops. He saw Christine first and leveled his weapon at her.

Joey screamed.

A hard, ear-shattering explosion rocked the room, and Christine was certain that she was in the last milliseconds of her life.

But it was the intruder who was hit. His shirt blossomed with an ugly red flower of blood.

Pete Lockburn had fired first. Now he fired again.

A spray of blood erupted from the intruder's shoulder. The stranger's shotgun spun out of his hands, and he stumbled backwards. Lockburn's third shot caught him in the neck, catapulting him off his feet. Already dead, he was pitched into a small foyer table; his head slammed backwards, striking a mirror above the table, cracking it, and then he collapsed in a gory heap.

As Joey bolted into Christine's arms, she shouted to Lockburn: 'There's another man! The study – '

Too late. The gunman who had killed Frank Reuther was already in the living room.

Lockburn whirled. Fast but not fast enough. The shotgun roared. Pete Lockburn was blown away.

Although he had been their dog less than a day, Chewbacca knew where his loyalties ought to lie. Snarling, teeth bared, he leapt at the gunman, bit the intruder's left leg, sank his fangs in deep and held tight.

The man cried out, raised the shotgun, slammed the heavy butt down on top of the retriever's golden head. The dog yelped and crumpled in a heap.

147

'No!' Joey said, as if the loss of a second pet was worse than the prospect of his own slaughter.

Sobbing in pain, obviously frightened, the gunman said, 'God help me, God help me, God help me,' and he turned the 20-gauge on Christine and Joey.

She saw that he, like the bearded man, did not really appear to be mad or degenerate or evil. The ferocity of the terror that gripped him was the most unusual thing about him. Otherwise, he was quite ordinary. Young, in his early twenties. Slightly overweight. Fair-skinned, with a few freckles and rain-soaked reddish hair that was plastered to his head. His ordinariness was the very thing that made him so scary; if *this* man could become a mindless killer under the influence of Grace Spivey, then the old woman could corrupt anyone; no one could be trusted; any one might be an assassin in her thrall.

He pulled the trigger.

There was only a dry click.

He had forgotten that both barrels were empty.

Whimpering and squealing as if *he* were the one in danger, the killer fumbled in his jacket pocket and withdrew a pair of shotgun shells.

With a strength and agility born of terror, Christine scooped Joey up and ran, not toward the front door and the street beyond, for they would surely die out there, but toward the stairs and the master bedroom, where she had left her purse – the purse in which she'd been carrying her own pistol. Joey clung desperately to her, and he seemed to weigh nothing at all; she was briefly possessed with a more-than-human power, and the stairs succumbed to her pumping legs. Then, almost at the top, she stumbled, nearly fell, grabbed at the banister, cried out in despair.

But it was a good thing she had stumbled, for, in that same moment, the gunman below opened fire, discharging both barrels. Two waves of buckshot smashed into the railing at the top of the stairs, reducing the oak handrail to splinters, tearing plaster from the wall, blowing out the ceiling light up there at the very place she would have been is she hadn't misstepped.

As the killer reloaded yet again, Christine plunged ahead, into the upstairs hall. For a moment she hesitated, clutching Joey, swaying, disoriented. This was her own house, more familiar to her than any place in the world, but tonight it was alien; the angles and proportions and lighting in the rooms seemed wrong, different. The hallway, for instance, appeared infinitely long, with distorted walls like a passageway in a carnival maze. She blinked and tried to repress the heart-hammering panic that twisted her perceptions; she hurried forward and made it to the master bedroom door.

Behind her, from the stairway, came the sound of the killer's footsteps as he raced after her, favouring his bitten leg.

She stepped into the bedroom, slammed the door behind her, latched it, put Joey down. Her purse was on the nightstand. She grabbed it just as the assassin reached the door and rattled the knob. Her fingers were too frantic; for a moment she couldn't work the zipper. Then she had her purse open, the gun in hand.

Joey had crawled into a corner, beside the highboy. He cringed, trying to make himself even smaller than he was.

The bedroom door shook and partially dissolved in a storm of buckshot. A hole opened on the right side of it. One hinge was torn out of the frame; it spun into the air, bounced off a wall, clattered across the top of the dresser.

Holding her pistol in both hands, painfully aware that she wasn't holding it steady, Christine swung toward the door.

Another blast ruined the lock, and the door swung inward, hanging on only one hinge.

The young, red-haired killer stood in the doorway, looking even more terrified than Christine felt. He was gibbering senselessly. His hands were shaking worse than hers. Snot hung from one of his nostrils, but he seemed unaware of it.

She pointed the pistol at him, pulled the trigger.

Nothing happened.

The safety was on.

The assassin seemed startled to find her armed. His shotgun was empty again. He dropped it and pulled a revolver from the waistband of his trousers.

She heard herself saying, 'No, no, no, no, no,' in a chant of pure fear as she fumbled for the two safeties on the pistol. She snapped off both of them, pulled the trigger again and again and again.

The thunder of her own gunfire, booming off the walls around her, was the sweetest sound she'd ever heard.

The intruder went to his knees as the bullets ripped into him, then sprawled on his face. The revolver fell out of his limp hand.

Joey was crying.

Christine cautiously approached the body. Blood was soaking into the carpet around it. With one foot she prodded the man. He was dead weight.

She went to the door, looked into the shadowy hall, which was littered with fragments of the stairway railing and splinters of glass from the light fixture that had been struck by shotgun pellets. The carpet was spotted with blood from the dead gunman's bitten leg; he had left a trail from the head of the stairs.

She listened. No one moved or spoke downstairs. There were no footsteps.

Had there been just two assassins?

She wondered how many bullets she had left. The magazine held ten. She thought she had fired five. Five left.

Joey's sobbing subsided. 'M-Mom?'

'*Sshhh*,' she said.

They both listened.

Wind. Thunder. Rain on the roof, tapping the windows.

Four men dead. That realization hit her, and she felt nausea uncoiling in her stomach. The house was a slaughter pen, a graveyard.

Wind-stirred, a tree branch scraped against the house. Inside, the funereal silence deepened.

Finally she looked at Joey.

He was bleached white. His hair hung in his face. His eyes looked haunted. In a moment of terror, he had bitten his lip, and a thread of blood had sewn a curving red seam down his chin, along his jawline, and part of the way down his neck. As always, she was shocked by the sight of his blood. However, considering what had almost happened to him, this injury could be borne.

The cemetery stillness lost its cold grip on the night. Outside, along the street, there were shouts, not of anger but of fear and curiosity, as neighbors at last ventured out of their homes. In the distance a siren swelled.

PART THREE
The Hounds

Satan hasn't a single salaried helper;
the Opposition employs a million.

> — Mark Twain

The hounds, the hounds
come baying at his heels.
The hounds, the hounds!
The breath of death he feels.

> — *The Book of Counted Sorrows*

26

As the authorities went about their work, Christine and Joey waited in the kitchen because that was one of the few rooms in the house that wasn't splashed with blood.

Christine had never seen so many policemen in one place before. Her house was crowded with uniformed men, plainclothes detectives, police lab technicians, a police photographer, a coroner and his assistant. Initially, she had welcomed the lawmen because their presence gave her a feeling of security, at last. But after a while she wondered if one of them might be a follower of Mother Grace and the Church of the Twilight. That notion didn't seem far-fetched. In fact, the logical assumption was that a militant religious cult, determined to force its views upon society at large, would make a special point of planting its people in various law-enforcement agencies and converting those who were already employed in that capacity. She remembered Officer Wilford, the born-again Christian who had disapproved of her language and manner of dress, and she wondered if perhaps Grace Spivey had been the mid-wife of his 'rebirth.'

Paranoia.

But considering the situation, perhaps a measure of paranoia was not a sign of mental illness; maybe, instead, it was prudent, a necessity for survival.

As rain continued to spatter the windows and as thunder shoved its way roughly through the night outside, she

watched the cops warily, regarded each unusual move
with suspicion. She realized that she couldn't go through
the rest of her life distrusting everyone; that would require
a constant watchfulness and a level of tension that would
utterly drain her physical, emotional, and mental energies.
It would be like living a life entirely on a high wire.
For the moment, however, she couldn't relax; she
remained on guard, alert, her muscles half tensed, ready
to spring at anyone who made a threatening move toward
Joey.

Again, the boy's resiliency surprised her. When the
police had first arrived, he had seemed to be in shock. His
eyes had been glazed, and he hadn't been willing or able
to speak. The sight of so much bloody violence and the
threat of death had left a mark on him that, for a while,
had seemed disturbingly profound. She knew this
experience would scar him for life; there was no escaping
that. But for a time she had been afraid that the harrowing
events of the past couple of hours would render him
catatonic or precipitate some other dangerous form of
psychologic withdrawal. But eventually he had come out
of it, and she had encouraged him by getting his battery-
powered Pac-Man game and playing it with him. The
electronic Pac-Man music theme and the beeping sounds
made by the cookie-gobbling yellow circle on the game
board made a bizarre counterpoint to the grimness of
murder and the seriousness of the homicide investigation
being conducted around them.

Joey's recovery had also been helped by Chewbacca's
miraculous recovery from the blow to the head that one
of the assassins had delivered with the butt of a shotgun.
The dog had been knocked unconscious, and his scalp had
been skinned a bit, but the mild bleeding had stopped in
response to pressure which Christine applied with antiseptic
pads. There were no signs of concussion. Now the pooch

was almost as good as new, and he stayed close to them, lying on the floor by Joey's chair, occasionally rising and looking up at the Pac-Man game, cocking his head, trying to figure out what the noisy device was.

She was no longer so sure that this dog's strong resemblance to Brandy was a bad thing. To endure the horror and turmoil, Joey needed reminders of more placid times, and he needed a sense of continuity that, like a bridge, would let him cross this period of chaos with his wits intact. Chewbacca, largely because of his resemblance to Brandy, could serve both those functions.

Charlie Harrison was in and out of the kitchen every ten or fifteen minutes, checking up on them and on the two new bodyguards he had stationed with them. One man, George Swarthout, sat on a tall stool by the kitchen phone, drinking coffee, watching Joey, watching the police who came in and out, watching Christine as she watched the police. The other, Vince Fields, was outside on the patio, guarding the rear approach to the house. It wasn't likely that any of Grace Spivey's people would launch a second attack while the house was swarming with cops, but the possibility couldn't be ruled out altogether. After all, kamikaze missions had a certain popularity with religious fanatics.

On each of his visits to the kitchen, Charlie kidded with Joey, played a game of Pac-Man, scratched behind Chewbacca's ears, and did whatever he could to lift the boy's spirits and keep his mind off the carnage in the rest of the house. When the police wanted to question Christine, Charlie stayed with Joey and sent her into another room, so the boy wouldn't have to listen to such gruesome talk. They wanted to question Joey, too, but Charlie managed their interrogation of the boy and kept it to a minimum. Christine realized that it wasn't easy for him to be such a rock, such a font of good spirits; he had lost two of his men, not only employees but friends. She was grateful that he seemed determined to conceal his own horror, tension, and grief for Joey's sake.

At eleven o'clock, just as Joey was tiring of Pac-Man, Charlie came in, pulled up a chair to the kitchen table, sat down, and said, 'Those suitcases you packed this morning –'

'Still in my car.'

'I'll have them put in mine. Go pack whatever else you might need for . . . say . . . a week. We'll be leaving here as soon as you're ready.'

'Where are we going?'

'I'd rather not tell you just now. We could be overheard.'

Had he, too, considered the possibility that one of Grace Spivey's people might be working as a cop? Christine wasn't sure whether his paranoia made her feel better or worse.

Joey said, 'We gonna hole up in a hideout somewhere?'

'Yep,' Charlie said. 'That's exactly what we're going to do.'

Joey frowned. 'The witch has magic radar. She'll find us.'

'Not where I'm taking you,' Charlie said. 'We've had a sorcerer cast a spell on the place so she can't detect it.'

'Yeah?' Joey said, leaning forward, fascinated. 'You know a sorcerer?'

'Oh, don't worry, he's a good guy,' Charlie said. 'He doesn't do black magic or anything like that.'

'Well, sure,' the boy said. 'I wouldn't figure a private eye would work with an *evil* sorcerer.'

Christine had a hundred questions for Charlie, but she didn't think it was a good idea to ask any of them in front of Joey and perhaps disturb his fragile equilibrium. She went upstairs, where the coroner was overseeing the removal of the red-haired killer's body, and she packed another suitcase. Downstairs, in Joey's room, she packed a second case for him, then, after a brief hesitation, stuffed some of his favorite toys in another bag.

She was gripped and shaken by the unsettling feeling that she would never see this house again.

Joey's bed, the *Star Wars* posters on his wall, his collection of plastic action figures and spaceships seemed slightly faded, as if they were not really here, as if they were objects in a photograph. She touched the bedpost, touched a doll, put a hand to the cool surface of the blackboard that stood in one corner, and she could feel those things beneath her fingers, but still, somehow, they didn't seem real any more. It was a strange, cold, augural feeling that left a hollowness within her.

No, she thought. I'll be back. Of course I will.

But the feeling of loss remained with her as she walked out of her son's room.

Chewbacca was taken out first and put into the green Chevy.

Then, in raincoats, shepherded by Charlie and his men, they left the house, and Christine shuddered when the cold, stinging rain struck her face.

Newspapermen, television camera teams, and a van from an all-news radio station awaited them. Powerful camera lights snapped on as soon as Christine and Joey appeared. Reporters jostled one other for the best position, and all of them spoke at once:

'Mrs. Scavello — '

' — a moment, please — '

' — just one question — '

She squinted as the lights lanced painfully at her eyes.

' — who would want to kill you and — '

' — is this a drug case — '

She held Joey tightly. Kept moving.

'— do you —'

'— can you —'

Microphones bristled at her.

'— have you —'

'— will you —'

A kaleidoscope of strange faces formed and reformed in front of her, some in shadow, some unnaturally pale and bright in the backsplash of the camera lights.

'— tell us what it feels like to live through —'

She got a glimpse of the familiar face of a man from KTLA's 'Ten O'clock News.'

'— tell us —'

'— what —'

'— how —'

'— why —'

'— terrorists or whatever they were?'

Cold rain trickled under the collar of her coat.

Joey was squeezing her hand very hard. The newsmen were scaring him.

She wanted to scream at them to get away, stay away, shut up.

They crowded closer.

Jabbered at her.

She felt as if she were making her way through a pack of hungry animals.

Then, in the crush and babble, an unfamiliar and unfriendly face loomed: a man in his fifties, with gray hair and bushy gray eyebrows. He had a gun.

No!

Christine couldn't get her breath. She felt a terrible weight on her chest.

It couldn't be happening again. Not so soon. Surely, they wouldn't attempt murder in front of all these witnesses. This was madness.

Charlie saw the weapon and pushed Christine and Joey out of the way.

At that same instant, a newswoman also saw the threat and tried to chop the gun out of the assailant's hand, but took a bullet in the thigh for her trouble.

Madness.

People screamed, and cops yelled, and everyone dropped to the rainsoaked ground, everyone but Christine and Joey, who ran toward the green Chevy, flanked by Vince Fields and George Swarthout. She was twenty feet from the car when something tugged at her, and pain flashed along her right side, just above the hip, and she knew she had been shot, but she didn't go down, didn't even stumble on the rain-slick sidewalk, just plunged ahead, gasping for breath, heart pounding so hard that each beat hurt her, and she held on to Joey, didn't look back, didn't know if the gunman was pursuing them, but heard a tremendous volley of shots, and then someone shouting, 'Get me an ambulance!'

She wondered if Charlie had shot the assailant.

Or had Charlie been shot instead?

That thought almost brought her to a stop, but they were already at the Chevy.

George Swarthout yanked open the rear door of the car and shoved them inside, where Chewbacca was barking excitedly.

Vince Fields ran around to the driver's door.

'On the floor!' Swarthout shouted. 'Stay down!'

And then Charlie was there, piling in after them, half on top of them, shielding them.

The Chevy's engine roared, and they pulled away from the curb with a shrill screeching of tires, rocketed down the street, away from the house, into the night and the rain, into a world that couldn't have been more completely hostile if it had been an alien planet in another galaxy.

27

Kyle Barlowe dreaded taking the news to Mother Grace, although he supposed she had already learned about it through a vision.

He entered the back of the church and stood there for a while, filling the doorway between the narthex and the nave, his broad shoulders almost touching both jambs. He was gathering strength from the giant brass cross above the altar, from the Biblical scenes depicted in the stained-glass windows, from the reverent quietude, from the sweet smell of incense.

Grace sat alone, on the left side of the church, in the second pew from the front. If she heard Barlowe enter, she gave no indication that she knew he was with her. She stared straight ahead at the cross.

At last Barlowe walked down the aisle and sat beside her. She was praying. He waited for her to finish. Then he said, 'The second attempt failed, too.'

'I know,' she said.

'What now?'

'We follow them.'

'Where?'

'Everywhere.' She spoke softly at first, in a whisper he could barely hear, but gradually her voice rose and gained power and conviction, until it echoed eerily off the shadow-hung walls of the nave. 'We give them no peace, no rest, no haven, no quarter. We must be pitiless, relentless, unsleeping, unshakable. We will be hounds. The hounds of Heaven. We will bay at their heels, lunge for their throats, and bring them to ground, sooner or later, here or there, when God wills it. We shall win. I am sure of it.'

She had been staring intently at the cross as she spoke, but now she turned her colorless gray eyes on him, and as always he felt her gaze penetrating to the core of him, to his very soul.

He said, 'What do you want me to do?'

'For now, go home. Sleep. Prepare yourself for the morning.'

'Aren't we going after them again tonight?'

'First, we must find them.'

'How?'

'God will lead. Now go. Sleep.'

He stood, stepped into the aisle. 'Will you sleep, too? You need your rest,' he said worriedly.

Her voice had faded to a reedy whisper once more, and there was exhaustion in it. 'I can't sleep, dear boy. An hour a night. Then I wake, and my mind is filled with visions, with messages from the angels, contacts from the spirit world, with worries and fears and hopes, with glimpses of the promised land, scenes of glory, with the awful weight of the responsibilities God has settled upon me.' She wiped at her mouth with the back of one hand. 'How I wish I *could* sleep, how I *long* for sleep, for surcease from all these demands and anxieties! But He has transformed me so that I can function without sleep during this crisis. I will not sleep well again until the Lord wills it. For reasons I don't understand, He needs me awake, *insists* upon it, gives me the strength to endure without sleep, keeps me alert, almost *too* alert.' Her voice was shaking, and Barlowe imagined it was both awe and fear that put the tremor in it. 'I tell you, dear Kyle, it's both glorious and terrible, wonderful and frightful, exhilarating and exhausting to be the instrument of God's will.'

She opened her purse, withdrew a handkerchief, and blew her nose. Suddenly she noticed that the hankie was stained brown and yellow, disgustingly knotted and crusted with dried snot.

'Look at this,' she said, indicating the handkerchief. 'It's horrible. I used to be so neat. So clean. My husband, bless his soul, always said my house was cleaner than a hospital operating room. And I was always very conscious of grooming; I dressed well. And I *never* would have carried a revolting handkerchief like this, never, not before the Gift was given to me and crowded out so many ordinary thoughts.' Tears glimmered in her gray eyes. 'Sometimes . . . I'm frightened . . . grateful to God for the Gift, yes . . . grateful for what I've gained but frightened about what I've lost . . .'

He wanted to understand what it must be like for her, to be the instrument of God's will, but he couldn't comprehend her state of mind or the mighty forces working within her. He did not know what to say to her, and he was depressed that he couldn't comfort her.

She said, 'Go home, sleep. Tomorrow, perhaps, we'll kill the boy.'

28

In the car, speeding through the storm-sodden streets, Charlie insisted on having a look at Christine's wound, although she said it wasn't serious. He was relieved to discover that she was right; she had only been grazed; the bullet had left a shallow furrow, two inches long, just above her hip. It was more of an abrasion than a wound, mostly cauterized by the heat of the bullet; the slug wasn't in her, and there was only minor bleeding. Nevertheless, they stopped at an all-night market, where they picked up alcohol and iodine and bandages, and Charlie dressed the wound while Vince, behind the wheel, got them on the road again. They switched from street to street, doubled back, circled through the rain-lashed darkness, like a flying insect reluctant to light anywhere for fear of being swatted, crushed.

They took every possible precaution to insure that they weren't followed, and they didn't arrive at the safe house in Laguna Beach until almost one o'clock in the morning. It was halfway up a long street, with (in daylight) a view of the ocean; a small place, almost a bungalow, two bedrooms and one bath; quaint, about forty years old but beautifully maintained, with a trellised front porch, gingerbread shutters; shrouded in bougainvillaea that grew up one wall and most of the way across the roof. The house belonged to Henry Rankin's aunt, who was vacationing in Mexico, and there was no way Grace Spivey or anyone from the Church of the Twilight could know about it.

Charlie wished they had come here earlier, that he had never allowed Christine and Joey to return to their own house. Of course, he'd had no way of knowing that Grace Spivey would take such drastic and violent action so soon. Killing a dog was one thing, but dispatching assassins armed with shotguns, sending them boldly into a quiet residential neighborhood . . . well, he hadn't imagined she was *that* crazy. Now he had lost two of his men, two of his *friends*. An emotional acid, part grief and part self-reproach, ate at him. He had known Pete Lockburn for nine years, Frank Reuther for six, and liked both of them a great deal. Although he knew he wasn't at fault for what had happened, he couldn't help blaming himself; he felt as bleak as a man could feel without contemplating suicide.

He tried to conceal the depth of his grief and rage because he didn't want to upset Christine further. She was distraught about the murders and seemed determined to hold herself, in part, accountable. He tried to reason with her: Frank and Pete knew the risk when they took the job; if she hadn't hired Klemet-Harrison, the bodies now on the way to the morgue would be hers and Joey's, so she'd done the right thing by seeking help. Regardless of the arguments he presented, she couldn't shake off her dark sense of responsibility.

Joey had fallen asleep in the car, so Charlie carried him through the slanting rain, through the drizzling night quiet of the Laguna hills, into the house. He put him down on the bed in the master bedroom, and the boy didn't even stir, only murmured softly and sighed. Together, Charlie and Christine undressed him and put him under the covers.

'I guess it won't hurt if he misses brushing his teeth just one night,' she said worriedly.

Charlie couldn't suppress a smile, and she saw him smiling, and she seemed to realize how ironic it was to be fretting about cavities only hours after the boy had escaped three killers.

She blushed and said, 'I guess, if God spared him from the bullets, He'll spare him from tooth decay, huh?'

'It's a good bet.'

Chewbacca curled up at the side of the bed and yawned heartily. He'd had a rough day, too.

Vince Fields came to the doorway and said, 'Where do you want me, boss?'

Charlie hesitated, remembering Pete and Frank. He had put them in the line of fire. He didn't want to put Vince in the line of fire, too. But, of course, it was ridiculous of him to think that way. He couldn't tell Vince to hide in the back of the closet where it was safe. It was Vince's job to *be* in the line of fire if necessary; Vince knew that, and Charlie knew that, and they both knew it was Charlie's job to give the orders, regardless of the consequences. So what was he waiting for? Either you had the guts to accept the risks in this job, or you didn't.

166

He cleared his throat and said, 'Uh . . . I want you right here, Vince. Sitting on a chair. Beside the bed.'

Vince sat down.

Charlie took Christine to the small tidy kitchen, where George Swarthout had made a large pot of coffee and had poured cups for himself and Vince. Charlie sent George to the living room windows, to keep watch on the street, poured some of the coffee for himself and Christine.

'Miriam — Henry's aunt — is a brandy drinker. Would you like a slug in that coffee?'

'Might be a good idea,' Christine said.

He found the brandy in the cabinet by the refrigerator and laced both cups of coffee.

They sat across from each other at a small table by a window that looked out on a rain-hammered garden where, at the moment, only shadows bloomed.

He said, 'How's your hip?'

'Just a twinge.'

'Sure?'

'Positive. Listen, what happens now? Will the police make arrests?'

'They can't. The assailants are all dead.'

'But the woman who sent them isn't dead. She's a party to attempted murder. A conspirator. She's as guilty as they were.'

'We've no proof Grace Spivey sent them.'

'If all three of them are members of her church —'

'That would be an important lead. The problem is, how do we prove they were church members?'

'The police could question their friends, their families.'

'Which they would definitely do if they could *find* their friends and families.'

'What do you mean?'

'None of those three gunmen was carrying identification.

167

No wallets, no credit cards, no driver's licenses, no nothing.'

'Fingerprints. Couldn't they be identified by their fingerprints?'

'Of course, the police will be following up on that. But unless those men were in the army or have criminal records or once held a security job that required them to be fingerprinted, their prints won't be on file anywhere.'

'So we might *never* know who they were?'

'Maybe not. And until we can identify them, there's no way to trace them back to Grace Spivey.'

She scowled as she drank some of her coffee and brandy, mulling over the situation, trying to see what they might have missed, trying to come up with a way to link the killers with the Church of the Twilight. Charlie could tell her that she was wasting her time, that Grace Spivey had been too careful, but she had to reach that conclusion on her own.

Finally she said, 'The man who attacked us in front of the house . . . was he the one who was driving the van?'

'No. He's not the man I watched through binoculars.'

'But if he was in that van, even as a passenger, maybe it's still parked down the street from my house.'

'Nope. The police looked for it. No white van anywhere in the neighborhood. Nothing at all that would point to The True Word or to the Church of the Twilight.'

'What about their weapons?'

'Those are being checked out, too. But I expect they weren't purchased legitimately. There'll be no way to find out who bought them.'

Her face soured by frustration, she said, 'But we know Grace Spivey threatened Joey, and we know one of her people has been following us in a van. After what happened tonight, isn't that reason enough for the cops to at least go talk to her?'

'Yes. And they will.'

'When?'

'Now. If they haven't already. But she'll deny everything.'

'They'll keep a watch on her?'

'Nope. No point in it, anyway. They might be able to watch her, but they can't keep tabs on everyone who's a member of her church. That would require a lot more manpower than they have. Besides, it'd be unconstitutional.'

'Then we're right back where we started,' she said miserably.

'No. Eventually, maybe not right away but in time, one of those nameless dead men or one of their guns or the pictures I took of the man in the van will give us a concrete connection with Grace Spivey. These people aren't perfect. Somewhere, they've overlooked a detail, made a mistake, and we'll capitalize on it. They'll make other mistakes, too, and sooner or later we'll have enough evidence to nail them.'

'Meanwhile?'

'You and Joey will lay low.'

'Here?'

'For the time being.'

'They'll find us.'

'No.'

'They will,' she said grimly.

'Not even the police know where you are.'

'But your people know.'

'We're on *your* side.'

She nodded, but he could see that she still had something to say, something she really didn't want to say but something she couldn't contain, either.

'What is it? What're you thinking?' he prodded.

'Isn't it possible that one of your people belongs to the Church of the Twilight?'

The question startled him. He hand-picked his people, knew them, liked them, trusted them. 'Impossible.'

'After all, your agency had a run-in with Spivey. You rescued those two little children from her cult, snatched them away from their mother. I'd think maybe Grace Spivey would be wary of you, wary enough to plant someone in your organization. She could've converted one of your men.'

'No. Impossible. The first time she tried to contact one of them, he'd report it to me immediately.'

'Maybe it's one of your new employees, someone who was a Spivey disciple before he ever came to work for you. Have you hired anyone new since you snatched those kids?'

'A few people. But our employees have to undergo a rigorous background investigation before we hire them —'

'Membership in the church could be hidden, kept secret.'

'It'd be difficult.'

'I notice you've stopped saying "impossible".'

She'd made him uneasy. He liked to believe that he always thought of everything, prepared for every contingency. But he hadn't thought of this, primarily because he knew his people too well to entertain the notion that any of them was weak-minded enough to sign up with a crackpot cult. Then again, people were strange, especially these days, and the only thing about them that could surprise you was if they *never* surprised you.

He sipped his coffee and said, 'I'll have Henry Rankin run entirely new checks on everyone who's joined us since the Spivey case. If something was missed the first time, Henry'll find it. He's the best there is.'

'And you're sure you can trust Henry?'

'Jesus, Christine, he's like my brother!'

'Remember Cain and Abel.'

'Listen, Christine, a little suspicion, a touch of paranoia — that's good. I encourage it. Makes you more cautious.

But you can go too far. You've got to trust someone. You can't handle this alone.'

She nodded, looked down at her half-finished coffee and brandy. 'You're right. And I guess it's not very charitable of me to worry about how trustworthy your people are when two of them have already died for me.'

'They didn't die for you,' he said.

'Yes, they did.'

'They only—'

'Died for me.'

He sighed and said nothing more. She was too sensitive a woman not to feel some guilt about Pete Lockburn and Frank Reuther. She would just have to work it out by herself — the same way he would.

'All right,' she said. 'So while Joey and I are lying low, what'll you be doing?'

'Before we left your house, I called the rectory at the church.'

'*Her* church?'

'Yeah. She wasn't in. But I asked her secretary to arrange a meeting for tomorrow. I made her promise to call Henry Rankin tonight, no matter how late, and let him know when I'm to be there.'

'Walking into the lion's den.'

'It's not quite that dramatic or dangerous.'

'What do you expect to gain by talking to her?'

'I don't know. But it seems the next logical step.'

She shifted in her chair, picked up her coffee, put it down without taking a drink, and chewed nervously on her lower lip. 'I'm afraid that . . .'

'What?'

'I'm afraid, if you go to her . . . somehow she'll make you tell her where we are.'

'I'm not that easy,' he said.

'But she might use drugs or torture or—'

'Believe me, Christine, I can handle myself and I can handle this old woman and her pack of crazies.'

She stared at him for a long time.

Her eyes were mesmerizingly beautiful.

At last she said, 'You can. I know it. You can handle them. I have a lot of faith in you, Charlie Harrison. It's an . . . instinct. I feel good about you. I know you're capable. I don't doubt you. Really I don't. But I'm still scared.'

At 1:30, someone from Klemet-Harrison brought Charlie's gray Mercedes to the house in Laguna Beach, so he could drive himself home when he was ready. At 2:05, grainy-eyed and bone-weary, he looked at his watch, said, 'Well, I guess I'll be going,' and went to the sink to rinse out his coffee cup.

When he put his cup in the rack to dry and turned, she was standing at the kitchen window, beside the door, staring out at the dark lawn. She was hugging herself.

He went to her. 'Christine?'

She turned, faced him.

'You okay?' he asked.

She nodded, being brave. 'Just a chill.'

Her teeth chattered when she spoke.

On impulse, he put his arms around her. Without a hint of reservation, she came against him, allowed herself to be held, her head on his shoulder. Then her arms slipped around him, too, and they were linked, and nothing had ever been better than hugging her. Her hair was against his cheek, her hands on his back, her body molded to him, her warmth piercing him, the scent of her filling him. The embrace had the electrifying quality of a new and longed-for experience and, at the same time, it was a comfortable, familiar sharing. It was difficult to believe he had known her less than one day. He seemed to have *wanted* her much

172

longer than that — and, of course, he had, though until he'd seen her he hadn't known it was her that he had wanted for so many years.

He could have kissed her then. He had the desire and the nerve to put a hand under her chin and lift her face and press his lips to hers, and he knew she wouldn't resist, might even welcome it. But he did no more than hug her because he sensed the time wasn't exactly right for the commitment that a passionate kiss implied. Now, it would be a kiss that she sought partly out of fear, partly out of a desperate need to be reassured. When at last he did kiss her, he wanted it to be for other reasons entirely: desire, affection, love. He wanted the start to be perfect for them.

When she finally let go of him, she seemed self-conscious. She smiled shyly and said, 'Sorry. Didn't mean to get shaky on you. I've got to be strong. I know it. There's no room for weakness in this situation.'

'Nonsense,' he said gently. 'I needed a hug, too.'

'You did?'

'Everyone could use a teddy bear now and then.'

She smiled at him.

He hated to leave her. All the way out to the car, with the wind tearing at his coat and the rain battering his bare head, he wanted to turn around and go back in there and tell her that something special was happening between them, something that shouldn't happen this fast, something like you saw in the movies but never in real life. He wanted to tell her now, even if it was the wrong time, because in spite of all his reassuring talk, he didn't know for sure that he would be able to handle Spivey and her crazies; there was a possibility, however slim, that he would never get another chance, never see Christine Scavello again.

He lived in the hills of North Tustin, and he was almost halfway home, cruising a lonely stretch of Irvine

Boulevard, thinking about Frank Reuther and Pete Lockburn, when the events of the past few hours became too much to handle, and he was suddenly short of breath. He had to pull to the berm and stop. There were orange groves on one side of the roadway, strawberry fields on the other side, and darkness all around. At this hour, there was no traffic. Slumped back in his seat, he stared at the rain-spattered windshield where the water made ghostly, speckled patterns in the backsplash of his own headlight beams, brief-lived patterns erased by the metronomically thumping windshield wipers. It was unnerving and dispiriting to realize that human lives could be erased as suddenly and easily as those rain patterns on the glass. He wept.

In all its years of operation, Klemet-Harrison had lost only one other man in the line of duty. He had been killed in an automobile accident while he was working, although it was unconnected to his assignment and could have taken place as easily on his own time. A few men had been shot at over the years, mostly by estranged husbands who were determined to harass their wives in spite of court orders restraining them from doing so; and a couple of guys had even been hit. But until now no one had been *murdered*, for God's sake. The private investigation business was far less violent, far less dangerous than it was portrayed on television and in the movies. Sometimes you got roughed up a bit or had to rough up someone else, and there was always the *potential* for violence, but the potential was rarely realized.

Charlie wasn't afraid for himself, but he was afraid for his men, the people who worked for him and relied upon him. When he had taken this case, maybe he had gotten them into something he shouldn't have. Maybe, by signing on to protect Christine and Joey, he had also signed death warrants for himself and his associates. Who knew what to expect when you were dealing with religious fanatics? Who knew how far they would go?

On the other hand, everyone who worked with him knew the risks, even though they usually expected better odds than these. And what kind of detective agency would they be, what kind of bodyguards would they be if they walked away from the first really nasty case they handled? And how could he back down on his word to Christine Scavello? He wouldn't be able to face himself in the morning if he left her defenseless. Besides, he was more certain than ever that he was, with irrational but not entirely involuntary haste, falling in love with her.

In spite of the rain booming on the roof and the thumping of the windshield wipers, the night was unbearably silent in the oppressively humid car; there was a dearth of *meaningful* sound, just the random noises of the storm which, by their very randomness, reminded him of the chasm of chaos above which his life and all other lives unfolded. That was a thought on which he preferred not to dwell at the moment.

He pulled back onto the road, accelerated, and sent up twin plumes of spray from a deep puddle, heading toward the hills, and home.

29

Christine hadn't expected to be able to sleep. She stretched out on the bed where Joey lay like a stone, but she figured she would just wait there with her eyes closed, resting, until he woke. She must have dropped off instantly.

She came around once during the night and realized the rain had stopped. The silence was profound.

George Swarthout was sitting in a chair in the corner, reading a magazine in the soft glow of a table lamp with a mother-of-pearl shade. She wanted to speak to him, wanted to know if everything was all right, but she hadn't the strength to sit up or even talk. She closed her eyes and drifted down into darkness again.

She came fully awake before seven o'clock, feeling fuzzy-headed after only four and a half hours of sleep. Joey was snoring softly. She left George watching over her son, went into the bathroom, and took a long, hot shower, wincing when water got under the bandage on her hip and elicited a stinging pain from her still-healing wound.

She finally stepped out of the shower, toweled dry, applied a new bandage, and was pulling on her clothes when she sensed that Joey was in trouble, right now, terrible trouble; she felt it in her bones. She thought she heard him scream above the rumbling of the bathroom's exhaust fan. Oh Jesus *no*. He was being slaughtered out there in the bedroom, hacked to pieces by some Bible-thumping maniac. Her stomach tightened, and her skin goose-pimpled, and in spite of the moaning bathroom fan she thought she heard something else, a thump, a clubbing sound. They must be beating him, too, stabbing and beating him, and her lungs blocked up, and she knew it, *knew* Joey was dead, my God, and in a wild panic she pulled up the zipper on her jeans, didn't even finish buttoning her blouse, stumbled out of the bathroom, shoeless, with her wet hair hanging in glossy clumps.

She had imagined everything.

The boy was safe.

He was awake, sitting up in bed, listening wide-eyed as George Swarthout told him a story about a magic parrot and the King of Siam.

Later, worried that her mother would hear about their

problems on the news or read about them in the papers, she called, but then wished she hadn't. Evelyn listened to all the details, was properly shocked, but instead of offering much sympathy, she launched into an interrogation that surprised and angered Christine.

'What did you do to these people?' Evelyn wanted to know.

'What people?'

'The people at this church.'

'I didn't do anything to them, Mother. They're trying to do it to *us*. Didn't you hear what I said?'

'They wouldn't pick on you for no reason,' Evelyn said.

'They're crazy, Mother.'

'Can't all of them be crazy, a whole churchful of people.'

'Well, they are. They're bad people, Mother, real bad people.'

'Can't all of them be bad. Not *religious* people like that. Can't all of them be after you just for the fun of it.'

'I told you why they're after us. They've got this crazy idea that Joey —'

'That's what you *told* me,' Evelyn said, 'but that can't be it. Not really. There must be something else. Must be something you did that made them angry. But even if they're angry, I'm sure they're not trying to kill anybody.'

'Mother, I *told* you, they came with guns, and men were killed —'

'Then the people who had guns weren't these church people,' Evelyn said. 'You've got it all wrong. It's someone else.'

'Mother, I haven't got it all wrong. I —'

'Church people don't use guns, Christine.'

'These church people do.'

'It's someone else,' Evelyn insisted.

'But —'

177

'You have a grudge against religion,' Evelyn said. 'Always have. A grudge against the Church.'

'Mother, I don't hold any grudges — '

'That's why you're so quick to blame this on religious people when it's plainly the work of someone else, maybe political terrorists like on the news all the time, or maybe you're involved in something you shouldn't be and now it's getting out of hand, which wouldn't surprise me. Are you involved in something, Christine, like drugs, which they're always killing themselves over, like you see on TV, dealers shooting each other all the time — is it anything like that, Christine?'

She imagined she could hear the grandfather clock ticking monotonously in the background. Suddenly, she couldn't breathe well.

The conversation progressed in that fashion until Christine couldn't stand any more. She said she had to go, and she hung up before her mother could protest. Evelyn hadn't even said, 'I love you,' or 'be careful,' or 'I'm worried about you,' or 'I'll do anything I can to help.'

Her mother might as well be dead; their relationship certainly was.

At seven-thirty, Christine made breakfast for George, Vince, Joey, and herself. She was buttering toast when the rain began to fall again.

The morning was so drab, the clouds so low, the light so dim and gray that it might have been the end rather than the beginning of the day, and the rain came out of that somber sky with gutter-flooding force. Fog still churned outside, and without any sun it probably would hang on all day, barely dissipate, and get blindingly thick tonight. This was the time of year when relentless trains of storms could assault California, moving in from the Pacific, pounding the coastal areas until creeks swelled over their

178

banks and reservoirs topped out and hillsides began to slide, carrying houses into the bottoms of the canyons with deadly swiftness. From the look of it, they were probably in the process of being run over by one of those storm trains right now.

The prospect of a long stretch of bad weather made the threat from the Church of the Twilight even more frightening. When winter rains closed in like this, streets were flooded, and freeways jammed up beyond belief, and mobility was curtailed, and California seemed to shrink, the mountains contracting toward the coast, squeezing the land in between. When the rainy season was at its worst, California acquired a claustrophobic aspect that you never read about in tourist brochures or see on postcards. In weather like this, Christine always felt a little trapped, even when she wasn't being hounded by well-armed lunatics.

When she took a plate of bacon and eggs to Vince Fields, where he was stationed by the front door, she said, 'You guys must be tired. How long can you keep this up?'

He thanked her for the food, glanced at his watch, and said, 'We only have about an hour to go. The replacement team will be here by then.'

Of course. A replacement team. A new shift. That should have been obvious to her, but it hadn't been. She had grown accustomed to Vince and George, had learned to trust them. If either of them had been a member of the Church of the Twilight, she and Joey would have been dead by now. She wanted them to stay, but they couldn't remain awake and on guard forever. Foolish of her not to have understood that.

Now she had to worry about the new men. One of *them* might have sold his soul to Grace Spivey.

She returned to the kitchen. Joey and George Swarthout were having breakfast at the semicircular pine table which could accommodate only three chairs. She sat down in front of her own plate, but suddenly she wasn't hungry any more. She picked at her food and said, 'George, the next shift of bodyguards — '

'Be here soon,' he said around a mouthful of eggs and toast.

'Do you know who Charlie . . . who Mr. Harrison is sending?'

'You mean their names?'

'Yes, their names.'

'Nope. Could be any of several fellas. Why?'

She didn't know why she would feel better if she knew their names. She wasn't familiar with Charlie's staff. Their names would mean nothing to her. She wouldn't be able to tell that they were Grace Spivey's people just by their names. She wasn't being rational.

'If you know any of our people and would prefer to have them work a shift here, you should tell Mr. Harrison,' George said.

'No. I don't know anybody. I just . . . well . . . never mind. It wasn't important.'

Joey seemed to sense the nature of her fear. He stopped teasing Chewbacca with a piece of bacon, put one small hand on Christine's arm, as if to reassure her the way he'd seen Charlie do, and said, 'Don't worry, Mom. They'll be good guys. Whoever Charlie sends, they'll be real good.'

'The best,' George agreed.

To George, Joey said, 'Hey, tell Mom the story about the talking giraffe and the princess who didn't have a horse.'

'I doubt if it's exactly your mother's kind of story,' George said, smiling.

'Then tell me again,' Joey said. 'Please?'

As George told the fairytale — which seemed to be of his own creation — Christine's attention drifted to the rainy day beyond the window. Somewhere out there, two of Charlie's men were coming, and she was increasingly certain that at least one of them would be a disciple of the Spivey creature.

Paranoia. She knew that half her problem was psychological. She was worrying unnecessarily. Charlie had warned her not to go off the deep end. She wouldn't be much good to either Joey or herself if she started seeing boogeymen in every shadow. It was just the damned lousy weather, closing in on them, the rain and the morning fog, weaving a shroud around them. She felt trapped, suffocated, and her imagination was working overtime.

She was aware of all that.

It didn't matter.

She couldn't talk herself out of her fear. She knew that something bad was going to happen when the two men showed up.

30

At eight o'clock Tuesday morning, Charlie met Henry Rankin in front of the Church of the Twilight: a Spanish-style structure with stained-glass windows, red tile roof, two bell towers, and a broad expanse of steps leading up to six massive carved oak doors. Rain slanted at the doors, streamed off the steps, making oily puddles on the cracked and canted sidewalk. The doors needed to be refinished, and the building needed new stucco; it was shabby and neglected, but that was in keeping with the neighborhood, which had been deteriorating for decades. The church had once been the home of a Presbyterian congregation, which had fled ten blocks north, to a new site, where there weren't so many abandoned stores, adult bookshops, failing businesses, and crumbling houses.

'You look wiped out,' Henry said. He stood at the foot of the church steps, holding a big black umbrella, frowning as Charlie approached under an umbrella of his own.

'Didn't get to bed until three-thirty,' Charlie said.

'I tried to make this appointment for later,' Henry said. 'This was the only time she would see us.'

'It's all right. If I'd had more time, I'd have just lain there, staring at the ceiling. Did the police talk to her last night?'

Henry nodded. 'I spoke with Lieutenant Carella this morning early. They questioned Spivey, and she denied everything.'

'They believe her?'

'They're suspicious, if only because they've had their own problems with more than a few of these cults.'

Each time a car passed in the street, its tires hissed on the wet pavement with what sounded like serpentine anger.

'Have they been able to put a name to any of those three dead men?'

'Not yet. As for the guns, the serial numbers are from a shipment that was sent from the wholesaler in New York to a chain of retail sporting goods outlets in the Southwest, two years ago. The shipment never arrived. Hijacked. So these guns were bought on the black market. No way to trace who sold or purchased them.'

'They cover their tracks well,' Charlie said.

It was time to talk to Grace Spivey. He wasn't looking forward to it. He had little patience for the psychotic babble in which these cult types frequently spoke. Besides, after last night, anything was possible; they might even risk committing murder on their own doorstep.

He looked at his car, by the curb, where one of his men, Carter Rilbeck, was waiting behind the wheel. Carter would wait for them and send for help if they weren't out in half an hour. In addition, both Charlie and Henry were packing revolvers in shoulder holsters.

The rectory was to the left of the church, set back from the street, beyond an unkempt lawn, between two coral trees in need of trimming, ringed by shrubbery that hadn't been thinned or shaped in months. Like the church, the rectory was in ill-repair. Charlie supposed that if you really believed the end of the world was imminent — as these Twilighters claimed to believe — then you didn't waste time on such niceties as gardening and house painting.

The rectory porch had a creaking floor, and the doorbell made a thin, harsh, irregular sound, more animal than mechanical.

The curtain covering the window in the center of the door was abruptly drawn aside. A florid-faced, overweight woman with protuberant green eyes stared at them for a long moment, then let the curtain fall into place, unlocked the door, and ushered them into a drab entry hall.

When the door was closed and the susurrous voice of the storm faded somewhat, Charlie said, 'My name is—'

'I know who you are,' the woman replied curtly. She led them back down the hall to a chamber on the right, where the door was ajar. She opened the door all the way and indicated that they were to enter. She didn't come with them, didn't announce them, just closed the door after them, leaving them to their own introductions. Evidently, common courtesy was not an ingredient in the bizarre stew of Christianity and doomsday prophecy that Spivey's followers had cooked up for themselves.

Charlie and Henry were in a room twenty feet long and fifteen feet wide, sparsely and cheaply furnished. Filing cabinets lined one wall. In the center were a simple metal table on which lay a woman's purse and an ashtray, one metal folding chair behind the table, and two chairs in front of it. Nothing else. No draperies at the windows. No tables or cabinets or knick-knacks. There were no lamps, either, just the ceiling fixture, which cast a yellowish glow that, blending with the gray storm light coming through the tall windows, gave the room a muddy look.

Perhaps the oddest thing of all was the complete lack of religious objects: no paintings portraying Christ, no plastic statues of Biblical figures or angels, no needlepoint samplers bearing religious messages, none of the sacred objects — or kitsch, depending on your point of view — that you expected to find among cult fanatics. There had been none in the hallway, either, or in any of the rooms they had passed.

Grace Spivey was standing at the far end of the room, at a window, her back to them, staring out at the rain.

Henry cleared his throat.

She didn't move.

Charlie said, 'Mrs. Spivey?'

Finally she turned away from the window and faced them. She was dressed all in yellow: pale yellow blouse, a gay yellow polka-dot scarf knotted at her neck, deep yellow skirt, yellow shoes. She was wearing yellow bracelets on each wrist and half a dozen rings set with yellow stones. The effect was ludicrous. The brightness of her outfit only accentuated the paleness of her puffy face, the withered dullness of her age-spotted skin. She looked as if she were possessed by senile whimsy and thought of herself as a twelve-year-old girl on the way to a friend's birthday party.

Her gray hair was wild, but her eyes were wilder. Even from across the room, those eyes were riveting and strange.

She was curiously rigid, shoulders drawn up tight, arms straight down at her sides, hands curled into tight fists.

'I'm Charles Harrison,' Charlie said because he'd never actually met the woman before, 'and this is my associate, Mr. Rankin.'

As unsteady as a drunkard, she took two steps away from the window. Her face twisted, and her white skin became even whiter. She cried out in pain, almost fell, caught herself in time, and stood swaying as if the floor were rolling under her.

'Is something wrong?' Charlie asked.

'You'll have to help me,' she said.

He hadn't figured on anything like this. He had expected her to be a strong woman with a vital, magnetic personality, a take-charge type who would keep them off balance from the start. Instead it was she who was off balance, and quite literally.

She was standing in a partial crouch now, as if pain were bending her in half. She was still stiff, and her hands were still fisted.

Charlie and Henry went to her.

'Help me to that chair before I fall,' she said weakly. 'It's my feet.'

Charlie looked down at her feet and was shocked to see blood on them. He took her left arm, and Henry took her right, and they half carried her to the chair that stood behind the metal table. As she sat down, Charlie realized there was a bleeding wound on the bridge of each foot, just above the tongue of each shoe, twin holes, as if she had been stabbed, not by a knife but by something with a very narrow blade — perhaps an ice pick.

'Can I get you a doctor?' he asked, disconcerted to find himself being so solicitous to her.

'No,' she said. 'No doctor. Please sit down.'

'But –'

'I'll be all right. I'll be fine. God watches over me, you know. God is good to me. Sit. Please.'

Confused, they went to the two chairs on the other side of the table, but before either of them could sit, the old

185

woman opened her fisted hands and held her palms up to them. 'Look,' she said in a demanding whisper. 'Look at *this*! Behold *this*!'

The gruesome sight stopped Charlie from sitting down. In each of the woman's palms, there was another bleeding hole, like those in her feet. As he stared at her wounds, the blood began to ooze out faster than before.

Incredibly, she was smiling.

Charlie glanced at Henry and saw the same question in his friend's eyes that he knew must be in his own: *What the hell is going on here?*

'It's for you,' the old woman said excitedly. She leaned towards them, stretching her arms across the table, holding her hands out to them, urging them to look.

'For us?' Henry said, baffled.

'What do you mean?' Charlie asked.

'A sign,' she said.

'Sign?'

'A holy sign.'

Charlie stared at her hands.

'Stigmata,' she said.

Jesus. The woman belonged in an institution.

A chill worked its way assiduously up Charlie's spine and curled at the base of his neck, flicking its icy tail.

'The wounds of Christ,' she said.

What have we walked into? Charlie wondered.

Henry said, 'I better call a doctor.'

'No,' she said softly but authoritatively. 'These wounds ache, yes, but it's a sweet pain, a good pain, a cleansing pain, and they won't become infected; they'll heal well on their own. Don't you understand? These are the wounds Christ endured, the holes made by the nails that pinned Him to the cross.'

She's mad, Charlie thought, and he looked uneasily at the door, wondering where the florid-faced woman had gone. To get some other crazies? To organize a death squad? A human sacrifice? They had the nerve to call *this* Christianity?

'I know what you're thinking,' Grace Spivey said, her voice growing louder, stronger. 'You don't think I look like a prophet. You don't think God would work through an old, crazy-looking woman like me. But that *is* how He works. Christ worked with the outcasts, befriended the lepers, the prostitutes, the thieves, the deformed, and sent them forth to spread His word. Do you know why? Do you *know*?'

She was speaking so loudly now that her voice rebounded from the walls, and Charlie was reminded of a television evangelist who spoke in hypnotic rhythms and with the projection of a well-trained actor.

'Do you know why God chooses the most unlikely messenger?' she demanded. 'It's because He wants to test you. *Anyone* could bring himself to believe the preachings of a pretty-boy minister with Robert Redford's face and Richard Burton's voice! But only the righteous, only those who truly want to believe in the Word . . . only those with enough *faith* will recognize and accept the Word regardless of the messenger!'

Her blood was dripping on the table. Her voice had risen until it vibrated in the window glass.

'God is testing you. Can you hear His message regardless of what you think of the messenger? Is your soul pure enough to allow you to *hear*? Or is there corruption within you that makes you deaf?'

Both Charlie and Henry were speechless. There was a mesmerizing quality to her tirade that was numbing and demanding of attention.

'Listen, listen, listen!' she said urgently. 'Listen to what I *tell* you. God visited these stigma upon me the moment you rang the doorbell. He has given you a *sign*, and that can mean only one thing: You aren't yet in Satan's thrall, and the Lord is giving you a chance to *redeem* yourselves. Apparently you don't realize what the woman is, what her *child* is. If you knew and still protected them, God wouldn't be offering you redemption. Do you know what they are? Do you *know*?'

Charlie cleared his throat, blinked, freed himself from the fuzziness that had briefly affected his thoughts. 'I know what you think they are,' Charlie said.

'It's not what I think. It's what I know. It's what God has told me. The boy is the Antichrist. The mother is the black Madonna.'

Charlie hadn't expected her to be so direct. He was sure she would deny any interest in Joey, just as she had denied it to the police. He was startled by her forthrightness and didn't know what to make of it.

'I know you're not recording this conversation,' she said. 'We have instruments that would have detected a recorder. I would have been alerted. So I can speak freely. The boy has come to rule the earth for a thousand years.'

'He's just a six-year-old boy,' Charlie said, 'like any other six-year-old boy.'

'No,' she said, still holding her hands up to reveal the blood seeping from her wounds. 'No, he is more, worse. He must die. We must kill him. It is God's wish, God's work.'

'You can't really mean –'

She interrupted him. 'Now that you have been told, now that God has made the truth clear to you, you must cease protecting them.'

'They're my clients,' Charlie said. 'I –'

'If you persist in protecting them, you're damned,' the old woman said worriedly, begging them to accept redemption.

'We have an obligation –'

'Damned, don't you see? You'll rot in Hell. All hope lost. Eternity spent in suffering. You must listen. You must learn.'

He looked into her fevered eyes, which challenged him with berserk intensity. His pity for her was mixed with a disgust that left him unable and unwilling to debate with her. He realized it had been pointless to come. The woman was beyond the reach of reason.

He was now more afraid for Christine and Joey than he had been last night, when one of Grace Spivey's followers had been shooting at them.

She raised her bleeding palms an inch or two higher. 'This sign is for you, for *you*, to convince you that I am, in fact, a herald bearing a true message. Do you see? Do you believe now? Do you *understand*?'

Charlie said, 'Mrs. Spivey, you shouldn't have done this. Neither of us is a gullible man, so it's all been for nothing.'

Her face darkened. She curled her hands into fists again.

Charlie said, 'If you used a nail that was at all rusty or dirty, I hope you'll go immediately to your doctor and get tetanus shots. This could be very serious.'

'You're lost to me,' she said in a voice as flat as the table to which she lowered her bleeding hands.

'I came here to try to reason with you,' Charlie said. 'I see that's not possible. So just let me warn you –'

'You belong to Satan now. You've had your chance –'

' – if you don't back off –'

' – and you've thrown your chance away –'

' – if you don't leave the Scavellos alone –'

' – and now you'll pay the terrible price!'

' – I'll dig into this and hang on. I'll keep at it come Hell or high water, until I've seen you put on trial, until I've seen your church lose its tax exemption, until everyone knows you for what you really are, until your followers lose their faith in you, and until your insane little cult is crushed. I mean it. I can be as relentless as you, as determined. I can finish you. Stop while you have a chance.'

She glared at him.

Henry said, 'Mrs. Spivey, will you put an end to this madness?'

She said nothing. She lowered her eyes.

'Mrs. Spivey?'

No response. Charlie said, 'Come on, Henry. Let's get out of here.'

As they approached the door, it opened, and an enormous man entered the room, ducking his head to avoid rapping it on the frame. He had to be almost seven feet tall. He had a face from a nightmare. He didn't seem real; only images from the movies were suitable to describe him, Charlie thought. He was like a Frankenstein monster with the hugely muscled body of Conan the Barbarian, a shambling hulk spawned by a bad script and a low budget. He saw Grace Spivey weeping, and his face knotted with a look of despair and rage that made Charlie's blood turn to icy slush. The giant reached out, grabbed Charlie by the coat, and nearly hauled him off the floor.

Henry drew his gun, and Charlie said, 'Hold it, hold it,' because although the situation was bad it wasn't necessarily lethal.

The big man said, 'What'd you do to her? What'd you do?'

'Nothing,' Charlie said. 'We were — '

'Let them go,' Grace Spivey said. 'Let them pass, Kyle.' The giant hesitated. His eyes, like hard bright sea creatures hiding deep under a suboceanic shelf, regarded Charlie with a pure malignant fury that would have given nightmares to the devil himself. At last he let go of Charlie, lumbered toward the table at which the woman sat. He spotted blood on her hands and wheeled back toward Charlie.

'She did it to herself,' Charlie said, edging toward the door. He didn't like the wheedling note in his own voice, but at the moment there didn't seem to be room for pride. To give in to a macho urge would be ironclad proof of feeble-mindedness. 'We didn't touch her.'

'Let them go,' Grace Spivey repeated.

In a low, menacing voice, the giant said, 'Get out. Fast.'

Charlie and Henry did as they were told.

The florid-faced woman with the protruding green eyes was waiting at the front of the rectory. As they hurried down the hallway, she opened the door. The instant they stepped onto the porch, she slammed the door behind them and locked it.

Charlie went out into the rain without putting up his umbrella. He turned his face toward the sky. The rain felt fresh and clean, and he let it hammer at him because he felt soiled by the madness in the house.

'God help us,' Henry said shakily.

They walked out to the street.

Dirty water was churning to the top of the gutter. It formed a brown lake out toward the intersection, and bits of litter, like a flotilla of tiny boats, sailed on the wind-chopped surface.

Charlie turned and looked back at the rectory. Now its grime and deterioration seemed like more than ordinary urban decay; the rot was a reflection of the minds of the building's occupants. In the dust-filmed windows, in the peeling paint and sagging porch and badly cracked stucco, he saw not merely ruin but the physical world's representation of human madness. He had read a lot of science fiction as a child, still read some now and then, so maybe that was why he thought of the Law of Entropy, which held that the universe and all things within it moved in only one basic direction — toward decay, collapse, dissolution, and chaos. The Church of the Twilight seemed to embrace entropy as the ultimate expression of divinity, aggressively promulgating madness, unreason, and chaos, reveling in it.

He was scared.

31

After breakfast, Christine called Val Gardner and a couple of other people, assured them that she and Joey were all right, but didn't tell any of them where she was. Thanks to the Church of the Twilight, she no longer entirely trusted her friends, not even Val, and she resented that sad development.

By the time she finished making her phone calls, two new bodyguards arrived to relieve Vince and George. One of them, Sandy Breckenstein, was tall and lean, about thirty, with a prominent Adam's apple; he brought to mind Ichabod Crane in the old Disney cartoon version of *The Legend of Sleepy Hollow*. Sandy's partner was Max Steck, a bull of a man with big-knuckled hands, a massive chest, a neck almost as thick as his head – and a smile as sweet as any child's.

Joey took an immediate liking to both Sandy and Max and was soon running back and forth from one end of the small house to the other, trying to keep company with both of them, jabbering away, asking them what it was like to be a bodyguard, telling them his charmingly garbled version of George Swarthout's story about the giraffe who could talk and the princess who didn't have a horse.

Christine was not as quick as Joey to place her confidence in her new protectors. She was friendly but cautious, watchful.

She wished she had a weapon of her own. She didn't have her pistol any more. The police had kept it last night until they could verify that it was properly registered. She couldn't very well take a knife from the kitchen drawer and walk around with it in her hand; if either Sandy or Max was a follower of Grace Spivey, the knife might not forestall violence but precipitate it. And if neither of them was a Twilighter, she would only offend and alienate them by such an open display of distrust. Her only weapons were wariness and her wits, which wouldn't be terribly effective if she found herself confronted by a maniac with a .357 Magnum.

However, when trouble paid a visit, shortly after nine o'clock, it did not come from either Sandy or Max. In fact, it was Sandy, keeping watch from a chair by a living room window, who saw that something was wrong and called their attention to it.

When Christine came in from the kitchen to ask him if he wanted more coffee, she found him studying the street outside with visible tension. He had risen from the chair, leaned closer to the window, and was holding the binoculars to his eyes.

'What is it?''she asked. 'Who's out there?'

He watched for a moment longer, then lowered the binoculars. 'Maybe nobody.'

'But you think there is.'

'Go tell Max to keep a sharp eye at the back,' Sandy said, his Adam's apple bobbling. 'Tell him the same van has cruised by the house three times.'

Her heartbeat accelerated as if someone had thrown a switch. 'A white van?'

'No,' he said. 'Midnight blue Dodge with a surfing mural on the side. Probably it's nothing. Just somebody who's not familiar with the neighborhood, trying to find an address. But . . . uh . . . better tell Max, anyway.'

She hurried into the kitchen, which was at the back of the house, and she tried to deliver the news to Max Steck calmly, but her voice had a tremor in it, and she couldn't control her hands, which made nervous, meaningless, butterfly gestures in the air.

Max checked the lock on the kitchen door, even though he had tested it himself when he'd first come on duty. He closed the blinds entirely on one window. He closed them halfway on the other.

Chewbacca had been lying in one corner, dozing. He raised his head and snorted, sensing the new tension in the air.

Joey was sitting at the table by the garden window, busily using his crayons to fill in a picture in a coloring book. Christine moved him away from the window, took him into the corner, near the humming refrigerator, out of the line of fire.

With the short attention span and emotional adaptability of a six-year-old, he had pretty much forgotten about the danger that had forced them to hide out in a stranger's house. Now it all came back to him, and his eyes grew big. 'Is the witch coming?'

'It's probably nothing to worry about, honey.'

She stooped down, pulled up his jeans, and tucked in his shirt, which had come half out of his waistband. His fear made her heart ache, and she kissed him on the cheek.

'Probably just a false alarm,' she said. 'But Charlie's men don't take any chances, you know.'

'They're super,' he said.

'They sure are,' she said.

Now that it looked as if they might actually have to put their lives on the line for her and Joey, she felt guilty about being suspicious of them.

Max shoved the small table away from the window, so he wouldn't have to lean over it to look out.

Chewbacca made an interrogatory whining sound in the back of his throat, and began to pad around in a circle, his claws ticking on the kitchen tile.

Afraid that the dog would get in Max's way at a crucial moment, she called to it, and then so did Joey. The animal couldn't have learned its new name yet, but it responded to tone of voice. It came to Joey and sat beside him.

Max peered through a chink between two of the slats in the blind and said, 'This damn fog sure is hanging on this morning.'

Christine realized that, in the fog and obscuring rain, the garden — with its azaleas, bushy oleander, veronicas, carefully shaped miniature orange trees, lilacs, bougainvillaea-draped arbor, and other shrubbery — would make it easy for someone to creep dangerously close to the house before being spotted.

In spite of his mother's reassurances, Joey looked up at the ceiling, toward the sound of rain on the roof, which was loud in this one-story house, and he said, 'The witch is coming. She's coming.'

32

Dr. Denton Boothe, both a psychologist and psychiatrist, was living proof that the heirs of Freud and Jung didn't have all the answers, either. One wall in Boothe's office was covered with degrees from the country's finest universities, awards from his colleagues in half a dozen professional organizations, and honorary doctorates from institutions of learning in four countries. He had written the most widely adopted and highly praised textbook on general psychology in thirty years, and his position as one of the most knowledgeable experts in the specialty of abnormal psychology was unchallenged. Yet Boothe, for all his knowledge and expertise, wasn't without problems of his own.

He was fat. Not just pleasantly plump. *Fat*. Shockingly, grossly overweight. When Charlie encountered Denton Boothe ('Boo' to friends), after not having seen him for a few weeks, he was always startled by the man's immensity; he never seemed to remember him as being *that* fat. Boothe stood five-eleven, Charlie's height, but he weighed four hundred pounds. His face did a good imitation of the moon. His neck was a post. His fingers were like sausages. Sitting, he overflowed chairs.

Charlie couldn't understand why Boothe, who could uncover and treat the neuroses even of those patients highly resistant to treatment, could not deal with his own compulsive eating. It was a puzzlement.

But his unusual size and the psychological problems underlying it did nothing to change the fact that he was a delightful man, kind and amusing and quick to laugh. Although he was fifteen years older than Charlie and infinitely better educated, they had hit it off on first encounter and had been friends for several years, getting together for dinner once or twice a month, exchanging gifts at Christmas, making an effort to keep in touch that, sometimes, surprised both of them.

Boo welcomed Charlie and Henry into his office, part of a corner suite in a glass high-rise in Costa Mesa, and insisted on showing them his latest antique bank. He collected animated banks with clockwork mechanisms that made a little adventure out of the deposit of each coin. There were at least two dozen of them displayed at various points in the office. This one was an elaborate affair the size of a cigar humidor; standing on the lid were hand-painted metal figurines of two bearded gold prospectors flanking a comically detailed donkey. Boo put a quarter in the hand of one prospector and pushed a button on the side of the bank. The prospector's hand came up, holding the coin out to the second prospector, but the donkey's hinged head lowered, and its jaws clamped shut on the quarter, which the prospector relinquished. The donkey raised its head again, and the quarter dropped down its gullet and into the bank underneath, while the prospectors shook their heads in dismay. The name on the donkey's saddlebags was Uncle Sam.

'It was made in 1903. So far as anyone knows, there are only eight working models in the world,' Boo said proudly. 'It's titled "The Tax Collector," but I call it "There Is No Justice in a Jackass Universe." '

Charlie laughed, but Henry looked baffled.

They adjourned to a corner of the room where large comfortable armchairs were grouped around a glass-topped coffee table. Boo's chair groaned softly as he settled into it.

Being a corner office, the room had two exterior walls that were largely glass. Because this building faced away from the other high-rise structures in Costa Mesa, toward one of the few remaining tracts of agricultural land in this part of the county, there seemed to be nothing outside but a gray void composed of churning clouds, gauzy veils of lingering fog, and rain that streamed down the glass walls in a vertical river. The effect was disorienting, as if Boothe's office didn't exist in this world but in an alternate reality, another dimension.

'You say this is about Grace Spivey?' Boothe asked.

He had a special interest in religious psychoses and had written a book about the psychology of cult leaders. He found Grace Spivey intriguing and intended to include a chapter about her in his next book.

Charlie told Boo about Christine and Joey, about their encounter with Grace at South Coast Plaza and the attempts on their lives.

The psychologist, who didn't believe in being solemn with patients, who used cajolery and humor as part of his therapy, whose face seldom played host to a frown, was now scowling. He said, 'This is bad. Very bad. I've always known Grace is a true believer, not just a phony, mining the religious rackets for a buck. She's always been convinced that the world really was coming to an end. But I never believed she was sunk this deep in psychotic fantasy.' He sighed and looked out at his twelfth-floor view of the storm. 'You know, she talks a lot about her "visions," uses them to whip her followers into a frenzy. I've always thought that she doesn't really have them, that she merely *pretends* to have them because she realizes they're a good tool for making converts and keeping disciples in line. By using the visions, she can have God tell her people to do the things *she* wants them to do, things they might not accept if they didn't think the orders were coming straight down from Heaven.'

'But if she's a true believer,' Henry said, 'how would she justify fakery to herself?'

'Oh, easily, easily,' the psychologist said, looking away from the rain-filled February morning. 'She'd justify it by saying she was only telling her followers things that God would've told them, anyway, if He actually *had* appeared to her in visions. The second possibility, which is more disturbing, is that she actually *is* seeing and hearing God.'

'You don't mean literally seeing Him,' Henry said, surprised.

'No, no,' Boo said, waving one pudgy hand. He was an agnostic, flirting with atheism. He sometimes told Charlie that, considering the miserable state of the world, God must be on extended vacation in Albania, Tahiti,

Cleveland or some other remote corner of the universe, where the news just wasn't getting to Him. He said, 'I mean that she's seeing and hearing God, but, of course, He's merely a figment of her own sick mind. Psychotics, if they're far enough over the line, often have visions, sometimes of a religious nature and sometimes not. But I wouldn't have thought Grace had gone that far round the bend.'

Charlie said, 'She's so far gone that they don't even have Taco Bells where she's at.'

Boo laughed, not as heartily as Charlie would have liked, but he did laugh, which was better than the scowl that made Charlie nervous. Boo had no pretensions about his profession and held nothing sacred; he was as likely to use the term 'fruitcake' as 'mentally disturbed.' He said, 'But if Grace has slipped her moorings altogether, then there's something about this situation that's hard to explain.'

To Henry, Charlie said, 'He loves to explain things. A born pedant. He'll explain beer to you while you're trying to drink it. And don't ask him to explain the meaning of life, or we'll be here until our retirement funds start to pay off.'

Boothe remained uncharacteristically solemn. 'It isn't the meaning of life that puzzles me right now. You say Grace has gone round the bend, and it certainly sounds as if you may be correct. But you see, if she really believes all this Antichrist stuff, and she's willing to kill an innocent child, then she's evidently a paranoid schizophrenic with apocalyptic fantasies and delusions of grandeur. But it's hard to imagine someone in that condition would be able to function as an authority figure or conduct the business of her cult.'

'Maybe someone else is running the cult,' Henry said. 'Maybe she's just a figurehead now. Maybe someone else is using her.'

Boothe shook his head. 'It's damned difficult to use a

paranoid schizophrenic the way you're suggesting. They're too unpredictable. But if she's really turned violent, has begun to *act* on her doomsday prophecies, she doesn't *have* to be crazy. Could be another explanation.'

'Such as?' Charlie asked.

'Such as . . . maybe her followers are disillusioned with her. Maybe the cult is falling apart, and she's resorting to these drastic measures to renew her disciples' excitement and keep them faithful.'

'No,' Charlie said. 'She's nuts.' He told Boo about his macabre meeting with Grace just a short while ago.

Boothe was startled. 'She actually drove nails into her hands?'

'Well, we didn't see her do it,' Charlie admitted. 'Maybe one of her followers wielded the hammer. But she obviously cooperated.'

Boo shifted, and his chair creaked. 'There's another possibility. The spontaneous appearance of crucifixion stigmata on the hands and feet of psychotics with religious persecution complexes is a rare phenomenon but not entirely unheard of.'

Henry Rankin was astonished. 'You mean they were *real*? You mean . . . *God* did that to her?'

'Oh, no, I don't mean to imply this was a genuine holy sign or anything of that sort. God had nothing to do with it.'

'I'm glad to hear you say that,' Charlie told him. 'I was afraid you were suddenly going mystical on me. And if there are two things I'd never expect you to do, one is to go mystical on me, and the other is to become a ballet dancer.'

The worried look on the fat man's face did not soften.

Charlie said, 'Jesus, Boo, I'm already scared, but if the situation worries *you* this much, I'm not half as frightened as I ought to be.'

Boothe said, 'I *am* worried. As for the stigmata phenomenon, there is some evidence that, in a Messianic frenzy, a psychotic may exert a control on his body . . . on tissue structure . . . an almost, well, psychic control that medical science can't explain. Like those Indian holy men who walk on hot coals or lie on nails and *prevent* injury by an act of will. Grace's wounds would be the other side of that coin.'

Henry, who liked everything to be reasonable and orderly and predictable, who expected the universe to be as neat and well pressed as his own wardrobe, was clearly disturbed by talk of psychic abilities. He said, 'They can make themselves bleed just by thinking about it?'

'They probably don't even have to think about it, at least not consciously,' Boo said. 'The stigmata are the result of a strong unconscious desire to be a religious figure or symbol, to be venerated, or to be a part of something bigger than self, something cosmic.' He folded his hands on his ample stomach. 'For instance . . . how much do you know about the supposed miracle at Fatima?'

'Not much,' Charlie said.

'The Virgin Mary appeared to a lot of people there, thousands of people,' Henry said, 'back in the twenties, I think.'

'A stunning and moving divine visitation − or one of the most incredible cases of mass hysteria and self-hypnosis ever recorded,' Boo said, clearly favoring the second explanation. 'Hundreds of people reported seeing the Virgin Mary and described a turbulent sky seething with all the colors of the rainbow. Among those in the huge crowd, two people developed crucifixion stigmata; one man's hands began to bleed, and nail holes appeared in a woman's feet. Several people claimed to have spontaneously acquired tiny punctures in a ring around their heads, as if from a crown of thorns. There's a documented case of an onlooker weeping tears of blood; subsequent medical examination showed no eye damage whatsoever, no possible source of blood. In short, the mind is still largely an uncharted sea. There are mysteries in here' — he tapped his head with one thick finger — 'that we may never understand.'

Charlie shivered. It was creepy to think Grace had descended so far into madness that she could make her body bleed spontaneously for the sole purpose of lending substance to her sick fantasies.

'Of course,' Boo said, 'you're probably right about the hammer and nails. Spontaneous crucifixion stigmata are rare. Grace probably did it to herself — or had one of her people do it.'

The rain streamed down the walls of glass, and a miserably wet black bird swooped close, seeking escape from the cold downpour, then darted away an instant before crashing through the window.

Considering what Boothe had told them about tears of blood and mentally-inflicted stigmata, Charlie said, 'I think I've stumbled across the meaning of life.'

'What's that?' Boo asked.

'We're all just actors in a cosmic horror film in God's private movie theater.'

'Could be,' Boo said. 'If you read your Bible, you'll see that God can think up more horrible punishments than anything Tobe Hooper or Steven Spielberg or Alfred Hitchcock ever dreamed of.'

33

With his binoculars, Sandy Breckenstein had gotten the license plate number the third time the blue Dodge van with the surfing murals had driven by the house. While Christine Scavello had hurried into the kitchen to report the presence of a suspicious vehicle to Max, Sandy had phoned Julie Gethers, the police liaison at Klemet-Harrison, and had asked her to get a make on the Dodge.

While he waited for a response from Julie, he stood tensely by the window, binoculars in hand.

Within five minutes, the van made a fourth pass, heading up the hill this time.

Sandy used the binoculars and saw, indistinctly, two men behind the rain-washed windshield.

They seemed to be studying this house in particular.

Then they were gone. Sandy almost wished they'd parked out front. At least there he could keep an eye on them. He didn't like having them out of sight.

While Sandy stood at the window, chewing on his lip, wishing he had become a certified public accountant like his father, Julie at HQ made contact with the Department of Motor Vehicles and then with the Orange County Sheriff's Department. Thanks to computerization at both agencies, the information was obtained quickly, and she returned Sandy's call in twelve minutes. According to the DMV, the blue van was registered to Emanuel Luis Spado of Anaheim. According to the Sheriff's office, which shared hot sheet data with all other police agencies in the county, Mr. Spado had reported his vehicle stolen as of six o'clock this morning.

As soon as he had that information, Sandy went into

the kitchen to share it with Max, who was equally uneasy about it.

'It's trouble,' Max said bluntly.

Christine Scavello, who had moved her son out of the line of fire, into the corner by the refrigerator, said, 'But it doesn't belong to the church.'

'Yeah, but it could've been someone from the church who stole it,' Sandy said.

'To put distance between the church and any attack they might make on us here,' Max explained.

'Or it could just be coincidence that someone in a stolen van is cruising this street,' the woman said, though she sounded as if she didn't believe it.

'Never met a coincidence I liked,' Max said, keeping a watch on the garden behind the house.

'Me neither,' Sandy said.

'But how did they find us?' Christine demanded.

'Beats me,' Sandy said.

'Damned if I know,' Max said. 'We took every precaution.'

They all knew the most likely explanation: Grace Spivey had an informer planted at Klemet-Harrison. None of them wanted to say it. The possibility was too unnerving.

'What'd you tell them at HQ?' Max asked.

'To send help,' Sandy said.

'You think we should wait for it?'

'No.'

'Me neither. We're sitting ducks here. This place was a good idea only as long as we figured they'd never find it. Now, our best chance is to get out, get moving, before they know we've spotted them. They won't be expecting us to suddenly pull up and light out.'

Sandy agreed. He turned to Christine. 'Get your coats on. You can take only two suitcases, 'cause you'll have to carry them both. Max and I can't be tied down with luggage on the way to the car; we've got to keep our hands free.'

The woman nodded. She looked stricken. The boy was pale and waxy. Even the dog seemed to be worried; it sniffed the air, cocked its head, and made a peculiar whining noise.

Sandy didn't feel so good himself. He knew what had happened to Frank Reuther and Pete Lockburn.

34

Thunder shook the window-walls.

Rain fell harder than ever.

Heat streamed from the ceiling vents, but Charlie couldn't get rid of a chill that made his hands clammy.

Denton Boothe said, 'I've talked with people who knew Grace before this religious fanaticism. Many of them mention how close she and her husband were. Married forty-four years, she idolized the man. Nothing was too good for her Albert. She kept his house exactly as he liked it, cooked only his favorite foods, did everything the way he preferred. The only thing she was never able to give him was the thing he would have liked the most — a son. At his funeral, when she broke down, she kept saying, over and over, "I never gave him a son." It's conceivable that, to Grace, a male child — *any* male child — is a symbol of her failure to give her husband what he most desired. While he was alive, she could make up for that failure by treating him like a king, but once he was gone she had no way to atone for her barrenness, and perhaps she began to hate little boys. Hate them, then fear them, then fantasize that one of them was the Antichrist, here to destroy the world. It's an understandable if regrettable progression for psychosis.'

Henry said, 'If I recall, they did adopt a daughter —'

'The one who had Grace committed for psychiatric evaluation when this Twilight business first came up,' Charlie said.

'Yes,' Boo said. 'Grace sold her house, liquidated investments, and put the money into this church. It was irrational, and the daughter was correct in seeking to preserve her mother's estate. But Grace came through the psychiatric evaluation with flying colors —'

'How?' Charlie wondered.

'Well, she was cunning. She knew what the psychiatric examiner was looking for, and she had sufficient control of herself to hide all those attitudes and tendencies that would have set off the alarm bells.'

'But she *was* liquidating property to form a church,' Henry said. 'Surely the doctor could see that wasn't the act of a rational person.'

'On the contrary. Provided she understood the risks of her actions and had a firm grip on all the potential consequences, or at least as long as she convinced the examining doctor that she had a firm grip, the mere fact that she wanted to give everything to God's work would not be sufficient to declare her mentally incompetent. We have religious liberty in this country, you know. It's an important constitutional freedom, and the law steps respectfully around it in cases like this.'

'You've got to help me, Boo,' Charlie said. 'Tell me how this woman thinks. Give me a handle on her. Show me how to turn her off, how to make her change her mind about Joey Scavello.'

'This kind of psychopathic personality is not frightened, shaky, about to collapse. Just the opposite. With a cause

206

she believes in, supported by delusions of grandeur that are intensely religious in nature . . . well, despite appearances to the contrary, she's a rock, utterly resistant to pressure and stress. She lives in a reality that she made for herself, and she's made it so well that there's probably no way you can shake it or pull it apart or cause her to lose faith in it.'

'Are you saying I can't change her mind?'

'I would think it's impossible.'

'Then how do I make her back off? She's a flake; there must be an easy way to handle her.'

'You're not listening — or you don't want to hear what I'm telling you. You mustn't make the mistake of assuming that, just because she's psychotic, she's vulnerable. This sort of mental problem carries with it a peculiar strength, an ability to withstand rejection, failure, and all forms of stress. You see, Grace evolved her psychotic fantasy for the sole purpose of protecting herself from those things. It's a way of armoring herself against the cruelties and disappointments of life, and it's damned good armor.'

Charlie said, 'Are you telling me she has no weaknesses?'

'Everyone has weaknesses. I'm just telling you that, in Grace's case, finding them won't be easy. I'll have to look over my file on her, think about it a while . . . Give me a day at least.'

'Think fast,' Charlie said, getting to his feet, 'I've got a few hundred homicidal religious fanatics breathing down my neck.'

At the door, as they were leaving his office, Boo said, 'Charlie, I know you put quite a lot of faith in me sometimes —'

'Yeah, I've got a Messiah complex about you.'

Ignoring the joke, still unusually somber, Boo said, 'I just don't want you to pin a lot of hope on what I might be able to come up with. In fact, I might not be able to come up with anything. Right now, I'd say there's only one answer, one way to deal with Grace if you want to save your clients.'

'What's that?'

'Kill her,' Boo said without a smile.

'You certainly aren't one of those bleeding-heart psychiatrists who always want to give mass murderers a second chance at life. Where'd you get your degree — Attila the Hun School of Head-Shrinking?'

He very much wanted Boo to joke with him. The psychiatrist's grim reaction to the story of his meeting with Grace this morning was so out of character that it unsettled Charlie. He needed a laugh. He needed to be told there was a silver lining somewhere. Boo's gray-faced sobriety was almost scarier than Grace Spivey's flamboyant ranting.

But Boo said, 'Charlie, you know me. You know I can find something humorous in *anything*. I chuckle at dementia praecox in certain situations. I am amused by certain aspects of death, taxes, leprosy, American politics, and cancer. I've even been known to smile at reruns of "Lavern & Shirley" when my grandchildren have insisted I watch with them. But I see nothing to laugh at here. You are a dear friend, Charlie. I'm frightened for you.'

'You don't really mean I should kill her.'

'I know you couldn't commit cold-blooded murder,' Boothe said. 'But I'm afraid Grace's death is the only thing that might redirect these cultists' attention away from your clients.'

'So it'd be helpful if I *was* capable of cold-blooded murder.'

'Yes.'

'Helpful if I had just a *little* killer in me.'

'Yes.'

'Jesus.'

'A difficult state of affairs,' Boo agreed.

35

The house had no garage, just a carport, which meant they had to expose themselves while getting in the green Chevy. Sandy didn't like it, but there was no other choice except to stay in the house until reinforcements arrived, and his gut instinct told him that would be a mistake.

He left the house first, by the side door, stepping directly into the open carport. The roof kept the rain from falling straight down on him, and latticework covered with climbing honeysuckle kept it from slanting in through the long side of the stall, but the chilly wind drove sheets of rain through the open end of the structure and threw it in his face.

Before giving the all-clear signal for Christine and Joey to come outside, he went to the end of the carport, into the driveway, because he wanted to make sure no one was lurking in front of the house. He wore a coat but went without an umbrella in order to keep his hands free, and the rain beat on his bare head, stung his face, trickled under his collar. No one was at the front door or along the walk or crouching by the shrubbery, so he called back to the woman to get into the car with the boy.

He took a few more steps along the driveway in order to have a look up and down the street, and he saw the blue Dodge van. It was parked a block and a half up the hill, on the other side of the street, facing down toward the house. Even as he spotted it, the van swung away from the curb and headed toward him.

Sandy glanced back and saw that Christine, lugging two suitcases and accompanied by the dog, had just reached the car, where the boy had opened the rear door for her. 'Wait!' he shouted to them.

He looked back at the street. The van was coming fast now. Too damned fast.

'Into the house!' Sandy shouted.

The woman must have been wound up tight because she didn't even hesitate, didn't ask what was wrong, just dropped the suitcases, grabbed her son, and headed back the way she'd come, toward the open door in which Max now stood.

The rest of it happened in a few seconds, but terror distorted Sandy Breckenstein's time sense, so that it seemed as though minutes passed in an unbearably extended panic.

First, the van surprised him by angling all the way across the street and entering the driveway of the house that was two doors uphill from this one. But it wasn't stopping there. It swung out of that driveway almost as soon as it entered, not back into the street but onto the grass. It roared across the lawn in front of that house, coming this way, tearing up grass, casting mud and chunks of sod in its wake, squashing flowers, knocking over a birdbath, engine screaming, tires spinning for a moment but then biting in again, surging forward with maniacal intent.

What the hell—

The passenger door of the van flew open, and the man on that side threw himself out, struck the lawn, and rolled.

Sandy thought of rats deserting a doomed ship.

The van plowed through the picket fence between the lawn and the next property.

Behind Sandy, Max yelled, 'What's happening?'

Now only one house separated the Dodge from this property.

Chewbacca was barking furiously.

The driver gave the van more gas. It was coming fast, like an express train, like a rocket.

The intent was clear. Crazy as it seemed, the van was going to ram the house in which they'd been hiding.

'Get out!' Sandy shouted back toward Christine and Joey and Max. 'Out of the house, away from here, *fast*!'

Max plunged out of the house, and the three of them — and the dog — fled toward the back yard, which was the only way they could go.

Uphill, the Dodge swerved to avoid a jacaranda in the neighboring yard and struck the fence between this property and that one.

Sandy had already turned away from the van. He was already running back along the side of the house.

Behind him, the picket fence gave way with a sound like cracking bones.

Sandy raced through the carport, past the car, leaping over the abandoned suitcases, yelling at the others to hurry, for God's sake *hurry*, screaming at them to get out of the way, urging them into the rear lawn, and then toward the back fence, beyond which lay a narrow alley.

But they didn't get all the way to the rear of the small lot before the van rammed into the house with a tremendous crash. A split second later, an ear-pulverizing explosion shook the rain-choked day, and for a moment it sounded as if the sky itself was falling, and the earth rose violently, fell.

The van had been packed full of explosives!

The blast picked Sandy up and pitched him, and he felt a wave of hot air smash over him, and then he was tumbling across the lawn, through a row of azaleas, into the board fence by the alleyway, jarring his right shoulder, and he saw fire where the house had been, fire and smoke, shooting up in a dazzling column, and there was flying debris, a lot of it — chunks of masonry, splintered boards, roofing shingles, lath and plaster, glass, the padded back of an armchair that was leaking stuffing, the cracked lid of a toilet seat, sofa cushions, a piece of carpeting — and he tucked his head down and prayed that he wouldn't be struck by anything heavy or sharp.

As debris pummeled him, he wondered if the driver of the van had leaped out as the man on the passenger's side had done. Had he jumped free at the last moment — or had he been so committed to murdering Joey Scavello that he had remained behind the wheel, piloting the Dodge all the way into the house? Maybe he was now sitting in the rubble, flesh stripped from his bones, his skeletal hands still clutching the fire-blackened steering wheel.

The explosion was like a giant hand that slammed Christine in the back. Briefly deafened by the blast, she was thrown away from Joey, knocked down. In a temporary but eerie silence, she rolled through a muddy flower bed, crushing dense clusters of bright red and purple impatiens, aware of billowing waves of superheated air that seemed to vaporize the falling rain for a moment. She cracked a knee painfully against the low brick edging that ringed the planting area, tasted dirt, and came to rest against the side of the arbor, which was thickly entwined with bougainvillaea. Still in silence, cedar shingles and shattered pieces of stucco and unidentifiable rubble fell on her and on the garden around her. Then her hearing began to return when the toaster, which she had so recently used when making breakfast, clanged onto the grass and noisily hopped along for some distance, as if it were a living thing, trailing its cord like a tail. An enormously heavy object, perhaps a roof beam or a large chunk of masonry, slammed down into the roof of the ten-foot-long, tunnel-like arbor, collapsing it. The wall against which she was leaning sagged inward, and torn bougainvillaea runners drooped over her, and she realized how close she had come to being killed.

'Joey!' she shouted.

He didn't answer. She pushed away from the ruined arbor, onto her hands and knees, then staggered to her feet, swaying.

'Joey!'

No answer.

Foul-smelling smoke poured across the lawn from the demolished house; combined with the lingering fog and the wind-whipped rain, it reduced visibility to a few feet. She couldn't see her boy, and she didn't know where to look, so she struck off blindly to her left, finding it difficult to breathe because of the acrid smoke and because of her own panic, which was like a vise squeezing her chest. She came upon the scorched and mangled door of the refrigerator, forced her way between two miniature orange trees, one of which was draped in a tangled bed sheet, and walked across the rear door of the house, which was lying flat on the grass, thirty feet from the frame in which it had once stood. She saw Max Steck. He was alive, trying to extricate himself from the thorny trailers of several rose bushes, among which he had been tossed. She moved past him, still calling Joey, still getting no answer, and then, among all the other rubble, her gaze settled on a strangely unnerving object. It was Joey's E.T. doll, one of his favorite toys, which had been left behind in the house. The blast had torn off both of the doll's legs and one of its arms. Its face was scorched. Its round little belly was ripped open, and stuffing bulged out of the rent. It was only a doll, but somehow it seemed like a harbinger of death, a warning of what she would find when she finally located Joey. She began to run, keeping the fence in sight, circling the property, frantically searching for her son, tripping, falling, pushing up again, praying that she would find him whole, alive.

'Joey!'

Nothing.'*Joey!*'
Nothing.
The smoke stung her eyes. It was hard to see.
'*Joooeeeeey!*'
Then she spotted him. He was lying at the back of the property, near the gate to the alley, face down on the rain-soaked grass, motionless. Chewbacca was standing over him, nuzzling his neck, trying to get a response out of him, but the boy wouldn't respond, couldn't, just lay there, still, so very still.

36

She knelt and nudged the dog out of the way.

She put her hands on Joey's shoulders.

For a moment she was afraid to turn him over, afraid that his face had been smashed in or his eyes punctured by flying debris.

Sobbing, coughing as another tide of smoke lapped out from the burning ruins behind them, she finally rolled him gently onto his back. His face was unmarked. There were smears of dirt but no cuts or visible fractures, and the rain was swiftly washing even the dirt away. She could see no blood. Thank God.

His eyelids fluttered. Opened. His eyes were unfocused.

He had merely been knocked unconscious.

The relief that surged through her was so powerful that it made her feel buoyant, as if she were floating inches off the ground.

She held him, and when his eyes finally cleared, she checked him for concussion by holding up three fingers in front of his face and asking him how many he saw.

He blinked and looked confused.

'How many fingers, honey?' she repeated.

He wheezed a few times, getting smoke out of his lungs, then said, 'Three. Three fingers.'

'Now how many?'

'Two.'

Having freed himself from the thorn-studded rose bushes, Max Steck joined them.

To Joey, Christine said, 'Do you know who I am?'

He seemed puzzled, not because he had trouble finding the answer but because he couldn't figure out why she was asking the question. 'You're Mom,' he said.

'And what's your name?'

'Don't you know my name?'

'I want to see if you know it,' she said.

'Well, sure, I know it,' he said. 'Joey. Joseph. Joseph Anthony Scavello.'

No concussion.

Relieved, she hugged him tight.

Sandy Breckenstein crouched beside them, coughing smoke out of his lungs. His forehead was cut above his left eye, and blood sheathed one side of his face, but he wasn't seriously hurt.

'Can the boy be moved?' Breckenstein asked.

'He's fine,' Max Steck said.

'Then let's get out of here. They may come nosing around to see if the explosives took care of us.'

Max unlatched the gate, pushed it open.

Chewbacca dashed through, into the alleyway, and the rest of them followed.

It was a narrow alley, with the back yards of houses on both sides of it, as well as a garage here and there, and lots of garbage cans awaiting pickup. There were no gutters or drains, and water streamed down the width of the one-lane passage, rushing toward storm culverts at the bottom of the hill.

As the four of them sloshed into the middle of the shallow stream, trying to decide which way to go, another gate opened two doors up the hill, and a tall man in a hooded yellow rain slicker came out of another yard. Even in the rain and the gloom, Christine could see that he was carrying a gun.

Max brought up his revolver, gripping it in both hands, and shouted, 'Drop it!'

But the stranger opened fire.

Max fired, too, three shots in quick succession, and he was a much better marksman than his enemy. The would-be assassin was hit in the leg and fell even as the sound of the shots roared up the hillside. He rolled, splashing through the rivulet, his yellow rain slicker flapping like the wings of an enormous and brightly colored bird. He collided with two garbage cans, knocked them over, half-disappeared under a spreading mound of refuse. The gun flew out of his hand, spun along the macadam.

They didn't even wait to see if the man was dead or alive. There might be other Twilighters nearby.

'Let's get out of this neighborhood,' Max said urgently. 'Get to a phone, call this in, get a backup team out here.'

With Sandy and Chewbacca leading the way and Max bringing up the rear, they ran down the hill, slipping and sliding a bit on the slick macadam but avoiding a fall.

Christine looked back a couple of times.

The wounded man had not gotten up from the garbage in which he'd landed.

No one was pursuing them.

Yet.

They turned right at the first corner, raced along a flat street that ran across the side of the hill, past a startled mailman who jumped out of their way. A ferocious wind sprang up, as if giving chase. As they fled, the wind-shaken trees tossed and shuddered around them, and the brittle branches of palms clattered noisily, and an empty soda can tumbled along at their heels.

After two blocks, they left the flat street and turned into another steeply sloped avenue. Overhanging trees formed a tunnel across the roadway and added to the gloom of the sunless day, so that it almost seemed like evening rather than morning.

Breath burned in Christine's throat. Her eyes still stung from the smoke they had left behind them, and her heart was beating so hard and fast that her chest ached. She didn't know how much farther she could go at this pace. Not far.

She was surprised that Joey's little legs could pump this fast. The rest of them weren't keeping back much on account of the boy; he could hold his own.

A car was coming up the hill, headlights stabbing out before it, cutting through the thinning mist and the deep shadows cast by the huge trees.

Christine was suddenly sure that Grace Spivey's people were behind those lights. She grabbed Joey by one shoulder, turned him in another direction.

Sandy shouted at her to stay with him, and Max shouted something she couldn't make out, and Chewbacca began barking loudly, but she ignored them.

Didn't they see death coming?

She heard the car's engine growing louder behind her. It sounded feral, hungry.

Joey stumbled on a canted section of sidewalk, went down, skidding into someone's front yard.

She threw herself on him to protect him from the gunfire she expected to hear at any second.

The car drew even with them. The sound of its laboring engine filled the world.

She cried out, '*No!*'

But the car went by without stopping. It hadn't been Grace Spivey's people, after all.

Christine felt foolish as Max Steck helped her to her feet. The entire world wasn't after them. It only seemed that way.

37

In downtown Laguna Beach, in an Arco Service Station they took shelter from the storm and from Grace Spivey's disciples. After Sandy Breckenstein showed the manager his PI license and explained enough of the situation to gain cooperation, they were allowed to bring Chewbacca into the service bay, as long as they tied him securely to a tool rack. Sandy didn't want to let the dog outside, not only because it would get wet — it was already soaked and shivering — but because there was a possibility, however insignificant, that Spivey's people might be cruising around town, looking for them, and might spot the dog.

While Max stayed with Christine and Joey at the rear of the service bays, away from doors and windows, Sandy used the pay phone in the small, glassed-in sales room. He called Klemet-Harrison. Charlie wasn't in the office. Sandy spoke with Sherry Ordway, the receptionist, and explained enough of their situation to make her understand the seriousness of it, but he wouldn't tell her where they were or at what number they could be reached. He doubted that Sherry was the informant who was reporting to the Church of the Twilight, but he could not be absolutely sure where her loyalties might lie.

He said, 'Find Charlie. I'll only talk to him.'

'But how's he going to know where to reach you?' Sherry asked.

'I'll call back in fifteen minutes.'

'If I can't get hold of him in fifteen minutes –'

'I'll call back every fifteen minutes until you do,' he said, and hung up.

He returned to the humid service bays, which smelled of oil and grease and gasoline. A three-year-old Toyota was up on one of the two hydraulic racks, and a fox-faced man in gray coveralls was replacing the muffler. Sandy told Max and Christine that it was going to take a while to reach Charlie Harrison.

The pump jockey, a young blond guy, was mounting new tires on a set of custom chrome wheels, and Joey was watching, fascinated by the specialized power tools, obviously bubbling over with questions but trying not to bother the man with more than a few of them. The poor kid was soaked to the skin, muddy, bedraggled, yet he wasn't complaining or whining as most children would have been doing in these circumstances. He was a damn good kid, and he seemed able to find a positive side to any situation; in this case, getting to watch tires being mounted appeared to be sufficient compensation for the ordeal he had just been through.

Seven months ago, Sandy's wife, Maryann, had given birth to a boy. Troy Franklin Breckenstein. Sandy hoped his son would turn out to be as well behaved as Joey Scavello. Then he thought: If I'm going to wish for anything, maybe I'd better wish that I live long enough to see Troy grow up, whether or not he's well behaved.

When fifteen minutes had passed, Sandy returned to the sales room out front, went to the phone by the candy machine, and called Sherry Ordway at HQ. She had beeped Charlie on his telepage, but he hadn't yet called in.

The rain bounced off the macadam in front of the station, and the street began to disappear under a deep puddle, and the pump jockey finished another tire, and Sandy was jumpier than ever when he called the office a third time.

Sherry said, 'Charlie's at the police lab with Henry Rankin, trying to find out if forensics discovered anything about those bodies at the Scavello house that would help him tie them to Grace Spivey.'

'That sounds like a long shot.'

'I guess it's the best he has,' Sherry said.

That was more bad news.

She gave him the number where Charlie could be reached, and he jotted it down in a small notebook he carried.

He dialed the forensics lab, asked for Charlie, and had him on the line right away. He told him about the attack on Miriam Rankin's house, laying it out in more detail than he'd given Sherry Ordway.

Charlie had heard the worst of it from Sherry, but he still sounded shocked and dismayed by how quickly Spivey had located the Scavellos.

'They're both all right?' he asked.

'Dirty and wet, but unhurt,' Sandy assured him.

'So we've got a turncoat among us,' Charlie said.

'Looks that way. Unless you were followed when you left their house last night.'

'I'm sure we weren't. But maybe the car we used had a bug on it.'

'Could be.'

'But probably not,' Charlie said. 'I hate to admit it, but we've probably got a mole in our operation. Where are you calling from?'

Instead of telling him, Sandy said, 'Is Henry Rankin with you?'

'Yeah. Right here. Why? You want to talk to him?'

'No. I just want to know if he can hear this.'

'Not your side of it.'

'If I tell you where we are, it's got to stay with you. Only you,' Sandy said. He quickly added: 'It's not that I have reason to suspect Henry of being Spivey's plant. I don't. I trust Henry more than most. The point is, I don't really trust *anyone* but you. You, me — and Max, because if it was Max, he'd already have snuffed the kid.'

'If we do have a bad apple,' Charlie said, 'it's most likely a secretary or bookkeeper or something like that.'

'I know,' Sandy said. 'But I've got a responsibility to the woman and the kid. And my own life's on the line here, too, as long as I'm with them.'

'Tell me where you are,' Charlie said. 'I'll keep it to myself, and I'll come alone.'

Sandy told him.

'This weather . . . better give me forty-five minutes,' Charlie said.

'We're not going anywhere,' Sandy said.

He hung up and went out to the garage to be with the others.

When the rains had first come, yesterday evening, there had been a brief period of lightning, but none in the past twelve hours. Most California storms were much quieter than those in other parts of the country. Lightning was not a common accompaniment of the rains here, and wildly violent electrical storms were rare. But now, with its hills grown dangerously soggy and with the threat of mudslides at hand, with its streets awash, with its coastline hammered by wind-whipped waves almost twice as high as usual, Laguna Beach was suddenly assaulted by fierce bolts of lightning as well. With a crash of accompanying thunder that shook the walls of the building, a cataclysmic bolt stabbed to earth somewhere nearby, and the gray day was

221

briefly, flickeringly bright. With strobelike effect, the light pulsed through the open doors of the garage and through the dirty high-set windows, bringing a moment of frenzied life to the shadows, which twisted and danced for a second or two. Another bolt quickly followed with an even harder clap of thunder, and loose windows rattled in their frames, and then a third bolt smashed down, and the wet macadam in front of the station glistened and flashed with scintillant reflections of nature's bright anger.

Joey had drifted away from his mother, toward the open doors of the garage bays. He winced at the crashes of thunder that followed each lightning strike, but he seemed pretty much unafraid. When the skies calmed for a moment, he looked back at his mother and said, 'Wow! God's fireworks, huh, Mom? Isn't that what you said it is?'

'God's fireworks,' Christine agreed. 'Better get away from there.'

Another bolt arced across the sky, and the day outside seemed to leap as the murderous current jolted through it. This one was worse than all the others, and the blast from it not only rattled windows and made the walls tremble, but seemed to shake the ground as well, and Sandy even felt it in his *teeth*.

'Wow!' the boy said.

'Honey, get away from that open door,' Christine said.

The boy didn't move, and in the next instant he was silhouetted by a chain of lightning strikes far brighter and more violent than anything yet, so dazzling and shocking in their power that the pump jockey was startled enough to drop a lug wrench. The dog whimpered and tried to hide under the tool rack, and Christine scurried to Joey, grabbed him, and brought him back from the open doorway.

'Aw, Mom, it's pretty,' he said.

Sandy tried to imagine what it would be like to be young again, so young that you hadn't yet realized how much there was to fear in this world, so young that the word 'cancer' had no definition, so young that you hadn't any real grip on the meaning of death or the inevitability of taxes or the horror of nuclear war or the treacherous nature of the clot-prone human circulatory system. What would it be like to be that young again, so young that you could watch storm lightning with delight, unaware that it might find its way to you and fry your brains in one ten-thousandth of a second? Sandy stared at Joey Scavello and frowned. He felt old, only thirty-two but terribly old.

What bothered him was that he couldn't remember *ever* having been that young and free of fear, though surely he had been just as innocent of death when he was six. They said that animals lived their lives with no sense of mortality, and it seemed terribly unjust that men didn't have the same luxury. Human beings couldn't escape the knowledge of their death; consciously or subconsciously, it was with them every hour of every day. If Sandy could have had a word with this religious fanatic, this Grace Spivey, he would have wanted to know how she could have such faith in — and devotion for — a God who created human beings only to let them die by one horrible means or another.

He sighed. He was getting morbid, and that wasn't like him. At this rate he would need more than his usual bottle of beer before bed tonight — like a *dozen* bottles. Still . . . he would like to ask Grace Spivey that question.

38

Shortly before noon, Charlie arrived in Laguna Beach, where he found Sandy, Max, Christine, Joey and the dog waiting for him in the service station.

Joey ran to him, met him just inside the garage door, shouting, 'Hey, Charlie, you shoulda seen the house go boom, just like in a war movie or somethin'!'

Charlie scooped him up and held him. 'I expected you to be mad at us for slipping up. I thought you'd insist on hiring Magnum again.'

'Heck, no,' the boy said. 'Your guys were great. Anyway, how could you've known it was gonna turn into a war movie?'

How indeed?

Charlie carried Joey to the rear of the garage, where the others stood in the shadows between shelves of spare parts and stacks of tires.

Sandy had told him that the woman and the boy were all right, and of course he believed Sandy, but his stomach finally unknotted only now that he saw them with his own eyes. The wave of relief that washed through him was a physical and not just emotional force, and he was reminded — though he didn't *need* reminding — of just how important these two people had become to him in such a short period of time.

They were a miserable-looking group, pretty much dried out by now, but rumpled and mud-streaked, hair lank and matted. Max and Sandy looked rough, angry, and dangerous, the kind of men who cleared out a bar just by walking into it.

It was a tribute to Christine's beauty, and an indication of its depth, that she looked almost as good now as when she was scrubbed and fresh and neatly groomed. Charlie remembered how it had felt to hold her, last night in the kitchen of Miriam Rankin's little house, just before he'd gone home, and he wanted to hold her again, felt a warm melting *need* to hold her, but in front of his men he could do nothing but put Joey down, take her hand in both of his, and say, 'Thank God you're all right.'

Her lower lip quivered. For a moment she looked as if she would lean against him and cry. But she kept control of herself and said, 'I keep telling myself it's just a nightmare . . . but I can't wake up.'

Max said, 'We ought to get them out of here *now*, out of Laguna.'

'I agree,' Charlie said. 'I'll take them right now, in my car. After we've left, you two call the office, tell Sherry where you are, and have a car sent out. Go back up the hill to Miriam's house — '

'There's not anything left of it,' Sandy said.

'That was one hell of a blast,' Max confirmed. 'The van must've been packed wall to wall with explosives.'

'There might not be anything left of the house,' Charlie said, 'but the cops and fire department are still up there. Sherry's been checking into it with the Laguna Beach police, and I talked with her on the phone, coming down here. Report to the cops, help them any way you can, and find out what they've come up with.'

'Did they find the guy in the alley, the one I shot?' Max asked.

'Nope,' Charlie said. 'He got away.'

'He'd have to have crawled. I shot him in the leg.'

'Then he crawled,' Charlie said. 'Or there was a third man around who helped him escape.'

'Third?' Sandy said.

'Yeah,' Charlie said. 'Sherry says the second man stayed with the van all the way into the house.'

'Jesus.'

'They *are* kamikazes,' Christine said shakily.

'There mustn't have been anything left of him but a lot of little pieces,' Max said and would have said more, but Charlie stopped him by nodding toward the boy, who was listening, mouth agape.

They were silent, contemplating the van driver's violent

225

demise. The rain on the roof was like the solemn drums in a funeral cortege.

Then the mechanic switched on a power wrench, and all of them jumped at the sudden, clangorous noise.

When the mechanic switched the wrench off, Charlie looked at Christine and said, 'Okay, let's get out of here.'

Suspiciously studying everything that moved in the rain-battered day, Max and Sandy accompanied them to the gray Mercedes in front of the service station. Christine sat up front with Charlie, and Joey got in back with Chewbacca.

Sitting behind the steering wheel, speaking to Sandy and Max through the open window, Charlie said, 'You did a damned fine job.'

'Almost lost them,' Sandy said, turning aside the praise.

'Point is — you didn't,' Charlie said. 'And you're safe, too.'

If another of his men had died so soon after the deaths of Pete and Frank, he wasn't sure how he could have handled it. From here on, only he would know where Christine and Joey were. His men would be working on the case, trying to link the Church of the Twilight to these murders and attempted murders, but only he would know the whereabouts of their clients until Grace Spivey was somehow stopped. That way, the old woman's spies wouldn't be able to find Christine and Joey, and Charlie wouldn't have to worry about losing another man. His own life was the only one he would be risking.

He put up his window, locked all the doors with the master switch, and drove away from the service station.

Laguna was actually a lovely, warm, clean, vital beach town, but today it seemed drab, cloaked in rain and gray mist and mud. It made Charlie think of graveyards, and it seemed to close in around them like the descending lid of a coffin. He breathed a bit easier when they were out of town, heading north on the Pacific Coast Highway.

Christine turned and looked at Joey, who was sitting quietly in the back of the car. Brandy . . . no, *Chewbacca* was lying on the seat, his big furry head in the boy's lap. Joey was listlessly petting the dog and staring out the window at the ocean, which was choppy and wind-tossed in front of a dense wall of ash-gray fog moving shorewards from half a mile out. His face was almost expressionless, almost blank, but not quite. There was a subtle expression, something she had never seen on his face before, and she couldn't read it. What was he thinking? Feeling? She had already asked him twice if he was all right, and he had said he was. She didn't want to nag him, but she was worried.

She wasn't merely concerned about his physical safety, although that fear gnawed at her. She was also worried about his mental condition. If he did survive Grace Spivey's demented crusade against him, what emotional scars would he carry with him for the rest of his life? It was impossible that he would come through these experiences unmarked. There would have to be psychological consequences.

Now he continued to stroke the dog's head but in a hypnotic fashion, as if not fully aware that the animal was there with him, and he stared at the ocean beyond the window.

Charlie said, 'The police want me to bring you in for more questioning.'

'The hell with them,' Christine said.

'They're more inclined to help now—'

'It took all these deaths to get their attention.'

'Don't write them off. Sure, we'll do a better job of protecting you than they can, and we might turn up something that'll help them nail Grace Spivey for all this. But now that they've got a homicide investigation under way, they'll do most of the work leading up to the indictment and convictions. They'll be the ones to stop her.'

'I don't trust the cops,' she said flatly. 'Spivey probably has people planted there.'

'She can't have infiltrated every police force in the country. She doesn't have that many followers.'

'Not every police force,' Christine said. 'Just those in the towns where she carries on her fund raising and seeks out her converts.'

'The Laguna Beach police want to talk to you, too, of course, about what happened this morning.'

'To hell with them, too. Even if none of them belongs to the Church of the Twilight, Spivey might be expecting me to show up at police headquarters; she might have people watching, waiting to cut us down the minute we step out of the car.' She had a sudden terrible thought and said: 'You're not taking us to any police station, are you?'

'No,' he said. 'I only said they want to talk to you. I didn't say I thought it was a good idea.'

She sagged back against the seat. '*Are* there any good ideas?'

'Got to keep your chin up.'

'I mean, what're we going to do now? We have no clothes, nothing but what we've got on our backs. My purse and credit cards. That's not much. We've got nowhere to stay. We don't dare go to our friends or anywhere else we're known. They've got us on the run like a couple of wild animals.'

'It's not quite that bad,' he said. 'Hunted animals don't have the luxury of fleeing in a Mercedes Benz.'

She appreciated his attempt to make her smile, but she couldn't find the will to do so.

The *thump-thump-thump* of the windshield wipers sounded like a strange, inhuman heartbeat.

Charlie said, 'We'll go into L.A., I think. The Church

of the Twilight does some work in the city, but most of its activities are centered in Orange and San Diego Counties. There're fewer of Grace's people floating around in L.A., so there'll be less chance of anyone accidentally spotting us. In fact, almost no chance at all.'

'They're everywhere,' she said.

'Be optimistic,' he said. 'Remember little ears.'

She glanced back at Joey, a pang of guilt cutting through her at the realization that she might be frightening him. But he seemed not to have been paying attention to the conversation in the front seat. He still stared out the window, not at the ocean any longer but at the array of shops along the highway in Corona Del Mar.

'In L.A., we'll buy suitcases, clothes, toiletries, whatever you need,' Charlie said.

'Then?'

'We'll have dinner.'

'Then?'

'Find a hotel.'

'What if one of her people works at the hotel?'

'What if one of her people is mayor of Peking?' Charlie said. 'We'd better not go to China, either.'

She found a weak smile for him, after all. It wasn't much, but it was all she had in her, and she was surprised she could respond even that well.

'I'm sorry,' she said.

'For what? Being human? Human and afraid?'

'I don't want to get hysterical.'

'Then don't.'

'I won't.'

'Good. Because there *are* favorable developments.'

'Such as?'

'One of the three dead men from last night — the red-head you shot — has been identified. His name's Pat O'Hara. They were able to get positive ID on him because he's a professional burglar with three arrests and one conviction on his record.'

'Burglar?' she said, baffled by this unexpected introduction of a more ordinary criminal element.

'The cops have done better than come up with a name for him. They can also tie him to Grace.'

She sat up straight, startled. 'How?'

'His family and friends say he joined the Church of the Twilight eight months ago.'

'Then there it is!' she said, excited. 'There's what they need to go after Grace Spivey.'

'Well, they've gone back to the church to talk to her again, of course.'

'That's all? Just talk to her?'

'At this point, they don't have any proof —'

'O'Hara was one of hers!'

'But there's no proof he was acting on her say-so.'

'They all do what she tells them, exactly what she tells them.'

'But Grace claims her church believes in free will, that none of her people is any more *controlled* than Catholics or Presbyterians, no more brainwashed than any Jew in any synagogue.'

'Bullshit,' she said softly but with feeling.

'True,' he said. 'But it's damned hard to prove it, especially since we can't put our hands on any ex-members of the church who might tell us what it's like in there.'

Some of her excitement drained away. 'Then what good does it do us to have O'Hara identified as a Twilighter?'

'Well, it gives some substance to your claims that Grace is harassing you. The cops take your story a whole lot more seriously now than they first did, and that can't hurt.'

'We need more than that.'

'There's a little something else.'

'What?'

'O'Hara — or maybe it was the other guy who came with him — left something outside your house. An airline flight bag. There were burglary tools in it, but there were others things, too. A large plastic jar full of a colorless liquid that turned out to be ordinary water. They don't know why it was there, what purpose it was meant to serve. More of interest was a small brass cross — and a copy of the Bible.'

'Doesn't that prove they were there on some crackpot religious mission?'

'Doesn't prove it, no, but it's interesting, anyway. It's one more knot in the hangman's noose, one more little thing that helps build a case against Grace Spivey.'

'At this rate we'll have her in court by the turn of the century,' Christine said sourly.

They were traveling MacArthur Boulevard now, climbing and descending a series of hills that took them past Fashion Island, past hundreds of million-dollar homes, a marshy area of back-water from Newport Bay, and fields of tall grass that bent with the driving rain and then stood straight up and quivered as the erratic storm wind abruptly changed directions. In spite of the fact that it was midday, most of the cars in the oncoming lane had their headlights on.

Christine said, 'The police know what Grace Spivey teaches — about the coming of Twilight, doomsday, the Antichrist?'

'Yes. They know all of it,' Charlie said.

'They know she thinks the Antichrist is already among us?'

'Yes.'

'And they know that she's spent the past few years searching for him?'

'Yes.'

'And that she intends to kill him when she finds him?'

231

'She's never said as much in a speech or in any of the religious literature she's had published.'

'But that *is* what she intends. We know it.'

'What we know and what we can prove are two different things.'

'The police should be able to see that this is why she's fixated on Joey and —'

'Last night, when the police questioned her, she denied knowing you and Joey, denied the scene at South Coast Plaza. She says she doesn't understand what you have against her, why you're trying to smear her. She said she hadn't found the Antichrist yet and didn't even think she was close. They asked her what she would do if she ever found him, and she said she'd direct prayer against him. They asked if she would try to kill him, and she pretended to be outraged by the very idea. She said she was a woman of God, not a criminal. She said prayer would be enough. She said she'd chain the devil in prayer, bind him up with prayers, drive him back to Hell with nothing but prayer.'

'And of course they believed her.'

'No. I talked to a detective this morning, read the report of their session with her. They think she's unbalanced, probably dangerous, and ought to be considered the primary suspect in the attempts on your lives.'

She was surprised.

He said, 'You see? You've got to be more positive. Things *are* happening. Not as fast as you'd like, no, because there are procedures the police must follow, rules of evidence, constitutional rights that must be respected —'

'Sometimes it seems like the only people who have constitutional rights are the criminals among us.'

'I know. But we've got to work within the system as best we can.'

They passed the Orange County Airport and got on the San Diego Freeway, heading north toward Los Angeles.

Christine glanced back at Joey. He was no longer staring out the window or petting the dog. He was slumped down in a corner of the back seat, eyes closed, mouth open, breathing softly and deeply. The motion of the car had lulled him to sleep.

To Charlie, she said, 'What worries me is that while *we* have to work within the system, slowly and carefully, that Spivey bitch doesn't have any rules holding her back. She can move fast and be brutal. While we're treading carefully around her rights, she'll kill us all.'

'She might self-destruct first,' he said.

'What do you mean?'

'I went to the church this morning. I met her. She's completely around the bend, Christine. Utterly irrational. Coming apart at the seams.'

He told her about his meeting with the old woman, about the bloody stigmata on her hands and feet.

If he intended to reassure her by painting a picture of Grace Spivey as a babbling lunatic teetering on the edge of collapse, he failed. The intensity of the old woman's madness only made her seem more threatening, more predictable, more relentless than ever.

'Have you reported this to the cops?' Christine asked. 'Have you told them that she threatened Joey to your face?'

'No. It would just be my word against hers.'

He told her about his discussion with Denton Boothe, his friend the psychologist. 'Boo says a psychotic of this sort has surprising strength. He says we shouldn't expect her to collapse and solve this problem for us — but then *he* didn't see her. If he'd been there with me and Henry, in her office, when she held up her bleeding hands, he'd know she can't hold it together much longer.'

'Did he have any suggestions, any ideas about how to stop her?'

'He said the best way was to kill her,' Charlie said, smiling.

Christine didn't smile.

He glanced away from the rain-swept freeway long enough to gauge her reaction, then said, 'Of course, Boo was joking.'

'Was he really?'

'Well . . . no . . . he sort of meant it . . . but he knew it wasn't an option we could seriously consider.'

'Maybe it *is* the only answer.'

He looked at her again, his brow creased with worry. 'I hope *you're* joking.'

She said nothing.

'Christine, if you could somehow get her with a gun, if you killed her, you'd only wind up in prison. The state would take Joey away from you. You'd lose him anyway. Killing Grace Spivey isn't the answer.'

She sighed and nodded. She didn't want to argue about it.

But she wondered . . .

Maybe she would end up in prison, and maybe they would take Joey away from her, but as least he would still be *alive*.

When Charlie pulled the Mercedes off the freeway at the Wilshire Boulevard ramp, on the west side of L.A., Joey woke and yawned noisily and wanted to know where they were.

'Westwood,' Charlie said.

'I never been to Westwood,' Joey said.

'Oh?' Charlie said. 'I thought you were a man of the world. I thought you'd been everywhere.'

'How could I have been everywhere?' the boy asked. 'I'm only six.'

'Plenty old enough to've been everywhere,' Charlie said.

'Why, by the time I was six, I'd been all the way from my home in Indiana clear to Peoria.'

'Is that a dirty word?' the boy asked suspiciously.

Charlie laughed and saw that Christine was laughing, too.

'Peoria? No, that's not a dirty word; it's a place. I guess you aren't a man of the world after all. A man of the world would know Peoria as well as he'd know Paris.'

'Mom, what's he talking about?'

'He's just being silly, honey.'

'That's what I thought,' the boy said. 'Lots of detectives act that way sometimes. Jim Rockford's silly like that sometimes, too.'

'That's where I picked it up,' Charlie said. 'From good old Jim Rockford.'

They parked the car in the underground garage beside the Westwood Playhouse, across the street from UCLA, and went shopping for clothes and necessities in Westwood Village, putting everything on credit cards. In spite of the circumstances, in spite of the weather, it was a rather pleasant excursion. There were overhangs or awnings in front of all the stores, and they could always find a dry place to tie Chewbacca while they went inside to browse. The incredible downpour, which was the main topic of conversation among all the salesclerks, helped explain Joey's and Christine's rumpled and bedraggled appearance; no one looked at them askance. Charlie made jokes about some of the clothes they tried on, and Joey held his nose as if detecting a pungent odor when Charlie pretended to consider a loud orange sportshirt, and after a while it almost seemed as if they were an ordinary family on an ordinary outing in a world where all the religious fanatics were over in the Middle East somewhere, fighting over their oil and their mosques. It was nice to think that the three of them were a unit, sharing special bonds, and

Charlie felt another surge of that domestic yearning that had never come upon him until he had met Christine Scavello.

They made two trips back to the car to put their purchases in the trunk. When Christine and Joey had everything they needed, they went to a couple of stores to outfit Charlie, as well. Because he didn't want to risk returning to his own house, where he might pick up a tail, he bought a suitcase, toiletries, and three days worth of clothes.

Several times they saw people on the street who seemed to be watching them or were otherwise suspicious, but in each instance the danger proved to be imaginary, and gradually they relaxed a bit. They were still watchful, alert, but they no longer felt as if there were armed maniacs lurking around every corner.

They finished shopping just as the stores were closing, and by the time they found a cozy-looking restaurant — nothing fancy but with lots of satiny-looking dark wood and stained-glass windows, and a menu rich with fattening specialties like potato skins stuffed with cheese and bacon — it was almost five-thirty. It was early for dinner, but they hadn't eaten lunch, and they were starved.

They ordered drinks, and then Christine took Joey to the ladies' room with her, where both of them washed up a bit and changed into some of the new clothes they'd bought.

While they were thus engaged, Charlie used a pay phone to ring the office. Sherry was still at her desk, and she put him through to Henry Rankin, who'd been awaiting his call, but Henry didn't have much news to report. From the results of lab tests, the police believed the stolen blue Dodge van had been carrying a couple of cases of a moldable plastic explosive favored by more than one branch of the United States armed forces, but they couldn't possibly work back to the point at which the stuff had been purchased or stolen. Henry's Aunt Miriam had been reached in Mexico, was shocked at the news that her house was gone, but didn't blame Henry. She didn't seem disposed to return early from her trip, partly because there wasn't anything left to salvage from the rubble anyway, partly because insurance would cover the loss, partly because she had always taken bad news well, but mainly because she had encountered an interesting man in Acapulco. His name was Ernesto. Those were the only recent developments.

'I'll check in twice a day to see how the case is progressing and to make suggestions,' Charlie said.

'If I have any news about Aunt Miriam and Ernesto, I'll save that for you, too.'

'I'd appreciate it.'

They were both silent a moment, neither of them in a mood to carry the joke any further.

Finally Henry said, 'You think it's wise for you to try to protect them all by yourself?'

'It's the only way.'

'I find it hard to believe Spivey has someone planted here, but I'm putting everyone under the microscope, looking for the disease. If one of them's a Twilighter, I'll find him.'

'I know you will,' Charlie said. He wasn't going to mention that another operative, Mike Specovitch, was checking up on Henry, at Charlie's orders, while Henry was checking up on everyone else. He felt guilty about that betrayal of trust, even though it was unavoidable.

'Where are you now?' Henry asked.

'The Australian outback,' Charlie said.

'What? Oh. None of my business, huh?'

'I'm sorry, Henry.'

'That's all right. You're playing it the only way you

possibly can,' Henry said, but he sounded slightly wounded by Charlie's distrust.

Depressed about the way this case was fracturing the much-valued camaraderie among his employees, Charlie hung up and returned to the table. The waitress was just putting down his vodka martini. He ordered another one even before sipping the first, then took a look at the menu.

Christine returned from the ladies' room in tan corduroy jeans and a green blouse, carrying a bag filled with their old clothes and a few toiletries. Joey wore blue jeans and a cowboy shirt of which he was particularly proud. Their outfits were in need of a steam iron, but they were cleaner and fresher than the clothes they had been wearing since fleeing Miriam Rankin's doomed house in Laguna Beach. Indeed, regardless of the wrinkles in her blouse, Christine looked no worse than stunning, and Charlie's heart lifted again at the sight of her.

By the time they left the restaurant, carrying two hamburgers for Chewbacca, night had settled in completely, and the rain had let up. A light drizzle was falling, and the humid air was oppressively heavy, but it no longer seemed as if they should start building an ark. The dog smelled the burgers, sensed they were for him, and insisted on being fed before they got back to the garage. He gobbled both sandwiches right there in front of the restaurant, and Christine said, 'You know, he even has Brandy's manners.'

'You always said Brandy had no manners,' Joey reminded her.

'That's what I mean.'

Now that the storm seemed to be subsiding, the sidewalks along Westwood Boulevard were filling up with students from UCLA on their way to dinner or a movie, window-shoppers, and theater-goers killing some time before heading to the Playhouse. Californians have little or no tolerance for rain, and after a storm like this one, they always burst forth, eager to be out and around, in an almost festive mood. Charlie was sorry it was time to leave; the Village seemed like an oasis of sanity in a deranged world, and he was thankful for the respite it had provided.

The parking garage had been almost full when they'd arrived this afternoon, and they'd had to leave the car on the lowest level. Now, as they took the elevator down to the bottom of the structure, they were all in a better state of mind than they would have thought possible only a few hours ago. There was nothing like good food, a couple of drinks, and several hours of walking freely on public streets without being shot at to convince you that God was in His heaven and that all was right with the world.

But it was a short-lived feeling. It ended when the elevator doors opened.

The lights immediately beyond the doors were all burned out. There were lights glowing some distance to the left and others to the right, revealing rows of cars and drab concrete walls and massive roof-supporting pillars, but directly in front of the elevator, there was darkness.

How likely was it that three or four lights would be out all at the same time?

That unsettling question flashed into Charlie's mind the moment the door slid open, and before he could react, Chewbacca began to bark at the shadows beyond the doors. The dog was shockingly ferocious, as if possessed by a sudden black rage, yet he didn't rush out of the elevator to pursue the object of his anger, and that was a sure sign that something very bad was waiting out there for them.

Charlie reached toward the elevator control board.

Something whizzed into the cab and slammed into the back wall, two inches from Christine's head. A bullet. It tore a hole through the metal panel. The sound of the shot was almost like an afterthought.

'Down!' Charlie shouted, and hit the CLOSE DOOR button, and another shot slammed into the doors as they started to roll shut, and he punched the button for the top floor, and Chewbacca was still barking, and Christine was screaming, and then the doors were completely shut, and the cage was on its way up, and Charlie thought he heard a last futile shot as they rose out of the concrete depths.

The killers hadn't planned on the dog reacting so quickly and noisily. They had expected Christine and Joey to come out of the elevator, and they hadn't been prepared to hit their quarry within the cab itself. Otherwise, the shot would have been more carefully placed, and Joey or his mother — or both — would already be dead.

With any luck, the only gunmen were those on the lowest level of the garage. But if they had planned for this contingency, for the possibility that their prey would be forewarned and would not get out of the elevator, then they might have stationed others on the upper floor. The cab might stop rising at any level, and the door might open, and another hit squad might be waiting there.

But how did they find us? Charlie asked himself desperately as Christine picked herself up from the floor. In Christ's name, *how*?

He was still packing his own gun, which he'd taken to the Church of the Twilight this morning, and he drew it, aimed at the doors in front of them.

The cab didn't stop until it reached the top floor of the garage. The doors opened. Yellowish lights. Gray concrete walls. Gleaming cars parked in narrow spaces. But no men with guns.

'Come on!' Charlie said.

They ran because they knew the men on the bottom floor of the garage must be coming up quickly behind them.

39

They ran to Hilgarde Avenue, then beyond it, away from UCLA and the commercial area of Westwood, into an expensive and quiet residential neighborhood. Charlie welcomed each convocation of shadows, but dreaded the pools of light surrounding every streetlamp, because here they were the only people on the sidewalks and easily spotted. They turned several times, seeking concealment in the upper-class warren of lushly landscaped streets. Gradually he began to think they had lost their pursuers, though he knew he wouldn't feel entirely safe for a long time to come.

Although the rain had subsided to little more than a light mist, and although they were all wearing raincoats, they were wet and cold again by the time Charlie began looking for transportation. Automobiles were parked along the street, and he moved down the block, under the dripping coral trees and palms, stealthily trying doors, hoping no one was watching from any of the houses. The first three cars were locked up tight, but the driver's door on the fourth, a two-year-old yellow Cadillac, opened when he tried it.

He motioned Christine and Joey into the car. 'Hurry.'

She said, 'Are the keys in it?'

'No.'

'Are you stealing it or what?'

'Yes. Get in.'

'I don't want you breaking the law and winding up in prison because of me and – '

'*Get in!*' he said urgently.

The velour-covered bench seat in front accommodated

the three of them, so Christine put Joey in the middle, apparently afraid to let him get even as far away as the rear seat. The dog got in back, shaking the rain off his coat and spraying everyone in the process.

The glove compartment contained a small, detachable flashlight that came with the car and that was kept, except when needed, in a specially designed niche where its batteries were constantly recharged. Charlie used it to look under the dashboard, below the steering wheel, where he located the ignition wires. He hot-wired the Cadillac, and the engine turned over without hesitation.

No more than two minutes after he had opened the car door, they pulled away from the curb. For the first block, he drove without headlights. Then, confident they had gotten away unnoticed, he snapped on the lights and headed up toward Sunset Boulevard.

Christine said, 'What if the cops stop us?'

'They won't. The owner probably won't report it stolen until morning. And even if he discovers it's gone ten minutes from now, it won't make the police hot sheets for a while.'

'But they might stop us for speeding—'

'I don't intend to speed.'

'— or some other traffic violation—'

'What do you think I am — a stunt driver?'

'Are you?' Joey asked.

'Oh, sure, better than Evel Knievel,' Charlie said.

'Who?' the boy asked.

'God, I'm getting old,' Charlie said.

'Are we gonna get in a car chase like on TV?' Joey asked.

'I hope not,' Charlie said.

'Oh, I'd like that,' the boy said.

Charlie checked the rearview mirror. There were two cars behind him. He couldn't tell what make they were or anything about them. They were just pairs of headlights in the darkness.

Christine said, 'But sooner or later, the car *will* end up on the hot sheets –'

'We'll have parked it somewhere and taken another car by then,' Charlie said.

'*Steal* another one?'

'I'm sure not going to Hertz or Avis,' he said. 'A rental car can be traced. They might find us that way.'

Jesus, listen to me, he thought. Pretty soon I'm going to be like Ray Milland in *Lost Weekend*, imagining a threat in every corner, seeing giant bugs crawling out of the walls.

He turned left at the next corner. So did both of the cars behind him.

'How did they find us?' Christine asked.

'Must've planted a transmitter on my Mercedes.'

'When would they've done that?'

'I don't know. Maybe when I was at their church this morning.'

'But you said you left a man in your car while you went in there, someone who could call for help if you didn't come back out when you were supposed to.'

'Yeah. Carter Rilbeck.'

'So he'd have seen them trying to plant a transmitter.'

'Unless, of course, he's one of them,' Charlie said.

'Do you think he could be?'

'Probably not. But maybe they planted the bug before that. As soon as they knew you'd hired me.'

At Hilgarde, he turned right.

So did both of the cars behind him.

To Christine, he said, 'Or maybe Henry Rankin is a Twilighter, and when I called him from the restaurant a while ago, maybe he got a trace on the line and found out where I was.'

'You said he's like a brother.'

243

'He is. But Cain was like a brother to Abel, huh?'

He turned left on Sunset Boulevard, with UCLA on the left now and Bel Air on the hills to the right.

Only one of the cars followed him.

She said, 'You sound as if you've become as paranoid as I am.'

'Grace Spivey gives me no choice.'

'Where are we going?' she asked.

'Farther away.'

'Where?'

'I'm not sure yet.'

'We spent all that time buying clothes and things, and now a lot of it's gone,' she said.

'We can outfit ourselves again tomorrow.'

'I can't go home; I can't go to work; I can't take shelter with any of my friends – '

'I'm your friend,' Charlie said.

'We don't even have a car now,' she said.

'Sure we do.'

'A stolen car.'

'It's got four wheels,' he said. 'It runs. That's good enough.'

'I feel like we're the cowboys in one of those old movies where the Indians trap them in a box canyon and keep pushing them farther and farther toward the wall.'

'Remember who always won in those movies,' Charlie said.

'The cowboys,' Joey said.

'Exactly.'

He had to stop for a red traffic light because, as luck would have it, a police cruiser was stopped on the other side of the intersection. He didn't like sitting there, vulnerable. He used the rearview mirror and the side mirror to keep a watch on the car that had followed them, afraid that someone would get out of it while they were immobilized here — someone with a shotgun.

In a weary voice that dismayed Charlie, Christine said, 'I wish I had your confidence.'

So do I, he thought wryly.

The light changed. He crossed the intersection. Behind him, the unknown car fell back a bit.

He said, 'Everything'll seem better in the morning.'

'And where will we be in the morning?' she asked.

They had come to an intersection where Wilshire Boulevard lay in front of them. He turned right, toward the freeway entrance, and said, 'How about Santa Barbara?'

'Are you serious?'

'It's not that far. A couple hours. We could be there by nine-thirty, get a hotel room.'

The unknown car had turned right at Wilshire, too, and was still on his tail.

'L.A.'s a big city,' she said. 'Don't you think we'd be just as safe hiding out here?'

'We probably would,' he said. 'But I wouldn't *feel* as safe, and I've got to settle us down somewhere that feels right to me, so I can relax and think about the case from a calmer perspective. I can't function well in a constant panic. They won't expect us to go as far away from my operations as Santa Barbara. They'll expect me to hang around, at least as close as L.A., so I know we'll be safe up there.'

He drove onto the entrance ramp of the San Diego Freeway, heading north. Checked the rearview mirror. Didn't see the other car yet. Realized he was holding his breath.

She protested. 'You didn't bargain for this much trouble, this much inconvenience.'

'Sure I did,' he said. 'I thrive on it.'

'Of course you do.'

'Ask Joey. He knows all about us private detectives. He knows we just *love* danger.'

'They do, Mom,' the boy said. 'They love danger.'

Charlie looked at the rearview mirror again. No other car had come onto the freeway behind him. They weren't being followed.

They drove north into the night, and after a while the rain began to fall heavily again, and there was fog. At times, because of the mist and rain that obscured the landscape and the road ahead, it seemed as if they weren't driving through the real world at all but through some haunted and insubstantial realm of spirits and dreams.

40

Kyle Barlowe's Santa Ana apartment was furnished to suit his dimensions. There were roomy Lay-Z-Boy recliners, a big sectional sofa with a deep seat, sturdy end tables, and a solidly built coffee table on which a man could prop his feet without fear of the thing collapsing. He had searched a long time, in countless used furniture stores, before he'd found the round table in the dining alcove; it was plain and somewhat battered, maybe not too attractive, but it was a little higher than most dining tables and gave him the kind of leg room he required. In the bathroom stood a very old, very large claw-foot tub, and in the bedroom he had one big dresser that he'd picked up for forty-six bucks and a king-size bed with an extra-long custom mattress that accommodated him, though with not an inch to spare. This was the one place in the world in which he could be truly comfortable.

But not tonight.

He could not be comfortable when the Antichrist was still alive. He could not relax, knowing that two assassination attempts had failed within the past twelve hours.

He paced from the small kitchen to the living room, into the bedroom, back to the living room again, pausing to look out windows. Main Street was eerily lit by sickly yellow street-lamps, as well as by red and blue and pink and purple neon, all bleeding together, disguising the true colors of every object, giving the shadows fuzzy electric edges. Passing cars spewed up phosphorescent plumes of water that splashed back to the pavement, like rhinestone sequins. The falling rain looked silvery and molten, though the night was far from hot.

He tried watching television. Couldn't get interested in it.

He couldn't keep still. He sat down, got up right away, sat in another chair, got up, went into the bedroom, stretched out on the bed, heard an odd noise at the window, got up to investigate, realized it was only rainwater falling through the downspout, returned to bed, decided he didn't want to lie down, returned to the living room.

The Antichrist was still alive.

But that wasn't the only thing that was making him nervous. He tried to believe nothing else was bothering him, tried to pretend he was only worried about the Scavello boy, but finally he had to admit to himself that another thing was chewing at him.

The old need. Such a fierce need. The NEED. He wanted—

No!

It didn't matter what he wanted. He couldn't have it. He couldn't surrender to the NEED. He didn't dare.

He dropped to his knees in the middle of the living room and prayed to God to help him resist the weakness in him.

He prayed hard, prayed with all his might, with all his attention and devotion, prayed with such teeth-grinding intensity that he began to sweat.

He still felt the old, despicable terrifying urge to mangle someone, to pummel and twist and claw, to hurt somebody, to *kill*.

In desperation, he got up and went into the kitchen, to the sink, and turned on the cold water. He put the stopper in the drain. He got ice cubes from the refrigerator and added them to the growing pool. When the sink was almost full, he turned the spigot off and lowered his head into the freezing water, forced himself to stay there, holding his breath, face submerged, skin stinging, until he finally had to come up, gasping for air. He was shivering, and his teeth were chattering, but he still felt the violence building in him, so he put his head under again, waiting until his lungs were bursting, came up sputtering and spitting, and now he was frigid, quaking uncontrollably, but still the urge to do violence swelled unchecked.

Satan was here now. Must be. Satan was here and dredging up the old feelings, pushing Kyle's face in them, tempting him, trying to get him to toss away his last chance at salvation.

I won't!

He stormed through the apartment trying to detect exactly where Satan was. He looked in closets, opened cabinets, pulled aside the draperies to check behind them. He didn't actually expect to *see* Satan, but he was sure he would at least sense the devil's presence somewhere, invisible though the demon might be. But there was nothing to be found. Which only meant the devil was clever at concealing himself.

When he finally gave up searching for Satan, he was in the bathroom, and he caught a glimpse of himself in the mirror: eyes wild, nostrils dilated, jaw muscles popping, lips bloodless and skinned back over his crooked yellow teeth. He thought of the Phantom of the Opera. He thought of Frankenstein's monster and a hundred other tortured, unhuman faces from a hundred other films he had seen on 'Chiller Theater.'

The world hated him, and he hated the world, all of them, the ones who laughed, who pointed, the women who found him repulsive, all the —

No. God. Please. Don't let me think about these things. Get my mind off this subject. Help me. Please.

He couldn't look away from his Boris Karloff-Lon Chaney-Rhondo Hatten face, which filled the age-spotted mirror.

He never missed those old horror movies when they were on TV. Many nights he sat alone in front of his black-and-white set, riveted by the ghastly images, and when each picture ended, he went into the bathroom, to this very mirror, and looked at himself and told himself that he wasn't *that* ugly, wasn't *that* frightening, not as bad as the creatures that crept out of primeval swamps or came from beyond the stars or escaped from mad scientists' laboratories. By comparison, he was almost ordinary. At worst, pathetic. But he could never believe himself. The mirror didn't lie. The mirror showed him a face made for nightmares.

He smiled at himself in the mirror, tried to look amiable. The result was awful. The smile was a leer.

No woman would ever have him unless he paid, and even some whores turned him down. Bitches. All of them. Rotten, stinking, heartless bitches. He wanted to make one of them hurt. He wanted to bring his pain to one of them, hammer his pain into some woman and leave it in her, so that for a short while, at least, there would be no pain in him.

No. That was bad thinking. Evil thinking.

Remember Mother Grace.

Remember the Twilight and salvation and life everlasting.

But he wanted. He needed.

He found himself at the door of his apartment without being able to recall how he'd gotten there. He had the door half open. He was on his way out to find a prostitute. Or someone to beat up. Or both.

No!

He slammed the door, locked it, put his back to it, and looked frantically around his living room.

He had to act quickly to save himself.

He was losing his battle against temptation. He was whimpering now, shuddering and mewling. He knew that in a second or two he would open the door again, and this time he would leave, go hunting . . .

In panic, he rushed to a small bookshelf, pulled out one of the inspiration volumes from his collection of a hundred such titles, tore out a fistful of pages and threw them onto the floor, tore out more pages, and more, until only the covers of the book remained, and then he ripped those apart, too. It felt good to mutilate something. He was gasping and shuddering like a horse in distress, and he seized another book, tore it to pieces, pitched the fragments behind him, grabbed another book, demolished it, then another, another . . .

When he regained his senses, he was on the floor, weeping softly. Twenty ruined books, thousands of ripped pages, were heaped around him. He got up, pulled out his handkerchief, wiped his eyes. Got to his knees, stood. He wasn't shaking any more. The NEED was gone.

Satan had lost.

Kyle had not surrendered to temptation, and now he knew why God wanted men like him to fight the battle of the Twilight. If God built His army strictly of men who had never sinned, how could He know that they would be able to resist the devil's entreaties? But by choosing men like me, Kyle thought, men with no resistance to sin, giving us a second chance at salvation, by making us prove ourselves, God has acquired an army of *tempered* soldiers.

He looked up at the ceiling but didn't see it. Instead he saw the sky beyond, saw into the heart of the universe. He said, 'I'm worthy. I've climbed out of the sewer of sin, and I've proved I'll never sink back down. If what You want is for me to handle the boy for You, I'm worthy now. Give me the boy. Let me have the boy. Let me.'

He felt the NEED surging in him again, the desire to choke and rend and crush, but this time it was a purer emotion, the clean white holy desire to be God's gladiator.

It occurred to him that God was asking him to do the very thing he most wanted to avoid. He didn't *want* to kill again. He didn't want to harm people any more. He was finally gaining a small measure of respect for himself, finally saw the dim but real possibility that he might one day live in peace with the rest of the world — and now God wanted him to kill, wanted him to use his rage against selected targets.

Why? he asked in sudden, silent misery. Why do *I* have to be the one? I used to thrive on the NEED, but now it scares me, and it *should* scare me. Why must I be used this way; why not in some other way?

That was what Mother Grace called 'wrong-thought,' and he tried to wipe it out of his mind. You never challenged God like that. You just accepted what He wanted. God was mysterious. Sometimes He was harsh, and you couldn't understand why He demanded so much of you. Like why He wanted you to kill . . . or why He'd made you a freak in the first place when He could just as easily have made you handsome.

No. That was more wrong-thought.

Kyle cleaned up the ravaged books. He poured a glass of milk. He sat down by his telephone. He waited for Grace to call and say that it was time for him to be the hammer of God.

PART FOUR
The Chase

Everything that deceives also enchants.

— Plato

There's no escape
From death's embrace,
though you lead it on
a merry chase.

The dogs of death
enjoy the chase.
Just see the smile
on each hound's face.

The chase can't last;
the dogs must feed.
It will come to pass
with terrifying speed.

— *The Book of Counted Sorrows*

41

In Ventura, they abandoned the yellow Cadillac. They searched along another residential street until Charlie found a dark blue Ford LTD whose owner had been unwise enough to leave the keys in the ignition. He drove the LTD only two miles before stopping again, in a poorly lit parking lot behind a movie theater, where he removed the license plates and tossed them in the trunk. He took the plates off a Toyota parked nearby and put those on the LTD.

With a little luck, the Toyota's owner wouldn't notice that his plates were missing until tomorrow, perhaps later. Once he did notice, he might not bother reporting the incident to the police, at least not immediately. Anyway, the police wouldn't put stolen plates on the hot sheet the way they would if the entire car was stolen, wouldn't have every cop in the state looking for just a pair of tags, and wouldn't be likely to connect this small crime with the bigger theft of the LTD. They'd treat the plate-nabbing report as just a case of vandalism. Meanwhile, the stolen LTD would have new tags and a new identity, and it would, in effect, cease to be a hot car.

They left Ventura, heading north, and reached Santa Barbara at 9:50 Tuesday night.

Santa Barbara was one of Charlie's favorite getaway places when the pressures of work became overwhelming. He usually stayed at either the Biltmore or the Montecito

Inn. This time, however, he chose a slightly shabby motel, The Wile-Away Lodge, at the east end of State Street. Considering his well-known taste for the finer things in life, this was about the last place anyone would look for him.

There was a kitchenette unit available, and Charlie took it for a week, signing the name Enoch Flint to the register and paying cash in advance, so he wouldn't have to show the clerk a credit card.

The room had turquoise draperies, burnt-orange carpet, and bedspreads in a loud purple and yellow pattern; either the decorator had been limited by a tight budget and had bought whatever was available within a certain price range – or he had been a blind beneficiary of the Equal Opportunity Employment Act. The pair of queen-size beds had mattresses that were too soft and lumpy. A couch converted into a third bed, which looked even less comfortable. The furniture was mismatched and well used. The bathroom had an age-yellowed mirror, lots of cracked floor tiles, and a vent fan that wheezed asthmatically. In the kitchen alcove, out of sight from the bedroom, there were four chairs and a table, a sink with a leaky faucet, a battered refrigerator, a stove, cheap plates and cheaper silverware, and an electric percolator with complimentary packets of coffee, Sanka, sugar, and non-dairy creamer. It wasn't much, but it was cleaner than they had expected.

While Christine put Joey to bed, Charlie brewed a pot of Sanka.

When she came into the kitchenette a few minutes later, Christine said, 'Mmmmm, that smells heavenly.'

He poured two cups for them. 'How's Joey?'

'He was asleep before I finished tucking him in. The dog's on the bed with him, and I usually don't allow that, but, what the hell, I figure any day that starts out with a bomb attack and goes downhill from there is a day you should be allowed to have your dog on your bed.'

They sat at the kitchen table, by a window that presented a view of one end of the motel parking lot and a small swimming pool ringed by a wrought-iron fence in need of paint. The wet macadam and the parked cars were splashed with orange neon light from the motel's sign. The storm was winding down again.

The coffee was good, and the conversation was better. They talked about everything that came to mind — politics, movies, books, favorite vacation spots, work, music, Mexican food — everything but Grace Spivey and the Twilight. They seemed to have an unspoken agreement to ignore their current circumstances. They desperately needed a respite.

But, to Charlie, their conversation was much more than that; it was a chance to learn about Christine. With the obsessive curiosity of a man in love, he wanted to know every detail of her existence, every thought and opinion, no matter how mundane.

Maybe he was only flattering himself, but he suspected that his romantic interest in her was matched by her interest in him. He hoped that was the case. More than anything, he wanted her to want him.

By midnight, he found himself telling her things he had never told anyone before, things he had long wanted to forget. They were events he thought had lost the power to hurt him, but as he spoke of them he realized the pain had been there all the while.

He talked about being poor in Indianapolis, when there wasn't always enough food or enough heat in the winter because the welfare checks were used first for wine, beer, and whiskey. He spoke of being unable to sleep for fear that the rats infesting their tumble-down shack would get up on the bed with him and start chewing on his face.

He told her about his drunken, violent father, who had beaten his mother as regularly as if that were a husband's duty. Sometimes the old man had beaten his son, too, usually when he was too drunk and unsteady to do much damage. Charlie's mother had been weak and foolish, with her own taste for booze; she hadn't wanted a child in the first place, and she had never interfered when her husband struck Charlie.

'Are your mother and father still alive?' Christine asked.

'Thank God, no! Now that I've done well, they'd be camping on my doorstep, pretending they'd been the best parents a kid ever had. But there was never any love in that house, never any affection.'

'You've come a long way up the ladder,' Christine said.

'Yeah. Especially considering I didn't expect to live long.'

She was looking out at the parking lot and swimming pool. He turned his eyes to the window, too. The world was so quiet and motionless that they might have been the only people in it.

He said, 'I always thought my father would kill me sooner or later. The funny thing is, even way back then, I wanted to be a private detective because I saw them on TV – Richard Diamond and Peter Gunn – and I knew they were never afraid of anything. I was always afraid of everything, and more than anything else I wanted not to be afraid.'

'And now, of course, you're fearless,' she said with irony.

He smiled. 'How simple it seems when you're just a kid.'

A car pulled into the lot, and both of them stared at it until the doors opened and a young couple got out with two small children.

Charlie poured more Sanka for both of them and said, 'I used to lie in bed, listening to the rats, praying that both my parents would die before they got a chance to kill me, and I became real angry with God because He didn't answer that prayer. I couldn't understand why He would let those two go on victimizing a little kid like me. I couldn't defend myself. Why wouldn't God protect the defenseless? Then, when I got a little older, I decided God couldn't answer my prayers because God was good and wouldn't ever kill anyone, not even moral rejects like my folks. So I started praying just to get out of that place. "Dear God, this is Charlie, and all I want is to some day get out of here and live in a decent house and have money and not be scared all the time." '

He suddenly recalled a darkly comic episode he hadn't thought about in years, and he laughed sharply at the bizarre memory.

She said, 'How can you laugh about it? Even though I know things turned out pretty well for him, I still feel *terrible* for that little boy back there in Indianapolis. As if he's still there.'

'No, no. It's just I . . . remembered something else, something that is funny in a grim sort of way. After a while, after I'd been praying to God for maybe a year, I got tired of how long it took for a prayer to be answered, and I went over to the other side for a while.'

'Other side?'

Staring out the window as a squall of rain whirled through the darkness, he said, 'I read this story about a man who sold his soul to the devil. He just one day wished for something he really needed, said that he'd sell his soul for it, and *poof*, the devil showed up with a contract to sign. I decided the devil was much more prompt and efficient than God, so I started praying to the devil at night.'

'I assume he never showed up with a contract.'

'Nope. He turned out to be as inefficient as God. But then one night it occurred to me that my parents were sure to wind up in Hell, and if I sold my soul to the devil I'd wind up in Hell, too, right there with my folks, for eternity, and I was so frightened I got out of bed in the dark, and I prayed with all my might for God to save me. I told Him I understood he had a big backlog of prayers to answer, and I said I realized it might take a while to get around to mine, and I groveled and begged and pleaded for Him to forgive me for doubting Him. I guess I made some noise because my mother came in my room to see what was up. She was as drunk as I'd ever seen her. When I told her I was talking to God, she said, "Yeah? Well, tell God your daddy's out with a whore somewhere again, and ask Him to make the bastard's cock fall off." '

'Good heavens,' Christine said, laughing but shocked. He knew she wasn't shocked by the word or by his decision to tell her this story; she was shaken, instead, by what his mother's casual crudity revealed about the house in which he'd been raised.

Charlie said, 'Now, I was only ten years old, but I'd lived all my life in the worst part of town, and my parents would never be mistaken for Ozzie and Harriet, so even then I knew what she was talking about, and I thought it was the funniest thing I'd ever heard. Every night after that, when I'd be saying my prayers, sooner or later I'd think of what my mother had wanted God to do to my father, and I'd start to laugh. I couldn't finish a prayer without laughing. After a while, I just stopped talking to God altogether, and by the time I was twelve or thirteen I knew there probably wasn't any God or devil and that, even if there was, you have to make your own good fortune in this life.'

She told him more about her mother, the convent, the work that had gone into Wine & Dine. Some of her stories were almost as sad as parts of his youth, and others were funny, and all of them were the most fascinating stories he had ever heard because they were *her* stories.

Once in a while, one of them would say they ought to be getting some sleep, and they both really were exhausted, but they kept talking anyway, through two pots of Sanka. By 1:30 in the morning, Charlie realized that a compelling desire to know each other better was not the only reason they didn't want to go to bed. They were also afraid to sleep. They often glanced out the window, and he realized they both expected to see a white Ford van pull into the motel parking lot.

Finally he said, 'Look, we can't stay up all night. They can't find us here. No way. Let's go to bed. We need to be rested for what's ahead.'

She looked out the window. She said, 'If we sleep in shifts, one of us will always be awake to keep a guard.'

'It's not necessary. There's no way they could have followed us.'

She said, 'I'll take the first shift. You go to sleep, and I'll wake you at . . . say four-thirty.'

He sighed. 'No. I'm wide awake. You sleep.'

'You'll wake me at four-thirty, so I can take over?'

'All right.'

They took their dirty coffee cups to the sink, rinsed them — then were somehow holding each other and kissing gently, softly. His hands moved over her, lightly caressing, and he was stirred by the exquisite shape and texture of her. If Joey had not been in the same room, Charlie would have made love to her, and it would have been the best either of them had ever known. But all they could do was cling to each other in the kitchenette, until at last the frustration outweighed the pleasure. Then she kissed him three times, once deeply and twice lightly on the corner of his mouth, and she went to bed.

When the lights were out, he sat at the table by the window and watched the parking lot.

He had no intention of waking Christine at four-thirty. Half an hour after she joined Joey in bed, when Charlie was sure she was asleep, he went silently to the other bed.

Waiting for sleep to overtake him, he thought again of what he'd told Christine about his childhood, and for the first time in more than twenty-five years, he said a prayer. As before, he prayed for the safety and deliverance of a little boy, though this time it was not the boy in Indianapolis, whom he had once been, but a boy in Santa Barbara who by chance had become the focus of a crazy old woman's hatred.

Don't let Grace Spivey do this, God. Don't let her kill an innocent child in Your name. There can be no greater blasphemy than that. If You really exist, if You really care, then surely this is the time to do one of Your miracles. Send a flock of ravens to pluck out the old woman's eyes. Send a mighty flood to wash her away. Something. At least a heart attack, a stroke, something to stop her.

As he listened to himself pray, he realized why he had broken the silence between God and himself after all these years. It was because, for the first time in a long time, on the run from the old woman and her fanatics, he felt like a child, unable to cope, in need of help.

42

In Kyle Barlowe's dream he was being murdered: a faceless adversary was stabbing him repeatedly, and he knew he was dying, yet it didn't hurt and he wasn't afraid. He didn't fight back, just surrendered, and in that acquiescence he discovered the most profound sense of peace he had ever known. Although he was being killed, it was a pleasant dream, not a nightmare and a part of him somehow knew that not *all* of him was being killed, just the bad part of him, just the old Kyle who had hated the world, and when that part of him was finally disposed of he would be like everyone else, which is the only thing he had ever wanted in life. To be like everyone else . . .

The telephone woke him. He fumbled for it in the darkness.

'Hello?'

'Kyle?' Mother Grace.

'It's me,' he said, sleep instantly dispelled.

'Much has been happening,' she said.

He looked at the illuminated dial of the clock. It was 4:06 in the morning.

He said, 'What? What's been happening?'

'We've been burning out the infidels,' she said cryptically.

'I wanted to *be* there if anything was going to happen.'

'We've burned them out and salted the earth so they can't return,' she said, her voice rising.

'You promised me. I wanted to *be* there.'

'I haven't needed you — until now,' Mother Grace said.

He threw off the covers, sat up on the edge of the bed, grinning at the darkness. 'What do you want me to do?'

'They've taken the boy away. They're trying to hide him from us until his powers increase, until he's untouchable.'

'Where have they taken him?' Kyle asked.

'I don't know for sure. As far as Ventura. I know that much. I'm waiting for more news or for a vision that'll clarify the situation. Meanwhile, we're going north.'

'Who?'

'You, me, Edna, six or eight of the others.'

'After the boy?'

'Yes. You must pack some clothes and come to the church. We're leaving within the hour.'

'I'll be there right away,' he said.

'God bless you,' she said, and she hung up.

Barlowe was scared. He remembered the dream, remembered how *good* it had felt in that dream, and he thought he knew what it meant: He was losing his taste for violence, his thirst for blood. But that was no good because, now, for the first time in his life, he had an opportunity to use that talent for violence in a good cause. In fact his salvation depended upon it.

He must kill the boy. It was the right thing. He must not entirely lose the bitter hatred that had motivated him all his life.

The hour was late; Twilight drew near. And now Grace needed him to be the hammer of God.

43

Wednesday morning, rain was no longer falling, and the sky was only half obscured by clouds.

Charlie got up first, showered, and was making coffee by the time Christine and Joey woke.

Christine seemed surprised that they were still alive. She didn't have a robe, so she wrapped a blanket around herself and came into the kitchen looking like an Indian squaw. A beautiful Indian squaw. 'You didn't wake me for guard duty,' she said.

'This isn't the marines,' Charlie said, smiling, determined to avoid the panic that had infected them yesterday.

When they were too keyed up, they didn't act; they only *re*acted. And that was the kind of behavior that would eventually get them killed.

He had to think; he had to plan. He couldn't do either

if he spent all his time looking nervously over his shoulder. They were safe here in Santa Barbara, as long as they were just a little cautious.

'But we were all asleep at the same time,' Christine said.

'We needed our rest.'

'But I was sleeping so deeply . . . they could've broken in here, and the first thing I would've known about it was when the shooting started.'

Charlie looked around, frowning. 'Where's the camera? Are we filming a Sominex commercial?'

She sighed, smiled. 'You think we're safe?'

'Yes.'

'Really?'

'We made it through the night, didn't we?'

Joey came into the kitchen, barefoot, in his underpants, his hair tousled, his face still heavy with sleep. He said, 'I dreamed about the witch.'

Charlie said, 'Dreams can't hurt you.'

The boy was solemn this morning. There was no sparkle in his bright blue eyes. 'I dreamed she used her magic to turn you into a bug, and then she just stepped on you.'

'Dreams don't mean anything,' Charlie said. 'I once dreamed I was President of the United States. But you don't see any Secret Service men hanging around me, do you?'

'She killed . . . in the *dream* she killed my mom, too,' Joey said.

Christine hugged him. 'Charlie's right, honey. Dreams don't mean anything.'

'Nothing I've *ever* dreamed about has ever happened,' Charlie said.

The boy went to the window. He stared out at the parking lot. He said, 'She's out there somewheres.'

Christine looked at Charlie. He knew what she was thinking. The boy had thus far been amazingly resilient, bouncing back from every shock, recovering from every horror, always able to smile one more time. But maybe he had exhausted his resources; maybe he wasn't going to bounce back very well any more.

Chewbacca padded into the kitchenette, stopped at the boy's side, and growled softly.

'See?' Joey said. 'Chewbacca knows. Chewbacca knows she's out there somewheres.'

The boy's usual verve was gone. It was disturbing to see him so gray-faced and bereft of spirit.

Charlie and Christine tried to kid him into a better mood, but he was having none of it.

Later, at nine-thirty, they ate breakfast in a nearby coffee shop. Charlie and Christine were starved, but they repeatedly had to urge Joey to eat. They were in a booth by one of the big windows, and Joey kept looking out at the sky, where a few strips of blue seemed like gaily colored ropes holding the drab clouds together. He looked as glum as a six-year-old could look.

Charlie wondered why the boy's eyes were drawn repeatedly to the sky. Was he expecting the witch to come sailing in on her broom?

Yes, in fact, that was probably just what he was worried about. When you were six years old, it wasn't always possible to distinguish between real and imaginary dangers. At that age you *believed* in the monster-that-lives-in-the-closet, and you are convinced that something even worse was crouching under your bed. To Joey, it probably made as much sense to search for broomsticks in the sky as to look for white Ford vans on the highway.

Chewbacca had been left in the car outside the coffee shop. When they were finished with breakfast, they brought him an order of ham and eggs, which he devoured eagerly.

'Last night it was hamburgers, this morning ham and eggs,' Christine said. 'We've got to find a grocery store and buy some real dog food before this mutt gets the idea that he's always going to eat this well.'

They went shopping again for clothes and personal effects in a mall just off East State Street. Joey tried on some clothes, but listlessly, without the enthusiasm he had shown yesterday. He said little, smiled not at all.

Christine was obviously worried about him. So was Charlie.

They were finished shopping before lunch. The last thing they bought was a small electronic device at Radio Shack. It was the size of a pack of cigarettes, a product of the paranoid '70s and '80s that would not have had any buyers in a more trusting era: a tap detector that could tell you if your telephone line was being monitored by a recorder or a tracing mechanism of any kind.

In a phone booth near the side entrance of Sears, Charlie unscrewed the earpiece on the handset, screwed on another earpiece that came with the tap detector. He removed the mouthpiece, used a car key to short the inhibitor that made it impossible to place a long-distance call without operator assistance, and dialed Klemet-Harrison in Costa Mesa, toll-free. If his equipment indicated a tap, he'd be able to hang up in the first fraction of a second after the connection was made and, most likely, cut the line before anyone had a chance even to determine that the call was from another area code.

The number rang twice, then there was a click on the line.

The meter in Charlie's hand gave no indication of a tap.

But instead of Sherry Ordway's familiar voice, the call was answered by telephone company recording: 'The number you have dialed is no longer in service. Please consult your directory for the correct number or dial the operator for . . .'

Charlie hung up.

Tried it again.

He got the same response. With a presentiment of disaster chewing at him, he dialed Henry Rankin's home number. It was picked up on the first ring, and again the meter indicated no tap, but this time the voice was not a recording.

'Hello?' Henry said.

Charlie said, 'It's me, Henry. I just called the office —'

'I've been waiting here by the phone, figuring you'd try me sooner or later,' Henry said. 'We got trouble, Charlie. We got lots of trouble.'

From outside the booth, Christine couldn't hear what Charlie was saying, but she could tell something bad had happened. When he finally hung up and opened the folding door, he was ashen.

'What's wrong?' she asked.

He glanced at Joey and said, 'Nothing's wrong. I talked to Henry Rankin. They're still working on the case, but there's nothing new to report yet.'

He was lying for Joey's sake, but the boy sensed it just as Christine did, and said, 'What'd she do now? What'd the witch do now?'

'Nothing,' Charlie said. 'She can't find us, so she's throwing tantrums down there in Orange County. That's all.'

'What's a tantrum?' Joey asked.

'Don't worry about it. We're okay. Everything's ticking along as planned. Now let's go back to the car, find a supermarket, and stock up on groceries.'

Walking through the open-air mall and all the way out to the car, Charlie looked around uneasily, with a visible tension he hadn't shown all morning.

Christine had begun to accept his assurances that they were safe in Santa Barbara, but now fear crawled up out of her subconscious and took possession of her once more.

As if it were an omen of renewed danger, the weather worsened again. The sky began to clot up with black clouds.

They found a supermarket, and as they shopped, Joey moved down the aisles ahead of them. Ordinarily, he scampered ahead, searching for items on their shopping list, eager to help. Today he moved slowly and studied the shelves with little interest.

When the boy was far enough away, Charlie said softly, 'Last night my offices were torched.'

'Torched?' Christine said. There was suddenly a greasy, roiling feeling in her stomach. 'You mean . . . burned?'

He nodded, taking a couple of cans of Mandarin orange slices from the shelf and putting them in the shopping cart. 'Everything's . . . lost . . . furniture, equipment, all the files . . . gone.' He paused while two women with carts moved past them. Then: 'The files were in fire-proof cabinets, but someone got the drawers open anyway, pulled out all the papers, and poured gasoline on them.'

Shocked, Christine said, 'But in a business like yours, don't you have burglar alarms – '

'Two systems, each independent of the other, both with backup power sources in case of a blackout,' Charlie said.

'But that sounds fool-proof.'

'It was supposed to have been, yeah. But her people got through somehow.'

Christine felt sick. 'You think it was Grace Spivey.'

'I know it was Grace. You haven't heard everything that happened last night. Besides, it had to be her because there's such a quality of rage about it, such an air of desperation, and she must be angry and desperate right now because we've given her the slip. She doesn't know

269

where we've gone, can't get her hands on Joey, so she's striking out wherever she can, flailing away in a mad frenzy.'

She remembered the Henredon desk in his office, the Martin Green paintings, and she said, 'Oh, dammit, Charlie, I'm so sorry. Because of me, you've lost your business and all your —'

'It can all be replaced,' he said, although she could see that the loss disturbed him. 'The important files are on microfilm and stored elsewhere. They can be recreated. We can find new offices. Insurance will cover most everything. It's not the money or the inconvenience that bothers me. It's the fact that, for a few days at least, until Henry gets things organized down there, my people won't be able to keep after Grace Spivey — and we won't have them behind us, supporting us. Temporarily, we're pretty much on our own.'

That *was* a disturbing thought.

Joey came back with a can of pineapple rings. 'Can I have these, Mom?'

'Sure,' she said, putting the can in the cart. If it would have brought a smile to his small glum face, she'd have allowed him to get a whole package of Almond Joys or some other item he was usually not permitted to have.

Joey went off to scout the rest of the aisle ahead.

To Charlie, Christine said, 'You mentioned that something else happened last night . . .'

He hesitated. He put two jars of applesauce in the cart. Then, with a look of sympathy and concern, he said, 'Your house was also torched.'

Instantly, without conscious intent, she began to catalogue what she had lost, the sentimental as well as the truly valuable things that this act of arson had stolen from her: all Joey's baby pictures; the fifteen-thousand-dollar oriental carpet in the living room, which was the first expensive thing she'd owned, her first gesture of self-indulgence after the years of self-denial her mother had demanded of her; photographs of Tony, her long-dead brother; her collection of Lalique crystal . . .

For an awful moment she almost burst into tears, but then Joey returned to say that the dairy case was at the end of this aisle and that he would like some cottage cheese to go with the pineapple rings. And Christine realized that losing the oriental carpets, the paintings, and even the old photographs was of little importance as long as she still had Joey. He was the only thing in her life that was irreplaceable. No longer on the verge of tears, she told him to get the cottage cheese.

When Joey moved away again, Charlie said, 'My house, too.'

For a moment she wasn't sure she understood. 'Burned?'

'To the ground,' he said.

'Oh my God.'

It was too much. Christine felt like a plague-carrier. She had brought disaster to everyone who was trying to help her.

'Grace is desperate, you see,' Charlie said excitedly. 'She doesn't know where we've gone, and she really thinks that Joey is the Antichrist, and she's afraid she's failed in her God-given mission. She's furious and frightened, and she's striking out blindly. The very fact that she's done these things means we're safe here. Better than that, it means she's rapidly destroying herself. She's gone too far. She's stepped way, way over the line. The cops can't help but connect those three torchings with the murders at your place last night and with the bomb at Miriam Rankin's house in Laguna. This is now the biggest story in Orange County, maybe the biggest story in the whole state. She can't go around blowing up houses, burning them down. She's brought *war* to Orange County, for Christ's sake, and no one's going to tolerate that. The cops are going to come down hard on her now. They're going to be grilling her and everyone in her church. They'll go over her affairs with a microscope. She'll have made a mistake last night; she'll have left incriminating evidence. Somewhere. Somehow. One little mistake is all the cops need. They'll seize on it and pull her alibi apart. She's done for. It's only a matter of time. All we've got to do is lie low here for a few days, stay in the motel, and wait for the Church of the Twilight to fall apart.'

'I hope you're right,' she said, but she wasn't going to get her hopes up. Not again.

Joey returned with the cottage cheese and stayed close to them for a while, until they entered an aisle that contained a small toy section, where he drifted away to look at the plastic guns.

Charlie said, 'We'll finish shopping, get a bunch of magazines, a deck of cards, a few games, whatever we need to keep us occupied for the rest of the week. After we've taken everything back to the room, I'll get rid of the car – '

'But I thought it wouldn't turn up on any hot sheets for a few days yet. That's what you said.'

He was trying not to look grim, but he couldn't keep the worry out of either his face or his voice. He took a package of Oreos from the cookie section and put them in the cart. 'Yeah, well, according to Henry, the cops have already found the yellow Cadillac we abandoned in Ventura, and they've already linked it with the stolen LTD and the missing plates. They lifted fingerprints from the Caddy, and because my prints are on file with my PI license application, they made a quick connection.'

'But from what you said, I didn't think they ever worked that fast.'

'Ordinarily, no. But we had a piece of bad luck.'

'Another one?'

'That Cadillac belongs to a state senator. The police didn't treat this like they would an ordinary stolen car report.'

'Are we jinxed or what?'

'Just a bit of bad luck,' he said, but he was clearly unnerved by this development.

Across the aisle from the cookies were potato chips, corn chips, and other snack foods, just the stuff she tried to keep Joey away from. But now she put potato chips, cheese puffs, and Fritos in the cart. She did it partly because she wanted to cheer Joey up — but also because it seemed foolish to deny themselves anything when the time left to them might be very short.

'So now the cops aren't just looking for the LTD,' she said. 'They're looking for you, too.'

'There's worse,' he said, his voice little more than a whisper.

She stared at him, not sure she wanted to hear what he had to tell her. During the last couple of days, she'd had the feeling they were all caught in a vise. For the past few hours, the jaws of the vise had loosened a bit, but now Grace Spivey was turning the handle tight again.

He said, 'They found my Mercedes in the garage in Westwood. A phone tip sent them to it. In the trunk . . . they found a dead body.'

Stunned, Christine said, 'Who?'

'They don't know yet. A man. In his thirties. No identification. He'd been shot twice.'

'Spivey's people killed him and put him in your car?' she asked, keeping an eye on Joey as he checked out the toy guns at the end of the aisle.

'Yeah. That's what I figure. Maybe he was in the garage when they attacked us. Maybe he saw too much and had to be eliminated, and they realized they could use his body to put the police on my tail. Now Grace doesn't have just her thousand or two thousand followers out looking for us; she's got every cop in the state helping with the search.'

They were at a standstill now, speaking softly but intently, no longer pretending to be interested only in groceries.

'But surely the police don't think *you* killed him.'

'They have to assume I'm involved somehow.'

'But won't they realize it's related to the church, to that crazy woman —'

'Sure. But they might think the guy in my trunk is one of her people and that I've eliminated him. Or even if they do suspect I'm being framed, they've still got to talk to me. They've still got to put a warrant out for me.'

The whole world was after them now. It seemed hopeless. Like a toxic chemical, despair settled into her bones, leeching her strength. She just wanted to lie down, close her eyes, and sleep for a while.

Charlie said, 'Come on. Let's get the shopping done, take everything back to the motel, and then dump the car. I want to hole up inside before some cop spots our license plates or recognizes me.'

'Do you think the police know we headed for Santa Barbara after we left Ventura?'

'They can't know for sure. But they've got to figure we were running from L.A., moving north, so Santa Barbara's a good bet.'

As they went up and down the remaining aisles, as they checked out and paid for the groceries, Christine found it difficult to breathe. She felt as if a spotlight were trained on them. She kept waiting for sirens and alarms.

Joey became even more lethargic and solemn than before. He sensed that they were hiding something from him, and maybe it wasn't good to withhold the truth, but she decided it would be worse to tell him that the witch had burned down their house. That would convince him they were never going back, never going home again, which might be more than he could handle.

It was almost more than *she* could handle.

Because maybe it was the truth. Maybe they'd never be able to go home again.

44

Charlie drove the LTD into the motel lot, parked in the slot in front of their unit — and saw movement at the small window in the kitchenette. It might have been his imagination, of course. Or it might have been the maid. He didn't think it was either.

Instead of switching the engine off, he immediately threw the LTD into reverse and began backing out of the parking space.

Christine said, 'What's wrong?'

'Company,' he said.

'What? Where?'

In the rear seat, in a voice that was the essence of terror, Joey said, 'The witch.'

In front of them, as they backed away from it, the door to their unit began to open.

How the hell did they find us so soon? Charlie wondered.

Not wanting to waste the time required to turn the car around, he kept it in reverse and backed rapidly toward the avenue in front of the motel.

Out in the street, a white van appeared and swung to the curb, blocking the exit from the Wile-Away Lodge.

Charlie saw it in the rearview mirror, jammed on the brakes to avoid hitting it.

He heard gunfire. Two men with automatic weapons had come out of the motel room.

'Get down!'

Christine looked back at Joey. 'Get on the floor!' she told him.

'You too,' Charlie said, tramping on the accelerator again, pulling on the steering wheel, angling away from the van behind them.

She popped her seatbelt and crouched down, keeping her head below the windows.

If a bullet came through the door, she'd be killed anyway.

There wasn't anything Charlie could do about that. Except get the hell out of there.

Chewbacca barked, an ear-rupturing sound in the closed car.

Charlie reversed across the lot, nearly sideswiping a Toyota, clipping one corner of the wrought-iron fence that encircled the swimming pool. There was no other exit to the street, but he didn't care. He'd make an exit of his own. He drove backwards, over the sidewalk and over the curb. The undercarriage scraped, and Charlie prayed the fuel tank hadn't been torn open, and the LTD slammed to the pavement with a jolt. The engine didn't cut out. *Thank God*. His heart pounding as fast as the sedan's six cylinders, Charlie kept his foot on the accelerator, roaring backwards into State Street, tires screaming and smoking, nearly hitting a VW that was coming up the hill, causing half a dozen other vehicles to brake and wheel frantically out of his path.

The white Ford van pulled away from the motel exit, which it had been blocking, drove into the street again, and tried to ram them. The truck's grille looked like a big grinning mouth, a shark's maw, as it bore down on them. Two men were visible beyond the windshield. The van clipped the right front fender of the LTD, and there was a tortured cry of shredding metal, a shattering of glass as the car's right headlight was pulverized. The LTD rocked from the blow, and Joey cried out, and the dog bleated, and Charlie almost bit his tongue.

Christine started to rise to see what was happening, and Charlie shouted at her to stay down as he shifted gears and drove forward, east on State, swinging wide around the back of the white van. It tried to ram him in reverse, but he got past it in time. He expected the crumpled fender to obstruct the tire and eventually bring them to a stop, but it didn't. There were a few clanging-tinkling sounds as broken pieces of the car fell away, but there was no grinding noise of the sort that an impacted tire or an obstructed axle would make.

He heard more gunfire. Bullets thudded into the car, but none of them entered the passenger compartment. Then the LTD was moving fast, pulling out of range.

Charlie was grinding his teeth so hard that his jaws hurt, but he couldn't stop.

Ahead, at the corner, on the cross-street, another white Ford van appeared on their right, swiftly moving out from the shadows beneath a huge oak.

Jesus, they're everywhere!

The new van streaked toward the intersection, intent on blocking Charlie. To stay out of its way, he pulled recklessly into oncoming traffic. A Mustang swung wide of the LTD, and behind the Mustang a red Jaguar jumped the curb and bounced into the parking lot of a Burger King to avoid a collision.

The LTD had reached the intersection. The car was responding too sluggishly, though Charlie pressed the accelerator all the way to the floor.

From the right, the second van was still coming. It couldn't block him now; it was too late for that, so it was going to try to ram him instead.

277

Charlie was still in the wrong lane. The driver of an oncoming Pontiac braked too suddenly, and his car went into a slide. It turned sideways, came straight at them, a juggernaut.

Charlie eased up on the accelerator but didn't hit the brakes because he would lose his flexibility if he stopped completely and would only be delaying the moment of impact.

In a fraction of a second, he considered all his options. He couldn't swing left into the cross-street because it was crowded with traffic. He couldn't go right because the car was bearing down on him from that direction. He couldn't throw the van into reverse because there was lots of traffic behind him, and, besides, there was no time to shift gears and back up. He could only go forward as the Pontiac slid toward him, go forward and try to dodge the hurtling mass of steel that suddenly loomed as large as a mountain.

A strip of rubber peeled off one of the Pontiac's smoking tires, spun into the air, like a flying snake. In another fraction of a second, the situation changed: The Pontiac was no longer coming at him broadside, but was continuing to turn, turn, turn, until it had swiveled one hundred and eighty degrees from its original position. Now its back end pointed at the LTD, and, though it was still sliding, it was a smaller target than it had been. Charlie wrenched the steering wheel to the right, then left again, arcing around the careening Pontiac, which shrieked past with no more than an inch to spare.

The van rammed them. Fortunately, it caught only the last couple inches of the LTD. The bumper was torn off with a horrendous sound, and the whole car shuddered and was pushed sideways a couple of feet. The steering wheel abruptly had a mind of its own; it tore itself out of Charlie's grasp, spun through his clutching hands, burning

his palms, and he cried out in pain but got hold of it again.
Cursing, blinking back the tears of pain that briefly blurred
his vision, he got the car pointed eastward again, stood
on the accelerator, and kept going. When they were
through the intersection, he swung back into his own lane.
He hammered the horn, encouraging the car in front of
him to get out of his way.

The second white van — the one that had ripped away
their bumper — had gotten out of the mess at the
intersection and had followed them. At first it was two cars
back of them, then one; then it was right behind the LTD.

With the subsidence of gunfire, both Christine and Joey
sat up again.

The boy looked out the rear window at the van and said,
'It's the witch! I can see her! I can *see* her!'

'Sit down and put your seatbelt on,' Charlie told him.
'We might be making some sudden stops and turns.'

The van was thirty feet back but closing.

Twenty feet.

Chewbacca was barking again.

Belted in, Joey held the dog close and quieted it.

Traffic in front of them was closing up, slowing down.

Charlie checked the rearview mirror.

The van was only fifteen feet back of them.

Ten feet.

'They're going to ram us while we're moving,' Christine
said.

Barely touching the brakes, Charlie whipped the car to
the right, into a narrow cross-street, leaving the heavy
traffic and commercial development of State Street behind.
They were in an older residential neighborhood: mostly
bungalows, a few two-story houses, lots of mature trees,
cars parked on one side.

The van followed, but it dropped back a bit because it
couldn't make the turn as quickly as the LTD. It wasn't

DEAN R KOONTZ

as maneuverable as the car. That's what Charlie was counting on.

At the next corner he turned left, cutting his speed as little as possible, almost standing the LTD on two wheels, almost losing control in a wild slide, but somehow holding on, nearly clipping a car parked too close to the intersection. A block later he turned right, then left, then right, then right again, weaving through the narrow streets, putting distance between them and the van.

When they were not just one but *two* corners ahead of the van, when their pursuers could no longer see which way they were turning, Charlie stopped making random turns and began choosing their route with some deliberation, street by street, heading back toward State, then across the main thoroughfare and into the parking lot of another shopping center.

'We're not stopping here?' Christine said.

'Yeah.'

'But —'

'We've lost them.'

'For the moment, maybe. But they —'

'There's something I have to check on,' Charlie said.

He parked out of sight of the traffic on State Street, between two larger vehicles, a camper and a pickup truck.

Apparently, when the second white van had grazed the back of the LTD, tearing off the rear bumper, it had also damaged the exhaust pipe and perhaps the muffler. Acrid fumes were rising through the floorboards, into the car. Charlie told them to crank their windows down an inch or two. He didn't want to turn off the engine if he could help it; he wanted to be ready to move out at a moment's notice; but the fumes were just too strong, and he had to shut the car down.

Christine unhooked her seatbelt and turned to Joey. 'You okay, honey?'

280

The boy didn't answer.

Charlie looked back at him.

Joey was slumped down in the corner. His small hands were fisted tight. His chin was tucked down. His face was bloodless. His lips trembled, but he was too scared to cry, scared speechless, paralyzed with fear. At Christine's urging, he finally looked up, and his eyes were haunted, forty years too old for his young face.

Charlie felt sick and sad and weary at the sight of the boy's eyes and the tortured soul they revealed. He was also angry. He had the irrational urge to get out of the car right now, stalk back to State Street, find Grace Spivey, and put a few bullets in her.

The bitch. The stupid, crazy, pitiful, hateful, raving, disgusting old *bitch*!

The dog mewled softly, as if aware of its young master's state of mind.

The boy produced a similar sound and turned his eyes down to the dog, which put its head in his lap.

As if by magic, the witch had found them. The boy had said that you couldn't hide from a witch, no matter what you did, and now it seemed that he was correct.

'Joey,' Christine said, 'are you all right, honey? Speak to me, baby. Are you okay?'

Finally the boy nodded. But he still wouldn't — or couldn't — speak. And there was no conviction in his nod.

Charlie understood how the boy felt. It was difficult to believe that everything could have gone so terribly wrong in the span of just a few minutes.

There were tears in Christine's eyes. Charlie knew what she was thinking. She was afraid that Joey had finally snapped.

And maybe he had.

45

The churning black-gray clouds at last unleashed the pent-up storm that had been building all morning. Rain scoured the shopping center parking lot and pounded on the battered LTD. Sheet lightning pulsed across large portions of the dreary sky.

Good, Charlie thought, looking out at the water-blurred world.

The storm — especially the static caused by the lightning — gave them a little more cover. They needed all the help they could get.

'It has to be in here,' he said, opening Christine's purse, dumping the contents on the seat between them.

'But I don't see how it could be,' she said.

'It's the only place they could have hidden it,' he insisted, frantically stirring through the contents of the purse, searching for the most likely object in which a tiny transmitter might have been concealed. 'It's the only thing that's come with us all the way from L.A. We left behind the suitcases, my car . . . this is the only place it could've been hidden.'

'But no one could've gotten hold of my purse –'

'It might've been planted a couple of days ago, when you weren't suspicious or watchful, before all this craziness began,' he said, aware that he was grasping at straws, trying to keep his desperation out of his voice but not entirely succeeding.

If we aren't unwittingly carrying a transmitter, he thought, then how the hell did they find us so quickly? How the *hell*?

He looked out at the parking lot, turned and glanced out of the back window. No white vans. Yet.

Joey was staring out the side window. His lips were moving, but he wasn't making a sound. He looked wrung-out. A few raindrops slanted in through the narrow gap at the top of the window, struck the boy's head, but he didn't seem to notice.

Charlie thought of his own miserable childhood, the beatings he had endured at the hands of his father, the loveless face of his drunken mother. He thought about the other helpless children, all over the world, who became victims because they were too small to fight back, and a renewed, powerful current of anger energized him again.

He picked up a green malachite compact from the pile of stuff that had been in Christine's purse, opened it, lifted out the powder puff, took out the cake of powder, dropped them both in the litter bag that hung on the dashboard. He quickly examined the compact, but he couldn't see anything unusual about it. He hammered it against the steering wheel a couple of times, smashed it, examined the pieces, saw nothing suspicious.

Christine said, 'If we *have* been carrying a transmitter, something they've been able to home in on, it'd need a strong power source, wouldn't it?'

'A battery,' he said, taking apart her tube of lipstick.

'But surely it couldn't operate off a battery *that* small.'

'You'd be surprised what modern technology has made possible. Microminiaturization. You'd be surprised.'

Although all four of the windows were down an inch or two, letting in a bit of fresh air, the glass was steaming up. He couldn't see the parking lot, and that made him uneasy, so he started the engine again and switched on the defroster, in spite of the exhaust fumes that seeped in from the damaged muffler and tailpipe.

The purse contained a gold fountain pen and a Cross ballpoint. He took them both apart.

'But how far would something like that broadcast?' Christine asked.

'Depends on its sophistication.'

'More specifically?'

'A couple of miles.'

'That's all?'

'Maybe five miles if it was really good.'

'Not all the way to L.A.?'

'No.'

Neither of the pens was a transmitter.

Christine said, 'Then how'd they find us all the way up here in Santa Barbara?' While he carefully examined her wallet, a penlight, a small bottle of Excedrin, and several other items, he said, 'Maybe they have contacts in various police agencies, and maybe they learned about the stolen Caddy turning up in Ventura. Maybe they figured we were headed toward Santa Barbara, so they came up here and started cruising around, just hoping to strike it lucky, just driving from street to street in their vans, monitoring their receivers, until they got close enough to pick up the signal from the transmitter.'

'But we could have gone a hundred other places,' Christine said. 'I just don't see why they would've zeroed in on Santa Barbara so quickly.'

'Maybe they weren't just looking for us here. Maybe they had search teams working in Ventura and Ojai and a dozen other towns.'

'What are the odds of their finding us just by cruising around in a city this size, waiting to pick up our transmitter's signal?'

'Not good. But it could happen. It must have happened that way. How else would they find us?'

'The witch,' Joey said from the back seat. 'She has . . .

magic powers . . . witch powers . . . stuff like that.' Then
he lapsed into moody silence again, staring out at the rain.

Charlie was almost ready to accept Joey's childish
explanation. The old woman was inhumanly relentless and
seemed to possess an uncanny gift for tracking down her
prey. But of course it wasn't magic. There was a logical
explanation. A hidden, miniaturized transmitter made the
most sense. But whether it was a transmitter or something
else, they must figure it out, apply reason and common
sense until they found the answer, or they were never going
to lose the old bitch and her crazies.

The windows had unsteamed.

As far as Charlie could see, there were still no white vans
in the parking lot.

He had looked through everything in the purse without
finding the electronic device that he had been sure would
be there. He began to examine the purse itself, seeking
lumps in the lining.

'I think we should get moving again,' Christine said
nervously.

'In a minute,' Charlie said, using her nail file to rip out
the well-stitched seams in the handles of her purse.

'The exhaust fumes are making me sick,' she said.

'Open your window a little more.'

He found nothing but cotton padding inside the handles
of the purse.

'No transmitter,' she said.

'It's still got to be the answer.'

'But if not in my purse . . . where?'

'Somewhere,' he said, frowning.

'You said yourself that it *had* to be in the purse.'

'I was wrong. Somewhere else . . .' He tried to think.
But he was too worried about the white vans to think
clearly.

'We've got to get moving,' Christine said.

'I know,' he said.

He released the emergency brake, put the car in gear, and drove away from the shopping center, splashing through large puddles.

'Where now?' Christine asked.

'I don't know.'

46

For a while they drove aimlessly through Santa Barbara and neighboring Montecito, mostly staying away from main thoroughfares, wandering from one residential area to another, just keeping on the move.

Here and there, at an intersection, a confluence of overflowing gutters formed a lake that made passage difficult or impossible. The dripping trees looked limp, soggy. In the rain and mist, all the houses, regardless of color or style, seemed gray, drab.

Christine was afraid that Charlie had run out of ideas. Worse, she was afraid he had run out of hope. He didn't want to talk. He drove in silence, staring morosely at the storm-swept streets. Until now she hadn't fully realized how much she had come to depend upon his good humor, positive outlook, and bulldog determination. He was the glue holding her together. She never thought she would say such a thing about a man, any man, but she had to say it about Charlie: Without him, she would be lost.

Joey would speak when spoken to, but he didn't have much to say, and his voice was frail and distant like the voice of a ghost.

Chewbacca was equally lethargic and taciturn.

They listened to the radio, changing from a rock station to a country station, to one that played swing and other jazz. The music, regardless of type, sounded flat. The commercials were all ludicrous: When you were running from a pack of lunatics who wanted to kill you and your little boy, who cared whether one brand of motor oil, Scotch, blue jeans, or toilet tissue was better than another brand? The news was all weather, and none of it good: flooding in half a dozen towns between L.A. and San Diego; high waves smashing into the living rooms of expensive homes in Malibu; mud slides in San Clemente, Laguna Beach, Pacific Palisades, Montecito, and points north along the stormy coastline.

Christine's personal world had fallen apart, and now the rest of the world seemed dead set on following her example.

When Charlie finally stopped thinking and started talking, Christine was so relieved she almost wept.

He said, 'The main thing we've got to do is get away from Santa Barbara, find a safe place to hide out, and lie low until Henry can get the organization functioning again. We can't do anything to help ourselves until all my men are focused on Grace Spivey, putting pressure on her and on the others in that damned church.'

'So how do we get out of town?' she asked. 'This car's hot.'

'Yeah. Besides, it's falling apart.'

'Do we steal another set of wheels?'

'No,' he said. 'The first thing we need is cash. We're running out of money, and we don't want to use credit cards everywhere we go because that leaves a trail. Of course, it doesn't matter if we use cards *here* because they already know we're in Santa Barbara, so we'll start milking our plastic for all the cash in it.'

When at last Charlie swung into action, he moved with gratifying speed.

First they went to a telephone booth, searched the yellow pages, and made a note of the addresses of the nearest Wells Fargo and Security Pacific bank offices. In Orange County, Charlie had his accounts at the former, Christine at the latter.

At one Security Pacific office, Christine used her Visa card to get a cash advance of one thousand dollars, which was the maximum allowable. At another branch, she obtained a five-hundred-dollar advance on her Mastercard. At a third office, using her American Express Card she bought two thousand dollars worth of traveller's checks in twenty- and hundred-dollar denominations. Then, outside the same bank, she used her automatic teller card to obtain more cash. She was permitted to withdraw three hundred dollars at a time from the computerized teller, and she was allowed to make such withdrawals twice a day. Therefore, she was able to add six hundred bucks to the fifteen hundred that she had gotten from Visa and Mastercard. Counting the two thousand in traveller's checks, she had put together a bankroll of forty-one hundred dollars.

'Now let's see what I can add to that,' Charlie said, setting out in search of a Wells Fargo office.

'But this ought to be enough for quite a while,' she said.

'Not for what I've got in mind,' he said.

'What is it you've got in mind?'

'You'll see.'

Charlie always carried a blank check in his wallet. At the nearest Wells Fargo branch, after presenting an array of ID and after speaking at length with the manager, he withdrew $7,500 of the $8,254 in his personal checking account.

He was worried that the police might have informed his bank of the warrant for his arrest and that the Wells Fargo computer would direct any teller to call the authorities the moment he showed up to withdraw money. But luck was with him. The cops weren't moving quite as fast as Grace Spivey and her followers.

At other banks, he obtained cash advances on his Visa, Mastercard, Carte Blanche, and American Express cards.

Twice, in their travels back and forth across town, they saw police cruisers, and Charlie tried to duck out of their way. When it wasn't possible to duck, he held his breath, sure that the end had come, but they were not stopped. He knew they were swiftly running out of luck. At any moment a cop was going to notice their license plate number — or Spivey's people were going to make contact again.

Where was the transmitter if not in Christine's purse? There *had* to be a transmitter somewhere. It was the only explanation.

Minute by minute, his uneasiness grew until, at last, he found himself sheathed in a cold sweat.

By late afternoon, they had put together a kitty of more than fourteen thousand dollars.

Rain was still falling.

Darkness was settling in early.

'That's it,' Christine said. 'Even if there was some way to squeeze out a few hundred dollars more, the banks are all closed. So now what?'

They stopped at a small shopping center, where they bought a new purse for Christine, a briefcase in which Charlie could carry the neat stacks of cash they had amassed, and a newspaper.

A headline on the bottom half of the front page caught his attention: CULT LEADER SOUGHT IN WAKE OF ARSON, BOMBINGS.

He showed the story to Christine. Standing under an awning in front of a dress shop, they read the piece all the way through, while rain hissed and pattered and gurgled in the settling twilight. Their names – and Joey's were mentioned repeatedly, and the article said Charlie was wanted for questioning in a related homicide investigation, but fortunately there were no pictures.

'So the police aren't just looking for me,' Charlie said. 'They want to talk to Grace Spivey, too. That's some consolation, anyway.'

'Yeah, but they won't be able to pin anything on her,' Christine said. 'She's too slippery, too clever.'

'A witch isn't scared of cops,' Joey said grimly.

'Don't be pessimistic,' Charlie told them. 'If you'd seen her with those holes in her hands, if you'd heard her raving, you'd know she's teetering right on the edge. Wouldn't surprise me if she *bragged* about what she'd done next time the cops talk to her.'

Christine said, 'Listen, they're probably looking for her down in Orange County, or maybe in L.A., but not up here. Why don't we call the cops – anonymously, of course – and tell them she's in the neighborhood?'

'Excellent idea,' he said. He made the call from a pay phone and kept it brief. He spoke with a desk sergeant named Pulaski and told him that the incident at the Wile-Away Lodge, earlier in the day, had involved Grace Spivey and the Church of the Twilight. He described the white vans and warned Pulaski that the Twilighters were armed with automatic weapons. He hung up without answering any of the sergeant's questions.

When they were in the car once more, Charlie opened the paper to the classified ads, found the 'For Sale' section under the heading 'Automobiles,' and began reading.

The house was small but beautifully kept. It was a Cape Cod-style structure, unusual for California, pale blue with white shutters and white window frames. The lamps at the end of the walk and those on the porch pillars were brass ship's lamps with flame-shaped bulbs. It looked like a warm, snug haven against the storm and against all the other vicissitudes of life.

Charlie had a sudden longing for his own home, back in North Tustin. Belatedly, he felt the terrible impact of the news that Henry had given him this morning: His house, like Christine's, had been burned to the ground. He had told himself insurance would cover the loss. He had told himself there was no use crying over spilt milk. He had told himself that he had more important things to worry about than what he had lost in the fire. But now, no matter what he told himself, he could not dispel the dull ache that took possession of his heart. Standing here in the chilly February darkness, dripping rainwater, weary and worried, burdened by his responsibility for the safety of Christine and Joey (a crushing weight that grew heavier by the hour), he was overcome by a poignant yearning for his favorite chair, for the familiar books and furnishings of his den.

Stop it, he told himself angrily. There's no time for sentiment or self-pity. Not if we're going to stay alive.

His house was rubble.

His favorite chair was ashes.

His books were smoke.

With Christine, Joey, and Chewbacca, Charlie climbed the porch steps of the Cape Cod house and rang the bell.

The door was opened by a white-haired, sixtyish man in a brown cardigan sweater.

Charlie said, 'Mr. Madigan? I called a little while ago about – '

'You're Paul Smith,' Madigan said.

'Yes,' Charlie said.

'Come in, come in. Oh, you've got a dog. Well, just tie him up there on the porch.'

Looking past Madigan at the light beige carpet in the living room, Charlie said, 'Afraid we'll track up your carpet. Is that the station wagon there in the driveway?'

'That's it,' Madigan said. 'Wait a moment, and I'll get the keys.'

They waited in silence on the porch. The house was on a hill above Santa Barbara. Below, the city twinkled and shimmered in the darkness, beyond curtains of blowing rain.

When Madigan returned, he was wearing a raincoat, hood, and high-top galoshes. The amber light from the porch lamps softened the wrinkles in his face; if they had been making a movie and looking for a gentle grandfatherly type, Madigan would have been perfect casting. He assumed Christine and Joey were Charlie's wife and son, and he expressed concern about them being out in such foul weather.

'Oh, we're originally from Seattle,' Christine lied. 'We're used to duck weather like this.'

Joey had retreated even further into his private world. He didn't speak to Madigan, didn't smile when the old man teased him. However, unless you knew what an outgoing boy he usually was, his silence and solemnity seemed like nothing worse than shyness.

Madigan was eager to sell the Jeep wagon, though he didn't realize how obvious his eagerness was. He thought he was being cool, but he kept pointing out the low mileage (32,000), the like-new tires, and other attractive features.

After they had talked a while, Charlie understood the man's situation. Madigan had retired a year ago and had quickly discovered that Social Security and a modest pension were insufficient to support the lifestyle that he and his wife had maintained previously. They had two cars, a boat, the Jeep wagon, and two snowmobiles. Now they had to choose between boating and winter sports, so they were getting rid of the Jeep and snowmobiles. Madigan was bitter. He complained at length about all the taxes the government had sucked out of his pockets when he'd been a younger man. 'If they'd taken just ten percent less,' he said, 'I'd have had a pension that would've let me live like a king the rest of my life. But they took it and peed it away. Excuse me, Mrs. Smith, but that's exactly what they did: peed it away.'

The only light was from two lamps on the garage, but Charlie could see no visible body damage on the wagon, no sign of rust or neglect. The engine caught at once, didn't sputter, didn't knock.

'We can take it for a spin if you'd like,' Madigan said.

'That won't be necessary,' Charlie said. 'Let's talk a deal.'

Madigan's expression brightened. 'Come on in the house.'

'Still don't want to track up your carpet.'

'We'll go in by the kitchen door.'

They tied Chewbacca to one of the posts on the back porch, wiped their feet, shook the rain off their coats, and went inside.

The pale-yellow kitchen was cheery and warm.

Mrs. Madigan was cleaning and chopping vegetables on a cutting board beside the sink. She was gray-haired, round-faced, as much a Norman Rockwell type as her husband. She insisted on pouring coffee for Charlie and Christine, and she mixed up a cup of hot chocolate for Joey, who wouldn't speak or smile for her, either.

Madigan asked twenty percent too much for the Jeep, but Charlie agreed to the price without hesitation, and the old man had trouble concealing his surprise.

'Well . . . fine! If you come back tomorrow with a cashier's check—'

'I'd like to pay cash and take the Jeep tonight,' Charlie said.

'Cash?' Madigan said, startled. 'Well . . . um . . . I guess that'd be okay. But the paperwork—'

'Do you still owe the bank anything, or do you have the pink slip?'

'Oh, it's free and clear. I have the pink slip right here.'

'Then we can take care of the paperwork tonight.'

'You'll have to have an emissions test run before you'll be able to apply for registration in your name.'

'I know. I can handle that first thing in the morning.'

'But if there's some problem—'

'You're an honest man, Mr. Madigan. I'm sure you've sold me a first-rate machine.'

'Oh, it is! I've taken good care of her.'

'That's good enough for me.'

'You'll need to talk to your insurance agent—'

'I will. Meanwhile, I'm covered for twenty-four hours.'

The haste with which Charlie wanted to proceed, combined with the offer of cash on the spot, not only surprised Madigan but made him uneasy and somewhat suspicious. However, he was being paid eight or nine hundred more than he had expected to get, and that was enough to insure his cooperation.

Fifteen minutes later, they left in the Jeep wagon, and there was no way that Grace Spivey or the police could trace the sale to them if they didn't bother to file an application for registration.

Though rain was still falling, though an occasional soft pulse of lightning backlit the clouds, the night seemed less threatening than it had before they'd made their deal with Madigan.

'Why did it have to be a Jeep?' Christine asked as they found the freeway and drove north on 101.

'Where we're going,' Charlie said, 'we'll need four-wheel-drive.'

'Where's that?'

'Eventually . . . the mountains.'

'Why?'

'I know a place where we can hide until Henry or the police find a way to stop Grace Spivey. I'm part owner of a cabin in the Sierras, up near Tahoe.'

'That's so far away . . .'

'But it's the perfect place. Remote. It's a sort of time-sharing arrangement with three other owners. Each of us has several weeks there every year, and when none of us is using it, we rent it out. It was supposed to be a ski chalet, but it's hardly occupied during the worst of the winter because the road into it was never paved. It was planned to be the first of twenty chalets, and the county had promised to pave the road, but everything fell through after the first one was built. So now, there's still just a one-lane dirt track that's never plowed, and getting in there in the winter isn't easy. Bad investment, as it turned out, but now maybe I'll get my money's worth.'

'We keep running, running . . . I'm not used to running away from problems.'

'But there's nothing we can do here. It's all up to Henry and my other men. We've just got to stay out of sight, stay alive. And no one will ever look for us up in the mountains.'

From the back seat, in a low voice filled with weariness and resignation, Joey said, 'The witch will. She'll come after us. She'll find us. We can't hide from the witch.'

47

As usual, Grace could not sleep.

After leaving Santa Barbara and driving north for a while — ten of them in two white vans and one blue Oldsmobile — they had finally stopped at a motel in Soledad. They had lost the boy. Grace was certain he was still heading into the northern part of the state — she felt it in her bones — but she didn't know *where* in the north. She had to stop and wait for news — or holy guidance.

Before they checked into the motel, she had tried to put herself into a trance, and Kyle had done everything he could to help her, but she hadn't been able to break through the barrier between this world and the next. Something lay in her way, a wall she had never encountered before, a malignant and inhibiting force. She had been sure that Satan was there, in the back of the van, preventing her from entering the spirit realm. All her prayers had not been sufficient to dispel the devil and bring her close to God, as she had desired.

Defeated, they had stopped for the night at the motel and had taken dinner together in the coffee shop, most of them too weary and too scared to eat much or to talk. Then they had all gone to their separate rooms, like monks to cells, to pray and think and rest.

But sleep eluded Grace.

Her bed was firm and comfortable, but she was distracted by voices from the spirit realm. Even though she was not in a trance, they spoke to her from beyond, called out warnings that she could not quite understand, asked questions she could not quite discern. This was the first time since she had received the Gift that she was unable to commune with the spirit world, and she was both frustrated and afraid. She was afraid because she knew what this meant: The devil's power on earth was increasing rapidly; the Beast's confidence had grown to such an extent that he could now boldly interfere between Grace and her God.

Twilight was coming faster than expected.

The gates of Hell were swinging open.

Although she could no longer understand the spirit voices, although their cries were muffled and distorted, she detected an urgency in all of them, and she knew the abyss loomed ahead.

Maybe if she rested, got a little sleep, she would be stronger and better equipped to break through the barrier between this world and the next. But there was no rest. Not in these desperate times.

She had lost five pounds in the last few days, and her eyes stung from lack of sleep. She longed for sleep. But the incomprehensible spirit voices continued to assault her, a steady stream of them, a torrent, a flood of other-worldly messages. Their urgency infected her, pushed her to the brink of panic.

Time was running out. The boy was growing stronger.

Too little time to do all that was necessary.

Too little time. Maybe no time at all . . .

She was overwhelmed not only by voices but by visions, as well. As she lay in her bed, staring at the dark ceiling, the shadows abruptly came to life, and the folds of the night were transmuted into leathery black wings, and something hideous descended from the ceiling — *No!* — fell atop her, flapping and hissing, spitting in her face, something slimy and cold — *oh God, no, please!* — with breath that reeked of sulfur. She gagged and flailed and tried to cry out for help, but her voice failed her the way she had failed God. Her hands were pinned. She kicked. Her legs were pinned. She writhed. She bucked. Hard hands pawed at her. Pinched her. Struck her. An oily tongue lapped her face. She saw eyes of crimson fire glaring down at her, a grinning mouth full of viciously sharp teeth, a stoved-in nose, a nightmare visage that was partly human, partly porcine, partly like the face of a bat. She was finally able to speak but only in a whisper. She frantically called out some of the names of God, of saints, and those holy words had an effect on the shadow-demon; it shrank from her, and its eyes grew less bright, and the stench of its breath faded, and, mercifully, it rose from her, swooped up toward the ceiling, whirled away into a tenebrous corner of the room.

She sat up. Threw back the tangled covers. Scrambled to the edge of the bed. Reached for the nightstand lamp. Her hands were shaking. Her heart was hammering so hard that pain spread across her chest, and it seemed her breastbone would fracture. She finally switched on the bedside lamp. No demon crouched in the room. She turned on the other lamps, went into the bathroom.

The demon wasn't there, either.

But she knew it had been real, yes, terribly real, knew it wasn't just imagination or lunacy. Oh, yes. She knew. She knew the truth. She knew the awful truth –

– but what she *didn't* know was how she had gotten from the bathroom to the floor at the foot of the queen-size bed, where she next found herself. Apparently she had passed out in the bathroom and had crawled to the bed. But she couldn't remember anything. When she came to, she was naked, on her belly, weeping softly, clawing at the carpet.

Shocked, embarrassed, confused, she found her pajamas and pulled them on – and became aware of the serpent under the bed. Hissing. It was the most wicked sound she had ever heard. It slithered out from beneath the bed, big as a boa constrictor, but with the supremely evil head of a rattlesnake, the multi-faceted eyes of an insect, and venom-dripping fangs as big as hooked fingers.

Like the serpent in the Garden of Eden, this one spoke: 'Your God cannot protect you any more. Your God has abandoned you.'

She shook her head frantically: *no, no, no, no!*

With a sickening sinuosity, it coiled itself. Its head reared up. Its jaws fell open. It struck, biting her in the neck –

– and then, without knowing how she had come to be there, she found herself sitting, some time later, on a stool in front of the dresser mirror, staring into her own bloodshot, watery eyes. She shivered. Her eyes, even the flat reflection of them, contained something she didn't want to see, so she looked elsewhere in the mirror, at the reflection of her age-wrinkled throat, where she expected to find the mark of the serpent. There was no wound. Impossible. The mirror must be lying. She put one hand to her throat. She could not feel a wound, either. And she had no pain. The serpent hadn't bitten her, after all. Yet she remembered so clearly . . .

She noticed an ashtray in front of her. It was overflowing with cigarette butts. She was holding a smouldering cigarette in her right hand. She must have been sitting here an hour or more, smoking constantly, staring into the mirror – yet she couldn't remember any of it. What was happening to her?

She stubbed out the cigarette she'd been holding and looked into the mirror again, and she was shocked. She seemed to see herself for the first time in years. She saw that her hair was wild, frizzy, tangled, unwashed. She saw how sunken her eyes were, ringed with crepe-like flesh that had an unhealthy purplish tint. Her teeth, my God, they looked as if they hadn't been brushed in a couple of weeks;

they were yellow, caked with plaque! In addition to banishing sleep, the Gift had driven many other things out of her life; she was aware of that. However, until now, she hadn't been so painfully aware that the Gift — the visions, the trances, the communications with spirits — had caused her to *completely* neglect personal hygiene. Her pajamas were spotted with food and cigarette ashes. She raised her hands and looked at them with amazement. Her fingernails were too long, chipped, dirty. There were traces of dirt in her knuckles.

She had always valued cleanliness, neatness.

What would her Albert say if he could see her now?

For one devastating moment, she wondered if her daughter had been correct in having her hospitalized for psychiatric evaluation. She wondered if she was not a visionary after all, not a genuine religious leader, but simply a disturbed old woman, senile, plagued by bizarre hallucinations and delusions, deranged. Was the Scavello boy really the Antichrist? Or just an innocent child? Was Twilight actually coming? Or was her fear of the devil only a foolish old woman's demented fantasy? She was suddenly, gut-twistingly sure that her 'holy mission' was, in fact, merely the crusade of a pitiful schizophrenic.

No. She shook her head violently. *No!*

These despicable doubts were planted by Satan. This was her Gethsemane. Jesus had endured an agony of doubt in the Garden of Gethsemane, near the brook of Kedron. *Her* Gethsemane was in a more humble location: a nondescript motel in Soledad, California. But it was every bit as important a turning point for her as Jesus's experience in the garden had been for Him.

She was being tested. She must hold on to her faith in both God and herself. She opened her eyes. Looked in the mirror again. She still saw madness in her eyes. *No!*

She picked up the ashtray and threw it at her reflection,

smashing the mirror. Glass and cigarette butts rained over the dresser and the floor around it.

Immediately she felt better. The devil had been in the mirror. She had smashed the glass *and* the devil's hold on her. Self-confidence flooded into her once more.

She had a sacred mission.

She must not fail.

48

Charlie stopped at a motel shortly before midnight. They got one room with two king-size beds. He and Christine took turns sleeping. Although he was positive they couldn't have been followed, although he felt safer tonight than he had felt last night, he now believed that a watch must be kept at all times.

Joey slept fitfully, repeatedly waking from nightmares, shivering in a cold sweat. In the morning he looked paler than ever, and he spoke even less than before.

The rain had subsided to a light drizzle.

The sky was low, gray, bleak, and ominous.

After breakfast, when Charlie pointed the station wagon north again, toward Sacramento, Christine rode in the back seat with the boy. She read to him from some of the story books and comics they had bought yesterday. He listened but asked no questions, showed little interest, never smiled. She tried to engage him in a card game, but he didn't want to play.

Charlie was increasingly worried about Joey, increasingly frustrated and angry, too. He had promised to protect them and put a stop to Spivey's harassment. Now all he could do for them was help them run, tails between their legs, toward an uncertain future.

Even Chewbacca seemed depressed. The dog lay in the cargo area behind the rear seat, rarely stirring, rising only a few times to look out one of the windows at the soot-colored day, then slumping back down, out of sight.

They arrived in Sacramento before ten o'clock in the morning, located a large sporting goods store, and bought a lot of things they would need for the mountains: insulated sleeping bags in case the heating system in the cabin was not strong enough to completely compensate for winter's deep-freeze temperatures; rugged boots; ski suits — white for Joey, blue for Christine, green for Charlie; gloves; tinted goggles to guard against snow-blindness; knitted toboggan caps; snowshoes; weatherproof matches in watertight cans; an ax; and a score of other items. He also bought a Remington .20-gauge shotgun, and a Winchester Model 100 automatic rifle chambered for a .308 cartridge, which was a light but powerful weapon; he stocked up on plenty of ammunition, too.

He was sure Spivey wouldn't find them in the mountains.

Positive.

But just in case . . .

After a quick and early lunch at McDonalds, Charlie connected the electronic tap detector to a pay phone and called Henry Rankin. The line wasn't bugged, and Henry didn't have much news. The Orange County and Los Angeles papers were still filled with stuff about the Church of the Twilight. The cops were still looking for Grace Spivey. They were still looking for Charlie, too, and they were getting impatient; they were beginning to suspect he hadn't turned himself in because he actually was guilty of the murder about which they wanted to question him. They couldn't understand that he was avoiding them because

Spivey might have followers within the police department; they refused even to consider such a possibility. Meanwhile, Henry was busy getting the company back on its feet and was, for the time being, headquartering the agency in his own house. By tomorrow they would again be working fullsteam on the Spivey case.

At a service station, they used the rest rooms to change into the winter clothing they had purchased. The mountains were not far away.

In the Jeep wagon once more, Charlie headed east toward the Sierras, while Christine continued to sit in back, reading to Joey, talking to him, trying hard — but without much success — to draw him out of his shell.

The rain stopped.

The wind grew stronger.

Later, there were snow flurries.

49

Mother Grace rode in the Oldsmobile. Eight disciples followed in the two white vans. They were on Interstate 5 now, in the heart of California's farm country, passing between immense flat fields, where crops flourished even in the middle of winter.

Kyle Barlowe drove the Olds, now anxious and edgy, now bored and drowsy, sometimes oppressed by the tedium of the long drive and the rain-grayed landscape.

Although the church's sources of information — in various police departments and elsewhere — had no news about Joey Scavello and his mother, they headed north from Soledad because Grace said the boy and his protectors had gone that way. She claimed to have received a vision in the night.

Barlowe was pretty sure she'd had no vision and that she was just guessing. He knew her too well to be fooled. He understood her moods. If she'd really had a vision, she would be . . . euphoric. Instead, she was sullen, silent, grim. He suspected she was at a loss but didn't want to tell them that she was no longer in contact with the spirit world.

He was worried. If Grace had lost the ability to talk with God, if she could not journey to the other side to commune with angels and with the spirits of the dead, did that mean she was no longer God's chosen messenger? Did it mean that her mission no longer had His blessing? Or did it mean that the devil's power on earth had grown so dramatically that the Beast could interfere between Grace and God? If the latter were true, Twilight was very near, and the Antichrist would soon reveal himself, and a thousand-year reign of evil would begin.

He glanced at Grace. She was staring ahead, through the rain, at the arrow-straight highway, lost in thought. She looked older than she had last week. She had aged ten years in a few days. She seemed positively ancient. Her skin looked lifeless, brittle, gray.

Her face wasn't the only thing that was gray. All her clothes were gray, too. For reasons Barlowe didn't fully understand, she always dressed in a single color; he thought it had a religious significance, something to do with her visions, but he wasn't sure. He was accustomed to her monochromatic costumes, but this was the first time he had ever seen her in gray. Yellow, blue, fire-red, apple-red, blood-red, green, white, purple, violet, orange, pink, rose – yes, she had worn all of those, but always bright colors, never anything as somber as this.

She hadn't *expected* to dress in gray; this morning, after

leaving the motel, they'd had to go shopping to buy her gray shoes, gray slacks, a gray blouse and sweater because she had owned no gray clothes. She had been in great distress, almost hysterical, until she'd changed into a completely gray outfit. 'It's a gray day in the spirit world,' she had said. 'The energy is all gray. I'm not synchronized. I'm not in tune, not in touch. I've got to get in touch!' She had wanted jewelry, too, because she liked jewelry a lot, but it wasn't easy to find gray rings and bracelets and brooches. Most jewelry was bright. She'd finally had to settle for just a string of gray beads. Now it was odd to see her without a single ring on her pale, leathery hands.

A gray day in the spirit world.

What did that mean? Was that good or bad?

Judging from Grace's demeanor, it was bad. Very bad. Time was running out. That's what Grace had said this morning, but she hadn't been willing to elaborate. Time was running out, and they were lost, driving north on just a hunch.

He was scared. He still worried that it would be a terrible thing for him to kill anyone, that it would be backsliding into his old ways, even if he was doing it for God. He was proud of himself for resisting the violent impulses which he had once embraced, proud of the way he had begun to fit into society, just a little bit, and he was afraid that one murder would lead to another. Was it right to kill — even for God? He knew that was wrong-thought, but he couldn't shake it. And sometimes, when he looked at Grace, he had the unsettling notion that perhaps he had been wrong about her all along, that perhaps she wasn't God's agent — and that was *more* wrong-thought. The thing was . . . Grace had taught him that there were such things as moral values, and now he could not avoid applying them to everything he did.

Anyway, if Grace *was* right about the boy — and surely

she was — then time was running out, but there was nothing to be done but drive, wait for her to regain contact with the spirit world, and call the church in Anaheim once in a while to learn if there was any news that might help.

Barlowe put his foot down a little harder on the accelerator. They were already doing over seventy, which was maybe about as fast as they ought to push it in the rain, even on this long straight highway. But they were Chosen, weren't they? God *was* watching over them, wasn't He? Barlowe accelerated until the needle reached 80 on the speedometer. The two vans accelerated behind him, staying close.

50

The Jeep wagon was, as Madigan had promised, in fine shape. It gave them no trouble at all, and they reached Lake Tahoe on Thursday afternoon.

Christine was weary, but Joey had perked up a bit. He was showing some interest in the passing scene, and that was a welcome change. He didn't seem any happier, just more alert, and she realized that, until today, he had never seen snow before, except in magazine pictures, on TV, and in the movies. There was plenty of snow in Tahoe, all right. The trees were crusted and burdened with it; the ground was mantled with it. Fresh flurries sifted down from the steely sky, and according to the news on the radio, the flurries would build into a major storm during the night.

The lake, which straddled the state line, was partly in California and partly in Nevada. On the California side of the town of South Lake Tahoe, there were a great many motels – some of them surprisingly shabby for such a lovely and relatively expensive resort area – lots of touristy shops and liquor stores and restaurants. On the Nevada side, there were several large hotels, casinos, gambling in just about every form, but not as much glitz as in Las Vegas. Along the northern shore, there was less development, and the man-made structures were better integrated with the land than they were along the southern shore. On both sides of the border, and both in the north and south, there was some of the most beautiful scenery on the face of the earth, what many Europeans have called 'America's Switzerland': snow-capped peaks that were dazzling even on a cloudy day; vast, primeval forests of pine, fir, spruce, and other evergreens; a lake that, in its ice-free summer phase, was the cleanest, clearest, and most colorful in the world, iridescent blues and glowing greens, a lake so pure you could see the bottom as far as sixty and eighty feet down.

They stopped at a market on the north shore, a large but rustic building shadowed by tamarack and spruce. They still had most of the groceries they'd bought in Santa Barbara yesterday, the stuff they'd never had a chance to put in the refrigerator and cupboards at the Wile-Away Lodge. They'd disposed of the perishables, of course, and that was what they stocked up on now: milk, eggs, cheese, ice cream, and frozen foods of all kinds.

At Charlie's request, the cashier packed the frozen food in a sturdy cardboard box with a lid, separate from the goods that were not frozen. In the parking lot, Charlie carefully poked a few holes in the box. He had purchased nylon clothesline in the market, and with Christine's assistance, he threaded the rope through the holes and looped it around the box and secured it to the luggage rack on top of the Jeep. The temperature was below freezing; nothing carried on the roof would thaw on the way to the cabin.

As they worked (with Chewbacca watching interestedly from inside the Jeep), Christine noticed that a lot of the cars in the market lot were fitted with ski racks. She had always wanted to learn to ski. She often promised herself that she would take lessons with Joey one day, the two of them beginning and learning together, just as soon as he seemed old enough. It would have been fun. Now it was probably just one more thing they would never get to do together . . .

That was a damned grim thought. Uncharacteristically grim.

She knew she had to keep her spirits up, if only for Joey's sake. He would see her pessimism and would crawl away even deeper into the psychological hole he seemed to be digging for himself.

But she couldn't shake off the gloom that weighed her down. Her spirits had sunk, and there seemed to be no way to get them afloat again.

She told herself to enjoy the crisp, clean mountain air. But it just seemed painfully, bitingly cold. If a wind sprang up, the weather would be insufferable.

She told herself that the snow was beautiful and that she should enjoy it. It looked wet, cold, and forbidding.

She looked at Joey. He was standing beside her, watching as Charlie tied the final knot in the clothesline. He was more like a little old man than a child. He didn't make a snowball. He didn't stick out his tongue and catch snowflakes. He didn't run and slide on the icy portions of the parking lot. He didn't do any of the things a small boy could be expected to do when setting foot on a snow landscape for the first time in his life.

He's just tired, and so am I, Christine told herself. It's been a long day. Neither of us has had a restful night since last Saturday. Once we've had a good supper, once we've each gotten eight solid hours in the sack without nightmares and without waking up a dozen times to the imagined sound of footsteps . . . *then* we'll feel better. Sure we will. Sure.

But she couldn't convince herself either that she would feel better tomorrow or that their circumstances would improve. In spite of all the distance they'd driven and the remoteness of the haven toward which they were making their way, she did not feel safe. It wasn't just that there were a couple of thousand religious fanatics who, more than anything else, wanted them dead. That was bad enough. But there was also something curiously suffocating about the huge trees rising on all sides and pressing close from every direction, something claustrophobic about the way the mountains walled them in, an indefinable menace in the stark shadows and the gray winter light of this high fastness. She would never feel safe here.

But it wasn't just the mountains. She wouldn't have felt safer anywhere else.

They left the main road that circled the lake, turned onto a two-lane blacktop that rose up a series of steep slopes, past expensive homes and getaway chalets that were tucked back in among the densely packed and massive trees. If there hadn't been light in those houses, glowing warmly in the purple-black shadows beneath the trees, you wouldn't have known most of them were there. Even on the day-side of eventide, lights were needed here.

Snow was piled high on both sides of the road, and in some places new drifts reduced traffic to a single lane. Not that there were many other vehicles around: They passed only two − another Jeep Wagon with a plow on the front, and a Toyota Land Rover.

Near the end of the paved road, Charlie decided it would be a good idea to put the chains on the tires. Although a plow had been through recently, the drifts were inching farther across the pavement here than on the lower slopes, and there were bigger patches of ice. He pulled into a driveway, which ran across the face of the mountain and was level, stopped, and got the chains from the back. He required twenty minutes to complete the job, and he was unhappily aware of how fast the sunlight was fading from behind the snow-spitting clouds.

With chains clanking, they drove on, and soon the paved road ended in a one-lane dirt track. This, too, was plowed for the first half mile, but because it was narrower than the lower road, it tended to drift shut faster. Nevertheless, slowly but steadily, the Jeep clawed its way upward.

Charlie didn't attempt to keep a conversation going. There was no point in making the effort. Ever since they'd left Sacramento earlier in the day, Christine had become steadily less communicative. Now, she was almost as silent and withdrawn as Joey.

He was dismayed by the change in her, but he understood why she was having difficulty staving off depression. The mountains, which usually conveyed an uplifting feeling of openness and freedom, now seemed paradoxically restraining, oppressive. Even when they passed through a broad meadow and the trees fell back from the roadway, the mood of the landscape didn't change.

Christine was probably wondering if coming here had been a serious mistake.

Charlie was wondering, too.

But there had been nowhere else to go. With Grace's people looking for them, with the police searching for them throughout California, unable to trust the authorities or even Charlie's employees, they hadn't much choice but to go to ground in a place where no one would spot them, which meant a place with few people.

Charlie told himself that they had done the wisest thing,

that they had been cautious in the purchase of the Jeep, that they had planned well and had moved with admirable speed and flexibility, that they were in control of their destiny. They would probably be here only a week or so, until Grace Spivey was brought to heel either by his own men or the police.

But in spite of what he told himself, he felt as if they were out of control, fleeing in near-panic. The mountain seemed not a haven but a trap. He felt as if they had walked out on a gangplank.

He tried to stop thinking about it. He knew he wasn't being entirely rational. For the moment, his emotions had the upper hand. Until he could think calmly again, it was best to put Grace Spivey out of his mind as much as possible.

There were considerably fewer houses and cabins along the dirt lane than there had been along the paved road, and after a third of a mile there were none visible at all.

At the end of the first half mile the dirt road was no longer plowed. It vanished under several feet of snow. Charlie stopped the Jeep, pulled on the emergency brake, and switched off the engine.

'Where's the cabin?' Christine asked.

'Half a mile from here.'

'What now?'

'We walk.'

'In snowshoes?'

'Yep. That's why we bought 'em.'

'I've never used them before.'

'You can learn.'

'Joey—'

'We'll take turns carrying him. Then he can stay at the cabin while you and I come back for—'

'Stay there by himself?'

'He'll have the dog, and he'll be perfectly safe. Spivey

can't have known we were coming here; she's not around anywhere.'

Joey didn't object. He didn't even appear to hear what they'd said. He was staring out the window, but he couldn't be looking at anything because the glass was fogged by his breath.

Charlie got out of the station wagon and winced as the winter air bit at his face. It had grown considerably colder since they had left the market down by the lake. The snowflakes were enormous and falling faster than before. They spun down from the lowering sky on a gently shifting breeze that became a little less gentle, more insistent, even as he paused for a moment to look around at the forest. The trees shouldered against one another and seemed to be crouching, ready to pounce, at the edges of the meadow.

For some reason he thought of an old fairytale: *Little Red Riding Hood*. He could still remember the spooky illustration in the storybook he'd had when he'd been a child, a picture of Red making her way through a gloomy, wolf-haunted forest.

That made him think of Hansel and Gretel, lost in the woods.

And *that* made him think of witches.

Witches who baked children in ovens and ate them.

Jesus, he had never realized how gruesome some fairytales were!

The snowflakes had grown slightly smaller and were falling faster by the second.

Softly, softly, the wind began to howl.

Christine was surprised by how quickly she learned to walk in the cumbersome snowshoes, and she realized how difficult – and perhaps impossible – the journey would have been without them, especially with the heavy backpacks they carried. In some places, the wind had almost scoured the meadow bare, but in other places, wherever the land presented even the slightest wind-break, drifts had piled up eight, ten, or twelve feet deep, even deeper. And of course snow had filled in every gully and hole and basin in the land. If you were to attempt to cross an unseen depression without snowshoes, you might find yourself sinking down into a deep well of snow out of which it would be difficult or impossible to climb.

The gray afternoon light, which had a disconcerting artificial quality, played tricks with snow-glare and shadow, giving a false sense of distance, distorting shapes. Sometimes it even caused a mounting ridge of snow to look like a depression until she reached it and realized she must climb instead of descend as she'd expected.

Joey found it more difficult to adapt to snowshoes than she did, even though he had a small pair suitable for a child. Because the day was fast fading and because they didn't want to finish unloading the Jeep entirely in the dark, they didn't have time for him to learn snowshoeing right now. Charlie picked him up and carried him.

Chewbacca was a big dog but still light enough so he didn't break through the crust on top of the snow. He also had an instinct for avoiding places where the crust was thin or nonexistent, and he could often find his way around the deepest snow, moving from one wind-scoured spot to another. Three times he sank in; once he was able to dig his way up and out by himself, but twice he had to be helped.

From the abandoned Jeep, they went up a slope for three hundred yards, until they reached the end of the meadow. They followed the snow-hidden road into the trees, bearing right along the top of a broad ridge, with a table of forested land on their right and a tree-choked valley on their left. Even though nightfall was still perhaps an hour away, the valley dropped down through shades of gray and blue and purple, finally into blackness, and there were no spots of light down there, so she supposed there were no dwellings.

By now she knew that Charlie was a considerably more formidable man than either his size or general appearance would indicate, but she was nevertheless surprised by his stamina. Her own backpack was beginning to feel like a truckload of cement blocks, but though Charlie's pack was bigger and heavier than hers, he did not seem to be bothered by it. In addition, he carried Joey without complaint and stopped only once in the first quarter-mile to put the boy down and relieve cramping muscles.

After a hundred yards, the road angled away from the rim of the valley, moving across the mountain instead of uphill, but then turned and sloped upward again in another fifty yards. The trees became thicker and bigger and bushier, and in places the sheltered lane was so deep in shadow that night might as well have come already. In time they arrived at the foot of another meadow, broader than the one where they'd parked the Jeep, and about four hundred yards long.

'There's the cabin!' Charlie said, the words bursting out of him with plumes of crystallized breath.

Christine didn't see it.

He stopped, put Joey down again, and pointed. 'There. At the far end, just in front of the tree line. There's a windmill beside it.'

She saw the windmill first because her eye caught the movement of the spinning blades. It was a tall, skeletal mill, nothing picturesque about it, more like an oil derrick than anything a Dutchman would recognize, very businesslike and somewhat ugly.

Both the cabin and the mill blended well with the trees behind them, although she supposed they would be more visible earlier in the day.

'You didn't tell me there was a windmill,' she said. 'Does that mean electric light?'

'Sure does.' His cheeks, nose, and chin were pink from the cold, and he sniffed to clear a runny nose. 'And plenty of hot water.'

'Electric heat?'

'Nope. There's a limit to what a power mill can provide, even in a place as windy as this.'

The jacket snap at Joey's throat had come undone, and his scarf was loose. Christine stooped to make adjustments. His face was more red than pink, and his eyes were tearing from the cold.

'We're almost there, Skipper.'

He nodded.

After catching their breath, they started uphill once more, with Chewbacca bounding ahead as if he understood that the cabin was their final destination.

The place was constructed of redwood that had silvered slightly in the harsh weather. Though the cedar-shingled roof was steeply sloped, some snow clung to it anyway. The windows were frosted. Snow had drifted over the front steps and onto the porch.

They took off their snowshoes and gloves.

Charlie retrieved a spare key from a cleverly hidden recess in one of the porch posts. Ice cracked away from the door as he pulled it open, and the frozen hinges squealed briefly.

They went inside, and Christine was surprised by how lovely the cabin was. The downstairs consisted of one enormous room, with a kitchen occupying the far end, a long pine dining table just this side of the kitchen, and then a living area with a polished oak floor, braided rag rugs, comfortable dark green sofas and armchairs, brass lamps, paneled walls, draperies in a Scottish-plaid pattern that was dominated by greens to complement the sofas and chairs, and a massive rock fireplace almost as big as a walk-in closet. Half the downstairs was open all the way to the second-floor ceiling, and was overlooked by a gallery. Up there, three closed doors led to three other rooms: 'Two bedrooms and a bath,' Charlie said. The effect was rustic yet quite civilized.

A tiled area separated the front door from the oak floor of the living room, and that was where they removed their snow-crusted boots. Then they took an inspection tour of the cabin. There was some dust on the furniture, and the air smelled musty. There was no electricity because the breakers were all thrown in the fuse box, which was out in the battery room below the windmill, but Charlie said he would go out there and remedy the situation in a few minutes. Beside each of the three fireplaces – the big one in the living room and a smaller one in each of the bedrooms – were stacks of split logs and kindling, which Charlie used to start three fires. All the fireplaces were equipped with Heatolators, so the cabin would be reasonably warm even in the bitter heart of winter.

'At least no one's broken in and wrecked things,' he said.

'Is that a problem?' Christine asked.

'Not really. During the warmer months, when the road's open all the way, there's nearly always somebody staying here. When the road is snowed shut and there's no one here to look after the place, most would-be looters wouldn't even know there was a cabin this far into the woods. And the ones who *do* know . . . well . . . they probably figure the trek isn't worth what little they'd find to carry away. Still, first time you arrive each spring, you wonder if you're going to discover the place has been wrecked.'

The fires were building nicely, and the vents of the Heatolator in the downstairs mantel were spewing welcome draughts of warm air into the big main room.

Chewbacca had already settled down on the hearth there, head on his paws.

'Now what?' Christine asked.

Opening one of the backpacks and removing a flashlight from it, Charlie said, 'Now you and Joey take everything out of these bags while I go and see about getting us some electricity.'

She and Joey carried the backpacks into the kitchen while Charlie pulled his boots on again. By the time he had gone out to the windmill, they were stashing canned goods in the cabinets, and it almost seemed as if they were an ordinary family on an ordinary skiing holiday, getting settled in for a week of fun. Almost. She tried to instill a holiday mood in Joey by whispering happy songs and making little jokes and pretending that she was actually going to enjoy this adventure, but either the boy saw through her charade or he wasn't even paying attention to her, for he seldom responded and never smiled.

With the monotonous humming-churning of the windmill's propellers above him, Charlie used a shovel to clear the snow from the wooden doors that protected the steps that led down to the room under the windmill. He descended the two flights of steps that went rather deeply into the ground; the battery room was below the frost line. When he reached the bottom, he was in a hazy-blue darkness that robbed the whiteness from the snowflakes sifting down around him, so they looked as if they were bits of gray ash. He took the flashlight from his coat pocket and snapped it on. A heavy metal door stood in front of him. The cabin key worked this lock, too, and in a moment he was in the battery room, where everything appeared to be in order: cables; twenty heavy-duty, ten-year storage batteries lined up side by side on two sturdy benches; a concrete pallet holding all the machinery; a rack of tools.

A foul odor assaulted him, and he immediately knew the cause of it, knew he would have to deal with it, but first he went to the fuse box and pushed all the breakers from OFF to ON. That done, the wall switch by the door brought light to the two long fluorescent bulbs in the ceiling. The light revealed three dead, decaying mice, one in the middle of the room, the other two in the corner by the first battery bench.

It was necessary to leave tins of poisoned bait here, especially during the winter when mice were most likely to come seeking shelter, for if the rodents were left to their own devices they would eat the insulation from all the cables and wires, leaving a ruined electrical system by the time spring arrived.

The mouse in the middle of the small chamber had been dead a long time. The process of decomposition had pretty much run its course in the tiny corpse. There were bones, fur, scraps of leathery skin, little else.

The two in the corner were more recent casualties. The small bodies were bloated and putrescent. Their eye sockets were alive with squirming maggots. They had been dead only a few days.

Queasy, Charlie went outside, got the shovel, returned, scooped up all three of the creatures, took them out to the woods behind the mill, and pitched them off into the trees. Even when he had disposed of them, even though a blustery wind was huffing up the mountainside and scrubbing the world clean as it passed, Charlie couldn't get the stink of death out of his nostrils. Oddly, the smell stayed with him all the way back to the battery room, where, of course, it still hung on the damp musty air. He didn't have time for a really thorough inspection of the equipment, but he wanted to give it a quick once-over to be sure the mice had died before they had done any serious damage. The wires and cables were lightly nibbled in a few places, but there didn't seem to be any reason to worry that they'd lose their lights to rodent sabotage.

He had almost satisfied himself as to the system's integrity when he heard a strange, threatening noise behind him.

51

The day was melting into darkness. Color was seeping out of the landscape through which they drove, leaving the trees and hills and everything else as gray as the surface of the highway.

Kyle Barlowe switched on the headlights and hunched over the steering wheel of the Oldsmobile, grinning.

Now. Now they had something real to go on. Now they had a solid lead. Information. A logical plan. They weren't just going on a hunch and a prayer any more. They were no longer driving blind, heading north merely because it seemed like a good idea. They knew where the boy was, where he *must* be. *Now* they had a destination, and now Barlowe was beginning to believe in Mother Grace's leadership again.

She was in the seat beside him, slumped against the door, briefly lost in one of those short but mile-deep sleeps that came to her with decreasing frequency. Good. She needed her rest. The confrontation was coming. The showdown. When they were face to face with the devil, she would need all the energy she could muster.

And if Grace *wasn't* God's messenger, why had this vital information been conveyed to them? This proved she was right, meant well, told the truth, and should be obeyed.

For the moment his doubts had receded.

Barlowe looked in the rearview mirror. The two vans were still behind him. Crusaders. Crusaders on wheels instead of horseback.

52

When Charlie heard the strange noises behind him, he dropped into a defensive crouch as he turned. He expected to see Grace Spivey standing in the doorway to the battery room, but the disturbance had no human source. It was a rat.

The filthy thing was between him and the doorway, but he was sure it hadn't come in from the snow because part of what he had heard was the thump it made as it scurried out from under some machine. It was hissing, squeaking, glaring at him with bloody eyes, as if threatening to prevent his escape.

It was a damned big rat, but in spite of its size, which indicated that it had once been well fed, it didn't look healthy now. Its pelt wasn't smooth, but oily and matted and dull. There was something dark and crusted at its ears, probably blood, and there was bloody foam dripping from its mouth. It had been the poison. Now, pain-wracked and delirious, it might be a bold and vicious opponent.

And there was another, even less pleasant possibility to consider. Maybe it *hadn't* been the poison. Maybe the foam at its mouth was an indication of rabies. Could rodents carry rabies just as easily as dogs and cats? Every year in the California mountains, the state's vector control officers turned up a few rabid animals. Sometimes, portions of state parks were even put off limits until it could be ascertained whether there was a rabies epidemic.

This rat was most likely affected by the poison, not rabies. But if he was wrong, and if the rat bit him . . .

He wished he had brought the shovel back into the battery room after disposing of the three dead mice. He had no weapon except his revolver, and that was too powerful for this small job, like going hunting for pheasant with a cannon.

He straightened up from his crouch, and his movement agitated the rat. It came at him.

He jumped back against the wall.

It was coming fast, screeching. If it ran up his leg—

He kicked, catching it squarely with the reinforced toe of his boot. The kick threw it across the room, and it struck the wall, shrieking, and dropped to the floor on its back.

Charlie reached the door and was through it before the rat got on its feet. He climbed the stairs, picked up the shovel that was leaning against the base of the mill, and went back down.

The rat was just inside the open door to the battery room. It was making a continuous racket, a wailing-hissing-whining noise that Charlie found bone-chilling. It rushed him again.

He swung the shovel like a mallet, struck the rat, again, a third time, until it stopped making noise, then looked at it, saw it quivering, struck it again, harder, and then it was still and silent, obviously dead, and he slowly lowered the shovel, breathing hard.

How could a rat that size have gotten into the closed battery room?

Mice, yes, that was understandable, because mice needed only the smallest chink or crevice to get inside. But this rat was bigger than a dozen mice; it would require a hole at least three or four inches in diameter, and because the ceiling of the small room was of reinforced concrete, the walls of cinder block and mortar, there was no way the beast could have chewed open an entrance. And the door to the room was metal, inviolable and unviolated.

Could it have been locked in this past autumn, when the last vacationers closed up the place, or when the real estate management firm had come up to 'winterize' the cabin? No. It would have eaten the poison bait and would have been dead months ago. It had been poisoned recently; therefore, it had only recently gotten into the battery room.

He circled the chamber, searching for the rat's passage, but all he found were a couple of small chinks in the mortar where a mouse — but never anything larger — might have squirmed through after first gaining access to the air space between the double-thick block walls.

It was a mystery, and as he stood staring at the dead rat, he had the creepy feeling that the brief and violent encounter between him and this disgusting creature was more than it appeared to be, that it *meant* something, that the rat was a symbol of something. Of course, he had grown up with the terror of rats, which had infested the shack in which he had spent his childhood, so they would always have a powerful effect on him. And he couldn't help thinking of old horror comics and horror movies in which there'd been scenes in ancient graveyards with rats skulking about. Death. That's what rats usually symbolized. Death, decay, the revenge of the tomb. So maybe this was an omen. Maybe it was a warning that death — in the form of Grace Spivey — was going to come after them up here on the mountain, a warning to be prepared.

He shook himself. No. He was letting his imagination run away with him. Like in his office, on Monday, when he'd looked at Joey and thought he had seen only a bare skull where the boy's face should have been. That had been imagination — and this, too. He didn't believe in such things as omens. Death wouldn't find them here. Grace Spivey wouldn't discover where they had gone. Couldn't. Not in a thousand years.

Joey was not going to die.

The boy was safe.

They were all safe.

Christine didn't want to leave Joey alone in the cabin while she and Charlie returned to the Jeep for more of their supplies. She knew Grace Spivey wasn't near. She knew the cabin was safe, that nothing would happen in the short time she was gone. Nevertheless, she was terrified that they would find her little boy dead when they got back.

But Charlie couldn't carry everything by himself; it was wrong of her to expect him to do it. And Joey couldn't come along because he would slow them down too much now that the last of the daylight was rapidly fading and the storm was getting dangerously fierce. She had to go, and Joey had to stay. No choice.

She told herself it might even be good for him to be left alone with Chewbacca for a while, for it would be a demonstration of her and Charlie's confidence in the safety of their chosen hiding place. He might gain some self-assurance and hope from the experience.

Yet, after she hugged him, kissed him, reassured him, and left him on the green sofa in front of the fireplace, she almost could not find the strength to turn and leave. When she closed the cabin door and watched as Charlie locked it, she was nearly overcome by fear so strong it made her sick to her stomach. Moving off the porch, descending the snow-covered steps, she felt an aching weakness in her legs that was almost incapacitating. Each step away from the cabin was like a step taken on a planet with five times the gravity of this world.

The weather had deteriorated dramatically since they had come up the mountain from where they had parked the Jeep, and the extreme hostility of the elements gradually began to occupy her thoughts and push her fear toward the back of her mind. The wind was a steady twenty to thirty miles an hour, gusting to at least fifty at times, racing across the mountain with a banshee shriek, shaking the enormous trees. The snowflakes were no longer large and fluffy, but small, hard-driven by the wind, mounting up on the ground at a startling rate. They had not worn ski masks earlier, on the way up to the cabin, but Charlie had insisted they wear them on the way down. And although she initially objected because the mask felt smothering, she was glad she had it, for the temperature had fallen drastically and now must be around zero or lower, even without taking into account the wind-chill factor. With the protection of the mask, icy needles of wind still managed to prick and numb her face; without it, she would surely have suffered frostbite.

When they reached the station wagon, daylight was fading as if the world was in a pot onto which a giant lid was being lowered. Snow was already drifted around the Jeep's tires, and the lock was half frozen and stubborn when Charlie tried the key in it.

They stuffed their backpacks full of cans and boxes of food, canned matches, ammunition for the guns, and other things. Charlie strung the three tightly rolled sleeping bags on a length of clothesline and tied one end of the line around his waist so he could drag the bags behind him; they were lightweight, made of a cold-resistant vinyl that would slide well on the snow, and he said he was sure they wouldn't give him much trouble. She carried the rifle, which was equipped with a shoulder strap, and Charlie carried the shotgun. Neither of them could handle a single additional item without buckling under the load, yet there was still more in the station wagon.

'We'll come back for it,' Charlie said, shouting to be heard above the roaring wind.

'It's almost dark,' she protested, having realized how easily you could become lost at night, in a blinding snowstorm.

'Tomorrow,' he said. 'We'll come back tomorrow.'

She nodded, and he locked the Jeep, although the foul weather was surely a sufficient deterrent to thieves. No self-respecting criminal, in the habit of living an easy life off the labors of others, would be out on a night like this.

They headed back toward the cabin, moving with considerably less speed than they had on the way down, slowed by the weight of what they carried, by the wind that hammered at them, and by the fact that they were now climbing instead of descending. Walking in snowshoes had been surprisingly easy — until now. As they made their way up the first meadow, the muscles in Christine's thighs began to pull, then those in her calves, and she knew that she would be stiff and sore in the morning.

The wind whipped up the snow that was already on the ground, dressed itself in crystalline cloaks and robes that flapped and swirled, formed whirling funnels that danced through the twilight. In the swiftly dying light, the snow devils seemed like spirits, cold ghosts roaming the lonely reaches of the top of the world.

The hills felt steeper than when she and Charlie had first made this trip with Joey and the dog. Her snowshoes were certainly twice as large as they had been then . . . and ten times heavier.

Darkness fell when they were in the woods, before they even reached the upper meadow. They were in no danger of getting lost because the snow-covered ground had a vague natural luminosity, and the clear swath of the road provided an unmistakable route through the otherwise densely packed trees.

However, by the time they reached the upper meadow, the storm's fury eliminated the advantage of the snow's slight phosphorescence. New snow was falling so heavily, and the wind was kicking up such thick clouds of old snow that, had there not been lights on at the cabin, they would without doubt have become disoriented and would have been in serious risk of wandering aimlessly, back and forth, around in circles, until they collapsed and died, less than four hundred yards from safety. The dim, diffuse, amber glow at the cabin windows was a welcome beacon. On those occasions when the gale-driven snow temporarily blocked that beacon, Christine had to resist panic, stop and wait until she glimpsed her target again, for when she kept on without being able to see the lights, she always headed off in the wrong direction within a few steps. Although she stayed close to Charlie, she frequently could not see him, either; visibility sometimes declined to no more than two or three feet.

The aching in her leg muscles grew worse, and the throbbing in her shoulders and back became unbearable, and the night's chill somehow found its way through all her layers of clothes, but though she cursed the storm she also welcomed it. For the first time in days, she was beginning to feel safe. This wasn't just a storm; it was a damned *blizzard*! They were shut off from the world now. Isolated. By morning they would be snowbound. The storm was the best security they could have. At least for the next day or so, Grace Spivey would not be able to reach them even if, by some miracle, she learned their whereabouts.

When they finally reached the cabin, they found Joey in a better mood than when they'd left. There was color in his face again. He was energetic and talkative for the first time in a couple of days. He even smiled. The change in him was startling and, for a moment, mysterious, but then it became clear that he took the same comfort from the storm as Christine did. He said, 'We'll be okay now, huh, Mom? A witch can't fly a broom in a blizzard, can she, huh?'

'Nope,' Christine assured him as she took off the backpack she'd been caring. 'All the witches are grounded tonight.'

'FWA rules,' Charlie said.

Joey looked at him quizzically. 'What's . . . FWA?'

'Federal Witch Administration,' Charlie said, pulling off his boots. 'That's the government agency that licenses witches.'

'You gotta have a license to be a witch?' the boy asked.

Charlie feigned surprise. 'Oh, sure, what'd you think – just anybody can be a witch? First, when a girl wants to be a witch, she's got to prove she has a mean streak in her. For instance, your mom would never qualify. Then a would-be witch has got to be ugly because witches are always ugly, and if a pretty lady like your mom wants to be a witch she's got to go have plastic surgery to make herself ugly.'

'Wow,' Joey said softly, wide-eyed. 'Really?'

'But that's not the worst of it,' Charlie said. 'The hardest thing if you want to be a witch is finding those tall, pointy black hats.'

'It is?'

'Well, just think about it once. You've gone shopping with your mom when she was buying clothes. You ever see any of those tall, pointy black hats in any stores you were ever in?'

The boy frowned, thinking about it.

'No, you haven't,' Charlie said as he carried one of the heavy backpacks into the kitchen. 'Nobody sells those hats because nobody wants witches coming in their stores all the time. Witches smell like the wings of bats and tails of newts and salamander tongue and all those other weird things they're always cooking in their cauldrons. Nothing will chase off a storekeeper's customers faster than a witch who reeks of boiled pig's snout.'

'Yuck,' Joey said.

'Exactly,' Charlie said.

Christine was so happy and relieved to see Joey acting like a six-year-old again that she had trouble holding back tears. She wanted to put her arms around Charlie, squeeze him tight, and thank him for his strength, for his way with children, for just being the man he was.

Outside, the wind howled and huffed and wailed and whistled.

Night hugged the cabin. Snow dressed it.

In the living room fireplace, the big logs sputtered and crackled.

They worked together to make dinner. Afterwards, they sat on the floor in the living room, where they played Old Maid and Tic-Tac-Toe, and Charlie told knock-knock jokes that Joey found highly amusing.

Christine felt snug. Secure.

53

In South Lake Tahoe, the snowmobile shop was about to close when Grace Spivey, Barlowe, and the eight others arrived. They had come from just down the street, where they had all purchased ski suits and other insulated winter clothing. They had changed into their new gear and now looked as if they belonged in Tahoe. To the surprise and delight of the owner of Mountain Country Snowmobile — a portly man whose name was Orley Treat and who said his friends called him 'Skip' — they purchased four Skidoos and two custom-designed flatbed trailers to haul them.

Kyle Barlowe and a churchman named George Westvec did most of the talking because Westvec knew a lot about snowmobiles, and Barlowe had a knack for getting the best price possible on anything he bought. His great size, forbidding appearance, and air of barely controlled violence gave him an advantage in any bargaining session, of course, but his negotiating skills were not limited to intimidation. He had a first-rate businessman's knack of sensing an adversary's strengths, weaknesses, limits, and intentions. This was something he had learned about himself only after Grace had converted him from a life of self-hatred and sociopathic behavior, and it was a discovery that was as gratifying as it was surprising. He was in Mother Grace's everlasting debt not only because she had saved his soul but because she had provided him the opportunity to discover and explore the talents which, without her, he would never have known were there, within himself.

Orley Treat, who was too beefy to have such a boyish nickname as 'Skip,' kept trying to figure out who they were. He kept asking questions of Grace and Barlowe and the others, such as whether they belonged to a club of some kind or whether they were all related.

Keeping in mind that the police were still interested in talking to Grace about certain recent events in Orange County, worried that one of the disciples would inadvertently say too much to Treat, Barlowe sent everyone but George Westvec to scout the nearby motels along the main road and find one with sufficient vacancies to accommodate them.

When they paid for the snowmobiles with stacks of cash, Treat gaped at their money in disbelief. Barlowe saw greed in the man's eyes, and figured Treat had already thought of a way to doctor his books and hide this cash from the IRS. Even though his curiosity had an almost physically painful grip on him, Treat stopped prying into their business because he was afraid of queering the deal.

The white Ford vans weren't equipped with trailer hitches, but Treat said he could arrange to have the welding done overnight. 'They'll be ready first thing in the morning . . . say . . . ten o'clock.'

'Earlier,' Grace said. 'Much earlier than that. We want to haul these up to the north shore come first light.'

Treat smiled and pointed to the showroom windows, beyond which winddriven snow was falling heavily in the sodium-glow of the parking lot lights. 'Weatherman's calling for maybe eighteen inches. Stormfront won't pass until four or five o'clock tomorrow morning, so the road crews won't have the highway open around to the north shore until ten, even eleven o'clock. No point you folks starting out earlier.'

Grace said, 'If you can't have the hitches on our trucks and the Skidoos ready to go by four-thirty in the morning, the deal's off.'

Barlowe knew she was bluffing because this was the only place they could get the machines they needed. But judging from the tortured expression on Treat's face, he took her threat seriously.

Barlowe said, 'Listen, Skip, it's only a couple of hours worth of welding. We're willing to pay extra to have it done tonight.'

'But I've got to prep the Skidoos and –'

'Then prep them.'

'But I was just closing for the day when you –'

'Stay open a couple more hours,' Barlowe said. 'I know

330

it's inconvenient. I appreciate that. I really do. But, Skip, how often do you sell four snowmobiles and two trailers in one clip?'

Treat sighed. 'Okay, it'll be ready for pickup at four-thirty in the morning. But you'll never get up to the north shore at that hour.'

Grace, George Westvec, and Barlowe went outside, where the others were waiting. Edna Vanoff stepped forward and said, 'We've found a motel with enough spare rooms to take us, Mother Grace. It's just a quarter of a mile up the road here. We can walk it easy.'

Grace looked up into the early-night sky, squinting as the snow struck her face and frosted her eyebrows. Long tangled strands of wet frizzy gray hair escaped the edges of her knitted hat, which she had pulled down over her ears. 'Satan brought this storm. He's trying to delay us. Trying to keep us from reaching the boy until it's too late. But God will get us through.'

54

By nine-thirty Joey was asleep. They put him to bed between clean sheets, under a heavy blue and green quilt. Christine wanted to stay in the bedroom with him, even though she wasn't ready for bed, but Charlie wanted to talk to her and plan for certain contingencies.

He said, 'You'll be all right by yourself, won't you, Joey?'

'I guess so,' the boy said. He looked tiny, elfin, under the huge quilt and with his head propped on an enormous feather pillow.

'I don't want to leave him alone,' Christine said.

Charlie said, 'No one can get him here unless they come up from downstairs, and we'll be downstairs to stop them.'

'The window —'

'It's a second-story window. They'd have to put a ladder up against the house to reach it, and I doubt they'd be carrying a ladder.'

She frowned at the window, undecided.

Charlie said, 'We're socked in here, Christine. Listen to that wind. Even if they knew we were in these mountains, even if they knew about this particular cabin — which they don't — they wouldn't be able to make it up here tonight.'

'I'll be okay, Mom,' Joey said. 'I got Chewbacca. And like Charlie said, it's against FWA rules for witches to fly in a storm.'

She sighed, tucked the covers in around her son, and kissed him goodnight. Joey wanted to give Charlie a goodnight kiss, too, which was a new experience for Charlie, and as he felt the boy's lips smack his cheek, a flood of emotions washed through him: a poignant sense of the child's profound vulnerability; a fierce desire to protect him; an awareness of the purity of the kid's affection; a heart-wrenching impression of innocence and sweet simplicity; a touching and yet quite frightening realization of the complete trust the boy had in him. The moment was so warm, so disarming and satisfying, that Charlie couldn't understand how he could have come to be thirty-six without having started a family of his own.

Maybe it had been his destiny to be here, waiting for Christine and Joey, when they needed him. If he'd had his own family, he wouldn't have been able to go to the wall for the Scavellos as he had done; these recent deeds, all beyond the call of duty, would have fallen to one of his men — who might not have been as clever or as committed as Charlie was. When Christine had walked into his office, he had been rocked by her beauty and by a feeling that they were meant to meet, one way or another, that they would have found each other in a different fashion if Grace Spivey hadn't acted to bring them together now. Their relationship seemed inevitable. And now it seemed equally inevitable and right that he should be Joey's protector, that he should one day soon become the child's legal father, that each night he should hear this small boy say, 'Goodnight, Daddy,' instead of 'Goodnight, Charlie.'

Destiny.

That was a word and a concept to which he had never given much thought. If anyone had asked him last week if he believed in destiny, he would probably have said he did not. Now, it seemed a simple, natural, and undeniable truth that all men and women had a destiny to fulfill and that his lay with this woman and this child.

They closed the heavy draperies at the bedroom window, and left a lamp on with a towel draped over the shade to soften the light. Joey fell asleep while they were arranging the towel. Chewbacca had curled up on the bed, too. Christine quietly motioned for the dog to get down, but it just stared mournfully at her. Charlie whispered that Chewbacca could stay where he was, and finally he and Christine retreated from the room with exaggerated stealth, leaving the door ajar an inch or two.

As they went downstairs she looked back a couple of times, as if having second thoughts about leaving the boy alone, but Charlie held her arm and steered her firmly to the table. They sat and had coffee and talked, while the wind moaned in the eaves and grainy snow tapped at the windows or hissed along the glass.

Charlie said, 'Now, once this storm is past and the roads are open farther down the mountain, I'll want to go into the market to use the pay phone, call Henry Rankin, see what's up. I'll be going in every two days, at least, maybe even every day, and when I'm gone I think you and Joey ought to hole up in the battery room, under the windmill. It —'

'No,' she said quickly. 'If you go down the mountain, we go with you.'

'It'll get tiring if it has to be done every day.'

'I can handle it.'

'But maybe Joey can't.'

'We won't stay here alone,' she said adamantly.

'But with the police looking for us, we'll be more noticeable as a group, more easily —'

'We go with you everywhere,' she said. 'Please. *Please.*'

He nodded. 'All right.'

He got a map that he had purchased at the sporting goods store in Sacramento, spread it out on the table, and showed her their back door escape route, which they would use if, against all odds, Spivey's people showed up, and if there was enough time to escape. They would go farther up the mountain, to the top of the next ridge, turn east into the valley that lay that way, find the stream at the bottom of the valley, and follow it south toward the lake. It was a journey of four or five miles — which would seem like a hundred in the snow-blanketed wilderness. But there would be good landmarks all the way and little chance of getting lost as long as they had the map and a compass.

Gradually, their conversation drifted away from Grace Spivey, and they talked about themselves, exploring each other's past, likes and dislikes, hopes and dreams, getting a better fix on each other than they'd had an opportunity to do thus far. In time they moved away from the table, switched off all the lights, and sat on the big sofa in front of the stone hearth, with nothing but the softly flickering firelight to hold back the shadows. Their conversation became more intimate, and more was said with fewer words, and finally even their silences conveyed a richness of information.

Charlie couldn't remember the first kiss; he just suddenly realized that they had been touching and kissing with increasing ardor for some time, and then his hand was on her breast, and he could feel her erect nipple through her blouse, hot upon the center of his palm. Her tongue moved within his mouth, and it was very hot, too, and her lips were searing, and when he touched her face with his fingertips the contact was so electrifying that it seemed as if sparks and smoke should issue from it. He had never wanted or needed a woman a fraction as much as he did Christine, and judging from the way her body arched against him and the way her muscles tensed, she wanted and needed him with a passion equal to his own. He knew that, in spite of their circumstances, in spite of the less than ideal trysting place that fate had provided, they would make love tonight; it was inevitable.

Her blouse was unbuttoned now. He lowered his mouth to her breasts.

'Charlie . . .' she said softly.

He licked her swollen nipples, first one, then the other, lovingly.

'No,' she said, but she did not push him away with any conviction, only halfheartedly, wanting to be convinced.

'I love you,' he said, meaning it. In just a few days, he had fallen in love with her exquisitely composed face, with her body, with her complex mind and wit, with her courage in the face of adversity, with her indomitable spirit, with the way she walked, with the way her hair looked in the wind . . .

'Joey . . .' she said.

'He's sleeping.'

'He might wake up . . .'

Charlie kissed her throat, felt the throbbing of her pulse against his lips. Her heart was beating fast. So was his.

'He might come out to the gallery . . . look down and see us,' she said.

He led her away from the firelight, to a long, deep sofa that was under the gallery overhang, out of sight. The shadows were deep and purple.

'We shouldn't,' she said, but she kept kissing his neck, his chin, lips, cheeks, and eyes. 'Even here . . . if he wakes up . . .'

'He'll call to us first,' Charlie said, breathless, aching with need. 'He won't just come down into a dark living room.'

She kissed his nose, each corner of his mouth, planted a chain of kisses along his jaw line, kissed his ear.

His hands moved over her body, and he thrilled to the perfect form and texture of her. Each sweet concavity and convexity, each enticing angle, the swell of breasts and hips, the taut flatness of belly, the ripeness of buttocks, the sleek roundness of thigh and calf — all of her seemed, to the millimeter, a precise definition of ideal femininity.

'All right,' she said weakly. 'But silently . . .'

'Not a sound,' he promised.

'Not a sound.'

'Not one small sound . . .'

The wind moaned at the window above the sofa, but he gave voice to his own intense pleasure only in his mind.

It's the wrong moment, she thought hazily. The wrong place. The wrong time. The wrong everything.

Joey. Might. Wake up.

But although it should matter, it didn't seem to, not much, not enough for her to resist.

He had said he loved her, and she had said she loved him, and she knew they had both meant it, that it was true, real. She didn't know for sure how long she had loved him, but if she thought about it hard enough she would probably be able to fix the precise moment in which respect and admiration and affection had been transformed into something better and more powerful. After all, she had known him only a few days; the moment of love's birth should not be difficult to pin down in that brief span of time. Of course, at the moment, she couldn't think hard about anything, or clearly; she was swept away, though such a condition was out of character for her.

In spite of their protestations of love, it wasn't merely love that induced her to cast caution aside and take the risk of being overheard in the midst of their passion: it was good, healthy lust, too. She had never wanted a man as much as she wanted Charlie. Suddenly she *had* to have him within her, couldn't *breathe* until he took her. His body was lean, the muscles hard and well defined; his sculpted shoulders, his rocklike biceps, smooth broad chest — everything about him excited her to an extent that she had never been excited before. Every nerve in her body was many times more sensitive than before; each kiss and touch, each stroke he took within her, was so explosively pleasurable that it bordered on pain, astonishing pleasure, pleasure that filled her and drove out everything else, every other thought, until she clung mindlessly to him, amazed at the abandon with which she embraced him, unable to understand or resist the primitive rutting fever that possessed her.

The need to be quiet, the oath of silence, had a strangely powerful erotic effect. Even when Charlie climaxed, he did not cry out, but gripped her hips and held her against him and arched his back and opened his mouth but remained mute, and somehow, by containing the cry he also contained his energy and virility, for he didn't lose his erection, not even for a moment, and they paused only to change positions, remaining welded together, but sliding around on the sofa until she was on top, and then she rode him with a pneumatic fluidity and a sinuous rhythm that was unlike anything he had ever known before, and he lost track of time and place, lost *himself* in the soft, silken, silent song of flesh and motion.

She had never in her life been so lacking in self-consciousness while making love. For long moments she forgot where she was, even who she was; she became an animal, a mindlessly copulating organism intent on taking pleasure, oblivious of all else. Only once was the hypnotic rhythm of their lovemaking interrupted, and that was when she was suddenly stricken by the feeing that Joey had come downstairs and was standing in the shadows, watching them, but when she lifted her head from Charlie's chest and looked around, she saw nothing but the shadowy forms of the furniture, backlit by the dying fire, and she knew she was only imagining things. Then love-lust-sex seized her again with a power that was startling and even scary, and she gave herself to the act, was unable to do anything else, was lost, utterly.

Before they were done, Charlie had been shaken by three orgasms and he had lost count of the number of times she had climaxed, but he didn't need a scorecard to know that neither of them had ever experienced anything like this in the past. When it was over, he was still trembling, and he felt drugged. They lay for a time, neither speaking, until they gradually became aware of the wind howling outside and realized that the dying fire had allowed a chill to creep back into the room. Then, reluctantly, they dressed and went upstairs, where they prepared the second bedroom for her.

'I should sleep with Joey and let you have this bed,' she said.

'No. You'll only wake him if you go in there now. The poor kid needs his rest.'

'But where will you sleep?' she asked.

'In the gallery.'

'On the floor?'

'I'll put a sleeping bag at the head of the stairs.'

For a moment anxiety replaced the dreaminess in her eyes. 'I thought you said there was no way they could get here tonight even if – '

He put a finger to her lips. 'There isn't any way. No way at all. But it wouldn't do for Joey to find me sleeping in your bed in the morning, would it? And most of the sofas downstairs are too soft for sleeping. So if I'm going to use a sleeping bag, I might as well put it at the head of the stairs.'

'And keep a gun at your side?'

'Of course. Even though I won't need it. I really won't, you know. So let's get you tucked in.'

When she was under the covers, he kissed her goodnight and backed out of the room, leaving her door ajar.

In the gallery, he looked at his watch and was startled to see how late it was. Could they have been making love for almost two hours? No. Surely not. There had been something frighteningly, deliciously animalistic about their coupling; they had indulged with an abandon and an intensity that stole the meaning from time, but he had never thought of himself as a rampaging stud, and he could not believe that he had performed so insatiably for so long. Yet his watch had never run fast before; surely it couldn't have gained an extra hour or more in just the past thirty minutes.

He realized he was standing there, alone, outside her bedroom door grinning like the Cheshire cat, full of self-satisfaction.

He built up the fire downstairs, carried a sleeping bag to the gallery and unrolled it, switched off the landing light, and slipped into the bedroll. He listened to the storm raging outside, but not for long. Sleep came like a great dark tide.

In the dream, he was tucking Joey into bed, straightening the covers, fluffing the boy's pillow, and Joey wanted to give him a goodnight kiss, and Charlie leaned over, but the boy's lips were hard and cold on his cheek, and when he looked down he saw the boy no longer had a face but just a bare skull with two staring eyes that seemed horribly out of place in that otherwise calcimine countenance. Charlie hadn't felt lips against his cheek but a fleshless mouth, cold teeth. He recoiled in terror. Joey threw back the covers and sat up in bed. He was a normal little boy in every respect except for having only a skull instead of a complete head. The skull's protuberant eyes fixed on Charlie, and the boy's small hands began unbuttoning his Space Raiders pajamas, and when his shallow little chest was revealed it began to split open, and Charlie tried to turn and run but couldn't, couldn't close his eyes either, couldn't look away, could only watch as the child's chest cracked apart and from it streamed a horde of red-eyed rats like the one in the battery room, ten and then a hundred and then a thousand rats, until the boy had emptied himself and had collapsed into a pile of skin, like a deflated balloon, and then the rats surged forward toward Charlie —

— and he woke, sweating, gasping, a scream frozen in his throat. Something was holding him down, constraining his arms and legs, and for a moment he thought it was rats, that they had followed him out of the dream, and he thrashed in panic until he realized he was in a zippered sleeping bag. He found the zipper, pulled the bag open, freed himself, and crawled until he came to a wall in the darkness, sat with his back to it, listening to his thunderous heartbeat, waiting for it to subside.

When at last he had control of himself, he went into Joey's room, just to reassure himself. The boy was sleeping peacefully. Chewbacca raised his furry head and yawned.

Charlie looked at his watch, saw that he had slept about four hours. Dawn was nearing.

He returned to the gallery. He couldn't stop shaking. He went downstairs and made some coffee.

He tried not to think about the dream, but he couldn't help it. He had never before had such a vivid nightmare, and the shattering power of it led him to believe that it had been less a dream than a clairvoyant experience, a foreshadowing of events to come. Not that rats were going to burst out of Joey. Of course not. The dream had been symbolic. But what it meant was that Joey was going to die. Not wanting to believe it, devastated by the very idea that he would fail to protect the boy, he was nevertheless unable to dismiss it as only a dream; he knew; he felt it in his bones: *Joey was going to die*. Maybe they were all going to die.

And now he understood why he and Christine had made love with such intensity, with such abandon and fiercely animalistic need. Deep down, they both had known that time was running out; subconsciously, they had felt death approaching, and they had tried to deny it in that most ancient and fundamental of life-affirming rituals, the ceremony of flesh, the dance done lying down.

He got up from the table, left his half-finished coffee, and went to the front door. He wiped at the frosted glass until he could look out at the snow-covered porch. He couldn't see much of anything, just a few whirling flakes and darkness. The worst of the storm had passed. And Spivey was out there. Somewhere. That's what the dream had meant.

55

By dawn the storm had passed.

Christine and Joey were up early. The boy was not as ebullient as he had been last night. In fact he was sinking back into gloom and perhaps despair, but he helped his mother and Charlie make breakfast, and he ate well.

After breakfast, Charlie suited up and went outside, alone, to sight-in the rifle that he had purchased yesterday in Sacramento.

More than a foot of new snow had fallen during the night. The drifts that sloped against the cabin were considerably higher than they had been yesterday, and a couple of first-floor windows were drifted over. The boughs of the evergreens dropped lower under the weight of the new snow, and the world was so silent it seemed like a vast graveyard.

The day was cold, gray, bleak. At the moment no wind blew.

He had fashioned a target out of a square of cardboard and two lengths of twine. He tied the target around the trunk of a Douglas Fir that stood a few yards downhill from the windmill, then backed off twenty-five yards and stretched out on his belly in the snow. Using one of the rolled-up sleeping bags as a makeshift bench rest, he aimed for the center of the target and fired three rounds, pausing between each to make sure the cross hairs were still lined up on the bull's-eye.

The Winchester Model 100 was fitted with a 3-power telescope sight which brought the target right up to him. He was firing 180-grain soft-point bullets, and he saw each of them hit home.

The shots cracked the morning stillness all across the mountain and echoed back from distant valleys. He got up, went to the target, and measured the point of average impact, which was the center point of the three hits. Then he measured the distance from the point of impact to the point of aim (which was the bull's-eye where he had lined up the cross hairs), and that figure told him how much adjustment the scope required. The rifle was pulling low and to the right. He corrected the elevation dial first, then the windage dial, then sprawled in the snow again and fired another group of three. This time he was gratified to see that every shot found the center of the target.

Because a bullet does not travel in a straight line but in a curving trajectory, it twice crosses the line of sight — once as it is rising and once as it is falling. With the rifle and ammunition he was using, Charlie could figure that any round he fired would first cross the line of sight at about twenty-five yards, then rise until it was about two and a half inches high of the mark at one hundred yards, then fall and cross the line of sight a second time at about two hundred yards. Therefore, the Winchester was now sighted-in for two hundred yards.

He didn't want to have to kill anyone.

He hoped killing wouldn't be necessary.

But now he was ready.

Christine and Charlie put on their snowshoes and backpacks and went down the mountain to the lower meadow to finish unloading the Jeep.

Charlie was carrying the rifle, slung over one shoulder.

She said, 'You're not expecting trouble?'

'No. But what's the use of having the gun if I don't always keep it close by?'

She felt better about leaving Joey alone this morning than she had last night, but she still wasn't happy about it. His high spirits had been short-lived. He was withdrawing again, retreating into his own inner world, and this change was even more frightening than it had been the last time it happened because, after his recovery yesterday evening, she had thought he was permanently back with them. If he withdrew into silence and despair again, perhaps he would slip even deeper than before, and perhaps this time he would not come out again. It *was* possible for a once perfectly normal, outgoing child to become autistic, cutting off most or all interaction with the real world. She'd read about such cases, but she'd never worried about it as much as she worried about diseases and accidents because Joey had always been such an open, joyous, communicative child. Autism had been something that could happen to other people's children, never to her extroverted little boy. But now . . . This morning he spoke little. He didn't smile at all. She wanted to stay with him every minute, hug him a lot, but she remembered that being left alone for a while last evening had convinced him that the witch must not be near, after all. Being left to his own resources this morning might have that same salutary effect again.

Christine didn't glance back as she and Charlie headed downhill, away from the cabin. If Joey was watching from a window, he might interpret a look back as an indication that she was afraid for him, and her own fear would then feed his.

Her breath took frosty form and wreathed her head. The air was bitterly cold, but because there was no wind, they didn't need to wear ski masks.

As first she and Charlie didn't speak, just walked, finding their way through the new soft snow, sinking in now and then in spite of the snowshoes, searching for a firmer crust, squinting because the glare of the snow was fatiguing to the eyes even under a sunless sky like this one.

However, as they reached the woods at the base of the meadow, Charlie said, 'Uh . . . about last night – '

'Me first,' she said quickly, speaking softly because the air was so still that a whisper carried as well as a shout. 'I've been sort of . . . well, a little embarrassed all morning.'

'About what happened last night?'

'Yes.'

'You're sorry it happened?'

'No, no.'

'Good. Because I'm sure not sorry.'

She said, 'I just want you to know . . . that the way I was last night . . . so eager . . . so aggressive . . . so . . .'

'Passionate?'

'It was more than passion, wouldn't you say?'

'I'd say.'

'My God, I was like . . . an animal or something. I couldn't get enough of you.'

'It was great for my ego,' he said, grinning.

'I didn't know your ego was deflated.'

'Wasn't. But I never thought of myself as God's gift to women, either.'

'But after last night you do, huh?'

'Absolutely.'

Twenty yards into the woods, they stopped and looked at each other and kissed gently.

She said, 'I just want you to understand that I've *never* been like that before.'

He feigned surprise and disappointment. 'You mean you're *not* sex crazy?'

'Only with you.'

'That's because I'm God's gift to women, I guess.'

She didn't smile. 'Charlie, this is important to me – that you understand. Last night . . . I don't know what got into me.'

'*I* got into you.'

'Be serious please. I don't want you to think I've been like that with other men. I haven't. Not ever. I did things with you last night that I've never done before. I didn't even know I *could* do them. I was really like a wild animal. I mean . . . I'm no prude but – '

'Listen,' he said, 'if you were an animal last night, then I was a *beast*. It's not like me to completely surrender control of myself like that, and it certainly isn't like me to be that well, demanding . . . rough. But I'm not embarrassed by the way I was, and you shouldn't be, either. We've got something special, something unique, and that's why we both felt able to let go the way we did. At times it was maybe crude – but it was also pretty terrific, wasn't it?'

'God, yes.'

They kissed again, but it was a brief kiss interrupted by a distant growling-buzzing.

Charlie cocked his head, listening.

The sound grew louder.

'Plane?' she said, looking up at the narrow band of sky above the tree-flanked lane.

'Snowmobiles,' Charlie said. 'There was a time when the mountains were always quiet, serene. Not any more. Those damned snowmobiles are everywhere, like fleas on a cat.'

The roar of engines grew louder.

'They wouldn't come up this far?' she asked worriedly.

'Might.'

'Sounds like they're almost on top of us.'

'Probably still pretty far off. Sound is deceptive up here; it carries a long way.'

'But if we do run into some snowmobilers – '

'We'll say we're renting the cabin. My name's Bob . . . mmm . . . Henderson. You're Jane Henderson. We live in Seattle. Up here to do some cross-country skiing and just get away from it all. Got it?'

'Got it,''she said.

'Don't mention Joey.'

She nodded.

They started downhill again.

The sound of snowmobile engines grew louder, louder – and then cut out one at a time, until there was once again only the deep enveloping silence of the mountains and the soft crunch and squeak of snowshoes in the snow.

When they reached the next break in the tree line, at the top of the lower meadow, they saw four snowmobiles and eight or ten people gathered around the Jeep, almost three hundred yards below. They were too far away for Christine to see what they looked like, or even whether they were men or women; they were just small, dark figures against the dazzling whiteness of the snowfield. The station wagon was half buried in drifted snow, but the strangers were busily cleaning it off, trying the doors.

Christine heard faint voices but couldn't understand the words. The sound of breaking glass clinked through the crisp cold air, and she realized they were not ordinary snowmobile enthusiasts.

Charlie pulled her backward, into the darkness beneath the trees, off to the left of the trail, and both of them nearly fell because snowshoes were not designed for dodging and running. They stood under a gigantic hemlock. Its spreading branches began about seven feet above the ground, casting shadows and shedding needles on the thin skin of snow that covered the earth beneath it. Charlie leaned against the enormous trunk of the tree and peered around it, past a couple of other hemlocks, between a few knobcone pines, toward the meadow and the Jeep. He unsnapped the binocular case that was clipped to his belt, took out the binoculars.

'Who are they?' Christine asked as she watched Charlie focus the glasses. Certain that she already knew the answer to her question but not wanting to believe it, not having the strength to believe it. 'Not just a group of people who like winter sports; that's for sure. They wouldn't go around busting the windows out of abandoned vehicles.'

'Maybe it's a bunch of kids,' he said, still focusing. 'Just out looking for a little trouble.'

'Nobody goes out in deep snow, comes this far up a mountain, just looking for trouble,' she said.

Charlie took two steps away from the hemlock, held the binoculars with both hands, peering downhill. At last he said, 'I recognize one of them. The big guy who came into her office at the rectory, just as Henry and I were leaving. She called him Kyle.'

'Oh Jesus.'

The mountain wasn't a haven, after all, but a dead end. A trap.

Suddenly the loneliness of the snow-blasted slopes and forests made their retreat to the cabin appear short-sighted, foolish. It seemed like such a good idea to get away from people, where they would not be spotted, but they had also removed themselves from all chance of help, from everyone who might have come to their assistance if they were attacked. Here, in these cold high places, they could be slaughtered and buried, and no one but their murderers would ever know what had happened to them.

'Do you see . . . *her*?' Christine asked.

'Spivey? I think . . . yeah . . . the only one still sitting in a snowmobile. I'm sure that's her.'

'But *how* could they find us?'

'Somebody who knew I was part owner of the cabin. Somebody remembered it and told Spivey's people.'

'Henry Rankin?'

'Maybe. Very few people know about this place.'

'But still . . . so quickly!'

Charlie said, 'Six . . . seven . . . nine of them. No. Ten. Ten of them.'

We're going to die, she thought. And for the first time since leaving the convent, since losing her religion, she wished that she had not turned entirely away from the Church. Suddenly, by comparison with the insanity of Spivey's cult beliefs, the ancient and compassionate doctrines of the Roman Catholic Church were immeasurably appealing and comforting, and she wished she could turn to them now without feeling like a hypocrite, wished she could beg God for help and ask the Blessed Virgin for her divine intercession. But you couldn't just reject the Church, put it entirely out of your life — then go running back when you needed it, and expect to be embraced without first making penance. God required your faith in the good times as well as the bad. If she died at the hands of Spivey's fanatics, she would do so without making a final confession to a priest, without the last rites or a proper burial in consecrated ground, and she was surprised that those things mattered to her and seemed important after all these years during which she had discounted their value.

Charlie put the binoculars back into the case, snapped it shut. He unslung the rifle from his shoulder. He said, 'You head back to the cabin. Fast as you can. Stay in the trees until you reach the bend in the trail. After that they can't see you from the lower meadow. Get Joey suited up. Pack some food in your knapsack. Do whatever you can to get ready.'

'You're staying here? Why?'

'To kill a few of them,' he said.

He unzipped one of the pockets in his insulated jacket. It was filled with loose cartridges. When he exhausted the rounds already in the rifle, he would be able to reload quickly.

She hesitated, afraid to leave him.

'Go!' he said. 'Hurry! We haven't much time.'

Heart racing, she nodded, turned, and made her way through the trees, heading upslope, shuffling as fast as the snowshoes would allow, which wasn't nearly fast enough, repeatedly raising her arms to push branches out of her way. She was thankful that the huge trees blocked the sun and prevented much undergrowth because it would have tangled in the snowshoes and snagged her ski suit and held her back.

Successful rifle shooting requires two things: the steadiest possible position for the gunman, and the letting-off of the trigger at exactly the right time and with the easiest possible pull. Very few riflemen — hunters, military men, whatever — are any good at all. Too many of them try to shoot off-hand when a better position is available, or they exert all the pull on the trigger in one swift movement that throws their aim entirely off.

A rifleman shoots best from a prone position, especially when he is aiming down a slope or into a basin. After taking off his snowshoes, Charlie moved to the perimeter of the forest, to the very edge of the meadow, and dropped to the ground. The snow was only about two inches deep here, for the wind came across the meadow from the west and scoured the land, pushing most of the snow eastward, packing it in drifts along that flank of the woods. The slope was steep at this point, and he was looking down at the people below, where they were still milling around the Jeep station wagon. He raised the rifle, resting it on the heel of the palm of his left hand; his left arm was bent, and the left elbow was directly under the rifle. In this position the rifle wouldn't wobble, for it was well supported by the bones of the forearm, which served as a pillar between the ground and the weapon.

He aimed at the dark figure in the lead snowmobile, though there were better targets, for he was almost certain it was Grace Spivey. Her head was above the vehicle's windscreen, which was one less thing to worry about: no chance of the shot being deflected by the Plexiglas. If he could take her out, the others might lose their sense of commitment and come apart psychologically. It ought to be devastating for a fanatic to see his little tin God die right in front of his eyes.

His gloved finger was curled around the trigger, but he didn't like the feel, couldn't get the right sense of it, so he stripped the glove off with his teeth, put his bare finger on the trigger, and that was a great deal better. He had the cross hairs lined up on the center of Grace Spivey's forehead because, at this distance, the bullet would fall past the sight line by the time it hit its target and would come in about an inch lower. With luck — right between her eyes. Without luck but with skill, it would still take her in the face or throat.

In spite of the sub-zero air, he was perspiring. Inside his ski suit, sweat trickled down from his armpits.

Could you call this self-defense? None of them had a gun on him at the moment. He wasn't in imminent danger of his life. Of course, if he didn't eliminate a few of them before they got closer, they would overwhelm him. Yet he hesitated. He had never before done anything this . . . cold blooded. A small inner voice told him that, if he resorted to an ambush of this sort, he would be no better than the monsters against which he found himself pitted. But if he didn't resort to it, he would eventually die — as would Christine and Joey.

The cross hairs were on Spivey's forehead.

Charlie squeezed the trigger but didn't take up all the pull in one tug because the initial pressure would throw the rifle off target just a little, so he kept the trigger mostly depressed, on the wire-edge of firing, until he brought the cross hairs back onto target, and then, almost as an after-thought but with a clean quick squeeze, he took up the last few ounces of pull. The rifle fired, and he flinched but not in anticipation of the blast, only in delayed reaction to it, by which time it was too late for the bullet to be deflected, for it was already out of the barrel. An anticipatory flinch was what you had to avoid, and the two-stage pull always fooled the subconscious a little, just enough that the muzzle blast was a slight surprise.

There was another surprise, a bad one, when he thought he saw Spivey lean forward in the snowmobile, reaching for something, lowering her profile, just as he let off the shot. Now, lining up the scope again, he couldn't see her, which meant either that he had hit her and that she had collapsed below the windscreen of the snowmobile — or that she had, indeed, bent down at the penultimate moment, saved by fate, and was now crouching out of the line of fire.

He immediately brought the rifle around on one of the others.

A man standing by the Jeep. Just turning this way in reaction to the shot. Not gifted with split-second reactions, confused, not fully aware of the danger.

Charlie fired. This time he was rewarded by the sight of his target pitching back, sprawling in the snow, dead or mortally wounded.

Moving at the edge of the woods, Christine had reached the bend in the open land and, out of sight of those below, had moved out onto the easier ground, when she heard a shot and then, a second or two later, another. She wanted to go back to Charlie, wanted to be there helping him, knew she couldn't do a damn thing for him. She didn't even have time to *look* back. Instead she doubled her efforts, huffing out a fog of breath, trying to walk lightly on the snow, breaking through the crust because of her haste, searching frantically for wind-scoured stretches of ground where she could make better time.

But what if something happened to Charlie? What if he was never able to rejoin her and Joey?

She wasn't an outdoors type. She wouldn't know how to survive in these wintry wastes. If they had to leave the cabin without Charlie, they'd get lost in the wilderness, either starve or freeze to death.

Then, as if nature was intent on honing Christine's fear to a razor's edge, as if in mocking glee, snow flurries began to fall again.

When the first man was hit and went down, most of the others dived for cover alongside the Jeep wagon, but two men started toward the snowmobiles, making perfect targets of themselves, and Charlie lined up on one of them. This shot, too, was well placed, taking the man high in the chest, pitching him completely over one of the snowmobiles, and when he went down in a drift he stayed there, unmoving.

The other man dropped, making a hard target of himself. Charlie fired anyway. He couldn't tell if he had scored this time because his prey was now hidden by a mound of snow.

He reloaded.

He wondered if any of them were hunters or ex-military men with enough savvy to have pinpointed his position. He considered moving along the tree line, finding another good vantage point, and he knew the shadows under the trees would probably cover his movement. But he had a hunch that most of them were not experienced in this sort of thing, were not cut out for guerrilla warfare, so he stayed where he was, waiting for one of them to make a mistake.

He didn't have to wait long. One of those who had taken shelter by the Jeep proved too curious for his own good. When half a minute had passed with no gunfire, the Twilighter rose slightly to look around, still in a half-crouch, ready to drop, probably figuring that a half-crouch made him an impossible target when, in fact, he was giving Charlie plenty at which to aim. Most likely, he also figured he could fall flat and hug the ground again at the slightest sound, but he was hit and dead before the sound of the shot could have reached him.

Three down. Seven left. Six — if he had also killed Spivey.

For the first time in his life, Charlie Harrison was glad that he had served in Vietnam. Fifteen years had passed, but battlefield cunning had not entirely deserted him. He felt the heart-twisting terror of both the hunter and the hunted, the battle stress that was like no other kind of stress, but he still knew how to use that tension, how to take advantage of that stress to keep himself alert and sharp.

The others remained very still, burrowing into the snow, hugging the Jeep and the snowmobiles. Charlie could hear them shouting to one another, but none of them dared move again.

He knew they would remain pinned down for five or ten minutes, and maybe he should get up now, head back to the cabin, use that lead time. But there was a chance that if he outwaited them he would get another clear shot the next time they regained a little confidence. For the moment, anyway, there was no danger of *losing* any advantage by staying put, so he remained at the perimeter of the woods. He reloaded again. He stared down at them, exhilarated by his marksmanship but wishing he wasn't so proud of it, savagely delighted that he had brought down three of them but also ashamed of that delight.

The sky looked hard, metallic. Light snow flurries were falling. No wind yet. Good. Wind would interfere with his shooting.

Below, Spivey's people had stopped talking. Preternatural silence returned to the mountain.

Time ticked by.

They were scared of him down there.

He dared to hope.

56

At the cabin, Christine found Joey standing in the living room. His face was ashen. He had heard the shooting. He knew. 'It's her.'

'Honey, get your ski suit on, your boots. We're going out soon.'

'Isn't it?' he said softly.

'We've got to be ready to leave as soon as Charlie comes.'

'*Isn't it her?*'

'Yes,' Christine said. Tears welled up in the boy's eyes and she held him. 'It'll be okay. Charlie will take care of us.'

She was looking into his eyes, but he was not looking into hers. He was looking *through* her, into a world other than this one, a place of his own, and the emptiness in his eyes sent a chill up her spine.

She had hoped that he could dress himself while she stuffed things into her backpack, but he was on the verge of catatonia, just standing there, face slack, arms slack. She grabbed his ski suit and dressed him, pulling it on over the sweater and jeans he already wore. She pulled two pair of thick socks onto his small feet, put his boots on for him, laced them up. She put his gloves and ski mask on the floor by the door, so she wouldn't forget them when it was time to leave.

As she went into the kitchen and began choosing food and other items for the backpack, Joey came with her, stood beside her. Abruptly he shook off his trance, and his face contorted with fear, and he said, 'Brandy? Where's Brandy?'

'You mean Chewbacca, honey.'

'Brandy. I mean *Brandy*!'

Shocked, Christine stopped packing, stooped beside him, put a hand to his face. 'Honey . . . don't do this . . . don't worry your mommy like this. You remember. I know you do. You remember . . . Brandy's dead.'

'No.'

'The witch –'

'*No!*'

' – killed him.'

He shook his head violently. 'No. No! Brandy!' He called desperately for his dead dog. 'Brandy! *Braaannndeeeee!*'

She held him. He struggled. 'Honey, please, please . . .'

At that moment Chewbacca padded into the kitchen to see what all the commotion was about, and the boy wrenched free of Christine, seized the dog joyfully, hugged the furry head. 'Brandy! See? It's Brandy. He's still here. You lied. Brandy's not hurt. Brandy's okay. Nothin' wrong with good old Brandy.'

For a moment Christine couldn't breathe or move because pain immobilized her, not physical pain but emotional pain, deep and bitter. Joey was slipping away. She thought he had accepted Brandy's death, that all of this had been settled when she'd forced him to name the dog Chewbacca instead of Brandy Two. But now . . . When she spoke his name, he didn't respond or look at her, just murmured and cooed to the dog, stroked it, hugged it. She shouted his name; still he didn't respond.

She should never have let him keep this look-alike. She should have made him take it back to the pound, should have made him choose another mutt, anything but a golden retriever.

Or maybe not. Maybe there was nothing she could have done to save his sanity. No six-year-old could be expected to hold himself together when his whole world was crumbling around him. Many adults would have cracked sooner. Although she had tried to pretend otherwise, the boy's emotional and mental problems had been inevitable.

A good psychiatrist would be able to help him. That's what she told herself. His retreat from reality wasn't permanent. She had to believe that was true. She had to *believe*. Or there was no point in going on from here.

She lived for Joey. He was her world, her *meaning*. Without him . . .

The worst thing was that she didn't have time to hold and cuddle and talk to him now, which was something he desperately needed and something she needed, as well. But Spivey was coming, and time was running out, so she had to ignore Joey, turn away from him when he needed her most, get control of herself, and ram things into the backpack. Her hands shook, and tears streamed down her face. She had never felt worse. Now, even if Charlie saved Joey's life, she might still lose her boy and be left with only the living but empty shell of him. But she kept on working, yanking open cupboard doors, looking for things they would need when they went into the woods.

She was filled with the blackest hatred for Spivey and the Church of the Twilight. She didn't just want to kill them. She wanted to torture them first. She wanted to make the old bitch scream and beg for mercy; the disgusting, filthy, rotten, crazy old *bitch*!

Softly, cooingly, Joey said, 'Brandy . . . Brandy . . . Brandy,' and stroked Chewbacca.

57

Seven minutes passed before any of Spivey's people dared rise up to test whether Charlie was still sighting down on them.

He was, and he opened fire. But though this was the opportunity he had been waiting for, he was sloppy, too tense and too eager. He jerked the trigger instead of squeezing it, threw the sights off target, and missed.

Instantly, there was return fire. He had figured they were armed, but he hadn't been absolutely sure until now. Two rifles opened up, and the fire was directed towards the upper end of the meadow. But the first rounds entered the woods fifty yards to the left of him; he heard them cracking through the trees. The next shots hit closer, maybe thirty-five yards away, still to his left, but the gunmen kept shooting, and the shots grew closer. They knew in general − though not precisely − where he was, and they were trying to elicit a reaction that would pinpoint his location.

As the shots came closer, he put his head down, pressed into the thinning shadows at the edge of the forest. He heard bullets slamming through the branches directly overhead. Scraps of bark, a spray of needles, and a couple pine cones rained down around him, and a few bits and pieces even fell on his back, but if the riflemen below were also hoping for a lucky hit, they would be disappointed.

The fire slowly moved off to his right, which indicated they knew only that the shots had come from above and did not know for sure which corner of the meadow harbored their assailant.

Charlie raised his head, lifted the rifle again, brought his eye to the scope — and discovered, with a start, that their shooting had another purpose, too. It was meant to cover two Twilighters who were running pell-mell for the forest at the east end of the meadow.

'*Shit!*' he said, quickly trying to line up a shot on one of the two. But they were moving fast, in spite of the drifting snow, kicking up clouds of crystalline flakes. Just as he got the cross hairs on one of them, both men plunged into the darkness between the trees and were gone.

The Twilighters down by the Jeep stopped firing.

Charlie wondered how long it would take the two in the woods to work their way up through the trees and come in behind him. Not long. There wasn't a lot of underbrush in these forests. Five minutes. Less.

He could still do some damage, even if those remaining in the meadow did not show themselves. He brought one of the snowmobiles into the bull's-eye in his scope and pumped two rounds through the front of it, hoping to smash something vital. If he could put them on foot, he would slow them down, make the chase more fair. He targeted the other snowmobile, pumped two slugs into the engine. The third machine was half hidden by the other two, offering less of a target, and he fired five times at that one, reloading the rifle as needed, and all his shooting finally made it possible for them to pinpoint him. They began blasting from below, but this time all the shots were coming within a few yards of him.

The fourth snowmobile was behind the Jeep, out of reach, so there was nothing more he could do. He put on the glove he had stripped off a few minutes ago, then slithered on his belly, deeper into the woods, until he found a big hemlock trunk to put between himself and the incoming bullets. He had taken off his snowshoes earlier, when he had needed to be in a prone position to get the most from his rifle. Now he put them on again, working as rapidly as possible, trying to make as little noise as he could, listening intently for any sounds made by the two men coming up through the eastern arm of the forest.

He had expected to hear or see them by this time, but now he realized they would be extremely cautious. They would figure he had seen them making a break for the trees, and they would be sure he was lying in wait for them. And they knew he enjoyed the advantage of familiarity with the terrain. They would move slowly, from one bit of cover to the next, thoroughly studying every tree and rock formation and hollow that lay ahead of them, afraid of an ambush. They might not be here for another five or even ten minutes, and once they got here they'd waste another ten minutes, at least, searching the area until they were sure he had pulled back. That gave him, Christine, and Joey maybe a twenty- or twenty-five-minute lead.

As fast as he could, he moved through the woods, heading toward the upper meadow and the cabin.

Snow flurries were still falling.

A wind had risen. The sky had darkened and lowered. It was still morning, but it felt like late afternoon. Hell, it felt later than that, much later; it felt like the end of time.

Chewbacca stayed beside Joey, as if he sensed that his young master needed him, but the boy no longer paid attention to the dog. Joey was lost in an inner world, oblivious of this one.

Biting her lip, repressing her concern for her son, Christine had finished stuffing provisions into her backpack, had made a pile of everything that ought to go into Charlie's pack, and had loaded the shotgun by the time he returned to the cabin. His face was flushed from the bitter air, and his eyebrows were white with snow, but for a moment his eyes were the coldest thing about him.

'What happened?' she asked as he came across the living room to the dining table, leaving clumps of melting snow in his wake.

'I blew them away. Like ducks in a barrel, for God's sake.'

Helping him off with his backpack and spreading it on the table, she said, 'All of them?'

'No. I either killed or badly wounded three men. And I might've nipped a fourth, but I doubt it.'

She began frantically packing things into the waterproof vinyl pack. 'Spivey?'

'I don't know. Maybe. Maybe I hit her. I don't know.'

'They're still coming?'

'They will be. We've got maybe a twenty minute head start.'

The pack was half full. She paused, a can of matches in her hand. Staring hard at him, she said. 'Charlie? What's wrong?'

He wiped at the melting snow trickling down from his eyebrows. 'I . . . I've never done anything like that. It was . . . slaughter. In the war, of course, but that was different. That was war.'

'So is this.'

'Yeah. I guess so. Except . . . when I was shooting them . . . I *liked* it. And even in the war, I never liked it.'

'Nothing wrong with that,' she said, continuing to stuff things into the backpack. 'After what they've put us through, I'd like to shoot a few of them, too. God, would I ever!'

Charlie looked at Joey. 'Get your gloves and mask on, Skipper.'

The boy didn't respond. He was standing by the table, his face expressionless, his eyes dead.

'Joey?' Charlie said.

The boy didn't react. He was staring at Christine's hands as she jammed various items into the second backpack, but he didn't really seem to be watching her.

'What's wrong with him?' Charlie asked.

'He . . . he just . . . went away,' Christine said, fighting back the tears that she had only recently been able to overcome.

Charlie went to the boy, put a hand under his chin, lifted his head. Joey looked up, toward Charlie but not at him, and Charlie spoke to him but without effect. The boy smiled vaguely, humorlessly, a ghastly smile, but even that wasn't meant for Charlie; it was for something he had seen or thought of in the world where he had gone, something that was light-years away. Tears shimmered in the corner of the boy's eyes, but the eerie smile didn't leave his face, and he didn't sob or make a sound.

'Damn,' Charlie said softly.

He hugged the boy, but Joey didn't respond. Then Charlie picked up the first backpack, which was already full, and he put his arms through the straps, shrugged it into place, buckled it across his chest.

Christine finished with the second pack, made sure all the flaps were securely fastened, and took that burden upon herself.

Charlie put Joey's gloves and ski mask on for him. The boy offered little or no assistance.

Picking up the loaded shotgun, Christine followed Charlie, Joey, and Chewbacca out of the cabin. She looked back inside before she closed the door. A pile of logs blazed in the fireplace. One of the brass lamps was on, casting a circle of soft amber light. The armchairs and sofas looked comfortable and enticing.

She wondered if she would ever sit in a chair again, ever see another electric light. Or would she die out there in the woods tonight, in a grave of drifted snow?

She closed the door and turned to face the gray, frigid fastness of the mountains.

Carrying Joey, Charlie led Christine around the cabin and into the forest behind it. Until they were into the screen of trees, he kept glancing around nervously at the open meadow behind them, expecting to see Spivey's people come into sight at the far end of it.

Chewbacca stayed a few yards ahead of them, anticipating their direction with some sixth sense. He struggled a bit with the snow until he reached the undrifted ground within the forest, and then he pranced ahead with an eager sprightliness, unhindered by rock formations, fallen timber, or anything else.

There was some brush at the edge of the forest, but then the trees closed ranks and the brush died away. The land rose, and the earth became rocky and difficult, except for a shallow channel that, in spring, was probably filled with run-off from the melting snowpack, pouring down from higher elevations. They stayed in the channel, heading north and west, which was the direction they needed to go. Their snowshoes were strapped to their backpacks because, for the next few hours, they would be mostly under the huge trees, where the mantle of snow was not particularly deep. In fact, in places, the boughs of the densely grown evergreens were so tightly interlaced that the ground beneath them was bare or virtually so.

Nevertheless, there was sufficient snow for them to leave a clear trail. He could have stopped and tried brushing away their tracks, but he didn't bother. Waste of time. The signs he would leave by trying to eradicate their footprints would be just as obvious as the footprints themselves, for the wind couldn't gain much force in the deepest part of the forest, at least not down here at floor level, and it would not soften and obliterate the brush marks. They could only press on, keep moving, and hope to outrun their pursuers. Perhaps later, if and when they crossed any stretches of open land, the increasing wind might be strong enough to help them out, obscure their passage.

If.

If they ever made it through this part of the woods and onto a stretch of open ground.

If they weren't brought down by Spivey's hounds in the next half hour or forty-five minutes.

If.

The woods were shadowy, and they soon found that the narrow eye holes of the ski masks limited their vision even further. They tripped and stumbled because they didn't see everything in their path, and at last they had to take the masks off. The sub-zero air nipped at them, but they would just have to endure it.

Charlie became acutely aware that their lead on Spivey's people was dwindling. They had been at the cabin almost five minutes. So they were now just fifteen minutes ahead of the pack, maybe even less. And because he couldn't move as fast as he wanted while carrying Joey, Charlie had little doubt that their lead was narrowing dangerously, minute by minute.

The land rose more steeply; he began to breathe harder, and he heard Christine panting behind him. His calves and thighs were knotted, beginning to ache already, and his arms were weary with the burden of the boy. The convenient channel began to curve eastward, which wasn't the way they needed to go. It was still heading more north than south, so they could continue to follow it for a short while, but soon he would have to put the boy down in order to make his way over considerably less hospitable terrain.

If they were going to escape, Joey would have to walk on his own.

But what if he wouldn't walk? What if he just stood there, staring, empty-eyed?

58

Grace crouched within the snowmobile, staying down out of the line of fire, though her old bones protested against her cramped position.

It was a black day in the spirit world. This morning, discovering this disturbing development, she thought she would not be able to dress in harmony with the spectral energies. She had no black clothes. There had never been a black day prior to this. Never. Fortunately, Laura Panken, one of her disciples, had a black ski suit, and they were nearly the same size, so Grace swapped her gray suit for Laura's black outfit.

But now she almost wished she weren't in contact with the saints and with the souls of the dead. The spectral energies radiating from them were uniformly unsettling, tinged with fear.

Grace was also assaulted with clairvoyant images of death and damnation, but these didn't come from God; they had another source, a taint of brimstone. With emotionally unsettling visions, Satan was trying to destroy her faith, to terrorize her. He wanted her to run, abandon the mission. She knew what the Father of Lies was up to. She knew. Sometimes, when she looked at the faces of those around her, she didn't see their real countenances but, instead, rotting tissue and maggot-ridden flesh, and she was shaken by these visions of mortality. The devil, as wise as he was evil, knew she would never give in to temptation, so he was trying to shatter her faith with a hammer of fear.

It wouldn't work. Never. She was strong.

But Satan kept trying. Sometimes, when she looked at the stormy sky, she saw *things* in the clouds: grinning goat heads, monstrous pig faces with protruding fangs. There were voices in the wind, too. Hissing, sinister voices made false promises, told lies, spoke of perverse pleasures, and their hypnotic descriptions of these unspeakable acts were rich in images of the mutant beauty of wickedness.

While she was crouched in the snowmobile, hiding from the rifleman at the top of the meadow, Grace suddenly saw a dozen huge cockroaches, each as large as her hand, crawling over the floor of the machine, over her boots, inches from her face. She almost leapt up in revulsion. That was what the devil wanted; he hoped she would present a better target and make an easy job of it for Charlie Harrison. She swallowed hard, choked on her revulsion, and remained pressed down in the small space.

She saw that each cockroach had a human head instead of the head of an insect. Their tiny faces, filled with pain and self-disgust and terror, looked up at her, and she knew these were damned souls who had been crawling through Hell until, moments ago, Satan had transported them here, to show her how he tortured his subjects, to prove his cruelty had no limits. She was so afraid that she almost lost control of her bladder. Staring at the beetles with human faces, she was supposed to wonder how God could permit the existence of Hell. That's what the devil meant for her to do. Yes. She was supposed to wonder if, by permitting Satan's cruelty, God was indeed cruel Himself. She was supposed to doubt the virtue of her maker. This vision was intended to bring despair and fear deep into her heart.

Then she saw that one beetle had the face of her dead husband, Albert. No. Albert was a good man. Albert had not gone to Hell. It was a lie. The tiny face peered up, screaming yet making no sound. No. Albert was a sweet man, sinless, a saint. Albert in Hell? Albert damned for eternity? God wouldn't do such a thing. She was looking forward to being with Albert again, in Heaven, but if Albert had gone the other way . . .

She felt herself teetering on the edge of madness.

No. No, no, no. Satan was lying. Trying to drive her crazy.

He'd like that. Oh, yes. If she was insane, she wouldn't be able to serve her God. If she even questioned her sanity, she would also be questioning her mission, her Gift, and her relationship with God. She must not doubt herself. She was sane, and Albert was in Heaven, and she had to repress all doubts, give herself completely to blind faith.

She closed her eyes and would not look at the things crawling on her boots. She could feel them, even through the heavy leather, but she gritted her teeth and listened to the rifle fire and prayed, and when eventually she opened her eyes, the cockroaches were gone.

She was safe for a while. She had pushed the devil away.

The rifle fire had stopped, too. Now, Pierce Morgan and Denny Rogers, the two men who had been sent into the woods to circle around behind Charlie Harrison, called from the upper end of the meadow. The way was clear. Harrison was gone.

Grace climbed out of the snowmobile and saw Morgan and Rogers at the top of the meadow, waving their arms. She turned to the body of Carl Rainey, the first man shot. He was dead, a big hole in his chest. The wind was drifting snow over his outflung arms. She knelt beside him.

Kyle eventually came to her. 'O'Conner is dead, too. And George Westvec.' His voice quaked with anger and grief.

She said, 'We knew some of us would be sacrificed. Their deaths were not in vain.'

The others gathered around: Laura Panken, Edna Vanoff, Burt Tully. They looked as angry and determined as they did frightened. They would not turn and run. They *believed*.

Grace said, 'Carl Rainey . . . is in Heaven now, in the arms of God. So are . . .' She had trouble remembering first names for O'Conner and Westvec, hesitated, once again wishing that the Gift did not drive so much else out of her mind. 'So are . . . George Westvec and . . . Ken . . . Ken . . . uh . . . Kevin . . . *Kevin* O'Conner . . . all in Heaven.'

Gradually the snow knitted a shroud over Rainey's corpse.

'Will we bury them here?' Laura Panken asked.

'Ground's frozen,' Kyle said.

'Leave them. No time for burials,' Grace said. 'The Antichrist is within our reach, but his power grows by the hour. We can't delay.'

Two of the Skidoos were out of commission. Grace, Edna, Laura, and Burt Tully rode in the remaining two, while Kyle followed them on foot to the top of the meadow where Morgan and Rogers were waiting.

A sadness throbbed through Grace. Three men dead.

They moved forward, proceeding in fits and starts, only when the way ahead had been scouted, wary of running into another ambush.

The wind had picked up. The snow flurries grew thicker. The sky was all the shades of death.

Soon she would be face to face with the child, and her destiny would be fulfilled.

PART FIVE
The Kill

Pestilence, disease, and war
haunt this sorry place.
And nothing lasts forever;
that's a truth we have to face.

We spend vast energy and time
plotting death for one another.
No one, nowhere, is ever safe.
Not father, child, or mother.

        — *The Book of Counted Sorrows*

By the pricking of my thumbs,
something wicked this way comes.

        — *MacBeth,*
William Shakespeare

Nothing saddens God more than the
death of a child.

        — Dr. Tom Dooley

59

Christine said, 'That's good. That's my boy,' as Joey followed Charlie up through the trees, heading for a broad set-back in the slope, halfway to the ridge line.

She had been afraid that he wouldn't walk on his own, would just stand like a zombie. But perhaps he was not as detached from reality as he seemed; he didn't talk, didn't meet her eye, seemed numb with fear, but apparently he was still enough in tune with this world to understand that he had to keep moving to avoid the witch.

His small legs were not strong, and his bulky ski suit hindered him a bit, and the ground was extremely steep in places, but he kept going, grabbing at rocks and at a few clumps of sparse brush to steady himself and pull himself along. He walked with increasing difficulty, crawled in some places, and Christine, following behind, often had to lift him over fallen timber or help him across a slippery, ice-crusted outcropping of rock. They couldn't move as fast with the boy as they could have without him, but at least they were covering some ground; if they'd had to carry him, they would have been brought to a complete halt.

Frequently, Chewbacca moved ahead of them, loping and scrabbling up the forested slopes as if he were not a dog at all but a wolf, at home in these primeval regions. Often, the retriever stopped above them and looked back, panting, with one ear raised in an almost comical expression. And the boy, seeing him, seemed to take heart and move forward with renewed effort, so Christine supposed she ought to be grateful the animal was with them, even if its resemblance to Brandy might have contributed to Joey's mental deterioration.

Indeed, she had begun to worry about the dog's chances of survival. Its coat was heavy, yes, but silky, not like the thick fur of a wolf or any other animal indigenous to these climes. Already, snow had frozen to the tips of the long hairs on its flanks and belly, as well as to part of its tail and to the furry tips of its ears. It didn't seem bothered yet, or too cold, but how would it feel an hour from now? Two hours? The pads of its feet were not made for this rugged terrain, either. It was a house pet, after all, accustomed to the easy life of suburbia. Soon its feet would be bruised and cut, and it would begin to limp, and instead of racing ahead it would be lagging behind.

If Chewbacca couldn't make it, if the poor mutt died out here, what would *that* do to Joey?

Kill him?

Maybe. Or send him irretrievably far off into his own silent, inner world.

For a couple of minutes, Christine heard a distant growling-buzzing below and behind them, and she knew it must be the snowmobiles roaring into the upper meadow, closing in on the cabin. That grim fact must have penetrated Joey's fog, too, because for a few minutes he made a gallant effort, moved faster, clawing and scrambling upward. When the sound of the snowmobiles died, however, so did his energy, and he resumed a slower, more labored pace.

They reached the set-back in the ridge and paused for breath, but none of them spoke because speaking required energy they could put to better use. Besides, there was nothing to talk about except how soon they might be caught and killed.

Several yards away, something broke from a vine-entangled clump of gnarled dogwood and dashed across the forest floor, startling them.

Charlie unslung his rifle.

Chewbacca stiffened, gave a short, sharp yip.

It was only a gray fox.

It vanished in the shadows.

Christine supposed it was on the trail of game, a squirrel or a snow rabbit or something. Life must be hard up here, in the winter. However, her sympathies lay not with the fox but with the prey. She knew what it was like to be hunted.

Charlie slung the rifle over his shoulder again, and they started climbing once more.

Above the set-back, on the last slope before the ridge line, the trees thinned out, and there was more snow on the ground, although not enough to require snowshoes. Charlie found a deer path, which followed the route of least resistance toward the flat top of the ridge. Where the track passed unavoidably through deep snow that might have given Joey trouble, the deer had cleared the way — there must have been dozens of them through here since the last big storm, tamping the snow with their hooves — and the boy was able to proceed with only a little slipping and sliding.

Chewbacca became excited by the scent of the deer that had come this way before them, whimpered and growled in the back of his throat, but didn't bark. She realized he hadn't once barked since leaving the cabin. Even when startled by the fox, he had made only a small sound that couldn't have carried far, as if he sensed that a bark would have been a beacon for the witch. Or maybe he just didn't have enough energy to climb and bark at the same time.

Each upward step not only put ground between them and their pursuers but seemed to take them into worse weather. It was as if winter were a geographic reality rather than an atmospheric condition, a real place rather than a season, and they were walking deeper into its frigid kingdom.

The sky seemed only inches higher than the treetops. The flurries had changed to heavy snow that slanted down between the pines and firs. By the time they reached the crest of the ridge, where there were no trees at all, Christine could see that a new storm had moved in and that, judging by this early stage, it was going to be even worse than last night's storm. The temperature was well below zero, and the wind was beginning to churn up from the valleys, driven by the rising thermals, blowing harder and gusting more fiercely even as they stood there, trying to catch their breath. Within a couple of hours, the mountain would be a white hell. And now they were without the warm refuge of the cabin.

Charlie didn't immediately lead them down into the next valley. He turned and, standing at the edge of the ridge, stared thoughtfully back the way they had come. Something was on his mind, a plan of some sort. Christine could tell that much, and she hoped it was a good plan. They were outnumbered and outgunned. They needed to be damned clever if they were going to win.

She stooped beside Joey. His nose was running, and the mucous had frozen to his upper lip and to one cheek. She wiped his face with her gloved hand, cleaning him as best she could, and she kissed each of his eyes, held him close, keeping his back to the wind.

He did not speak.

His eyes looked *through* hers, as before.

Grace Spivey, I will kill you, Christine thought, looking back the way they had come, into the woods. For what you've done to my little boy, I will blow your goddamned head off.

*   *   *

Squinting as the stinging wind blew snow into his face, Charlie surveyed the top of the ridge and decided it was just the place for an ambush. It was a long, treeless expanse, running roughly north and south, as narrow as fifteen feet in some places, as wide as thirty feet in others, mostly swept free of snow by the gales that punished its exposed contours. Rock formations, smoothed and carved by centuries of wind, thrust up all along the crest, providing a score of superb hiding places from which he could observe the ascending Twilighters.

At the moment there was no sign of Spivey's people. Of course, he could not see particularly far down into the shadowed woods. Although the trees were not as densely grown on the slope immediately under him as they were on the lower hills, nevertheless they appeared to close up into a wall no more than a hundred or a hundred and twenty yards below. Beyond that point, an army could have been approaching, and he would have been unable to see it. And the wind, whistling and moaning across the top of the ridge, evoked a noisy hissing and rustling from the branches of the enormous trees, masking any sounds that pursuers might have made.

Instinctively, however, Charlie sensed that the cultists were still at least twenty minutes behind, maybe even farther back. Climbing toward the top of the ridge, slowed down by Joey, Charlie had been sure they were losing precious lead time. But now he remembered that Spivey's gang would ascend cautiously, wary of another ambush, at least for the first quarter or half a mile, until their confidence returned. Besides, they had probably stopped to have a look in the cabin and had waited a few minutes there. He had plenty of time to arrange a little welcoming party for them.

He went to Christine and Joey, knelt beside them.

The boy was still detached, almost catatonic, even unaware of the dog rubbing affectionately against his leg.

To Christine, Charlie said, 'We'll head down into the next valley, as far we can go in five minutes, find a place for you to get out of the weather a little. Then I'll come straight back here and wait for them.'

'No.'

'I should be able to pick off at least one before they dive for cover.'

'No,' Christine said, shaking her head adamantly. 'If you're going to wait here for them, we wait with you.'

'Impossible. Once I've finished shooting, I want to be able to clear out fast, make a run for it. If you're here with me, we'll have to move slow. We'll lose too much of our lead on them.'

'I don't think we should separate.'

'It's the only way.'

'It scares me.'

'I've got to keep picking them off if I can.'

She bit her lip. 'It still scares me.'

'It won't be dangerous for me.'

'Like hell it won't.'

'No. Really. I'll be above them when I start shooting. I'll be well concealed. They won't know where the fire's coming from until it's too late, until I've already pulled out. I'll have all the advantages.'

'Maybe they won't even follow us up here.'

'They will.'

'It's not an easy hike.'

'We made it. They can, too.'

'But Spivey's an old woman. She isn't up to this sort of thing.'

'So they'll leave her behind at the cabin with a couple of guards, and the rest of them will come after us. I have to make it hard for them, Christine. I have to kill all of

376

them if I can. I swear to you, an ambush won't be dangerous. I'll shoot one or two of them and slip away before they even have a chance to spot my location and return my fire.'

She said nothing.

'Come on,' he said. 'We're wasting time.'

She hesitated, nodded, and got up. 'Let's go.'

She was one hell of a woman. He didn't know many *men* who would have come this far without complaint, as she had done, and he didn't think he knew any other woman who would consent to being left alone in the middle of this frozen forest under these circumstances, regardless of how necessary the separation might be. She had as much emotional strength and stability as she had beauty.

Not far north along the ridge line, he found where the deer trail continued, and they followed it down into the next valley. The path made two switchback turns to avoid the steepest slopes and take full advantage of the friendliest contours of the land. Charlie hoped to lead them most of the way to the bottom before turning back to set the trap for Spivey's people. In five minutes, however, because the deer trail added distance as well as ease to the journey downward, they had not reached the floor of the valley, were not even halfway there.

He found a place where the trail turned a corner and passed under a rock overhang, creating a protected hollow, not a full-fledged cave but the next best thing, out of the wind and out of what little snow sifted down through the trees. At the far end of the niche, opposite the curve in the trail, the hillside bulged out, forming a wall, so that the natural shelter was enclosed on three of its four sides.

'Wait here for me,' Charlie said. 'Better break off some of the dead branches toward the center of that big spruce over there, start a fire.'

'But you'll only be gone . . . what . . . twenty or twenty-five minutes? Doesn't seem like it's worth the effort to build a fire just for that long.'

'We've been moving ever since we left the cabin,' he said. 'We've continuously generated body heat. But sitting here, unmoving, you'll start to notice the cold more.'

'We're wearing insulated — '

'Doesn't matter. You'll probably still need the fire. If you don't, Joey will. He doesn't have an adult's physical resources.'

'All right. Or . . . we could keep moving, heading down along the deer trail, until you catch up with us.'

'No. It's too easy to get lost in these woods. There might be branches in the trail. You might even pass one without seeing it, but I might see it, and then I wouldn't know for sure which way you went.'

She nodded.

He said, 'Build the fire here, on the trail, but just out beyond the overhang. That way the smoke won't collect under here with you, but you'll still be able to feel the heat.'

'Won't they see the smoke?' Christine asked.

'No. They're still beyond the ridge, with no clear view of the sky.' He quickly unstrapped the snowshoes from his backpack. 'Doesn't matter if they see it, anyway. I'll be between you and them, and I hope to take out at least one of them, maybe two, and make them lie low for at least ten minutes. By the time they get started again, this fire'll be out, and we'll be on down in the valley.' He hurriedly slipped off his backpack, dropped it, kept only his rifle and pocketsful of ammunition. 'Now I've got to get back up there.'

She kissed him. Joey seemed unaware of his departure.

He headed back the way they had come, along the narrow deer path, not exactly running, but hurrying, because it was going to take longer to go up than it had to come down, and he didn't have a lot of time to waste.

Leaving Christine and Joey alone in the forest was the most difficult thing he had ever done.

Joey and Chewbacca waited under the rocky overhang while Christine went into the trees to collect dead wood for a fire. Underneath the huge spreading branches that were green and healthy, close to the trunks, the evergreen provided a lot of dead branches thick with old pine cones and crisp brown needles that would make excellent tinder. These were all dry because the upper, living branches stopped the snow far above. Furthermore, the weight of those snow-bent upper branches had cracked and splintered the dead wood underneath, so she found it relatively easy to wrench and break off the kindling she needed. She swiftly assembled a big pile of it.

In short order, with a squirt of lighter fluid and a single match, she had a roaring blaze in front of the cul-de-sac where she and Joey and the dog took shelter. As soon as she felt the warmth of the fire, she realized how deeply the cold had sunk into her bones in spite of all the winter clothing she wore, and she knew it would have been dangerous to wait here, unmoving, without the fire.

Joey slumped back against a wall of rock and stared at the fire with a blank expression, with eyes that looked like two flat ovals of polished glass, empty of everything except the reflection of the leaping flames.

The dog settled down and began to lick one paw, then the other. Christine wasn't sure if its feet were just bruised or cut, but she could see that it was hurting a little, even though it didn't whine or whimper.

Around them the stone began to absorb the heat from the bonfire, and because the wind didn't reach into the cul-de-sac, the air was soon surprisingly warm.

Sitting next to Joey, Christine pulled off her gloves, zipped open one of the pockets in her insulated jacket, and took out a box of shotgun shells. She opened the box and put it beside the gun, which was already loaded. That was in case Charlie never came back . . . and in case someone else did.

60

By the time Charlie reached the top of the ridge, he was short of breath, and a stabbing pain thrust rhythmically through his thighs and calves. His back and shoulders and neck ached as if the heavy pack was still strapped to him, and he repeatedly had to shift the rifle from hand to hand because the muscles in both arms were weary and aching, too.

He was not out of shape; back in Orange County, when life had been normal, he had gone to the gym twice a week, and he had run five miles every other morning. If *he* was beginning to tire, what must Christine and Joey feel like? Even if he could kill a couple more of Spivey's fanatics, how much longer could Christine and Joey go on?

He tried to put that question out of his mind. He didn't want to think about it because he suspected the answer would not be encouraging.

Running in a crouch because the wind along the ridge had grown violent enough to stagger him, he crossed the narrow rocky plateau. Snow was falling so thickly now that, on the treeless summit, visibility was reduced to fifteen or twenty yards, considerably less when the wind gusted. He had never seen such snow in his life; it seemed as if it were not just coming down in flakes but in cold-welded agglomerations of flakes, in clumps and wads. If he hadn't known exactly where he was going, he might have become disoriented, might have wasted precious time floundering back and forth on the ridge, but he moved unerringly to a jumble of weather-smoothed boulders along the crest and flopped down on his stomach at a place he had chosen earlier.

Here, he could lie at the very lip of the slope, in a gap between two lumpy outcroppings in a long series of granite formations, and look straight down a winding section of the deer trail that he and Christine and Joey had climbed and along which the Twilighters were certain to ascend. He inched forward, peered down into the trees, and was startled by movement hardly more than a hundred yards below. He quickly brought the rifle up, looked through the telescopic sight, and saw two people.

Jesus.

They were here already.

But only two? Where were the others?

He saw that this pair was moving up toward a blind spot in the trail, and he figured they must be the last in the party. The others, ahead of these two, had already gone around the bend and would soon reappear higher on the path.

Of the two who were in sight, the first was of average size, wearing dark clothing. The second was a strikingly tall man in a blue ski suit over which he was wearing a hooded brown parka, his face framed in a fringe of fur lining.

The giant in the parka must be the man Charlie had seen in Spivey's rectory office, the monster Kyle. Charlie shuddered. Kyle gave him the creeps every bit as much as Mother Grace did.

Charlie had expected to have to wait here a while, ten minutes or even longer, before they came into sight, but now they were almost on top of him. They must be climbing without pause, without scouting the way ahead, reckless, unafraid of an ambush. If he'd been a couple of minutes slower getting here, he would have walked right into them as they came over the crest.

The deer trail turned a corner. The two Twilighters moved out of sight behind a rock, around a stand of interlaced pines and fir.

His heart racing, he shifted his sights to the point at which the trail emerged from those trees. He saw an open stretch of about eight yards in which he would be able to draw down on his targets. The distance between him and them would be only about seventy yards, which meant each round would be approximately one and three-quarters inches high when it impacted, so he would need to aim for the lower part of the chest in order to put a slug through the heart. Depending on how close together the bastards were, as many as three of them might have moved into that clear area before the first would be drawing close to the next blind spot. But he didn't think he would be able to pick off all three, partly because each would be in the way of the other; one target would have to fall to give him a good line on the next. They were also sure to leap for cover as the first shot slammed through the woods. He might bring down the second one during that mad rush for shelter, but the third would be hidden before he could realign his sights.

He would hope for two.

The first appeared, stepping out of shadows into a gray fall of light that splashed down in a gap among the trees. He put the cross hairs on target, and he saw it was a woman. A rather pretty young woman. He hesitated. A second Twilighter appeared, and Charlie swung the scope on that target. Another woman, less pretty and not as young as the first.

Very clever. They were putting the females first in hope of foiling an ambush. They were counting on his having compunctions about killing women, compunctions *they* did not have. It was almost amusing. *They* were the churchfolk, and they believed they were God's agents and that he was an infidel, yet they saw no contradiction in the fact that his moral code might be more demanding and inviolable than theirs.

Their plan might have worked, too, if he hadn't served in Vietnam. But fifteen years ago he had lost two close friends, had almost died himself, when a village woman had come to greet them, smiling, and then had blown herself up when they stopped to talk with her. These were not the first fanatics he had ever dealt with, although the others had been motivated by politics rather than religion. No difference, really. Both politics and religion could sometimes be a poison. And he knew that the mindless hatred and the thirst for violence that infected a true believer could turn a woman into a rabid killer every bit as deadly as any *man* with a mission. Institutionalized madness and savagery knew no limitations as to gender.

He had Joey and Christine to consider. If he spared these women, they would kill the woman he loved and her son.

They'll kill me, too, he thought.

He was repelled by the need to shoot her, but he brought his sights back to the first woman, put the cross hairs on her chest. Fired.

She was lifted off her feet and pitched off the deer path. Dead, she slammed into the bristling branches of a black spruce, bringing a small avalanche of snow off its boughs and onto her head.

Then a bad thing happened.

Christine had just put more fuel on the fire and had settled down beside Joey again, under the rock overhang, when she heard the first rifle blast echo down through the forest.

Chewbacca raised his head, his ears pricking up.

Other shots were fired a second or so after the first, but they weren't from Charlie's rifle. There was a steady chatter of shots, a thunderous metallic *ack-ack-ack-ack* which she recognized from old movies, the blood-freezing voice of an automatic weapon, maybe a machine gun. It was a cold, ugly, terrifying sound, filling the forest, and she thought that, if Death laughed, this was how he would sound.

She knew Charlie was in trouble.

Charlie didn't even have time to line up the second shot before the machine gun chattered, scaring the hell out of him. For a moment the racket of automatic fire echoed and re-echoed from a hundred points along the mountain, and it was difficult to tell where it came from. But the events of the past few days had shown that his hard-learned war skills had not been forgotten and he quickly determined that the gunman was not on the slope below but on the ridge with him, north of his position.

They *had* sent a scout ahead, and the scout had laid a trap.

Pressing hard against the ground, trying to become one with the stone, Charlie wondered why the trap hadn't been sprung earlier. Why hadn't he been gunned down the moment he'd come onto the top of the ridge? Maybe the scout had been inattentive, looking the wrong way. Or maybe the heavy snow had closed around Charlie at just the right time, granting him a temporary cloak of invisibility. That was probably part of the explanation, anyway, because he remembered a particularly thick and whirling squall of snow just as he'd come over the crest.

The machine gun fell silent for a moment.

He heard a series of metallic clinks and a grating noise, and he figured the gunner was replacing the weapon's empty magazine.

Before Charlie could rise up and have a look, the man began to fire again. Bullets ricocheted off the boulders among which Charlie was nestled, spraying chips of granite, and he realized that none of the other shots had been nearly this close. The gunner had been pumping rounds into the rocks north of Charlie. Now the piercing whine of the ricochets moved away, south along the ridge line, and he knew the Twilighter was firing blind, unsure of his target's position.

There was, after all, a chance Charlie could get off the ridge alive.

He got his feet under him, still hiding behind the boulders, keeping low. He shuffled around a bit until he was facing north.

The gunner stopped firing.

Was he just pausing to study the terrain, moving to another position? Or was he changing magazines again?

If the former were the case, then the man was still armed and dangerous; if the latter, he was temporarily defenseless.

Charlie couldn't hear the noises he had heard when the magazine had been changed before, but he couldn't squat here and wait forever, so he jumped up anyway, straight up, and *there* was his nemesis, only twenty feet away, standing in the snow. It was a man in brown insulated pants and a dark parka, not changing the machine gun's magazine but squinting at the ridge plateau beyond Charlie — until Charlie popped up and caught his attention. He cried out and swung the muzzle of the machine gun toward Charlie.

But Charlie had the element of surprise on his side and got off a round first. It struck the Twilighter in the throat.

The man appeared to take a great jump backwards, swinging his automatic weapon straight up and letting off a useless burst of fire at the snow-filled sky as he collapsed.

His neck had been ripped apart, his spinal cord severed, and his head nearly taken off. Death had been instantaneous.

And in the instant Death embraced the machine gunner, as the sound of Charlie's shot split the cold air, he saw that there was a second man on the ridge, thirty feet behind the first and over to the right, near the rocky crest. This one had a rifle, and he fired even as Charlie recognized the danger.

As if battered by a sledgehammer, Charlie was spun around and knocked down. He struck the ground hard and lay behind the boulders, out of sight of the rifleman, out of the line of fire, safe but not for long. His left arm, left shoulder, and the left side of his chest suddenly felt cold, very cold, and numb. Although there was no pain yet, he knew he had been hit. Solidly hit. It was bad.

61

The screams brought Christine out of the cul-de-sac, past the dying fire, onto the trail.

She looked up toward the ridge. She couldn't see all the way to the top of the valley wall, of course. It was too far. The snow and the trees blocked her view.

The screaming went on and on. God, it was awful. In spite of the distance and the muting effect of the forest, it was a horrible, bloodcurdling shriek of pain and terror. She shivered, and not because of the cold air.

It sounded like Charlie.

No. She was letting her imagination run away with her. It could have been anyone. The sound was too far away, too distorted by the trees for her to be able to say that it was Charlie.

It went on for half a minute or maybe even longer. It *seemed* like an hour. Whoever he was, he was screaming his guts out up there, one scream atop the other, until *she* wanted to scream, too. Then it subsided, faded, as if the screamer suddenly had insufficient energy to give voice to his agony.

Chewbacca came out onto the trail and looked up toward the top of the valley.

Silence settled in.

Christine waited.

Nothing.

She returned to the sheltered niche, where Joey sat in a stupor, and picked up the shotgun.

It was a shoulder wound. Serious. His entire arm was numb, and he couldn't move his hand. Damned serious. Maybe mortal. He wouldn't know until he could get out of his jacket and thermal underwear and have a look at it — or until he began to pass out. If he lost consciousness in this bitter cold, he would die, regardless of whether the Twilighters came along to finish him off.

As soon as he realized he was hit, Charlie screamed, not because the pain was so bad (for there was no pain yet), and not because he was scared (though he was *damned* scared), but because he wanted the man who had shot him to *know* that he was hit. He shrieked as a man might if he were watching his own entrails pour out of a grievous wound in his stomach, screamed as if he knew he were dying, and as he screamed he turned onto his back, stretched out flat in the snow, pushed the rifle aside because it was of little use to him now that he no longer had two good hands. He unzipped his jacket, pulled the revolver out of his shoulder holster. Keeping the gun in his good right hand, he tucked that arm under him, so his body concealed the weapon. His useless left arm was flung out at his side, the hand turned with the palm up, limp. He began to punctuate his screams with desperate gasping sounds; then he let the screams subside, though putting an even more horrible groan into them. Finally he went silent.

The wind died down for a moment, as if cooperating with Charlie. The mountain was tomb-quiet.

He heard movement beyond the boulders that screened him from the gunman. Boots on snow-free stone. A few more quick footsteps. Then wary silence. Then a few more footsteps.

He was counting on this man being an amateur, like the guy with the machine gun. A pro would be shooting when he came around the granite formation. But an amateur would want to believe the screams, would be congratulating himself on a good kill, and would be vulnerable.

Footsteps. Closer. Very close now.

Charlie opened his eyes wide and stared straight up at the gray sky. The rock formation kept some of the falling snow out of his way, but flakes still dropped onto his face, onto his eyelashes, and he needed all of his will power to keep from blinking.

He let his mouth sag open, but he held his breath because it would spiral up in a frosty plume and thus betray him.

A second passed. Five seconds. Ten.

In another half minute or so, he would need to breathe. His eyes were beginning to water.

Suddenly this seemed like a bad plan. Stupid. He was going to die here. He had to think of something better, more clever. Then the Twilighter appeared, edging around the hump of granite.

Charlie stared fixedly at the sky, playing dead; therefore, he couldn't see what the stranger looked like; he was aware of him only peripherally. But he felt sure that his performance as a corpse was convincing, and well it should have been, for he had provided a liberal display of his own blood as stage dressing.

The gunman stepped closer, stood directly over him, looking down, grinning.

Charlie had to strain not to focus on him, had to continue to look straight through him. It wasn't easy. The eye was naturally drawn toward movement.

The stranger still had a rifle and was still on his feet, better armed and more agile than Charlie. If he realized Charlie was still alive, he could finish the job in a fraction of a second.

A beat.

Another.

Irrationally, Charlie thought: *He'll hear my heart!*

That irrational terror gave rise to a more realistic fear – the possibility that the gunman would see Charlie's pulse beating in his neck or temple. Charlie almost panicked at that thought, almost moved. But he realized that his coat and the attached hood concealed both his neck and his temples; he would not be betrayed by his own throbbing blood flow.

Then the Twilighter stepped past him, to the lip of the ridge, and shouted down to his fellow churchmen on the slope below. 'I got him! I got the son of a bitch!'

The moment the gunman's attention was elsewhere, Charlie rolled slightly to the left, freeing his right hand, which had been under his buttocks, bringing up the revolver.

The Twilighter gasped, began to turn.

Charlie shot him twice. Once in the side. Once in the head.

The man went over the brink, crashed through some brush, rolled down between the trees, and came to a stop against the broad trunk of a pine, dead before he even had a chance to scream.

Turning onto his stomach, Charlie pulled himself to the edge of the ridge and looked down. Some of Spivey's people had come out of hiding in response to the rifleman's shout of triumph. Apparently, not all of them realized their enemy was still alive. Most likely they thought the two subsequent shots had been fired by their own man, to make sure Charlie was dead, and they probably figured the body toppling off the crest was Charlie's. They didn't dive for cover again until he shouted, 'Bastards,' and squeezed off two rounds from the revolver. Then, like a pack of rats smelling a cat, they scuttled into safe dark places.

He loosed the remaining two rounds in the revolver, not expecting to hit anyone, not even taking aim, intending only to frighten them and force them to lie low for a while.

'I got both of them!' he shouted. 'They're both dead. How come they're both dead if God's on *your* side?'

No one below responded.

The shouting winded him. He waited a moment, drawing several deep breaths, not wanting them to hear any weakness in his voice. Then he shouted again: 'Why don't you stand up and let God stop the bullets when I shoot at you?'

No answer.

'That would prove something, wouldn't it?'

No answer.

He took several long, slow breaths.

He tried flexing his left hand, and the fingers moved, but they were still numb and stiff.

Wondering whether he had killed enough of them to make them turn back, he did a little arithmetic. He had killed two on the ridge top, one on the trail, three down in the meadow where they had huddled around the Jeep and the snowmobiles. Six dead. Six of ten. How many did that leave in the woods below him? Three? He thought he'd seen three others down there: another woman, Kyle, and the man who had been in front of Kyle, toward the end of the line. But wouldn't at least one of them have stayed behind with Mother Grace? Surely she wouldn't have remained alone at the cabin. And she wouldn't have been able to come up here, on such an arduous hike. Would she? Or was she there among the trees right now, only sixty or seventy yards away, crouching in the shadows like an evil old troll?

'I'm going to wait right here,' he shouted. He fished half a dozen cartridges out of a jacket pocket and, hampered by having only one good hand, reloaded the revolver.

'Sooner or later, you're going to have to move,' Charlie called down to them. 'You'll have to stretch your muscles, or you'll cramp up.' His voice sounded eerie in the snowy stillness. 'You'll cramp up, and you'll slowly start freezing to death.'

The anesthetizing shock of being shot was beginning to wear off. His nerves began to respond, and the first dull pain crept into his shoulder and arm.

'Any time you're ready,' he shouted, 'let's test your faith. Let's see if you *really* believe God is on your side. Any time you're ready, just stand up and let me take a shot at you, and let's see if God turns the bullets away.'

He waited half a minute, until he was sure they weren't going to respond, and then he holstered his revolver and eased away from the crest. They wouldn't know he had left. They might suspect, but they couldn't be sure. They would be pinned down for half an hour, maybe longer, before they finally decided to risk continuing their ascent. At least he hoped to God they would. He needed every minute he could get.

With the dull pain in his shoulder rapidly growing sharper, he belly-crawled all the way across the flat top of the ridge, moving like a crippled crab, and didn't stand up until he had reached the place where the land sloped down and the deer trail headed off through the trees.

When he tried to rise, he found his legs were surprisingly weak; they crumpled under him, and he dropped back to the ground, jarring his injured arm — Christ! — and felt a big black wave roaring toward him. He held his breath and closed his eyes and waited until the wave had passed, refusing to be carried away by it. The pain was not dull any longer; it was a stinging, burning, *gnawing* pain, as if a living creature had burrowed into his shoulder and was now eating its way out. It was bad enough when he was perfectly still, but the slightest movement made it ten times worse. However, he couldn't just lie here. Regardless of the pain, he had to get up, return to Christine. If he was going to die, he didn't want to be alone in these woods when his time came. Christ, that was inexcusably negative thinking, wasn't it? Mustn't think about dying. The thought is father to the deed, right? The pain was bad, but that didn't mean the wound was mortal. He hadn't come this far to give up so easily. There was a chance. Always a chance. He had been an optimist all his life. He had survived two abusive, drunken parents. He had survived poverty. He had survived the war. He would survive this, too, dammit. He crawled off the plateau, onto the deer trail. Just over the edge of the crest, he grabbed a branch on a spruce and pulled himself upright at last, leaning on the trunk of the tree for support.

He wasn't dizzy, and that was a good sign. After he had taken several deep breaths and had stood there against the tree for a minute, his legs became less rubbery. The pain from the wound did not subside, but he found that he was gradually adjusting to it; he either had to adjust or escape it by surrendering consciousness, which was a luxury he could not afford.

He moved away from the tree, gritting his teeth as the fire in his shoulder blazed up a bit higher, and he descended along the deer path, moving faster than he had thought he could, though not as fast as he had come down the first time, when Christine and Joey had been with him. He was in a hurry, but he was also cautious, afraid of slipping, falling, and further injuring his shoulder and arm. If he fell on his left side, he would probably pass out from the subsequent explosion of pain, and then he might not come around again until Spivey's people were standing over him, poking him with the barrel of a gun.

Sixty or seventy yards below the ridge, he realized he should have brought the machine gun with him. Perhaps there were a couple of spare magazines of ammunition on the dead gunner's body. That would even the odds a bit. With a machine gun, he might be able to set up another ambush and wipe out all of them this time.

He stopped and looked back, wondering if he should return for the weapon. The rising trail behind him looked steeper than he remembered it. In fact the climb appeared as challenging as the most difficult face on Mount Everest. He breathed harder just looking up at it. As he studied it, the path seemed to grow even steeper. Hell, it looked *vertical*. He didn't have the strength to go back, and he cursed himself for not thinking of the machine gun while he was up there; he realized he wasn't as clear-headed as he thought.

He continued downward.

Twenty yards farther along the trail, the forest seemed to spin under him. He halted and planted his legs wide, as if he could bring the carousel of trees to a stop just by digging in his heels. He *did* slow it down, but he couldn't stop it altogether, so he finally proceeded cautiously, putting one foot in front of the other with the measured deliberation of a drunkard trying to prove sobriety to a cop.

The wind had grown stronger, and it made quite a racket in the huge trees. Some of the tallest creaked as the higher, slenderer portions of their trunks swayed in the inconstant gusts. The woody branches clattered together, and the shaken evergreen needles clicked-rustled-hissed. The creaking grew louder until it sounded like a thousand doors opening on unoiled hinges, and the clicking and rustling and hissing grew louder, too, thunderous, until the noise was painful, until he felt as if he were inside a drum, and he staggered, stumbled, nearly fell, realized that most of the sound wasn't coming from the wind in the trees but from his own body, realized he was hearing his own blood roar in his ears as his heart pounded faster and faster. Then the forest began to spin again, and as it spun it pulled darkness down from the sky like thread from a spool, more and more darkness, and now the whirling forest didn't seem like a carousel but like a loom, weaving the threads of darkness into a black cloth, and the cloth billowed around him, settled over him, and he couldn't see where he was going, stumbled again, and fell—

Pain!

A bright blast.

Darkness.

Blackness.

Deeper than night.

Silence . . .

He was crawling through pitch blackness, frantically searching for Joey. He had to find the boy soon. He had learned that Chewbacca wasn't an ordinary dog but a robot, an evil construction, packed full of explosives. Joey didn't know the truth. He was probably playing with the dog right this minute. Any second now, Spivey would press the plunger, and the dog would blow up, and Joey would be dead. He crawled toward a gray patch in the darkness, and then he was in a bedroom, and he saw Joey sitting up in bed. Chewbacca was there, too, sitting up just like a person, holding a knife in one paw and fork in the other. The boy and the dog were both eating steak. Charlie said, 'For God's sake, what're you eating?' And the boy said, 'It's delicious.' Charlie got to his feet beside the bed and took the meat away from the boy. The dog snarled. Charlie said, 'Don't you see? The meat's been poisoned. They've poisoned you.' 'No,' Joey said, 'it's good. You should try some.' 'Poison! It's poison!' Then Charlie remembered the explosives that were hidden in the dog, and he started to warn Joey, but it was too late. The explosion came. Except it wasn't the dog that exploded. It was Joey. His chest blew open, and a horde of rats surged out of it, just like the rat in the battery room under the windmill, and they rushed at Charlie. He staggered backward, but they surged up his legs. They were all over him, scores of rats, and they bit him, and he fell, dragged down by their numbers, and his blood poured out of him, and it was cold blood, cold instead of warm, and he screamed —

— and woke, gagging. He could feel cold blood all over his face, and he wiped at it, looked at his hand. It wasn't actually blood; it was snow. He was lying on his back in the middle of the deer path, looking up at the trees and at a section of gray sky from which snow fell at a fierce rate. With considerable effort, he sat up. His throat was full of phlegm. He coughed and spat.

How long had he been unconscious?

No way to tell.

As far as he could see, the trail leading up toward the crest of the ridge was deserted. Spivey's people hadn't yet come after him. He couldn't have been out for long.

The pain in his arm and shoulder had sent questing tendrils across his back and chest, up his neck, into his skull. He tried to raise his arm and had some success, and he could move his hand a little without making the pain any worse.

He squirmed to the nearest tree and attempted to pull himself up, but he couldn't do it. He waited a moment, tried again, failed again.

Christine. Joey. They were counting on him.

He would have to crawl for a while. Just till his strength returned. He tried it, on hands and knees, putting most of his weight on his right arm, but demanding some help from his left, and to his surprise he was able to shuffle along at a decent pace. Where the angle of the slope allowed him to accept gravity's assistance, he slid down the trail, sometimes as far as four or five yards, before coming to a stop.

He wasn't sure how far he had to go before reaching the rocky overhang under which he had left Christine and Joey. It might be around the next bend — or it might be hundreds of yards away. He had lost his ability to judge distance. But he hadn't lost his sense of direction, so he crabbed down toward the valley floor.

A few minutes or a few seconds later, he realized he had lost his rifle. It had probably come off his shoulder when he'd fallen. He ought to go back for it. But maybe it had slipped off the trail, into some underbrush or into a jumble of rocks. It might not be easy to find. He still had his revolver. And Christine had the shotgun. Those weapons would have to be sufficient.

He crawled farther down the trail and came to a fallen tree that barred his way. He didn't remember that it had been here earlier, though it might have been, and he wondered if he had taken a wrong turn somewhere. But on the first two trips, he hadn't noticed any branches in the trail, so how could he have gone wrong? He leaned against the log —

— and he was in a dentist's office, strapped into a chair.

He had grown a hundred teeth in his left shoulder and arm, and as luck would have it all of them were in need of root canal work. The dentist opened the door and came in, and it was Grace Spivey. She had the biggest, nastiest drill he had ever seen, and she wasn't even going to use it on the teeth in his shoulder; she was going to bore a hole straight through his heart —

— and his heart was pounding furiously when he woke and found himself slumped against the fallen log.

Christine.

Joey.

Mustn't fail them.

He climbed over the log, sat on it, wondered if he dared to try walking, decided against it, and slipped down to his knees again. He crawled.

In a while his arm felt better.

It felt *dead*. That was better.

The pain subsided.

He crawled.

If he stopped for a moment and curled up and closed his eyes, the pain would go away altogether. He knew it would.

But he crawled.

He was thirsty and hot in spite of the frigid air. He paused and scooped up some snow and put it in his mouth. It tasted coppery, foul. He swallowed anyway because his throat felt as if it were afire, and the wretched-tasting snow was at least cool.

Now all he needed before moving on again was a moment's rest. The day wasn't bright; nevertheless, the gray light striking down between the trees hurt his eyes. If he could just close them for a moment, shut out the gray glare for a few seconds . . .

62

Christine didn't want to leave Joey and Chewbacca alone under the overhang, but she had no choice because she knew Charlie was in trouble. It wasn't just the extended gunfire that had worried her. It was partly the screaming, which had stopped some time ago, and partly the fact that he was taking so long. But mainly it was just a hunch. Call it woman's intuition: she *knew* Charlie needed her.

She told Joey she wouldn't go far, just up the trail a hundred yards or so, to see if there was any sign of Charlie. She hugged the boy, asked him if he would be all right, thought he nodded in response, but couldn't get any other reaction from him.

'Don't go anywhere while I'm gone,' she said.

He didn't answer.

'Don't you leave here. Understand?'

The boy blinked. He still wasn't focusing on her.

'I love you, honey.'

The boy blinked again.

'You watch over him,' she told Chewbacca.

The dog snorted.

She took the shotgun and went out onto the trail, past the dying fire. She glanced back. Joey wasn't even looking at her. He was leaning against the rock wall, shoulders hunched, head bowed, hands in his lap, staring at the ground in front of him. Afraid to leave him, but also afraid that Charlie needed her, she turned away and headed up the deer path.

The heat from the fire had done her some good. Her bones and muscles didn't feel as stiff as they had a while ago; there wasn't so much soreness when she walked.

The trees protected her from most of the wind, but she knew it was blowing furiously, for it made a wild and ghoulish sound as it raged through the highest branches. In those places where the forest parted to reveal patches of leaden sky, the snow came down so thick and fast that it almost seemed like rain.

She had gone no more than eighty yards, around two bends in the trail, when she saw Charlie. He was lying face-down in the middle of the path, head turned to one side.

No.

She stopped a few feet from him. She dreaded going closer because she knew what she would find.

He was motionless.

Dead.

Oh, Jesus, he was dead. They had killed him. She had loved him, and he had loved her, and now he had died for her, and she was sick with the thought of it. The somber, sullen colors of the day seeped into her, and she was filled with a cold grayness, a numbing despair.

But grief had to allow room for fear, as well, because now she and Joey were on their own, and without Charlie she didn't think they would make it out of the mountains. At least not alive. His death was an omen of their own fate.

She studied the woods around her, decided that she was alone with the body. Evidently, Charlie had been hurt up on the ridge top and had managed to come this far under his own steam. Spivey's fanatics were apparently still on the other side of the ridge.

Or maybe he had killed them all.

Slipping the shotgun strap over her shoulder, she went to him, reluctant to examine him more closely, not certain she had the strength to look upon his cold dead face. She knelt beside him — and realized that he was breathing.

Her own breath caught in her throat, and her heart seemed to miss a beat or two.

He *was* alive.

Unconscious but alive.

Miracles did happen.

She wanted to laugh but repressed the urge, superstitiously afraid that the gods would be displeased by her joy and would take Charlie from her, after all. She touched him. He murmured but didn't come around. She turned him onto his back, and he grumbled at her without opening his eyes. She saw the torn shoulder of his jacket and realized he had been shot. Around the wound, lumps of dark and frozen blood adhered to the shredded fabric. It was bad, but at least he wasn't dead.

'Charlie?'

When he didn't reply she touched his face and spoke his name again, and finally his eyes opened. For a moment they were out of focus, but then he fixed on her and blinked, and she saw that he was aware, sluggish and perhaps fuzzy-headed but not delirious.

'Lost it,' he said.

'What?'

'The rifle.'

'Don't worry about it,' she said.

'Killed three of them,' he said thickly.

'Good.'

'Where are they?' he asked worriedly.

'I don't know.'

'Must be near.'

'I don't think so.'

He tried to sit up.

Apparently, a dark current of pain crackled through him, for he winced and held his breath, and for a moment she thought he was going to pass out again.

He was too pale, corpse-white.

He squeezed her hand until the pain subsided a bit.

He said, 'Still others coming,' and this time he managed to sit up when he tried.

'Can you move?'

'Weak . . .'

'We've got to get out of here.'

'Was . . . crawling.'

'Can you walk?'

'Not by myself.'

'If you lean on me?'

'Maybe.'

She helped him to his feet, gave him support, and encouraged him to descend the path. They made slow, halting progress at first, then went a bit faster, and a couple of times they slipped and almost fell, but eventually they reached the overhang.

Joey didn't react to their arrival. But as Christine helped Charlie case to the ground, Chewbacca came over, wagging his tail, and licked Charlie's face.

The rock walls had absorbed a lot of heat from the fire, which was now little more than embers, and warmth radiated from the stone on all sides.

'Nice,' Charlie said.

His voice was too dreamy to suit Christine.

'Light-headed?' she asked.

'A little.'

'Dizzy?'

'Was. Not now.'

'Blurred vision?'

'Nothing like that.'

She said, 'I want to see that wound,' and she began taking off his jacket.

'No time,' he said, putting a hand on hers, stopping her from tending to him.

'I'll be quick about it.'

'No *time*!' he insisted.

'Listen,' she said, 'right now, with all the pain you're in, you can't move fast.'

'A damned turtle.'

'And you're losing your strength.'

'Feel like . . . a little kid.'

'But we have a pretty extensive first-aid kit, so maybe we can patch you up and alleviate some of the pain. Then maybe you can get on your feet and get moving faster. If so, we'll be damned glad we took the time.'

He thought about it, nodded. 'Okay. But . . . keep your ears open. They might not be . . . far away.'

She removed his quilted jacket, unbuttoned his shirt, slipped it off his injured shoulder, then unsnapped and pulled back the top of his insulated underwear, which was sticky with blood and sweat. There was an ugly hole in him, high in the left side of his chest, just below the shoulder bones. The sight of it gave her the feeling that live snakes were writhing in her stomach. The worst of the bleeding had stopped, but the flesh immediately around the wound was swollen, an angry shade of red. The skin color faded to purple farther away from the hole, then to a dead-pale white.

'Lot of blood?' he asked.

'There was.'

'Now?'

'Still bleeding a little.'

'Spurting?'

'No. If an artery had been hit, you'd be dead by now.'

'Lucky,' he said.

'Very.'

An exit wound scarred his back. The flesh looked just as bad on that side, and she thought she saw splinters of bone in the torn and bloody meat of him.

'Bullet's not in you,' she said.

'That's a plus.'

The first-aid kit was in his backpack. She got it out, opened a small bottle of boric acid solution and poured it into the wound. It foamed furiously for a moment, but it didn't sting as iodine or Merthiolate would have; with a slightly dreamy, detached air, Charlie watched it bubble.

She hastily packed some snow into a tin cup and set it to melt on the hot coals of the burnt-out fire.

He overcame his dreaminess, shook his head as if to clear it, and said 'Hurry.'

'Doing the best I can,' she said.

When the boric acid had finished working, she quickly dusted both the entry and exit wounds with a yellowish antibiotic powder, then with a mild, white anesthetizing powder. Now there was almost no bleeding at all. Taking off her gloves so she could work faster and better, she used cotton pads, gauze pads, and a two-inch-wide roll of gauze to fashion an unsatisfactory and somewhat amateurish bandage, but she fixed it in place with so much white adhesive tape that she knew it would stay put.

'Listen!' he said.

She was very still.

They listened, but there was only the wind in the trees.

'Not them,' she said.

'Not yet.'

'Chewbacca will warn us if anyone's coming.'

The dog was lying beside Joey, at ease.

The icy air had already leeched the stored-up warmth in the stone. Beneath the rocky overhang, the sheltered niche was growing cold again. Charlie was shivering violently.

She hurriedly dressed him, pulled up the zipper on his jacket, tugged his hood in place and tied it under his chin, then fetched the cupful of melted snow from the embers. The first-aid kit contained Tylenol, which was not nearly a strong enough pain-suppressant for his needs, but it was all they had. She gave him two tablets, hesitated, then a third. At first he had a bit of trouble swallowing, and that worried her, but he said it was just that his mouth and throat were so dry, and by the time he took the third tablet he seemed better.

He wouldn't be able to carry his backpack; they would have to abandon it.

She shook a few items out of her own bag in order to get the first-aid kit into it, secured all the flaps. She slipped her arms through the loops, buckled the last strap across her chest.

She was frantic to get moving. She didn't need a wrist watch to know they were running out of time.

63

Kyle Barlowe was a big man but not graceless. He could move stealthily and sure-footedly when he put his mind to it. Ten minutes after Harrison killed Denny Rogers and threw his body down from the crest of the ridge, Barlowe moved cautiously from the tangle of dead brush where he had been hiding, and slipped across the face of the slope to a spot where shadows lay like frozen pools of night. From the shadows he dashed catlike to a huge fallen tree, from there to a jagged snout of rock poking up from the hillside. He neither climbed nor descended the slope, moved only laterally, away from the area over which Harrison held dominion, leaving the others pinned down but, with luck, not for long.

After another ten minutes, when he was certain that he was well out of Harrison's sight, Barlowe became less circumspect, rushed boldly up the slope to the crest, crawled over it. He moved through a gap between two rock formations and stood up on the flat, wind-abraded top of the ridge.

He had a Smith & Wesson .357 Magnum in a shoulder holster. He unzipped his jacket long enough to get the revolver. The snow was coming down so hard that he couldn't see more than twenty feet, sometimes not even that far. The limited visibility didn't worry him. In fact, he figured it was a gift from God. He already knew the spot from which Harrison had been firing on them; he wouldn't have any difficulty finding it. But in the meantime the snow would screen him from Harrison — if the detective was still on the ridge, which was doubtful.

He moved southward, directly into the raging wind. It stung and numbed his face, made him squint. His eyes watered and his nose dripped. But it couldn't stagger him or knock him down; it would have more easily felled one of the massive trees along the ridge line.

In fifty yards he found Morgan Pierce's body. The staring but unseeing eyes did not look human, for they were sheathed by milky cataracts that were actually thin films of crazed ice. The eyebrows and lashes and mustache were frosted. The wind was industriously packing snow in the angles formed by the dead man's arms, legs, and bent neck.

Barlowe was surprised to see that Harrison had not taken Pierce's Uzi, a compact Israeli-made gun. He picked it up, hoping it hadn't been damaged by the snow. He decided he'd better not rely on the Uzi until he had a chance to test it, so he slung it over his shoulder and kept the .357 in his right hand.

Staying close to the granite outcroppings along the eastern crest of the ridge, he crept toward the place from which Harrison had shot at them, from which he had pitched Denny Rogers down the slope. The .357 thrust out in front of him, Barlowe eased around the boulder that formed the northern wall of Harrison's roost – and was not surprised to discover the detective was gone.

The nook between rock formations was somewhat protected from the wind; therefore, some snow had settled and remained within the niche. Brass glinted in the snow: several expended cartridges.

Barlowe also noticed blood on the rocks that formed the walls of that sheltered space: dark, frozen stains on the grayish granite.

He stooped, stared at the cartridges poking out of the white-mantled floor. He brushed away the soft, dry layer of new flakes that had fallen in the past half an hour or so, pushing the expended cartridges aside as well, and he found a lot more blood on the older layer of snow underneath. Denny Rogers' blood? Or was some of it Harrison's? Maybe Rogers *had* wounded the bastard.

He turned away from the eastern crest, stepped across the narrow ridge top, and began searching for the place at which the deer path continued into the next valley. Because the Antichrist and his guardians had followed the trail this far, it was logical to assume they'd continue to follow it down the far side of the ridge. The new snow didn't cling to the wind-blasted plateau, but it was piling up just over the edge of the crest, where the wind didn't hit as hard and where brush and rocks gave it drift points against which it could build, and it obscured the entrance to the deer path. He almost missed the trail, had to kick through a drift, but then saw both deer tracks and human footprints in the more meager carpet of snow under the trees.

He went down the slope a few yards, until he found what he had hoped for: spots of blood. There was no way this could be Denny Rogers' blood. No doubt about it now: Harrison was hurt.

64

Charlie was impressed but not surprised by how quickly and surely Christine took charge. She got them out on the trail and moving down toward the valley again.

Joey and Chewbacca followed them. The boy said nothing, shuffled along as if he felt they were wasting their time trying to escape. But he didn't stop, didn't fall back, stayed close. The dog took his cue from his master, padding along in silence, his head drooping, his eyes downcast.

Charlie expected to hear shouting on the trail behind them. Minute by minute, he was increasingly sure that gunfire would break out.

But the snow fell, the wind whooped, the trees creaked and rustled, and Spivey's people did not appear. He must have put a damned good scare into them with that last ambush. They must have stayed where he'd left them for at least half an hour, afraid to crawl out of hiding, and when they *had* begun to move, they must have proceeded to the ridge top with extreme caution.

It was too much to hope they had given up and turned back. They would never give up. He had learned that much about them, anyway. Denton Boothe, his fat psychologist friend, had been right: Only death would stop this breed of fanatic.

As it wound down the lower half of the valley wall, the deer trail took a more wandering route than before. They were not going to reach the bottom as fast as they had anticipated.

During the first twenty minutes, Charlie didn't need much help. For the most part the path was gentle and undemanding. A few times he had to grab a tree or put one hand against a pillar of rock to keep his balance, and twice, when the land sloped too steeply, he leaned on Christine, but he didn't hang on her constantly. In fact he got along considerably better than he had thought possible when they'd started out.

Although the Tylenol and the anesthetizing powder had taken the edge off the pain in his shoulder and arm, it was still bad. In fact, even softened by the drugs, it was so intense that he would have expected to be incapacitated by it, but he discovered he had more tolerance for pain than he had thought; he was adapting to it, grinding his teeth into calcium sand and cutting permanent lines of agony in his face, but adapting.

After twenty minutes, however, his strength began to ebb, and he needed Christine's help more often. They reached the valley floor in twenty-five minutes, by which time he was beginning to get slightly dizzy again. Five minutes later, when they came to the edge of a broad meadow, where twin hammers of snow and wind pounded the land, he had to stop and rest while still in the shelter of the woods. He sat under a pine and leaned against the trunk.

Joey sat beside him but said nothing, didn't even acknowledge his presence. Charlie was too weak to attempt to elicit a word or a smile from the boy.

Chewbacca licked his paws. They were bleeding a little.

Christine sat, too, and took out the map that Charlie had spread on the table at the cabin, yesterday, when he'd insisted on showing her how they would get out of the mountains if Spivey's people arrived and tried to corner them. Christ, how unlikely such a situation had seemed then, and how terribly inevitable it seemed now!

Christine had to fold and refold the map, keeping it small while she studied it, because the wind occasionally broke out of the meadow and lashed between the trees, reaching some distance into the dense forest to slap and poke and grab at everything in its path.

Beyond the perimeter of the woods, a fierce blizzard raged across the valley floor. The wind was from the southwest, roaring like an express train from one end of the valley to the other, harrying sheets of snow in front of it. The snow was so thick that, most of the time, you could see only about a third of the way across the meadow, where the world appeared to end in a blank white wall. But occasionally the wind subsided for a few seconds or briefly changed directions, and the hundreds of opaque curtains of snow fluttered and parted at the same instant, and in the distance you could see more trees crowding the other side of the meadow, and then the far wall of the somewhat narrow valley, and beyond that another faraway ridge crest where ice and rock shone like chrome even in the sunless gloom.

According to the map, a little creek cut through the middle of the meadow and ran the length of the valley. She looked up, squinted at the white maelstrom beyond the forest, but she couldn't see the creek out there, not even when the snow parted. She figured it was frozen over and covered with snow. If they followed the creek (instead of crossing the meadow into the next arm of the woods), they would eventually come to the upper end of a narrow draw that sloped down toward the lake, for this was a high valley that funneled southwest, and they were still far above Tahoe. Yesterday, when he had first brought out the map, Charlie had said they would follow this route if they had to leave the cabin and take to the wilds, but that had been before he was shot. It was a three- or four-mile hike to civilization from here, not a discouragingly long way — *if* you were in good physical condition. However, now that he was wounded and weak, and with a full-scale blizzard moving in, there was absolutely no hope of getting down to the lake by that route. In their circumstances, three or four miles was a journey every bit as epic as a trek across China.

She desperately searched the map for some other way out or for some indication of shelter, and after consulting the key several times to interpret the cartographer's symbols, she discovered the caves. They were along this same side of the valley, half a mile northeast of here. Judging by the map, the caves were a point of interest for those hardy hikers who were curious about ancient Indian wall paintings and who had a mania for collecting arrowheads. Christine could not determine whether it was just one or two small caves or an extensive network of them, but she figured they would be at least large enough to serve as a place to hide from both Spivey's fanatics and the murderous weather.

She moved closer to Charlie, put her head to his in order to be heard above the cacophonous wind, and told him what she had in mind. He was in complete agreement, and his confidence in her plan gave her more faith in it. She stopped worrying about whether going to the caves was a wise decision, and she *started* worrying about whether they would be able to make it there through the storm.

'We could walk northeast through the woods, following the base of the valley wall,' she told Charlie, 'but that would leave a trail.'

'Whereas, if we went out into the meadow before heading up the valley, if we traveled out there in the open, the storm would obliterate our tracks in no time.'

'Yes.'

'Spivey's people would lose us right here,' he said.

'Exactly. Of course, to reach the caves, we'd have to re-enter the woods farther north, but there's not a chance in a million that they'd pick up our trail again. For one

410

thing, they'll be expecting us to head *down* the valley, southwest, toward the lake, 'cause civilization is that direction.'

'Right.' He licked his cracked lips. 'There's nothing at all northeast of us but . . . more wilderness.'

'They won't look for us in that neighborhood — will they?' Christine asked.

'I doubt it,' he said. 'Let's get moving.'

'Walking out there in the open, in the wind and snow isn't going to be easy,' she said.

'I'm all right. I can make it.'

He didn't *look* as if he could make it. He didn't look as if he could even get up. His eyes were watery and bloodshot. His face was gaunt and shockingly pale, and his lips were bloodless.

'But you've got to . . . look out for Joey,' Charlie said. 'Better cut a piece of line . . . put him on a tether.'

That was a good suggestion. Out in the open field, visibility was only a dozen yards in the best moments, declining to less than four yards when the wind whipped up and the snow squalled. It would be easy for Joey to wander a few steps off course, and once they were separated, they would find it difficult if not impossible to locate each other again. She cut a length of rope from the coil that hung on her backpack and made a tether that allowed the boy six feet of play; she linked them, waist to waist.

Charlie repeatedly, nervously looked back the way they had come.

Christine was most disturbed by the fact that Chewbacca, too, was watching the trail along which they'd come. He was still lying down, still relatively calm, but his ears had perked up, and he was growling softly in the back of his throat.

She helped Charlie and Joey put on their ski masks

because they would need them now, whether or not the eye holes restricted their vision. She put on her own mask, replaced her hood, pulled the drawstring tight under her chin.

Joey rose without being told. She decided that was a good sign. He still seemed lost, detached, uninterested in what was happening around him, but at least on a subconscious level he knew it was time to go, which meant he wasn't *completely* beyond reach.

Christine helped Charlie get to his feet.

He looked bad.

This last half mile to the caves was going to be sheer torture for him. But there was nothing else they could do.

Keeping one hand on Charlie's good arm, ready to provide support if he needed it, tethered to Joey, she led them into the meadow. The wind was a raging beast. The air temperature was at least twenty below zero. The snowflakes were not really flakes any more; they had shrunk to tiny, crystal pellets that bounced off Christine's insulated clothing with a sharp ticking sound. If Hell was cold instead of hot, this was what it must be like.

65

Ashes and half-burned black branches were all that remained of the fire that had recently flourished in the middle of the deer path. Kyle Barlowe kicked at the charred detritus, scattering it.

He stepped under the rocky overhang and looked at the abandoned backpack. There were scraps of paper in one corner of the rocky niche, wrappers from prepackaged gauze bandages.

'You were right,' Burt Tully said. 'The man's been hurt.'

'Bad enough he can't carry his pack any more,' Barlowe said, turning away from the abandoned gear.

'But I'm still not sure we should go after him, just the four of us,' Tully said. 'We need reinforcements.'

'There's no time to go for them,' Kyle Barlowe said.

'But he . . . he's killed so many of us.'

'Are you turning yellow on us?'

'No, no,' Tully said, but he looked scared.

'You're a soldier now,' Barlowe said. 'With God's protection.'

'I know. It's just . . . this guy . . . Harrison . . . he's damned good.'

'Not as good as he was before Denny shot him.'

'But *he* shot Denny! He must still have a lot on the ball.'

Impatiently, Kyle said, 'You saw the place farther back on the trail, where he fell. There was more blood there, where she came and helped him.'

'But reinforcements –'

'Forget it,' Kyle said, pushing past him.

He had his doubts, too, and he wondered if he was being sharp with Burt only to push his own second-thoughts out of his mind.

Edna Vanoff and Mother Grace were waiting on the trail.

The old woman didn't look well. Her eyes were bloodshot, deeply sunken, pinched half shut by the sooty flesh that ringed them. She stood round-shouldered, bent at the waist, the very image of exhaustion.

Barlowe was amazed that she had come this far. He had wanted her to stay back at the cabin, with guards, but she had insisted on going farther into the mountains with them. He knew she was a vital woman, possessed of considerable strength and stamina for her age, but he was surprised by her unflagging progress through the woods. Occasionally they had to help her over a rough spot, and once he had even carried her for thirty yards or so, but for the most part she had made it on her own.

'How long ago did they leave this place?' Grace asked him, her voice as cracked and bloodless as her lips.

'Hard to say. Fire's cold, but in this weather the embers would cool off real fast.'

Burt Tully said, 'If Harrison is as badly wounded as we think, they can't be making good time. We must be closing on them. We can afford to go slowly, be careful, and make sure we don't walk into another ambush.'

Grace said, 'No, if they're close, let's hurry, get it over with.'

She turned, took one step, stumbled, fell.

Barlowe lifted her to her feet. 'I'm worried about you, Mother.'

She said, 'I'm fine.'

But Edna Vanoff said, 'Mother, you look . . . wrung out.'

'Maybe we should rest here a few minutes,' Burt said.

'No!' Mother Grace said. Her bloodshot eyes transfixed them, each in turn. 'Not a few minutes. Not even *one* minute. We don't dare give the boy a second more than we have to. I've told you . . . each second he lives, his power increases. I've told you a thousand times!'

Barlowe said, 'But Mother, if anything happens to you, the rest of us won't be able to go on.'

He flinched from the penetrating power of her eyes. And now her voice had a special quality that entered it only when she was having a vision, a piercing resonance that vibrated in his bones: 'If I fail, you *must* go on. You *will* go on. It's blasphemy to say your allegiance is to me rather than to God. You *will* go on until your own legs fail, until

414

you can't crawl another foot. And then you will *still* go on, or God will have no pity on you. No pity and no mercy. If you fail Him in this, He will let your souls be conscripted into the armies of *Hell*.'

Some people were not swayed when Mother Grace spoke to them in this manner. Some heard nothing but the ranting of an old fool. Some fled as if she were threatening them. Some laughed. But Kyle Barlowe had always been humbled. He was still enthralled by her voice.

But will I be enthralled and obedient when she finally tells me to kill the boy? Or will I resist the violence that I used to thrive upon? Wrong-thought.

They left the rocky overhang, headed down the deer trail, Barlowe leading, Edna Vanoff second, Mother Grace third, and Burt Tully bringing up the rear. The howling of the wind seemed like a great demonic voice, and to Barlowe it was a constant reminder of the malignant forces that were even now conspiring to take control of the earth.

66

Christine was beginning to think they would never get out of the meadow alive.

This was worse than a blizzard. It was a white-out, with the wind so strong it would have been a hurricane in a tropical climate, and with the snow coming down so hard and so fast that she couldn't see more than two or three feet ahead. The world had vanished; she was moving through a nightmare landscape without detail, a world composed solely of snow and gray light; she could not see the forest on any side. She couldn't always see Joey when he ranged to the end of the tether. It was terrifying. And although the light was gray and diffuse, there was an all-pervading glare that made her eyes burn, and she realized that the threat of snow-blindness was very real. What would they do if they had to feel their way through the meadow, sightless, seeking the northeast end of the valley by instinct alone? She knew the answer: They would die. She paused every thirty steps to look at the compass, sheltering it in her gloved hands, and although she tried to move always in a straight line, she found, on several occasions, that they were heading in the wrong direction, and she had to correct their course.

Even if they didn't get disoriented and lost, they could die out here if they didn't move fast enough, for it was colder than she had ever thought it could be, so cold that she wouldn't have been surprised if she had suddenly frozen solid, upright, in mid-stride.

She was worried sick about Joey, but he stayed on his feet and plodded along at her side long after she expected him to drop. His quasi-catatonic withdrawal was, ironically, of benefit to him in these circumstances; having tuned out the real world, he was less affected by the cold and wind than he otherwise might have been. Even so, the elements would take their toll of him in time. She would soon have to get him off the meadow, into the comparative shelter of the forest, whether or not they reached the area in which the caves were situated.

Charlie fared worse than the boy. He stumbled frequently, went to his knees a couple of times. After five minutes, he occasionally leaned on Christine for support. After ten minutes, he needed her more than occasionally. After fifteen, he required her support constantly, and they were slowed to little more than a shuffle.

She couldn't tell either him or Joey that she was soon going to head toward the woods, for the wind made conversation impossible. When she faced into the wind, her words were driven back into her throat even as she spoke them, and when she faced away from it, her words were torn like fragile cloth and scattered in meaningless syllables.

For long minutes she lost sight of Chewbacca, and several times she was certain she'd never see the dog again, but he always reappeared, bedraggled and obviously weak, but alive. His fur was crusted with ice, and when he appeared out of the surging rivers of snow, he seemed like a revenant journeying back from the far side of the grave.

The wind swept broad areas of the meadow almost clean of snow, leaving just a few well-packed inches in some places, but drifts piled up against even the smallest windbreaks and filled in gullies and depressions, creating traps that could not be seen or avoided. They had abandoned Charlie's snowshoes with his backpack, partly because his wounded shoulder prevented him from carrying them any longer and partly because he was no longer sufficiently sure-footed to use them. As a result, she and Joey couldn't use their snowshoes to go across the drifts because they had to follow a route Charlie could negotiate with them. At times she found herself suddenly wading in snow up to her knees, then up to mid-thigh and getting deeper, and she had to back-track and find a way around the drift, which wasn't easy when she couldn't see where the hell she was going. At other times, she stepped into holes that the snow had filled in; with no warning at all, from one step to the other, she was waist-deep.

She was afraid there might be an abrupt drop-off or a really deep sinkhole somewhere in the meadow. Sinkholes were not uncommon in mountain country like this; they had passed a few earlier in the day, seemingly bottomless holes, some ancient and ringed with water-smoothed limestone. If she took one misplaced step and plunged down into snow over her head, Charlie might not be able to get her out again, even if she didn't break a leg in the process. By the same token, she wasn't sure she could extricate them from a similar trap if they fell into it.

She became so concerned about this danger that she stopped and untied the tether from her waist. She was afraid of dragging Joey into a chasm with her. She coiled the line around her right hand; she could always let go, let it unravel, if she actually did sink into a trap.

She told herself that the things we fear most never happen to us, that it's always something else that brings us down, something totally unexpected – like Grace Spivey's chance encounter with them in the South Coast Plaza parking lot last Sunday afternoon. But when they were well into the meadow, when she was almost ready to lead them back toward the eastern forest again, the worst happened, after all.

Charlie had just found new reserves of strength and had let go of her arm when she put her foot down into suddenly deep snow and realized she had found the very thing she feared. She tried to throw herself backward, but she had been leaning forward to begin with, bent by the wind, and her momentum was all forward, and she couldn't change her balance in time. Unleashing a loud scream that the wind softened to a quiet cry, she dropped into snow over her head, struck bottom eight feet down, crumpling, with her left leg twisted painfully under her.

She looked up, saw the snow caving in above her. It was filling the hole she'd made when she'd fallen through it.

She was going to be buried alive.

She had read newspaper stories about workmen buried alive, suffocated or crushed to death, in caved-in ditches, no deeper than this. Of course, snow wasn't as heavy as dirt or sand, so she wouldn't be crushed, and she would be able to claw her way through it, and even if she couldn't get all the way out, she would still be able to breathe under the snow, for it wasn't as compact and suffocating as earth, but that realization did not alleviate her panic.

She jackknifed onto her feet an instant after hitting bottom, in spite of the pain in her leg, and she clawed for firm handholds, for the hidden side of the gully or pit into which she had stepped. But she couldn't find it. Just snow. Soft, yielding snow, infuriatingly insubstantial.

She was still screaming. A clump of snow fell into her open mouth, choking her. The pit was caving in above her, on all sides, pouring down around her, up to her shoulders, then up to her chin, *Jesus*, and she kept pushing the snow away from her head, desperate to keep her face and arms free, but it closed over her faster than she could dig it away.

Above, Charlie's face appeared. He was lying on the ground, leaning over the edge of the drop, looking down at her. He was shouting something. She couldn't understand what he was saying.

She flailed at the snow, but it weighed down on her, an ever-increasing cascade, pouring in from the drift all around, until at last her aching arms were virtually pinned at her sides. *No!* And still the snow collapsed inward, up to her chin again, up to her mouth. She sealed her lips, closed her eyes, sure that she was going under altogether, that it would cover her head, that Charlie would never be able to get her out, that this would be her grave. But then the cave-in ceased before her nose was buried.

She opened her eyes, looked up from the bottom of a white funnel, toward Charlie. The walls of snow were still, but at any moment they might tremble and continue to collapse on top of her.

She was rigid, afraid to move, breathing hard.

Joey. What about Joey?

She had released the tether (and Joey) as soon as she'd felt herself going into the pit. She hoped Charlie had stopped Joey before he, too, had plunged over the edge. In his trancelike state, the boy would not necessarily have halted just because she had gone under. If he had fallen into the drift, they would probably never find him. The snow would have closed over him, and they wouldn't be able to locate him by listening to his screams, not in this howling wind, not when his cries would be muffled by a few feet of snow.

She wouldn't have believed her heart could beat this fast or hard without bursting.

Above, Charlie reached down with his good arm, his hand open, making a come-to-me gesture with his fingers.

If she dug her arms free of the snow that now pinned them, she could grab hold of him, and together they could try to work her up and out of the hole. But in freeing her arms, she might trigger another avalanche that would cover her head with a couple of feet of snow. She had to be careful, move slowly and deliberately.

She twisted her right arm back and forth under the snow, packing the snow away from it, making a hollow space, then turned her palm up and clawed at the stuff with her fingers, loosening it, letting it slide back into the hollow by her arm, and in seconds she had made a tunnel up to the surface. She snaked her arm through the tunnel, and it came into sight, unhampered from fingertips to above the elbow. She reached straight up, gripped Charlie's extended hand. Maybe she would make it, after all. She clawed her other arm free, grabbed Charlie's wrist.

The snow around her shifted. Just a little.

Charlie began to pull, and she heaved herself up.

The white walls started falling in again. The snow sucked at her as if it were quicksand. Her feet left the ground as Charlie hauled her up, and she kicked out, frantically searching for the wall of the gully, struck it, tried to dig her feet in against it and use it to shove herself toward the top. He eased backwards, pulling her farther up. This must be agony for him, as the strain passed through his good arm and shoulder into his wounded shoulder, sapping whatever strength he had left. But it was working. Thank God. The sucking snow was letting go of her. She was now high enough to risk holding on to Charlie's arm with only one hand, while she grabbed at the brink of the gully with the other. Ice and frozen earth gave way under her clutching fingers, but she grabbed again, and this time she gripped something solid. With both Charlie and solid earth to cling to, she was able to lever herself up and out and onto her back, gasping, whimpering, with the unnerving feeling that she was escaping the cold maw of a living creature and had nearly been devoured by a beast composed of ice and snow.

Suddenly she realized that the shotgun, which had been slung from her shoulder when she'd fallen into the trap, had slipped off, or the strap had broken. It must still be in the pit. But the hole had closed up behind her when Charlie had pulled her out. It was lost.

It didn't matter. Spivey's people wouldn't be following them through the blizzard.

She got onto her hands and knees and crawled away from the snow trap, looking for Joey. He was there, on the ground, curled on his side, in a fetal position, knees drawn up, head tucked down.

Chewbacca was with him, as if he knew the boy needed his warmth, though the animal seemed to have no warmth to give. His coat was crusted with snow and ice, and there was ice on his ears. He looked at her with soulful brown eyes full of confusion, suffering, and fear.

She was ashamed she had blamed him, in part, for Joey's withdrawal and that she had wished she'd never seen him. She put one hand on his large head, and, even as weak as he was, he nuzzled her affectionately.

Joey was alive, conscious, but hurting bad. Impacted snow clogged his ski mask. If she didn't get him out of this wind soon, he would be frost-bitten. His eyes were even more distant than before.

She tried to get him to stand, but he couldn't. Although she was exhausted and shaky, although her left leg still hurt from the fall she had taken, she would have to carry him.

She dug the compass out of her pocket, studied it, and turned to face east-northeast, toward the section of woodland where the caves ought to be. She could see only five or six feet, and then the storm fell like a heavy drapery.

Surprised by the extent of her own stamina, she scooped Joey up, held him in both arms. A mother's instinct was to save her child, regardless of the cost to herself, and her maternal desperation had loosed some last meager store of adrenaline.

Charlie moved in beside her. He was on his feet, but he looked bad, almost as terrible as Joey.

'Got to get into the forest,' she shouted. 'Out of this wind!'

She didn't think he could have heard her, not with the banshee storm shrieking across the meadow, but he nodded as if he understood her intention, and they moved into the white-out, trusting in the compass to lead them to the comparative shelter of the mammoth trees, shuffling with exaggerated caution to avoid falling into another snow trap.

Christine looked back at Chewbacca. The dog was getting up to follow, but creakily. Even if he could regain his feet, there was almost no chance that he would make it to the trees with them. This would probably be the last glimpse she ever had of him; the storm would swallow him just as the snow-filled pit had tried to swallow her.

Each step was an ordeal.

Wind. Snow. Cruel cold.

Dying would be easier than going on.

That thought scared her and gave her the will to take a few more steps.

One good thing: There was no doubt that their trail would be completely erased. The raging wind and arctic-fierce snowfall would make it impossible for Spivey's fanatics to follow them.

Snow dropped from the sky as if it were being dumped out of huge bins, came hurtling down in sheets and clumps.

Another step. Another.

As if plating them with suits of armor, the wind welded the snow to their arms and legs and backs and chests, until their clothes were the same color as the landscape around them.

Something ahead. A dark shape. It materialized in the storm, then was blotted out by an even more furious squall of snow. It appeared again. Didn't fade away this time. And another one. Huge blobs of darkness, shadowy formations rising up beyond snowy curtains. Gradually they became clearer, better defined. Yes. A tree. Several trees.

They trudged at least fifty yards into the forest before they found a place where the interlacing branches of the evergreens were so thick overhead that a significant amount of snow was shut out. Visibility improved. They were free of the wind's brutal fists, as well.

Christine stopped, put Joey down, peeled off his snow-caked ski mask. Her heart twisted when she saw his face.

67

Kyle Barlowe, Burt Tully, and Edna Vanoff gathered around Grace at the edge of the forest, under the last of the evergreens. The wind licked at them from the meadow, as if hungry for their warmth. With her gloves off, Grace held her arms out, palms spread toward the meadow beyond the trees, receiving psychic impressions. The others waited silently for her to decide what to do next.

Out on the open floor of the valley, the fulminating blizzard was like an endless chain of dynamite detonations, a continuous roar, the violent waves of wind like concussions, the snow as thick as smoke. It was appropriate weather for the end of the world.

'They went this way,' Mother Grace said.

Barlowe already knew their quarry had left the forest here, for their tracks told him as much. Which direction they had gone after heading into the open was another question; although they had left here only a short while ago, their footprints had not survived much past the perimeter of the woods. He waited for Mother Grace to tell him something he could not discern for himself.

Worriedly studying the snow-lashed field in front of them, Burt Tully said, 'We can't go out there. We'd die out there.'

Suddenly Grace lowered her hands and backed away from the meadow, farther into the trees.

They moved with her, alarmed by the look of terror on her face.

'*Demons,*' she said hoarsely.

'Where?' Edna asked.

Grace was shaking. 'Out there . . .'

'In the storm?' Barlowe asked.

'Hundreds . . . thousands . . . waiting for us . . . hiding in the drifts . . . waiting to rise up . . . and destroy us . . .'

Barlowe looked out at the open fields. He could see nothing but snow. He wished he had Mother Grace's Gift. There were malevolent spirits near, and he could not detect them, and that made him feel frighteningly vulnerable.

'We must wait here,' Grace said, 'until the storm passes.'

Burt Tully was clearly relieved.

Barlowe said, 'But the boy —'

'Grows stronger,' Grace admitted.

'And Twilight?'

'Grows near.'

'If we wait —'

'We might be too late,' she said.

Barlowe said, 'Won't God protect us if we go into the meadow? Aren't we armored with His might and mercy?'

'We must wait,' was the only answer she gave him. 'And pray.'

Then Kyle Barlowe knew how late it really was. So late that they must be more vigilant than they had ever been before. So late that they could no longer be bold. Satan was now as strong and real a presence in this world as God Himself. Maybe the scales had not yet tipped in the devil's direction, but the balance was delicate.

68

Christine peeled off the boy's ice-crusted ski mask, and Charlie had to look away from the child's face when it was revealed.

I've failed them, he thought.

Despair flooded into him and brought tears to his eyes.

He was sitting on the ground, with his back to a tree. He rested his head against the trunk, too, closed his eyes, took several deep breaths, trying to stop shaking, trying to think positively, trying to convince himself that everything would turn out all right, failing. He had been an optimist all his life, and this recent acquaintance with soul-shaking doubt was devastating.

The Tylenol and the anaesthetic powder had had only slight effect on his pain, but even that minimal relief was fading. The pain in his shoulder was gaining strength again, and it was beginning to creep outward, as before, across his chest and up his neck and into his head.

Christine was talking softly and encouragingly to Joey, though she must have wanted to weep at the sight of him, as Charlie had done.

He steeled himself and looked at the boy again.

The child's face was red, lumpy, and badly misshapen from hives caused by the fierce cold. His eyes were nearly swollen shut; the edges of them were caked with a gummy, mucous-like substance, and the lashes were matted with the same stuff. His nostrils were mostly swollen shut, so he was breathing through his mouth, and his lips were cracked, puffy, bleeding. Most of his face was flushed an angry red, but two spots on his cheeks and one on the tip of his nose were gray-white, which might indicate frostbite, though Charlie hoped to God it wasn't.

Christine looked at Charlie, and her own despondency was evident in her troubled eyes if not in her voice. 'Okay. We've got to move on. Got to get Joey out of this cold. We've got to find those caves.'

'I don't see any sign of them,' Charlie said.

'They must be near,' she said. 'Do you need help getting up?'

'I can make it,' he said.

She lifted Joey. The boy didn't hold on to her. His arms hung down, limp. She glanced at Charlie.

Charlie sighed, gripped the tree, and got laboriously to his feet, quite surprised when he made it all the way up.

But he was even more surprised when, a second later, Chewbacca appeared, cloaked in snow and ice, head hung low, a walking definition of misery. When he had last seen the dog, out in the meadow, Charlie had been sure the animal would collapse and die in the storm.

'My God,' Christine said when she saw the dog, and she looked as startled as Charlie was.

It's important, Charlie thought. The dog pulling through — that means we're *all* going to survive.

He wanted very much to believe it. He tried hard to convince himself. But they were a long way from home.

The way things had been going for them, Christine figured they would be unable to find the caves and would simply wander through the forest until they dropped from exhaustion and exposure to the cold. But fate finally had a bit of luck in store for them, and they found what they were looking for in less than ten minutes.

The trees thinned out in the neighborhood of the caves because the land became extremely rocky. It sloped up in uneven steps of stone, in humps and knobs and ledges and set-backs. Because there were fewer trees, more snow found its way in here, and there were some formidable drifts at the base of the slope and at many points higher up, where a set-back or a narrower ledge provided accommodation. But there was more wind, too, whistling down from the tops of the surrounding trees, and large areas of rock were swept bare of snow. She could see the dark mouths of three caves in the lower formations, where she and Charlie might be able to climb, and there were half a dozen more visible in the upper formations, but those were out of reach. There might be more openings, now drifted shut and hidden, because this portion of the valley wall appeared to be a honeycomb of tunnels, caves, and caverns.

She carried Joey to a jumble of boulders at the bottom of the slope and put him down, out of the wind.

Chewbacca limped after them and slumped wearily beside his master. It was astonishing that the dog had made it all this way, but it was clear he would not be able to go much farther.

With a grateful sigh and a gasp of pain, Charlie lowered himself to the ground beside Joey and the dog.

The look of him scared Christine as much as Joey's tortured face. His bloodshot eyes were fevered, two hot coals in his burnt-out face. She was afraid she was going to wind up alone out here with the bodies of the only two people she loved, caretaker of a wilderness graveyard that would eventually become her own final resting place.

'I'll look in these caves,' she told Charlie, shouting to be heard now they were more or less in the open again. 'I'll see which is the best for us.'

He nodded, and Joey didn't react, and she turned away from them, clambered over the rocky terrain toward the first dark gap in the face of the slope.

She wasn't sure if this part of the valley wall was limestone or granite, but it didn't matter because, not being a spelunker, she didn't know which kind of rock made for the safest caves, anyway. Besides, even if these were unsafe, she would have to make use of them; she had nowhere else to go.

The first cave had a low, narrow entrance. She took the flashlight out of her backpack and went into that hole in the ground. She was forced to crawl on her hands and knees, and in some places the passage was tight enough to require some agile squirming. After ten or twelve feet, the tunnel opened into a room about fifteen feet on a side, with a low ceiling barely high enough to allow her to stand up. It was big enough to house them, but far from ideal. Other passages led off the room, deeper into the hillside, perhaps to larger chambers, but none of them was of sufficient diameter to let her through. She went out into the wind and snow again.

The second cave wasn't suitable, either, but the third was as close to ideal as she could expect to find. The initial passageway was high enough so she didn't have to crawl to enter, wide enough so she didn't have to squeeze. There was a small drift at the opening, but she stamped through it with no difficulty. Five feet into the hillside, the passage turned sharply to the right, and in another six feet it turned just as sharply back to the left, a double baffle that kept the wind out. The first chamber was about twenty feet wide and thirty or thirty-five feet long, as much as twelve to fifteen feet high at the near end, with a smooth floor, walls that were fractured and ragged in some places and water-smoothed in others.

To her right, another chamber opened off this one. It was smaller, with a lower ceiling. There were several stalactites and stalagmites that looked as if they had been formed from melted gray wax, and in a few places they met at the middle of the room to form wasp-waisted pillars. She shone the flashlight beam around, saw a passage at the far end of the second room and guessed it led to yet a third cave, but that was all she needed to know.

The first room had everything they required. Toward the back, the floor rose and the ceiling dropped down, and in the last five feet the floor shelved up abruptly, forming a ledge five feet deep and twenty feet wide, only four feet below the ceiling. Exploring this raised niche with her flashlight, Christine discovered a two-foot-wide hole in the rock above it, boring up into darkness, and she realized she had found a huge, natural fireplace with its own flue. The hole must lead into another cave farther up the hillside, and either that chamber or another beyond it would eventually vent to the outside; smoke would rise naturally toward the distant promise of open air.

Having a fire was important. They hadn't brought their sleeping bags with them because such bulky items would have slowed them down and because they had expected to reach the lake before nightfall, in which case they wouldn't have required bed-rolls. The blizzard and the bullet hole in Charlie's shoulder had changed their plans drastically, and now without sleeping bags to ward off the night chill and help conserve body heat, a fire was essential.

She wasn't worried about the smoke giving away their position. The forest would conceal it, and once it rose above the trees, it would be lost in the white whirling skirts of the storm. Besides, Spivey's fanatics would almost certainly be searching southwest, toward the end of the valley that led to civilization.

The chamber boasted one other feature that, at first, added to its appeal. One wall was decorated with a seven-foot-tall drawing, an Indian totem of a bear, perhaps a grizzly. It had been etched into the rock with a corrosive yellow dye of some sort. It was either crude or highly stylized; Christine didn't know enough about Indian totems to make the fine distinction. All she knew for sure was that drawings like this were usually meant to bring good luck to the occupants of the cave; the image of the bear supposedly embodied a real spirit that would provide protection. Initially, that seemed like a good thing. She and Charlie and Joey needed all the protection they could get. But as she paused a moment to study the sulfur-yellow bear, she got the feeling there was something threatening about it. That was ridiculous, of course, an indication of her shaky state of mind, for it was nothing but a drawing on stone. Nevertheless, on reappraisal, she decided she would have preferred another drab gray wall in place of the totem.

But she wasn't going to look for another cave just because she didn't like the decor of this one. The natural fireplace more than outweighed the previous occupants' taste in art. With a fire for heat and light, the cave would provide almost as much shelter as the cabin they had left behind. It would not be as comfortable, of course, but at the moment, she wasn't as concerned about comfort as she was worried about keeping her son, Charlie, and herself alive.

In spite of the stone floor that served as chair and bed, Charlie was delighted with the cave, and at the moment it seemed as luxurious as any hotel suite he'd ever occupied. Just being out of the wind and snow was an incomparable blessing.

For more than an hour, Christine gathered dead wood and crisp dry evergreen branches with which to make a fire and keep it going until morning. She returned to the cave again and again with armloads of fuel, making one stack for the logs and larger pieces of wood, another for the small stuff that would serve as tinder.

Charlie marveled at her energy. Could such stamina spring entirely from a mother's instinct to preserve her offspring's life? There seemed no other explanation. She should have collapsed long ago.

He knew he should switch the flashlight off each time she went outside, turn it on again only so she would be able to see when she came in with more wood, for he was concerned the batteries would go dead. But he left it burning, anyway, because he was afraid Joey would react badly to being plunged into total darkness.

431

The boy was in bad shape. His breathing was labored. He lay motionless, silent, beside the equally depleted dog.

As he listened to Joey's ragged breathing, Charlie told himself that finding the cave was another good sign, an indication their luck was improving, that they would recover their strength in a day or two and then head down toward the lake. But another, grimmer voice within him wondered if the cave was, instead, a tomb, and although he didn't want to consider that depressing possibility, he couldn't tune it out.

He listened, as well, to the drip-drip-drip of water in an adjacent chamber. The cold stone walls and hollow spaces amplified the humble sound and made it seem both portentous and strange, like a mechanical heartbeat or, perhaps, the tapping of one clawed finger on a sheet of glass.

The fire cast flickering orange light on the yellow bear totem, making it shimmer, and on drab stone walls. Welcome heat poured from the blazing pile of wood. The natural flue worked as Christine had hoped, drawing the smoke up into higher caves, leaving their air untainted. In fact, the drawing action of the fire took some of the dampness out of the air and eliminated most of the vaguely unpleasant, musty odor that had been in the dank chamber since she had first entered.

For a while they just basked in the warmth, doing nothing, saying nothing, even trying not to think.

In time Christine took off her gloves, lowered the hood of her jacket, then finally took off the jacket itself. The cave wasn't exactly toasty, and drafts circulated through it from adjacent caves, but her flannel shirt and long insulated underwear were now sufficient. She helped Charlie and Joey out of their jackets, too.

She gave Charlie more Tylenol. She lifted his bandage,

dusted in more powdered antibiotics and more of the anaesthetic as well.

He said he wasn't in much pain.

She knew he was lying.

The hives that afflicted Joey began, at last, to recede. The swelling subsided, and his misshapen face slowly regained its proportions. His nostrils opened, and he no longer needed to breathe through his mouth, although he continued to wheeze slightly, as if there was some congestion in his lungs.

Please, God, not pneumonia, Christine thought.

His eyes opened wider, but were still frighteningly empty. She smiled at him, made a couple of funny faces, trying to get a reaction out of him, all to no avail. As far as she could tell he didn't even see her.

Charlie didn't think he was hungry until Christine began to heat beans and Vienna sausages in the aluminum pot that was part of their compact mess kit. The aroma made his mouth water and his stomach growl, and suddenly he was shaking with hunger.

Once he began to eat, however, he filled up fast. His stomach bloated, and he found it increasingly difficult to swallow. The very act of chewing exacerbated the pain in his head, which doubled back along the lines of pain in his neck and all the way into the shoulder wound, making that ache worse, too. Finally the food lost its flavor, then seemed bitter. He ate about a fourth of what he first thought he could put away, and even the meager meal didn't sit well in his belly.

'You can't get more of it down?' Christine asked.

'I'll have more later.'

'What's wrong?'

'Nothing.'

'Do you feel nauseous?'

'No, no. I'm okay. Just tired.'

She studied him in silence for a moment, and he forced a smile for her sake, and she said, 'Well . . . whenever you're ready for more, I'll reheat it.'

As the fluttering fire made shadows leap and cavort on the walls, Charlie watched her feed Joey. The boy was willing to eat and able to swallow, but she had to mash up the sausages and beans, and spoon the stuff into his mouth as if she were feeding an infant instead of a six-year-old.

A grim sense of failure settled over Charlie once more.

The boy had fled from an intolerable situation, from a world of pure hostility, into a fantasy that he found more congenial. How far had he retreated into that inner world of his? Too far ever to come back?

Joey would take no more food. His mother was unhappy about how little he had eaten, but she couldn't force him to swallow even one more mouthful.

She fed the dog, too, and he had a better appetite than his master. Charlie wanted to tell her that they couldn't waste food on Chewbacca. If this storm was followed by another, if the weather didn't clear for a few days, they would have to ration what little provisions they had left, and they would regret every morsel that had been given to the dog. But he knew she admired the animal's courage and perseverance, and she felt its presence helped prevent Joey from slipping all the way down into deep catatonia. He didn't have the heart to tell her to stop feeding it. Not now. Not yet. Wait until morning. Maybe the weather would have changed by then, and maybe they would head southwest to the lake.

Joey's breathing worsened for a moment; his wheezing grew alarmingly loud and ragged.

Christine quickly changed the child's position, used her folded jacket to prop up his head. It worked. The wheezing softened.

Watching the boy, Charlie thought: Are you hurting as bad as I am, little one? God, I hope not. You don't deserve this. What you *do* deserve is a better bodyguard than I've been, and that's for damned sure.

Charlie's own pain was far worse than he let Christine know. The new dose of Tylenol and powdered anaesthetic helped, but not quite as much as the first dose. The pain in his shoulder and arm no longer felt like a living thing trying to chew its way out of him. *Now* it felt as if little men from another planet were inside him, breaking his bones into smaller and smaller splinters, popping open his tendons, slicing his muscles and pouring sulfuric acid over everything. What they wanted to do was gradually hollow him out, use acid to burn away everything inside him, until only his skin remained, and then they would inflate the limp and empty sack of skin and put him on exhibit in a museum back on their own world. That's how it felt, anyway. Not good. Not good at all.

Later, Christine went out to the mouth of the cave to get some snow to melt for drinking water, and discovered that night had fallen. They hadn't been able to hear the wind from within the cave, but it was still raging. Snow slanted down from the darkness, and the frigid, turbulent air hammered the valley wall with arctic fury.

She returned to the cave, put the pan of snow by the fire to melt, and talked with Charlie for a while. His voice was weak. He was in more pain than he wanted her to know, but she allowed him to think he was deceiving her because there wasn't anything she could do to make him more comfortable. In less than an hour, in spite of his pain, he was asleep, as were Joey and Chewbacca.

She sat between her son and the man she loved, with her back to the fire, looking toward the front of the cave, watching the shadows and reflections of the flames as they danced a frantic gavotte upon the walls. With one part of her mind she listened for unusual sounds, and with another part she monitored the respiration of the man and the boy, afraid that one of them might suddenly cease breathing.

The loaded revolver was at her side. To her dismay, she had learned that Charlie had no more spare cartridges in his jacket pockets. The box of ammo was in his backpack, which they had abandoned at the rocky overhang where she had patched his shoulder. She was furious with herself for having forgotten it. The rifle and shotgun were gone. The handgun was their only protection, and she had only the six shells that were in it.

The totem bear glowed on the wall.

At 8:10, as Christine finished adding fuel to the fire, Charlie began to groan in his sleep and toss his head on the pillow she had made from his folded jacket. He had broken out in a greasy sweat.

A hand against his forehead was enough to tell her that he had a fever. She watched him for a while, hoping he would quiet down, but he only got worse. His groans became soft cries, then less soft. He began to babble. Sometimes it was wordless nonsense. Sometimes he spat out words and disjointed, meaningless sentences.

At last he became so agitated that she got two more Tylenol tablets from the bottle, poured a cupful of water, and attempted to wake him. Although sleep seemed to be providing no comfort for him, he wouldn't come around at first, and when he finally did open his eyes they were bleary and unfocused. He was delirious and didn't seem to know who she was.

She made him take the pills, and he greedily swallowed the water, washing them down. He was asleep again even as she took the cup from his lips.

He continued to groan and mutter for a while, and although he was sweating heavily, he also began to shiver.

His teeth chattered. She wished they had some blankets.
She piled more wood on the fire. The cave was relatively
warm, but she figured it couldn't be *too* warm right now.

Around 10:00, Charlie grew quiet again. He stopped
tossing his head, stopped sweating, slept peacefully.

At least, she *told* herself it was sleep that had him. But
she was afraid it might be a coma.

Something squeaked.

Christine grabbed the revolver and bolted to her feet as
if the squeak had been a scream.

Joey and Charlie slept undisturbed.

She listened closely, and the squeak came again, more
than one short sound this time, a whole series of squeaks,
a shrill though distant chittering.

It wasn't a sound of stone or earth or water, not a dead
sound. Something else, something *alive*.

She picked up the flashlight. Heart pumping furiously,
holding the revolver out in front of her, she edged toward
the sound. It seemed to be coming from the cavern that
adjoined this one.

Soft as they were, the shrill cries nevertheless lifted the
hairs on the back of her neck because they were so eerie,
alien.

At the entrance of the next chamber, she stopped,
probing ahead with the beam of the flashlight. She saw
the waxy-looking stalactites and stalagmites, the damp rock
walls, but nothing out of the ordinary. The noises now
seemed to be coming from farther away, from a third
cavern or even a fourth.

As she cocked her head and listened more intently,
Christine suddenly understood what she was hearing. Bats.
A lot of them, judging by their cries.

Evidently, they always nested in another chamber,
elsewhere in the mountain, always entered and exited by

another route, for there was no sign of them here, no bat corpses or droppings. Okay. She didn't mind sharing the caves with them, just as long as they kept to their own neighborhood.

She returned to Charlie and Joey and sat down between them, put the gun aside, switched off the flashlight.

Then she wondered what would happen if Spivey's people showed up, blocked off the entrance to this cave, and left them no option but to head deeper into the mountain in search of another way out, a back door to safety. What if she and Charlie and Joey were forced to flee from cave to cave and eventually had to pass through that chamber in which the bats nested? It would probably be knee-deep in bat shit, and there would be hundreds — maybe *thousands* — of them hanging overhead, and a few of them or even *all* of them might have rabies, because bats were excellent carriers of rabies —

Stop it! she told herself angrily.

She had enough to worry about already. Spivey's lunatics. Joey. Charlie's wound. The weather. The long journey back to civilization. She couldn't add bats to the list. That was crazy. There was only a chance in a million that they would ever have to go near the bats.

She tried to relax.

She put more wood on the fire.

The squeaking faded.

The caves became silent again except for Joey's labored breathing and the crackle of the fire.

She was getting drowsy.

She tried every trick she could think of to keep herself awake, but sleep continued to close in on her.

She was afraid to let herself go under. Joey might take a turn for the worse while she was dozing. Or Charlie might need her, and she wouldn't know.

Besides, someone ought to stand guard.

Spivey's people might come in the night.

No. The storm. Witches weren't allowed to fly on their brooms in storms like this.

She smiled, remembering the way Charlie had joked with Joey.

The flickering firelight was mesmerizing . . .

Someone ought to stand guard, anyway.

Just a quick nap.

Witches . . .

Someone . . . ought to . . .

It was one of those nightmares in which she knew she was asleep, knew that what was happening was not real, but that didn't make it any less frightening. She dreamed that all the caves in the valley wall were connected in an elaborate maze, and that Grace Spivey and her religious terrorists had entered this particular cave from other chambers farther along the hillside. She dreamed they were preparing a human sacrifice, and the sacrifice was Joey. She was trying to kill them, but each time she shot one of them, the corpse divided into two *new* fanatics, so by murdering them she was only adding to their numbers. She became increasingly frantic and terrified, increasingly outnumbered, until all the caves within the valley wall were swarming with Spivey's people, like a horde of rats or cockroaches. And then, aware that she was dreaming, she began to suspect that Grace Spivey's followers were not only in the caves of the dream but in the *real* caves in the real world beyond sleep, and they were conducting a human sacrifice in *both* the nightmare and in reality, and if she didn't wake up and stop them, they were going to kill Joey for real, kill him while she slept. She struggled to free herself of sleep's iron grip, but she could not do it, could not wake up, and now in the dream they were going to cut the boy's throat. And in reality, beyond the dream?

69

When Christine woke in the morning, Joey was eating a chocolate bar and petting Chewbacca.

She watched him for a moment, and she realized tears were streaming down her cheeks. This time, however, she was crying because she was happy.

He seemed to be returning from his self-imposed psychological exile. He was in better physical shape, too. Maybe he was going to be all right. Thank God.

The swelling was gone from his face, replaced by a better — though not really healthy — color, and he was no longer having difficulty breathing. His eyes were still blank, and he continued to be withdrawn, but not nearly as far-off and pathetic as he had been yesterday.

The fact that he had gone to the supplies, had rummaged through them, and had found the candy for himself was encouraging. And he had apparently added wood to the fire, for it was burning brightly, though after being untended during the night it should have cooled down to just a bank of hot coals.

She crawled to him and hugged him, and he hugged her, too, though weakly. He didn't speak, wouldn't be bribed or teased or encouraged into uttering a single word. And he still wouldn't meet her eyes directly, as if he were not entirely aware that she was here with him; however, she had the feeling that, when she looked away from him, his intense blue eyes turned toward her and lost their slightly glazed and dreamy quality. She wasn't positive. She couldn't catch him at it. But she dared to hope that he was returning to her, slowly feeling his way back from the edge of autism, and she knew she must not rush him or push him too hard.

Chewbacca had not perked up as much as his young master, though he was a bit less weak and stringy looking than he had been last night. The pooch seemed to grow healthier and more energetic even as Christine watched the boy pet him, responding to each pat and scratch and stroke as if Joey's small hands had healing power. There was sometimes a wonderful, mysterious, deep sharing, an instant bonding in the relationships between children and their animals.

Joey held his candy bar out in front of him, turned it back and forth, and seemed to be staring at it. He smiled vaguely.

Christine had never wanted anything more than she had wanted to see him smile, and a smile came to her own face in sympathy with his.

Behind her, Charlie woke with a start, and she went to him. She saw at once that, unlike Joey and the dog, he had not improved. The delirium had left him, but in all other ways his condition had grown worse. His face was the color and texture of bread dough, greasy with sweat. His eyes appeared to have collapsed back into his skull, as if the supporting bones and tissues beneath them had crumpled under the weight of things he had seen. Forceful shivers shook him, and at times they grew into violent tremors only one step removed from convulsions.

He was partially dehydrated from the fever. His tongue clove to the roof of his mouth when he tried to speak.

She helped him sit up and take more Tylenol with a cup of water. 'Better?'

'A little,' he said, speaking only slightly louder than a whisper.

'How's the pain?'

'Everywhere,' he said.

Thinking he was confused, she said, 'I mean the pain in your shoulder.'

"Yeah. That's what . . . I mean. It's no longer . . . just in my shoulder. It feels like . . . it's *everywhere* now . . . all through me . . . head to foot . . . everywhere. What time is it?'

She checked her watch. 'Good heavens! Seven-thirty. I must've slept hours without stirring an inch, and on this hard floor.'

'How's Joey?'

'See for yourself.'

He turned his head and looked just as Joey fed a last morsel of chocolate to Chewbacca.

Christine said, 'He's mending, I think.'

'Thank God.'

With her fingers, she combed Charlie's damp hair back from his forehead.

When they'd made love at the cabin, she had thought him by far the most beautiful man she had ever known. She had been thrilled by the contour of each masculine muscle and bone. And even now, when he was shrunken and pale and weak, he seemed beautiful to her: His face was so sensitive, his eyes so caring. She wanted to lie beside him, put her arms around him, hold him close, but she was afraid of hurting him.

'Can you eat something?' she asked.

He shook his head.

'You should,' she said. 'You've got to build up your strength.'

He blinked his rheumy eyes as if trying to clear his vision. 'Maybe later. Is it . . . still snowing?'

'I haven't been outside yet this morning.'

'If it's cleared up . . . you've got to leave at once without me.'

'Nonsense.'

'This time of year . . . the weather might clear for only . . . a day or even just . . . a few hours. You've got to take advantage of good weather . . . the moment it comes . . . get out of the mountains . . . before the next storm.'

'Not without you.'

'Can't walk,' he said.

'You haven't tried.'

'Can't. Hardly . . . can talk.'

Even the effort at conversation weakened him. His breathing grew more labored word by word.

His condition frightened her, and the notion of leaving him alone seemed heartless.

'You couldn't tend the fire here, all by yourself,' she protested.

'Sure. Move me . . . closer to it. Within arm's reach. And pile up . . . enough wood . . . to last a couple of days. I'll be . . . Okay.'

'You won't be able to prepare and heat your food —'

'Leave me a couple . . . candy bars.'

'That's not enough.'

He scowled at her and, for a moment, managed to put more volume in his voice, forced a steely tone: 'You've *got* to go without me. It's the only way, dammit. It's best for you and Joey . . . and it's best for me, too, because I'm . . . not going to get out of here . . . without the help of a medical evacuation team.'

'All right,' she said. 'Okay.'

He sagged, exhausted by that short speech. When he spoke again, his voice was not only a whisper but a *quavering* whisper that sometimes faded out altogether on the ends of words. 'When you get down . . . to the lake . . . you can send help back . . . for me.'

'Well, it's all moot until I find out whether the storm has let up or not,' she said. 'I better go have a look.'

As she began to get up, a man's voice called to them from the mouth of the cave, beyond the double baffle of the entrance passage: 'We know you're in there! You can't hide from us! We know!'

Spivey's hounds had found them.

70

Acting instinctively, not hesitating to consider the danger of her actions, Christine snatched up the loaded revolver and sprinted across the cave toward the Z-shaped passage that led outside.

'*No!*' Charlie said.

She ignored him, came to the first bend in the passage, turned right without checking to see if anyone was there, saw only the close rock walls and a vague spot of gray light at the next turn, beyond which lay the last straight stretch of tunnel and then the open hillside. She rushed forth with reckless abandon because that was probably the last thing Spivey's people would expect of her, but also because she couldn't possibly proceed in any other fashion; she was not entirely in control of herself. The crazy, vicious, stupid bastards had driven her out of her home, and put her on the run, had cornered her here in a hole in the ground, and now they were going to kill her baby.

The unseen man shouted again: '*We know you're in there!*'

She had never before in her life been hysterical, but she was hysterical now, and she knew it, couldn't help it. In fact, she didn't care that she was hysterical because it felt *good*, damned good, just to let go, to give in to blind rage and a savage desire to spill blood, *their* blood to make *them* feel some pain and fear.

With the same irrational disregard for danger that she had shown when turning the first blind corner in the passageway, she now turned the second, and ahead of her was the last stretch of the tunnel, then open air, and a figure silhouetted in the gray morning light, a man in a parka with a hood pulled up on his head. He was holding a rifle — no, a machine gun — but he was pointing it more or less at the ground, not directly ahead into the tunnel, because he wasn't expecting her to rush straight out at him and make such an easy target of herself, not in a million years, but that was just what she was doing, like a crazy kamikaze, and to hell with the consequences. She took him by surprise, and as he started to raise the muzzle of the machine gun to cover her, she fired once, twice, three times, hitting him every time, because he was so close that it was almost impossible to miss him.

The first shot jolted him, seemed to lift him off his feet, and the second shot flung him backwards, and the third shot knocked him down. The machine gun flew out of his hands, and for a moment Christine had a hope of getting hold of it, but by the time she stepped out of the cave, that immensely desirable weapon was clattering down the rocky slope.

She saw that the snow had stopped falling, that the wind was no longer blowing, and that there were three people on the slope behind the man she had killed. One of the three, an incredibly big man, off to her left, was already diving for cover, reacting to the shots that had wasted his buddy, though that first body had just hit the ground and bounced and was not yet still. The other two Twilighters weren't as quick as the giant. A short stocky woman stood directly in front of Christine, no more than ten or twelve feet away, a perfect target, and Christine reflexively pulled off a shot, and that woman went down, too, her face exploding like a punctured balloon full of red water.

Although Christine had plunged along the passageway and out of the cave in silence, she began to scream now, uncontrollably, shouting invectives at them, yelling so loud that her throat hurt and her voice cracked, then screaming louder still. She was using words she had never used before, and she was shocked by what she heard spewing from her own lips, yet was unable to stop, because her rage had reduced her to inarticulate noises and mindless obscenities.

And as she screamed her lungs out, even as she saw the stocky woman's face exploding, Christine turned on the third Twilighter, the one to her right, twenty feet away, and she saw at once that it was Grace Spivey.

'You!' she shouted, her hysteria stoked by the sight of the crone. '*You! You crazy old bitch!*'

How could a woman of her age have the stamina to climb these ridges and battle the life-sapping weather of the high Sierras? Did her madness give her strength? Yes, probably. Her madness blocked all doubt, all weariness, just as it had shielded her from pain when she had punctured her hands and feet to fake crucifixion stigmata.

God help us, Christine thought.

The hag stood unmoving, unbent, arrogant, defiant, as if daring Christine to pull the trigger, and even from this distance, Christine felt the strange and riveting power of the old woman's eyes. Immune to the hypnotic effect of that mad gaze, she fired a shot, the revolver bucking in her hands. She missed even though the distance was not great, squeezed the trigger again, was surprised when she missed a second time at such close range, tried a third shot but discovered she was out of ammunition.

Oh, Jesus.

No more bullets. No other weapons. Jesus. Nothing but her bare hands.

Okay, I can do it, I can do it, bare hands, all right, I'll strangle the bitch, I'll tear her goddamned head off.

Sobbing, cursing, shrieking, carried forward on a crashing wave of terror, she started toward Spivey. But the other Twilighter, the giant, began shooting at her from behind some boulders, where he had taken cover. Shots exploded and then ricocheted off the rocks around her with a piercing whine. She sensed bullets cutting the air near her head. She realized she couldn't help Joey if she was dead, so she stopped, turned back toward the cave.

Another shot. Sharp chips of stone sprayed up from the point of impact.

She was still hysterical, but all that manic energy was suddenly redirected, away from rage and blood lust, toward the survival instinct. With the sound of gunfire behind her, she stumbled back to the cave. The giant left his hiding place and came after her. Slugs whacked into the stone beside her, and she expected to take one in the back. Then she was through the entrance to the caves, into the first stretch of the Z-shaped passageway, out of sight of the gunman, and she thought she was safe. But one last shot ricocheted around the corner from the first length of the tunnel and slammed into her right thigh, kicking her off her feet. She went down, landing hard on her shoulder, and saw darkness reach up for her.

Refusing to succumb to the numbing effect of the shock that followed being hit, gasping for breath, desperately fending off the welling darkness that pooled up behind her eyes, Christine dragged herself along the passageway.

She didn't think they would come straight in after her. They couldn't know that she possessed only one gun or that she was out of ammunition. They would be wary.

But they *would* come. Cautiously. Slowly.

Not slowly enough.

They were relentless, like a posse in a Western movie.

Sweating in spite of the cold air, heaving and pulling her leg along as if it were a hunk of concrete, she hitched herself into the cave, where Charlie and Joey waited in the capering light of the fire.'

'Oh, Christ, you've been shot,' Charlie said.

Joey said nothing. He was standing by the ledge on which the fire was burning, and the pulsing light gave his face a bloody cast. He was sucking on one thumb, watching her with enormous eyes.

'Not bad,' she said, trying not to let them see how scared she was. She pulled herself up against the wall, standing on one leg.

She put one hand on her thigh, felt sticky blood. She refused to look at it. If it was bleeding heavily, she'd need a tourniquet. But there wasn't time for first aid. If she paused to apply a tourniquet, Spivey or the giant might just walk in and blow her brains out.

She wasn't dizzy yet, and she was no longer in imminent danger of passing out, but she was beginning to feel weak.

She was still holding the empty, useless gun. She dropped it.

'Pain?' Charlie asked.

'No.' That much was true; she felt little or no pain at the moment, but she knew it would come soon.

Outside, the giant was yelling: 'Give us the boy! We'll let you live if you'll just give us the boy.'

Christine ignored him. 'I got two of the bastards,' she told Charlie.

'How many are left?' he asked.

'Two more,' she said, giving no additional details, not wanting Joey to know that Grace Spivey was one of the two.

Chewbacca had gotten to his feet and was growling in the back of his throat. Christine was surprised the dog could stand up, but he was far from recovered; he looked sick and wobbly. He wouldn't be able to do much fighting or protect Joey.

She spotted the knife from the mess kit, which lay between Joey and Charlie, at the far end of the room. She asked Joey to bring it to her, but he only stared, unmoving, and would not be coaxed into helping.

'No more ammo?' Charlie asked

'None.'

From outside: '*Give us the boy!*'

Charlie tried to inch toward the knife, but he was too weak and too tortured by pain to accomplish the task. The effort made him wheeze, and the wheezing developed into a wracking cough, and the cough left him limp with exhaustion and with bloody saliva on his lips.

Christine had a frantic sense of time running out like sand pouring from the bottom of a funnel.

'*Give us the Antichrist!*'

Although Christine couldn't move fast, she began to make her way to the other end of the room, following the wall and bracing herself against it, hopping on her uninjured leg. If she could get to the knife, then return to this end of the chamber, she could wait just this side of the passageway, around the corner, and when they came in she might be able to lurch forward and stab one of them.

She finally reached the supplies and bent down and picked up the knife — and realized how short the blade was. She turned it over and over in her hand, trying to convince herself that it was just the weapon she needed. But it would have to penetrate a parka and the clothes underneath before doing any damage, and it wasn't long enough. If she had a chance to stab at their faces . . . but they would have guns, and she didn't have much hope of carrying out a successful frontal assault.

Damn.

She threw the knife down in disgust.

'Fire,' Charlie said.

At first she didn't understand.

He raised one hand to his mouth and wiped at the bloody saliva that he continued to cough up. 'Fire. It's . . . a good . . . weapon.'

Of course. Fire. Better than a knife with a stubby little blade. Suddenly she thought of something that, used in conjunction with a burning brand, would be almost as effective as a gun.

In her wounded leg, a dull pain had begun to throb in time with her rapid pulse, but she gritted her teeth and stooped down beside the pile of supplies. Stooping was not easy, and involved a painful maneuver, and she dreaded having to stand up again, even though she had the wall against which to support herself. She poked through the items she had emptied out of the backpack yesterday, and in a few seconds she turned up the squeeze-can of lighter fluid, which they had bought in case they had trouble starting a fire in the fireplace at the cabin. She stashed the can in the right-hand pocket of her pants.

When she stood, the stone floor rolled under her. She grabbed the edge of the raised hearth and waited until the dizziness passed.

She turned to the fire, snatched a burning branch from between two larger logs, afraid it would sputter out when she removed it from the blaze, but the branch continued to burn, a bright torch.

Joey did not move or speak, but he watched with interest. He was depending on her. His life was entirely in her hands now.

She hadn't heard any shouting from outside in quite some time. That silence wasn't welcome. It might mean Spivey and the giant were on their way inside, already in the Z-shaped passage . . .

She embarked upon a return trip around the room, past Charlie, toward the passageway through which the Twilighters might come at any moment, taking the long route because in her condition it was safest. She was agonizingly aware of the precious seconds she was wasting, but she couldn't risk going straight across the room because if she fell she might pass out or extinguish the torch. She held the burning brand in her left hand, using the other to steady herself against the wall, limping instead of hopping because limping was faster, daring to use the injured leg a little, though pain shot all through her when she put much weight on her right foot. And although the pain still throbbed in sympathy with her pounding pulse, it was no longer dull; it was a burning-stinging-stabbing-pinching-twisting pain that was getting worse with each punishing beat of her heart.

She briefly wondered how much blood she was losing, but she told herself it didn't matter. If she wasn't losing a lot, she might be able to take one last stand against the Twilighters. If she was losing too much, if it was pouring from a major vein or spurting from a nicked artery, there was no use checking on it, anyway, because a tourniquet would not save her, not out here, miles from the nearest medical assistance.

By the time she made her way to the far end of the chamber and stopped next to the mouth of the entrance tunnel, she was light-headed and nauseated. She gagged and tasted vomit at the back of her throat, but she managed to choke it down. The rippling light of the fire, lapping at the walls, imparted an amorphous feeling to the cave, as if the chamber's dimensions and contours were in a constant state of flux, as if the stone were not stone at all but some strange plastic that continuously melted and reformed: the walls receded, now drew closer, too close, now receded again; a convexity of rock suddenly appeared where there had been a concavity; the ceiling bulged downward until it almost touched her head, then snapped back to its former height; the floor churned and rose and then slid down until it seemed it would drop out from under her completely.

In desperation she closed her eyes, squeezed them tight, bit her lip, and breathed deeply until she felt less faint. When she opened her eyes again, the chamber was solid, unchanging. She felt relatively stable, but she knew it was a fragile stability.

She pressed against the wall, into a shallow depression to one side of the passageway. Holding the torch in her left hand, she fumbled in her pocket with her right hand and withdrew the squeeze-can of lighter fluid. Gripping it with three fingers and her palm, she used her thumb and forefinger to screw off the cap, uncovering the rigid plastic nozzle. She was ready. She had a plan. A good plan. It *had* to be because it was the only plan she could come up with.

The big man would probably be the first into the cave. He would have a gun, probably the same semi-automatic rifle he had been using outside. The weapon would be thrust out in front of him, pointed straight ahead, waist-high. That was the problem: dousing him before he could turn the muzzle on her and pull the trigger. Which was something he could do in — what? — maybe two seconds. Maybe one. The element of surprise was her best and only hope. He might be expecting gunfire, knives but not *this*. If she squirted him with lighter fluid the instant he appeared, he might be sufficiently startled to lose a full second of action time, might lose another second or so in shock as he smelled the fluid and realized he had been sprayed with something highly flammable. That was all the time she would need to set him afire.

She held her breath, listened.

Nothing.

Even if she didn't get any fuel on the giant's skin, only managed to douse his parka, he would almost certainly drop the rifle in horror and panic, and slap at the fire.

She took a deep breath, held it, listened again.

Still nothing.

If she was able to squirt his face, it wouldn't be panic alone that caused him to drop the gun. He would be rocked by intense pain as his skin blistered and peeled off, and fire ate into his eyes.

Smoke coiled up from her torch and fanned out along the ceiling, seeking escape from the confining rock.

At the other end of the room, Charlie, Joey, and Chewbacca waited in silence. The weary dog had slumped back on his hind-quarters.

Come on, Spivey! *Come on*, damn you.

Christine did not have unqualified faith in her ability to use the lighter fluid and the torch effectively. She figured, at best, there was only one chance in ten that she could pull it off, but she wanted them to come anyway, right now, so she could get it over with. The waiting was worse than the inevitable confrontation.

Something cracked, snapped, and Christine jumped, but it was only the fire at the other end of the room, a branch crumbling in the flames.

Come on.

She wanted to peek around the corner, into the passageway, and end this suspense. She didn't dare. She'd lose the advantage of surprise.

She thought she could hear the soft ticking of her watch. It must have been imagination, but the sound counted off the seconds, anyway: *tick, tick, tick* . . .

If she doused the big man and set him afire without getting herself shot, she would then have to handle Spivey. The old woman was sure to have a gun of her own.

Tick, tick . . .

If the hag was right behind the giant, maybe the flash of fire and all the screaming would disconcert her. The old

453

woman might be confused enough for Christine to be able to strike again with more lighter fluid.

Tick, tick . . .

The natural flue sucked away the smoke from the main fire, but the smoke from Christine's torch rose to the ceiling and formed a noxious cloud. Now the cloud was slowly settling down into the room, fouling the air they had to breathe, hitching a ride on every vagrant current but not moving away fast enough. The stink wasn't bad yet, but in a few minutes they would start choking. The caverns were so drafty that there was little chance of suffocation, though an ordeal by smoke would only further weaken them. Yet she couldn't extinguish the torch; it was her only weapon.

Something better happen soon, she thought. Damned soon.

Tick, tick, tick . . .

Distracted by the problem of the smoke and by the imaginary but nonetheless maddening sound of time slipping away, Christine almost didn't react to the *important* sound when it came. A single click, a scraping noise. It passed before Christine realized it had to be Spivey or the big man.

She waited, tense, torch raised high, the can of lighter fluid extended in front of her, fingers poised to depress and pump the sides of the container.

More scraping noises.

A soft metallic sound.

Christine leaned forward from the shallow depression in which she had taken refuge, praying her bad leg would hold up and abruptly realized the noises hadn't come from the Z-shaped passageway but from the chamber that adjoined this one, from deeper in the hillside.

She glimpsed a hooded flashlight in the next cave, the beam spearing past a stalactite. Then it winked out.

No. This wasn't possible!

She saw movement at the brink of darkness where the other cave joined this one. An incredibly tall, broad-shouldered, hideously ugly man stepped from the gloom, into the edge of the wavering firelight, twelve or fifteen feet from Christine.

Too late, she understood that Spivey was coming at them through the network of caverns rather than through the more easily defended entrance tunnel. But how? How could they know which caves led toward this one? Did they have maps of the caves? Or did they trust to luck? How could they be *that* lucky?

It was crazy.

It wasn't *fair*.

Christine lurched forward, one step, two, out of the shadows in which she had been hiding.

The giant saw her. He brought up his rifle.

She squirted the lighter fluid at him.

He was too far away. The flammable liquid arced out seven or eight feet, but then curved down and spattered onto the stone floor, two or three feet short of him.

It must have been instantly clear to him that she wouldn't be attacking with such a crude weapon unless she had no more ammunition for the gun.

'Drop it,' he said coldly.

Her great plan suddenly seemed pathetic, foolish.

Joey. He was depending on her. She was his last defense. She tottered one step closer.

'*Drop it!*'

Before he could shoot, her bad leg gave out. She collapsed.

With despair and anguish hanging heavily on the single word, Charlie said, 'Christine!'

The can of lighter fluid spun across the floor, away from her and Charlie and Joey, coming to rest in an inaccessible corner.

She landed on her wounded thigh and screamed as a hand grenade of pain went off in her leg.

Even as she was collapsing, the torch fell from her hand and landed on the trail of fluid that she had squirted at the huge, ugly man. A line of fire whooshed up, briefly filling the cave with dazzling light, then fluttered and went out, causing no harm to anyone.

Snarling, teeth bared, Chewbacca charged the big man, but the dog was too weak to be effective. He got jawsful of parka, but the giant raised the semiautomatic rifle in both hands and brought it down butt-first into the dog's skull. Chewbacca emitted a short, sharp yelp and slumped at the giant's feet, either unconscious or dead.

Christine clung to consciousness, though tides of blackness lapped at her.

Grinning like a creature out of an old Frankenstein movie, the big man advanced into the room.

Christine saw Joey backing into the corner at the far end of the cave.

She had failed him.

No! There must be something she could do, Jesus, some decisive action she could still take, something that would dramatically turn the tables, something that would save them. There *must* be something. But she couldn't think of anything.

71

The huge man stepped farther into the cave. It was the monster Charlie had met at Spivey's rectory, the giant with the twisted face. The one the hag had called Kyle.

As he watched Kyle swagger into the chamber, and as he watched Christine cower from the grotesque intruder, Charlie was filled with equal measures of fear and self-loathing. He was afraid because he knew he was going to die in this dank and lonely hole, and he loathed himself for his weakness and incompetence, and ineffective performance. His parents had been weak and ineffectual, had retreated into a haze of alcohol to console themselves for their inability to cope with life, and from the time he was very young Charlie had promised himself that he would never be like them. He had spent a lifetime learning to be strong, always strong. He *never* backed away from a challenge, largely because his parents had *always* backed away. And he seldom lost a battle. He *hated* losing, his parents were losers, not him, not Charlie Harrison of Klemet-Harrison. Losers were weak in body and mind and spirit, and weakness was the greatest sin. But he couldn't deny his current circumstances; there was no escaping the fact that he was now half paralyzed with pain, weak as a kitten, and struggling to retain consciousness. There was no dodging the truth, which was that he had brought Christine and Joey to this place and this condition with the promise that he would help them, and his promise had been empty. They needed him, and he couldn't do anything for them, and now he was going to end his life by failing those he loved, which didn't make him a lot different from his alky father and his hate-riddled, drunken mother.

A part of him knew that he was being too hard on himself. He had done his best. No one could have done more. But he was *always* too hard on himself, and he wouldn't relent now. What mattered was not what he had *meant* to do but what he had, in fact, done. And what he had done was bring them face to face with Death.

Behind Kyle, another figure moved out of the archway between this chamber and the next. A woman. For a moment she was in shadows, then revealed in the Halloween-orange light of the fire. Grace Spivey.

With effort, Charlie turned his stiff neck, blinked to clear his blurred vision, and looked at Joey. The boy was in the corner, back to the wall, hands down at his sides with his palms pressing hard against the stone behind him, as if he could will his way into the rock and out of this room. His eyes seemed to bulge. Tears glistened on his face. There was no question that he had been pulled back from the fantasy into which he had tried to escape, no doubt that his attention was now fully commanded by this world, by the chilling reality of Grace Spivey's hateful presence.

Charlie tried to raise his arms because if he could raise his arms he might be able to sit up, and if he could sit up he might be able to stand, and if he could stand he could fight. But he couldn't raise his arms, neither of them, not an inch.

Spivey paused to look down at Christine.

'Don't hurt him,' Christine said, reduced to begging. 'For God's sake, don't hurt my little boy.'

Spivey didn't reply. Instead, she turned toward Charlie and shuffled slowly across the room. In her eyes was a look of maniacal hatred and triumph.

Charlie was terrified and repelled by what he saw in those eyes, and he looked away from her. He searched frantically for something that could save them, for a weapon or a course of action they had overlooked.

He was suddenly certain that there was still a way out, that they were not doomed, after all. It wasn't just wishful thinking, and it wasn't just a fever dream. He knew his own feelings better than that; he trusted his hunches, and this one was as real and as reliable as any he'd ever had before. *There was still a way out*. But where, how, *what*?

* * *

When Christine stared into Grace Spivey's eyes, she felt as if an ice-cold hand had plunged through her chest and had seized her heart in an arctic grip. For a moment she couldn't blink her eyes, couldn't swallow, couldn't breathe, couldn't *think*. The old woman was mad, yes, a raving lunatic, but there was power in her eyes, a perverse strength, and now Christine saw how Spivey might be able to make and hold converts to her insane crusade. Then the hag turned away from her, and Christine could breathe again, and she became aware, once more, of the searing pain in her leg.

Spivey stopped in front of Charlie and stared down at him.

She's purposefully ignoring Joey, Christine thought. He's the reason she has come all this way and has risked being shot, the reason she has struggled into these mountains through two blizzards, and now she's ignoring him just to savor the moment, relish the triumph.

Christine had nurtured a black hatred for Spivey; but now it was blacker than black. It pushed everything else out of her head; for just a few seconds it drove out even her love for Joey and became all-fulfilling, consuming.

Then the madwoman turned toward Jocy, and the hatred in Christine receded as conflicting waves of love, terror, remorse, and horror swept through her.

Something else swept through her, as well: the resurging feeling that there was still something that could be done to bring Spivey and the giant to their knees, if only she could think clearly.

At last Grace came face to face with the boy.

She became aware of the dark aura that surrounded him and radiated from him, and she was much afraid, for she might be too late. Perhaps the power of the Antichrist had grown too strong, and perhaps the child was now invulnerable.

There were tears on his face. He was still pretending to be only an ordinary six-year-old, small and scared and defenseless. Did he really think that she would be deceived by his act, that he had any chance at all of instilling doubt in her at this late hour? She had had moments of doubt before, as in that motel in Soledad, but those periods of weakness had been short-lived and were all behind her now.

She took a few steps toward him. He tried to squeeze farther back into the corner, but he was already jammed so tightly into the junction of the rock walls that he almost seemed to be a boy-shaped extrusion of them.

She stopped when she was only six or eight feet from him, and she said, 'You will not inherit the earth. Not for a thousand years and not even for one minute. I have come to stop you.'

The child didn't answer.

She sensed that his powers had not yet grown too strong for her, and her confidence soared. He was still afraid of her. She had reached him in time.

She smiled. 'Did you really think you could run away from me?'

His gaze strayed past her, and she knew he was looking at the battered dog.

'Your hellhound won't help you now,' she said.

He began to shake, and he worked his mouth in an effort to speak, and she could see him form the word 'Mommy,' but he was unable to make even the slightest sound.

From a sheath attached to her belt, she withdrew a long-bladed hunting knife. It was sharply pointed and had been stropped until it was as keen as a razor.

Christine saw the knife and tried to bolt up from the floor, but the savage pain in her leg thwarted her, and she collapsed back onto the stone even as the giant was bringing the muzzle of the rifle around to cover her.

Speaking to Joey, Spivey said, 'I was chosen for this task because of the way I dedicated myself to Albert all those years, because I knew how to give myself completely, unstintingly. That's how I've dedicated myself to this holy mission — without reservation or hesitation, with every ounce of my strength and will power. There was never any chance you would escape from me.'

Desperately trying to reach Spivey, trying to touch her on an emotional level, Christine said, 'Please, listen, *please*, you're wrong, all wrong. He's just a little boy, my little boy, and I love him, and he loves me.' She was babbling, suddenly inarticulate, and she was furious with herself for being unable to find words that would convince. 'Oh God, if you could only see how sweet and loving he is, you'd know you're all confused about him. You can't take him away from me. It would be so . . .*wrong*.'

Ignoring Christine, talking to Joey, Spivey held the knife out and said, 'I've spent many hours praying over this blade. And one night I saw the spirit of one of Almighty God's angels come down from the heavens and through the window of my bedroom, and that spirit still resides here, within this consecrated instrument, and when it cuts into you, it will be not just the blade rending your flesh but the angelic spirit, as well.'

The woman was stark raving mad, and Christine knew that an appeal to logic and reason would be as hopeless as an appeal to the emotions had been, but she had to try it, anyway. With growing desperation, she said, 'Wait! Listen. You're wrong. Don't you see? Even if Joey was what you say — which he isn't, that's just crazy — but even if he *was*, even if God wanted him dead, then why wouldn't *God* destroy him? If He wanted my little boy dead, why wouldn't He strike him with lightning or cancer or let him be hit by a car? God wouldn't need *you* to deal with the Antichrist.'

461

Spivey answered Christine this time but didn't turn to face her; the old woman's gaze remained on Joey. She spoke with a fervency that was scary, her voice rising and falling like that of a tent revivalist, but with more energy than any Elmer Gantry, with a rabid excitement that turned some words into animalistic growls, and with a soaring exaltation that gave other phrases a lilting songlike quality. The effect was terrifying and hypnotic, and Christine imagined that this was the same mysterious, powerful effect that Hitler and Stalin had had on crowds.

'When evil appears to us, when we see it at work in this troubled, troubled world, we can't merely fall to our *knees* and beg God to deliver us from it. Evil and vile temptation are a *test* of our faith and virtue, a *challenge* that we must face every day of our lives, in order to prove ourselves *worthy* of salvation and ascendance into Heaven. We cannot expect *God* to remove the yoke from us, for it is a yoke that *we* put upon ourselves in the first place. It is our sacred responsibility to *confront* evil and triumph over it, *on our own*, with those resources that Almighty God has given us. *That* is how we earn a place at His right hand, in the company of *angels*.'

At last the old woman turned away from Joey and faced Christine, and her eyes were more disturbing than ever. She continued her harangue:

'And you reveal your own ignorance and your *damning* lack of faith when you attribute cancer and death and other afflictions to our *Lord*, God of Heaven and earth. It was not *He* who brought evil to the earth and afflicted mankind with ten thousand scourges. It was *Satan*, the abominable *serpent*, and it was *Eve*, in the blessed garden of peace, who brought the knowledge of *sin* and *despair* to the generations that followed. We brought evil upon ourselves, and now that the *ultimate* evil walks the earth in this child's body, it is our responsibility to deal with it ourselves. It

462

is the *test of tests*, and the hope of all mankind rests with our ability to meet it!'

The old woman's fury had left Christine speechless, devoid of hope.

Spivey turned to Joey again and said, 'I smell your putrescent heart. I feel your radiant evil. It's a coldness that cuts right into my bones and vibrates there. Oh, I know you, all right. I *know* you.'

Fighting off panic that threatened to leave her as emotionally and mentally incapacitated as she was physically helpless, Christine wracked her mind for a plan, an idea. She was willing to try anything, no matter how pointless it seemed, *anything*, but she could think of nothing.

She saw that, in spite of his condition, Charlie had pulled himself into a sitting position. Weak as he was, overwhelmed by pain, any movement must have been an ordeal for him. He wouldn't have pulled himself up without reason — would he? Maybe he had thought of the course of action which continued to elude Christine. That's what she wanted to believe. That's what she hoped with all her heart.

Spivey reversed her grip on the knife, held the handle toward the ugly giant. 'It's time, Kyle. The boy's appearance is deceptive. He looks small and weak, but he'll be strong, he'll resist, and although I am Chosen, I'm not *physically* strong, not any more. It's up to you.'

An odd expression took possession of Kyle's face. Christine expected a look of triumph, eagerness, maniacal hatred, but instead he appeared . . . not worried, not confused, but a little of both . . . and hesitant.

Spivey said, 'Kyle, it's time for you to be the hammer of God.'

Christine shuddered. She scrambled across the floor toward the giant, so frightened that she could ignore the pain in her leg. She grabbed for the hem of his parka, hoping to unbalance him, topple him, and get the gun away from him, a hopeless plan considering his size and strength, but she didn't even have a chance to try it because he swung the butt of his rifle at her, just as he'd swung it at the dog. It slammed into her shoulder, knocking her back, onto her side, and all the air was driven from her lungs. She gasped for breath and put one hand to her damaged shoulder and began to cry.

With tremendous effort, nearly blacking out from the pain, Charlie sat up because he thought he might see the situation differently from a new position and might, finally, spot a solution they had overlooked. However, he still could not think of anything that would save them.

Kyle took the knife from Grace and gave her the rifle.

The old woman stepped out of the giant's way.

Kyle turned the knife over and over in his hand, staring at it with a slightly baffled expression. The blade glinted in the goblin light of the fire.

Charlie tried to pull himself up the five-foot-high face of the ledge that formed the hearth, with the notion of grabbing a burning log and throwing it. From the corner of her eye, Spivey saw him struggling with the dead weight of his own shattered body, and she pointed the rifle at him. She might as well have saved herself the trouble; he didn't have sufficient strength to reach the fire, anyway.

Kyle Barlowe looked at the knife in his hand, then at the boy, and he wasn't sure which scared him more.

He had used knives before. He'd cut people before, even killed them. It had been easy, and he had vented some of the rage that periodically built in him like a head of steam in a boiler. But he was not the same man that he had been then. He could control his emotions now. He understood himself at last. The old Kyle had hated everyone he met, whether he knew them or not, because inevitably they rejected him. But the new Kyle realized that his hatred did more harm to him than to anyone else. In fact, he now knew that he had not always been rejected because of his ugliness, but often because of his surliness and anger. Grace had given him purpose and acceptance, and in time he had discovered affection, and after affection had come the first indications of an ability to love and be loved. And now, if he used the knife, if he killed the boy, he might be launching himself on an inevitable slide back down to the depths from which he'd climbed. He feared the knife.

But he was afraid of the boy, too. He knew Grace had psychic power, for he had seen her do things that no ordinary person could have done. Therefore, she must be right when she said the boy was the Antichrist. If he failed to kill the demonic child, he would be failing God, Grace, and all mankind.

But wasn't he being asked to throw away his soul in order to gain salvation? Kill in order to be blessed? Did that make sense?

'Please don't hurt my little boy. *Please*,' Christine Scavello said.

Kyle looked down at her, and his quandary deepened. She didn't *look* like the dark Madonna, with the power of Satan behind her. She was hurt, scared, begging for mercy. He had hurt her, and he felt a pang of guilt at the injury he'd caused.

Sensing that something was wrong, Mother Grace said, 'Kyle?'

Turning to the boy, Kyle drew his knife hand back, so he would have all the power of his muscles behind the first blow. If he took the last few steps in a crouch, swung the knife in low, rammed the blade into the boy's guts, it would all be over in a few seconds.

The child was still crying, and his bright blue eyes were

transfixed by the point of the knife in Kyle's hand. His face was twisted into a wretched mask of terror, and sweat had broken out all over his pasty skin. His small body was slightly bent as if in anticipation of the pain to come.

'Strike him!' Mother Grace urged.

Questions raced through Kyle's mind. How can God be merciful and still make me bear the burden of my monstrous face? What kind of god would let me be saved from a meaningless life of violence and pain and hatred — just to force me to kill again? If God rules the world, why does He allow so much suffering and pain and misery? And how could it be any worse if Satan ruled?

'The devil is putting doubt in your mind!' Grace said. 'That's where it's coming from, Kyle, not from within you! From the devil!'

'No,' he told her. 'You taught me to always think about doing the right thing, to *care* about doing the right thing, and now I'm going to take a minute here, just a minute to *think*!'

'Don't think, just *do*!' she said. 'Or get out of my way and let me use this gun. How can you fail me now? After all I've done, how can you fail?'

She was right. He owed her everything. He would still be peddling dope, living in the gutter, consumed by hatred, if not for her. If he failed her now, where was his honor, his gratitude? In failing her, wouldn't he be sliding back into his old life almost as surely as if he used the knife as she demanded?

'Please,' Christine Scavello said. 'Oh, God, please don't hurt my baby.'

'Send him back to Hell forever!' Grace shouted.

Kyle felt as if he were being torn apart. He had been making moral judgments and value decisions for only a few years, not long enough for it to be an unconscious habit, not long enough to deal easily with a dilemma

466

like this. He realized that tears were spilling down his cheeks

The boy's gaze rose from the point of the blade.

Kyle met the child's eyes and was jolted by them.

'Kill him,' Grace said.

Kyle was shaking violently.

The boy was shaking, too.

Their gazes had not merely locked but . . . *fused* . . . so it seemed to Kyle that he could see not only through his own eyes but through the eyes of the boy, as well. It was an almost magical empathy, as if he were both himself and the child, both assailant and victim. He felt large and dangerous . . . yet small and helpless at the same time. He was suddenly dizzy and increasingly confused. His vision swam out of focus for a moment. Then he saw — or imagined that he saw — himself looming over the child, literally saw himself from the boy's point of view, as if *he* were Joey Scavello. It was a stunning moment of insight, strange and disorienting, almost a clairvoyant experience. Looking up at himself from the boy's eyes, he was shocked by his appearance, the savagery in his own face, by the madness of this attack. A chill swept up his spine, and he could not get his breath. This unflattering vision of himself was the psychic equivalent of a blow to the head with a ball-peen hammer, psychologically concussive. He blinked, and the moment of insight passed, and he was just himself again, though with a terrible headache and a lingering dizziness. Finally, he knew what he must do.

To Christine's surprise, the giant turned away from Joey and threw the knife into the flames beyond Charlie. Sparks and embers flew up like a swarm of fireflies.

'No!' Grace Spivey shouted.

'I'm through killing,' the big man said, tears pouring copiously down his cheeks, softening the hard and dangerous look of him much as rain on a windowpane blurs and softens the view beyond.

'No,' Spivey repeated.

'It's wrong,' he said. 'Even if I'm doing it for you . . . it's wrong.'

'The devil put this thought in your mind,' the old woman warned.

'No, Mother Grace. *You* put it there.'

'The devil!' she insisted frantically. 'The devil put it there!'

The giant hesitated, blotting his face with his big hands.

Christine held her breath and watched the confrontation with both hope and dread. If this Frankensteinian creature actually turned against his master, he might be a formidable ally, but at the moment he did not seem sufficiently stable to deliver them from their crisis. Though he had thrown the knife away, he appeared confused, in a mental and emotional turmoil, and even slightly unsteady on his feet. When he put his hands to his head and squinted through his tears, he seemed in pain, almost as if he had been blackjacked. He might, at any moment, turn on Joey and kill him, after all.

'The devil put this doubt in your mind,' Grace Spivey insisted, advancing on the giant, shouting at him. 'The devil, the devil, the *devil*!'

He took his tear-wet hands from his face and blinked at the old woman. 'If it was the devil, then he's not all bad. Not all bad if he wants me never to kill again.' He staggered toward the passageway that led out of the caves, stopped just this side of it, and leaned wearily against the wall, as if he needed a moment to recover from some exhausting task.

'Then *I'll* do it,' Spivey said furiously. She had been clutching the semiautomatic rifle by its shoulder strap. Now she took it in both hands. 'You're my Judas, Kyle Barlowe.

Judas. You've failed me. But God won't fail me. And I won't fail God the way you have, no, not me, not the Chosen, not *me*!'

Christine looked at Joey. He still stood in the corner, with his back against the stone, his arms raised now, his small pale palms flattened and turned outward, as if warding off the bullets that Grace Spivey would fire at him. His eyes were huge and frightened and fixed on the old woman as though she had hypnotized him. Christine wanted to shout at him to run, but it was pointless because Spivey was in his way and would surely stop him. Besides, where could he go? Outside, in the subzero air, where he would quickly succumb to exposure? Deeper in the caves, where Spivey would easily follow and soon find him? He was trapped, small and defenseless, with nowhere to hide.

Christine looked at Charlie, who was weeping with frustration at his own inability to help, and she tried to launch herself up at Grace Spivey, but she was defeated by her wounded leg and damaged shoulder, and finally, in desperation, she looked back at Kyle and said, 'Don't let her do it! For God's sake, don't let her hurt him!'

The giant only blinked stupidly at Christine. He seemed shell-shocked, in no condition to wrest the rifle out of Spivey's hands.

'Please, please, stop her,' Christine begged him.

'*You* shut up!' Grace warned, taking one threatening step toward Christine. Then, to Joey, she said, 'And don't you try using those eyes on me. It won't work with me. You can't get at me that way, not *any* way, not me. I can resist.'

The old woman was having some difficulty figuring how to fire the gun, and when she finally got a round off, it went high, smashed into the wall above Joey's head, almost striking the ceiling, the explosive report crashing back and forth in that confined area, one deafening echo laminated atop another. The thunderous noise and the recoil surprised

Spivey, jolting her frail body. She stumbled backwards two steps, fired again without meaning to, and that second bullet *did* strike the ceiling and ricocheted around the room.

Joey was screaming.

Christine was shouting, looking for something to throw, a weapon no matter how crude, but she could find nothing. The pain in her wounded leg was like a bolt fastening her to the stone, and she could only beat her hand on the floor in frustration.

The old woman moved in on Joey, holding the rifle awkwardly though with evident determination to finish the job this time. But something was wrong. She was either out of ammunition or the gun had jammed, for she began to struggle with the weapon angrily.

As the echoes of the second shot faded, a mysterious sound arose from deeper in the mountain, adding to the confusion, rising up from other caverns, a strange and frightening racket that Christine could almost but not quite identify.

The gun *had* jammed. Spivey managed to eject an expended cartridge that had been wedged in the chamber. The brass cylinder popped into the air, reflecting the firelight, and hit the floor with a faint clink and ping.

Wicka-wicka-wicka-wicka: The strange, leathery, flapping sound drew nearer, approaching from deeper in the mountain. The cool air vibrated with it.

Spivey half turned away from Joey to look at the entrance to the adjoining cave, through which she and the giant had entered a few minutes ago. 'No!' she said, and she seemed to know what was coming.

And in that instant Christine knew, too.

Bats.

A thunderous, flapping, whirling tornado of bats.

An instant later they swarmed out of the adjoining caves

and into this room, a hundred of them, two hundred, more, rising to the vaulted ceiling, screeching, industriously working their leathery wings, darting back and forth, a seething multitude of frenziedly whirling shadows at the upper reaches of the firelight.

The old woman screamed at them. She was speaking, but her words were lost in the drumlike roar of the swarm.

As one, the bats stopped shrieking. Only the rustling fluttering-hissing of wings sounded now. Their silence was so unnatural that it seemed worse than their screams.

No, Christine thought. *Oh, no!*

In the pall of this frightening assemblage, Spivey's maniacal self-confidence shattered. She fired two rounds at the nightmare flock, a senseless and, in fact, dangerous assault.

Whether provoked by the gunfire or otherwise motivated, the bats swooped down as if they were a single creature, a cloud of tiny black killing machines, all claws and teeth, and fell upon Grace Spivey. They slashed at her insulated ski suit, got tangled in her hair, sank their claws into her and hung on. She staggered across the cave, flailing her arms and whirling about, as if performing a macabre dance, or as if she thought she could take flight with them. Squealing, gagging, retching, she collided with one wall, rebounded from it, and still the beasts clung to her, darted, nipped.

Kyle Barlowe took two tentative steps toward her, halted, looking not so much afraid as bewildered.

Christine did not want to look, but she could not help it. She was transfixed by the horrible battle.

Spivey appeared to be wearing a garment composed of hundreds of flapping black rags. Her face vanished entirely beneath that tattered cloth. But for the flutter and scrape and tick of their wings, they maintained their eerie silence, though they moved even more frantically now, with malign intent. They tore her to pieces.

72

At last the bats were still.

Spivey was motionless, too.

For perhaps a minute, the bats were a living, black funeral shroud covering the body, quivering slightly like wind-rustled cloth. By the second, their unnatural silence grew more remarkable and unnerving. They did not quite look, behave, or seem like ordinary bats. Besides the astonishing timeliness of their appearance and the purposefulness of their attack, they had a quality — an *air* that was indefinably strange. Christine saw some of the small, dark, evil heads lift up, turn left and right and left again, crimson eyes blinking, and it seemed as if they were awaiting an order from the leader of their flock. Then, as if the order came in a voice only they could hear, they rose as one, in a sudden fluttering cloud, and flew back into other caverns.

Kyle Barlowe and Charlie were silent, stunned.

Christine would not look at the dead woman.

And she could not look away from her son. He was alive — unbelievably, amazingly, miraculously alive. After all the terror and pain they had been through, after death had seemed inevitable, she had difficulty believing this last-minute reprieve was real. Irrationally, she felt that if she looked away from Joey, even for a moment, he would be dead when she looked back again, and their extraordinary salvation would prove to be a delusion, a dream.

More than anything, she wanted to hold him, touch his hair, his face, hug him tight, feel the beat of his heart and the warmth of his breath on her neck. But her injuries prevented her from going to him, and he appeared to be in a state of shock that rendered him temporarily oblivious of her.

Far away in other caves, the bats must have begun to resume their familiar perches, for they squeaked again as if contesting with one another for favored positions. The eerie sound of them, which soon faded into silence once more, sent a chill through Christine, a chill that intensified when she saw her half-mesmerized son cock his head as if in understanding of the shrill language of those nightmare creatures. He was disturbingly pale. His mouth curved into what appeared to be a vague smile, but then Christine decided it was actually a grimace of disgust or horror engendered by the scene that he had just witnessed and that had left him in this semiparalytic stupor.

As the renewed cries of the bats gradually faded, fear uncoiled in Christine, though not because of what had happened to Grace Spivey. And she was not afraid that the bats would return and kill again. In fact, somehow, she knew they would not, and it was precisely that impossible knowledge that frightened her. She did not want to consider where it came from, to ponder just *how* she knew. She did not want to think about what it might mean.

Joey was alive. Nothing else mattered. The sound of the gun had drawn the bats, and by a stroke of luck — or through God's mercy — they had limited their attack to Grace Spivey. Joey was alive. *Alive.* She felt tears of joy suddenly burning in her eyes. Joey was alive. She must concentrate on that wonderful twist of fate, for it was from here that their future began, and she was determined that it would be a bright future full of love and happiness, with no sadness, no fear, and above all no *doubts.*

Doubt could eat at you, destroy happiness, turn love to bitterness. Doubt could even come between a mother and her much-loved son, producing an unbridgeable chasm, and she simply could not allow that to happen.

Nevertheless, unbidden and unwanted, a memory came to her: Tuesday, Laguna Beach, the Arco station service bay where they had waited for Charlie after barely escaping the bomb that destroyed Miriam Rankin's house; she and Joey and the two bodyguards standing by the stacks of tires, with the world outside caught in a fierce electrical storm so powerful that it seemed to signal the end of the world; Joey moving to the open garage door, fascinated by the lightning, one devastating bolt after another, unlike anything Christine had seen before, especially in southern California where lightning was uncommon; Joey regarding it without fear, as if it were only fireworks, as if . . . as if he knew it could not harm him. As if it were a *sign*? As if the preternatural ferocity of the storm was somehow a message that he understood and took hope from?

No. Nonsense.

She had to push such stupid thoughts out of her mind. That was just the kind of craziness that could infect you merely from association with the likes of Grace Spivey. My God, the old woman had been like a plague carrier, spreading irrationality, infecting everyone with her paranoid fantasies.

But what about the bats? Why had they come at exactly the right moment? Why had they attacked only Grace Spivey?

Stop it, she told herself. You're just . . . making something out of nothing. The bats came because they were frightened by the first two shots that the old woman fired. The sound was so loud it scared them, brought them out. And then . . . when they got here . . . well, she shot at them and made them angry. Yes. Of course. That was it.

Except . . . If the first pair of shots scared the bats, why didn't the third and fourth shots scare them again? Why didn't they fly away? Why did they attack her and dispose of her so . . . *conveniently*?

474

No.

Nonsense.

Joey was staring at the floor, still anemically pale, but he was beginning to emerge from his semi-catatonic state. He was nervously chewing on one finger, very much like a little boy who knew he had done something that would upset his mother. After a few seconds, he raised his head, and his eyes met Christine's. He tried to smile through his tears, but his mouth was still soft and loose with shock, with fear. He had never looked sweeter or more in need of a mother's love, and his weakness and vulnerability gave her heart a twist.

His vision clouded by pain, weak from infection and loss of blood, Charlie wondered if everything that had happened in the cave had actually transpired only in his fevered imagination.

But the bats were real. Their bloody handiwork lay only a few feet away, undeniable.

He assured himself that the bizarre attack on Grace Spivey had a rational, natural explanation, but he was not entirely convinced by his own assurances. Maybe the bats were rabid; that might explain why they had not fled from the sound of the gun but had, instead, been drawn to it, for all rabid animals were especially sensitive to − and easily angered by − bright lights and loud noises. But why had they bitten and clawed only Grace, leaving Joey, Christine, Barlowe, and Charlie himself untouched?

He looked at Joey.

The boy had come out of his quasi-autistic trance. He had moved to Chewbacca. He was kneeling by the dog, sobbing, wanting to touch the motionless animal, but afraid, making little gestures of helplessness with his hands.

Charlie remembered when, last Monday in his office, he had looked at Joey and had seen a fleshless skull instead of a face. It had been a brief vision, lasting only the blink of an eye, and he had shoved the memory of it to the back of his mind. If he had worried about it all, it was because he thought it might mean Joey was going to die; but he hadn't really believed in visions or clairvoyant revelations, so he hadn't worried much. Now he wondered if the vision had been real. Maybe it had not meant that Joey would die; maybe it had meant that Joey *was* death.

Surely such thoughts were proof only of the seriousness of his fever. Joey was Joey — nothing more, nothing worse, nothing strange.

But Charlie remembered the rat in the battery cellar, too, and the dream he had later that same night, in which rats — messengers of death — had poured forth from the boy's chest.

This is nuts, he told himself. I've been a detective too long. I don't trust anyone any more. Now I'm looking for deception and corruption in even the most innocent hearts.

Petting the dog, Joey began to speak, the words coming in groups, in breathless rushes, between sobs: 'Mom, is he dead? Is Chewbacca dead? Did . . . that bad man . . . did he kill Chewbacca?'

Charlie looked at Christine. Her face was wet with tears, and her eyes brimmed with a new flood. She seemed temporarily speechless. Contrasting emotions fought for possession of her lovely face: horror over the bloodiness of Spivey's death, surprise at their own survival, and joy at the sight of her unharmed child.

Seeing her joy, Charlie was ashamed that he had regarded the boy with suspicion. Yet . . . he was a detective, and it was a detective's job to be suspicious.

He watched Joey closely, but he didn't detect the radiant evil of which Spivey spoke, didn't feel that he was in the presence of something monstrous. Joey was still a six-year-old boy. Still a good-looking kid with a sweet smile. Still

able to laugh and cry and worry and hope. Charlie had
seen what had happened to Grace Spivey, yet he was not
in the least afraid of Joey because, dammit, he could not
just suddenly start believing in devils, demons, and the
Antichrist. He'd always had a layman's interest in science,
and he'd been an advocate of the space program from the
time he was a kid himself; he always had believed that
logic, reason, and science – the secular equivalent of
Christianity's Holy Trinity – would one day solve all of
mankind's problems and all the mysteries of existence,
including the source and meaning of life. And science could
probably explain what had happened here, too; a biologist
or zoologist, with special knowledge of bats, would most
likely find their behavior well within the range of
normality.

As Joey continued to crouch over Chewbacca, petting
him, weeping, the dog's tail stirred, then swished across
the floor.

Joey cried, 'Mom, look! He's alive!'

Christine saw Chewbacca roll off his side, get to his feet,
shake himself. He had appeared to be dead. Now he was
not even dizzy. He pranced up onto his hind feet, put his
forepaws up on his young master's shoulders, and began
licking Joey's face.

The boy giggled, ruffled the dog's fur. 'How ya doin',
Chewbacca? Good dog. Good old Chewbacca.'

Chewbacca? Christine wondered. Or Brandy?

Brandy had been decapitated by Spivey's people, had
been buried with honors in a nice pet cemetery in Anaheim.
But if they went back to that cemetery now and opened
the grave, what would they find? Nothing? An empty
wooden box? Had Brandy been resurrected and had he
found his way to the pound just in time for Charlie and
Joey to adopt him again?

Garbage, Christine told herself angrily. Junk thought. Stupid.

But she could not get those sick thoughts out of her head, and they led to other irrational considerations.

Seven years ago . . . the man on the cruise ship . . . Lucius Under . . . Luke.

Who had he *really* been?

What had he been?

No, no, no. Impossible.

She squeezed her eyes shut and put one hand to her head. She was so tired. Exhausted. She did not have the strength to resist those fevered speculations. She felt contaminated by Spivey's craziness, dizzy, disconnected, sort of the way victims of malaria must feel.

Luke. For years she had tried to forget him; now she tried to remember. He'd been about thirty, lean, well-muscled. Blond hair streak-bleached by the sun. Clear blue eyes. A bronze tan. White, perfectly even teeth. An ingratiating smile, an easy manner. He had been a charming but not particularly original mix of sophistication and simplicity, worldliness and innocence, a smooth-talker who knew how to get what he wanted from women. She'd thought of him as a surfer, for God's sake; that's what he had seemed like, the epitome of the young California surfer.

Even with her strength draining away through her wound and leaving her increasingly light-headed, even though her exhaustion and loss of blood had put her in a feeble state of mind that left her highly susceptible to Spivey's insane accusations, she could not believe that Luke had been Satan. The devil in the guise of a surferboy? It was too banal to be believable. If Satan were real, if he wanted a son, if he wanted her to bear that son, why wouldn't he simply have come to her in the night in his real form? She could not have resisted him. Why wouldn't he have taken her forthrightly, with much flapping of his wings and lashing of his tail?

Luke had drunk beer, and he'd had a passion for potato chips. He had urinated and showered and brushed his teeth like any other human being. Sometimes his conversation had been downright tedious, dumb. Wouldn't the devil at least have been unfailingly witty?

Surely, Luke had been Luke, nothing more, nothing less.

She opened her eyes.

Joey was giggling and hugging Chewbacca, so happy. So ordinary.

Of course, she thought, the devil might take a perverse pleasure in using me, *particularly* me, to carry his child.

After all, she was a former nun. Her brother had been a priest — and a martyr. She had fallen away from her faith. She had been a virgin when she'd given herself to the man on the cruise ship. Wasn't she a perfect means by which the devil could make a mockery of the *first* virgin birth?

Madness. She hated herself for doubting her child, for giving any credence whatsoever to Spivey's babbling.

And yet . . . hadn't her whole life changed for the better as soon as she had become pregnant with the boy? She had been uncommonly healthy — no colds, no headaches — and happy and successful in business. As if she were. . . . *blessed*.

Finally satisfied that his dog was all right, Joey disentangled himself from Chewbacca and came to Christine. Rubbing at his red eyes, sniffling, he said, 'Mom, is it over? Are we going to be okay? I'm still scared.'

She didn't want to look into his eyes, but to her surprise she found nothing frightening in them, nothing to make her blood run cold.

Brandy . . . no, *Chewbacca* came to her and nuzzled her hand.

'Mommy,' Joey said, kneeling beside her, 'I'm scared. What'd they do to you? What'd they do? Are you going to die? Don't die, please, don't die, Mommy, please.'

She put a hand to his face. He was afraid, trembling. But that was better than an autistic trance.

He slid against her, and after only a moment's hesitation, she held him with her good arm. Her Joey. Her son. Her *child*. The feel of him, snuggling against her, was marvelous, indescribably wonderful. The contact was better than any medicine could have been, for it revitalized her, cleared her head, and dissipated the sick images and insane fear that were Grace Spivey's perverse legacy. Hugging her child, feeling him cling to her in need of love and assurance, she was cured of Spivey's mad contagion. This boy was the fruit of her womb, a life she had given to the world, and nothing was more precious to her than he was — and always would be.

Kyle Barlowe had slid down to the floor, his back against the wall, and had buried his face in his hands to avoid staring at Mother Grace's hideous remains. But the dog came to Kyle, nuzzled him, and Kyle looked up. The mutt licked his face; its tongue was warm, its nose cold, like the tongue and nose of any dog. It had a clownish face. How could he ever have imagined that such a dog was a hound from Hell?

'I loved her like a mother, and she changed my life, so I stayed with her even when she went wrong, went bad, even when she started . . . to do really crazy things,' Kyle said, startled by the sound of his own voice, surprised to hear himself explaining his actions to Christine Scavello and Charlie Harrison. 'She had this power. No denying that. She . . . was like in the movies . . . clairvoyant. You know? Psychic. That's how she could follow you and the boy . . . not because God was guiding her . . . and not because the boy was the son of Satan . . . but because she was just . . . clairvoyant.' This was not something he had known until he heard himself speaking it. In fact, even now, he did not seem to know what he was going to say until the words came from him 'She had visions. I guess they weren't religious like I thought. Not from God. Not really. Maybe she knew that all along. Or maybe she misunderstood. Maybe she actually believed she *was* talking with God. I don't think she meant to do bad, you know. She could've misinterpreted her visions, couldn't she? But there's a big difference between being psychic and being Joan of Arc, huh? A big difference.'

Charlie listened to Kyle Barlowe wrestle with his conscience, and he was curiously soothed by the ugly giant's deep, remorseful voice. The soothing effect was partly due to the fact that Barlowe was helping them understand these recent events in a light less fantastic than that shed by Armageddon; he was showing them how it might be paranormal without being supernatural or cataclysmic. But Charlie was also affected and relaxed by the odd, soft, rumbling tones and cadences of the big man's voice, by a slight smokiness in the air, and by some indefinable quality of light or heat that made him receptive to this message, as a hypnotist's subject is receptive to suggestions of all kinds.

Kyle said, 'Mother Grace meant well. She just got confused there towards the end. Confused. And, God help me, I went along with her even though I had my doubts. Almost went too far. Almost . . . God help me . . . almost used the knife on that little boy. See, what it is . . . I think maybe your Joey . . . maybe he has a little psychic ability of his own. You know? Have you ever noticed it? Any indications? I think he must be a little like Mother Grace herself, a little bit clairvoyant or something, even if he doesn't know it, even if the power hasn't become obvious yet . . . and *that* was what she sensed in him . . . but she misunderstood it. That must be it. That must explain it. Poor Grace. Poor sweet Grace. She meant well. Can you believe that? She meant well, and so did I, and so did everyone in the church. She meant well.'

Chewbacca left Kyle and came to Charlie, and he let the dog nuzzle him affectionately. He noticed blood in its ears, and blood matting the fur *on* its ears, which meant Barlowe had hit it very hard with the butt of the rifle, terribly hard indeed, and yet it seemed completely recovered. Surely it had suffered a severe concussion. Yet it was not dizzy or disoriented.

The dog looked into his eyes.

Charlie frowned.

'She meant well. She meant well,' Kyle said, and he put his face in his hands and began to cry.

Cuddling with his mother, Joey said, 'Mommy, he scares me. What's he talkin' about? He scares me.'

'It's all right,' Christine said.

'He scares me.'

'It's okay, Skipper.'

To Charlie's surprise, Christine found the strength to sit up and hitch back a couple of feet, until she was leaning against the wall. She had seemed too exhausted to move, even to speak. Her face looked better, too, not quite so pale.

Still sniffling, wiping at his nose with his sleeve, wiping his eyes with one small fist, Joey said, 'Charlie? You okay?'

Although Spivey and her people no longer posed any threat, Charlie was still quite certain that he would die in this cave. He was in bad shape, and it would be hours yet before help could be summoned and could reach them. He would not last that long. Yet he tried to smile at Joey, and in a voice so weak it frightened him, he said, 'I'm okay.'

The boy left his mother and came to Charlie. He said, 'Magnum couldn't've done better than you did.'

Joey sat down beside Charlie and put a hand on him. Charlie flinched, but it was all right, perfectly all right, and then for a couple of minutes he lost consciousness, or perhaps he merely dropped off to sleep. When Charlie came to, Joey was with his mother again, and Kyle Barlowe seemed to be getting ready to leave. 'What's wrong?' Charlie asked. 'What's happening now?'

Christine was obviously relieved to see him conscious once more. She said, 'There's no way you and I can make it out of here on our feet. We'll have to be carried in litters. Mr. Barlowe is going for help.'

Barlowe smiled reassuringly. It was a ghastly expression on his cruelly formed face. 'The snow's stopped falling, and there's no wind. If I stay to the forest trails, I should be able to make it down to civilization in a few hours. Maybe I can get a mountain rescue back here before nightfall. I'm sure I can.'

'Are you taking Joey with you?' Charlie asked. He noticed that his voice was stronger than before; speaking did not require as much effort as it had done a few minutes ago. 'Are you getting him out?'

'No,' Christine said. 'Joey's staying with us.'

'I'll move faster without him,' Barlowe said. 'Besides, the two of you need him to put wood on the fire every now and then.'

Joey said, 'I'll take care of them, Mr. Barlowe. You can count on me. Chewbacca and me.'

The dog barked softly, once, as if in affirmation of the boy's pledge.

Barlowe favored the boy with another malformed smile, and Joey grinned at him in turn. Joey had accepted the giant's conversion with considerably greater alacrity than

Charlie had, and his trust seemed to be reciprocated and well placed.

Barlowe left them.

They sat in silence for a moment.

They did not even glance at Grace Spivey's corpse, as if it were only another formation of stone.

Clenching his teeth, preparing for an agonizing and most likely fruitless ordeal, Charlie tried pulling himself up into a sitting position. Although he had possessed insufficient strength to do it before, he now found the task remarkably easy. The pain from the bullet wound in his shoulder had dramatically subsided, much to his surprise, and was now only a dull ache which he could endure with little trouble. His other injuries provided a measure of discomfort, but were not bothersome or sapping of his energy as they had been. He felt somewhat . . . revitalized . . . and he knew that he would be able to hold onto life until the rescue team had arrived and had gotten them off the mountain to hospital.

He wondered if he felt better because of Joey. The boy had come to him, had laid a hand on him, and he had slept for a couple of minutes, and when he had regained consciousness he was . . . partially healed. Was that one of the child's powers? If so, it was an imperfect power, for Charlie had not been entirely or even mostly healed; the bullet wound had not knitted up; his bruises and lacerations had not faded; he felt only a little bit better. The very imperfection of the healing power − *if* it existed at all − seemed to argue for the psychic explanation that Barlowe had offered them. The inadequacy of it indicated that it was a power of which Joey was unaware, a paranormal ability expressed in an entirely unconscious manner. Which meant he was just a little boy with a special gift. Because if he was the Antichrist, he would possess unlimited and miraculous power, and he would quickly and

entirely heal both his mother and Charlie. Wouldn't he?
Sure he would.

Chewbacca returned to Charlie.

There was still blood crusted in the dog's ears.

Charlie stared into its eyes.

He petted it.

The bullet wound in Christine's leg had stopped bleeding,
and the pain had drained out of it. She felt clear-headed.
With each passing minute she developed a greater
appreciation of their survival, which was (she now saw)
a tribute — *not* to the intervention of supernatural forces,
but — to their incredible determination and endurance.
Confidence returned to her, and she began to believe, once
more, in the future.

For a few minutes, when she had been bleeding and
helpless, when Spivey had been looming over Joey,
Christine had surrendered to an uncharacteristic despair.
She had been in such a black mood that, when the angry
bats had responded to the gunfire and had attacked Spivey,
Christine had even briefly wondered if Joey was, after all,
what Spivey had accused him of being. Good heavens!
Now, with Barlowe on his way for help, with the worst
of her pain gone, with a growing belief in the likelihood
of her and Charlie's survival, watching Joey as he
fumblingly added a few branches to the fire, she could not
imagine how such dark and foolish fears could have seized
her. She had been so exhausted and weak and so
despondent that she had been susceptible to Spivey's insane
message. Though that moment of hysteria was past and
equilibrium restored, she was chilled by the realization that
even *she* had been, however briefly, fertile ground for
Spivey's lunacy.

How easily it could happen: one lunatic spreads her
delusions to the gullible, and soon there is a hysterical mob,

or in this case a cult, believing itself to be driven by the
best intentions and, therefore, armored against doubt by
steely self-righteousness. *There* was evil, she realized: not
in her little boy but in mankind's fatal attraction to easy,
even if irrational, answers.

From across the room, Charlie said, 'You trust
Barlowe?'

'I think so,' Christine said.

'He could have another change of heart on the way
down.'

'I think he'll send help,' she said.

'If he changes his mind about Joey, he wouldn't even
have to come back. He could just leave us here, let cold
and hunger do the job for him.'

'He'll come back, I bet,' Joey said, dusting his small
hands together after adding the branches to the fire. 'I
think he's one of the good guys, after all. Don't you,
Mom? Don't you think he's one of the good guys?'

'Yeah,' Christine said. She smiled. 'He's one of the good
guys, honey.'

'Like us,' Joey said.

'Like us,' she said.

Hours later, but well before nightfall, they heard the
helicopter.

'The chopper will have skis on it,' Charlie said. 'They'll
land in the meadow, and the rescue team will walk in from
there.'

'We're going home?' Joey asked.

Christine was crying with relief and happiness. 'We're
going home, honey. You better get your jacket and gloves,
start getting dressed.'

The boy ran to the pile of insulated sportswear in the
corner.

To Charlie, Christine said, 'Thank you.'

486

'I failed you,' he said.

'No. We had a bit of luck there at the end . . . Barlowe's indecision, and then the bats. But we wouldn't have gotten that far if it hadn't been for you. You were great. I love you, Charlie.'

He hesitated to reply in kind, for any embrace of her was also an embrace of the boy; there was no escaping that. And he was not entirely comfortable with the boy, even though he was trying hard to believe that Barlowe's explanation was the right one.

Joey went to Christine, frowning. The drawstring on his hood was too loose, and he could not undo the clumsy knot he had put it in. 'Mommy, why'd they have to put a *shoe*lace under my chin like this?'

Smiling, Christine helped him. 'I thought you were getting really good at tying shoelaces.'

'I am,' the boy said proudly. 'But they gotta be on my *feet*.'

'Well, I'm afraid we can't think of you as a big boy until you're able to tie a shoelace no matter *where* they put it.'

'Jeez. Then I guess I'll never be a big boy.'

Christine finished retying the hood string. 'Oh, you'll get there one day, honey.'

Charlie watched as she hugged her son. He sighed. He shook his head. He cleared his throat. He said, 'I love you, too, Christine. I really do.'

Two days later, in the hospital in Reno, after enduring the attention of uncountable doctors and nurses, after several interviews with the police and one with a representative of the press, after long phone conversations with Henry Rankin, after two nights of much-needed drug-induced sleep, Charlie was left to find unassisted rest on the third night. He had no difficulty getting to sleep, but he dreamed.

He dreamed of making love to Christine, and it was not a fantasy of sex but more a memory of their lovemaking at the cabin. He had never given himself so completely as he had to her that night, and the next day she had gone out of her way to tell him that she had done things with him that she had never contemplated doing with another man. Now, in the dream, they coupled with that same startling fervor and energy, casting aside all inhibitions. But in the dream, as it had been in reality, there was also something . . . *savage* about it, something fierce and animalistic, as if the sex they shared were more than an expression of love or lust, as if it were a . . . ceremony, a bonding, which was somehow committing him totally to Christine and, therefore, to Joey as well. As Christine straddled him, as he thrust like a bull deep within her, the floor under them began to split open and here the dream departed from reality and the couch began to slip into a widening aperture, and although both he and Christine recognized the danger, they could not do anything about it, could not cease their rutting even to save themselves, but continued to press flesh to flesh as the crack in the floor grew ever wider, as they became aware of something in the darkness below, something that was *hungry* for them, and Charlie wanted to pull away from her, flee, wanted to scream, but could not, could only cling to her and thrust within her, as the couch collapsed through the yawning hole, the cabin floor vanishing above them. And they fell away into –

He sat up in the hospital bed, gasping. The patient in the other bed grunted softly but did not rouse from his deep sleep.

The room was dark except for a small light at the foot of each bed and a vague moonglow at the window.

Charlie leaned back against the headboard.

488

Gradually, his rapid heartbeat and frantic breathing subsided.

He was damp with sweat.

The dream had brought back all his doubts about Joey. Val Gardner had flown up from Orange County and had taken Joey home with her this afternoon, and Charlie had been genuinely sorry to see the kid go. The boy had been so cute, so full of good humor and unconsciously amusing banter, that the hospital staff had taken him to their hearts, and his frequent visits had made the time pass more quickly and agreeably for Charlie. But now, courtesy of his nightmare, which was courtesy of his subconscious, he was in an emotional turmoil again.

Charlie had always thought of himself as a good man, a man who always did the right thing, who tried to help the innocent and punish the guilty. That was why he had wanted to spend his life playing Mr. Private Investigator. Sam Spade, Philip Marlowe, Lew Archer, Charlie Harrison: moral men, admirable men, maybe even heroes. So. So what if? What if *Joey* had called forth those bats? What if Chewbacca was Brandy, dead twice and resurrected by his master both times? What if Joey was less the unaware psychic that Barlowe believed and more the . . . more the demon that Spivey claimed? Crazy. But what if? What was a good man supposed to do in such a case? What was the right course of action?

Weeks later, on a Sunday evening in April, Charlie went to the pet cemetery where Brandy had been buried. He arrived after closing time, well after dark, and he took a pick and shovel with him.

The small grave with its little marker was right at the top of a knoll, where Christine had said it was, between two Indian laurels, where the grass looked silver in the light of a three-quarter moon.

BRANDY
BELOVED DOG
PET AND FRIEND

Charlie stood beside the plot staring down at it, not really wanting to proceed, but aware that he had no choice. He would not be at peace until he knew the truth.

The night-mantled graveyard full of eternally slumbering cats, dogs, hamsters, parrots, rabbits, and guinea pigs was preternaturally silent. The mild breeze was cool. The branches of the trees stirred slightly, but with only an infrequent rustle.

Reluctantly, he stripped off his lightweight jacket, put his flashlight aside, and set to work. The bullet wound in his shoulder had healed well, more quickly than the doctors had expected, but he was not yet back in shape, and his muscles began to ache from his labor. Suddenly his spade produced a hollow *thunk-clonk* when it struck the lid of a solidly made though unfinished and unadorned pine box, a little more than two feet below ground. A few minutes later he had bared the entire coffin; in the moonlight it was visible as a pale, undetailed rectangle surrounded by black earth.

Charlie knew that the cemetery offered two basic methods of burial: with or without coffin. In either case, the animal was wrapped in cloth and tucked into a zipped canvas bag. Evidently, Christine and Joey had opted for the full treatment, and one of those zipped bags now lay within this box.

But did the bag contain Brandy's remains or was it empty?

He perceived no stench of decomposition, but that was to be expected if the canvas sack was moisture-proof and tightly sealed.

He sat at the edge of the grave for a moment, pretending that he needed to catch his breath. Actually, he was just delaying. He dreaded opening the dog's casket, not because he was sickened by the thought of uncovering a maggot-riddled golden retriever but because he was sickened by the thought of *not* uncovering one.

Maybe he should stop right now, fill the grave, and go away. Maybe it did not matter *what* Joey Scavello was.

After all, there were those theologians who argued that the devil, being a fallen angel and therefore inherently good, was not evil in any degree but merely *different* from God.

He suddenly remembered something that he had read in college, a line from Samuel Butler, a favorite of his: *An apology for the devil — it must be remembered that we have heard only one side of the case. God has written all the books.*

The night smelled of damp earth.

The moon watched.

At last he pried the lid off the small casket.

Inside was a zipped sack. Hesitantly, he stretched out on the ground beside the grave, reached down into it, and put his hands on the bag. He played a macabre game of blindman's buff, exploring the contours of the thing within, and gradually convinced himself that it was the corpse of a dog about the size of a full-grown golden retriever.

All right. This was enough. Here was the proof he had needed. God knows *why* he had thought he needed it, but here it was. He had felt that he was being . . . *commanded* to discover the truth; he had not been driven only by curiosity, but by an obsessive compulsion that seemed to come from outside of him, a motivating urge that some might have said was the hand of God pushing him along, but which he preferred not to analyze or define. The past few weeks had been shaped by that urge, by an inner voice compelling him to make a journey to the pet cemetery. At last he had succumbed, had committed himself to this silly scheme, and what he had found was not proof of a hell-born plot but, instead, merely evidence of his own foolishness. Although there was no one in the pet cemetery to see him, he flushed with embarrassment. Brandy had not come back from the grave. Chewbacca was an altogether different dog. It had been stupid to suspect otherwise. This was sufficient evidence of Joey's innocence; there was no point in opening the bag and forcing himself to confront the disgusting remains.

He wondered what he would have done if the grave had been empty. Would he then have had to kill the boy, destroy the Antichrist, save the world from Armageddon? What utter balderdash. He could not have done any such thing, not even if God had appeared to him in flowing white robes, with a beard of fire, and with the death order written on tablets of stone. His own parents had been child-beaters, child-abusers, and he the victim. That was the one crime that most outraged him — a crime against a child. Even if the grave had been empty, even if that emptiness had convinced him that Spivey was right about Joey, Charlie could not have gone after the boy. He could not outdo his own sick parents by *killing* a child. For a while, maybe, he would be able to live with the deed because he would feel sure that Joey was *more* than just a little boy, was in fact an evil being. But as time went on, doubts would arise. He would begin to think that he had imagined the inexplicable behavior of the bats, and the empty grave would have less significance, and all the other signs and portents would seem to have been self-delusion. He would begin to tell himself that Joey wasn't demonic, only gifted, not possessed of supernatural powers but merely psychic abilities. He would inevitably determine that he had killed nothing evil, that he had destroyed a special but altogether innocent child. And then, at least for him, Hell on earth would be reality, anyway.

He lay face-down on the cool, damp ground.

He stared into the dog's grave.

The canvas-wrapped lump was framed by the pale pine boards. It was a perfectly black bundle that might have contained anything, but which his hands told him contained a dog, so there was no need to open it, no need whatsoever.

The tab of the bag's zipper was caught in a moonbeam. Its silvery glint was like a single, cold, staring eye.

Even if he opened the bag and found only rocks, or even if he found something worse, something unimaginably horrible that was proof positive of Joey's sulphurous origins, he could not act as God's avenger. What allegiance did he owe to a god who allowed so much suffering in the world to begin with? What of his own suffering as a child, the terrible loneliness and the beatings and the constant fear he had endured? Where had God been then? Could life be all that much worse just because there had been a change in the divine monarchy?

He remembered Denton Boothe's mechanical coin bank: *There is No Justice in a Jackass Universe*.

Maybe a change would bring justice.

But, of course, he did not believe the world was ruled by either God or the devil, anyway. He did not *believe* in divine monarchies.

Which made his presence here even more ridiculous.

The zipper tab glinted.

He rolled onto his back so he'd be unable to see the zipper shine.

He got to his feet, picked up the coffin lid. He would put it in place and fill in the grave and go home and be sensible about this situation.

He hesitated.

Damn.

Cursing his own compulsion, he put the lid down. He

reached into the grave, instead, and heaved out the bag. He ran the zipper the length of the sack, and it made an insectlike sound.

He was shaking.

He peeled back the burial cloth.

He switched on his flashlight, gasped.

What the hell – ?

With a trembling hand, he directed the flashlight beam at the small headstone and, in the quaverous light, read the inscription again, then threw the light on the contents of the bag once more. For a moment he did not know what to make of his discovery, but gradually the mists of confusion cleared, and he turned away from the grave, away from the decomposing corpse that produced a vile stench, and he stifled the urge to be thoroughly sick.

When the nausea subsided, he began to shake, but with laughter rather than fear. He stood there in the still of the night, on a knoll in a pet cemetery, a grown man who had been in the fanciful grip of a childish superstition, feeling like the butt of a cosmic joke, a good joke, one that tickled the hell out of him even though it made him feel like a prime jackass. The dog in Brandy's grave was an Irish setter, not a golden retriever, not Brandy at all, which meant the people in charge of this place had screwed up royally, had buried Brandy in the wrong grave and had unknowingly planted the setter in *this* hole. One canvas-wrapped dog is like another, and the undertaker's mixup seemed not only understandable but inevitable. If the mortician was careless or if, more likely, he nipped at the bottle now and then, the odds were high that a lot of dogs in the graveyard were buried under the wrong markers. After all, burying the family dog was not exactly as serious a matter as burying Grandma or Aunt Emma; the precautions were not quite as meticulous. Not quite! To locate Brandy's true resting place, he would have to track down the identity of the setter and rob a second grave, and as he looked out at the hundreds upon hundreds of low markers, he knew it was an impossible task. Besides, it did not matter. The pet mortician's screw-up was like a dash of cold water in the face; it brought Charlie to his senses. He suddenly saw himself as a parody of the hero in one of those old E.C. Horror Comics, haunting a cemetery in pursuit of . . . Of what? Dracula Dog? He laughed so hard that he had to sit down before he fell down.

They said the Lord worked in mysterious ways, so maybe the devil worked in mysterious ways, too, but Charlie simply could not believe that the devil was *so* mysterious, so subtle, so elaborately devious, so downright *silly* as to muddy the trail to Brandy's grave by causing a mixup in a pet cemetery's mortuary. A devil like that might try to buy a man's soul by offering him a fortune in baseball trading cards, and such a demon was not to be taken seriously.

How and why *had* he taken this so seriously. Had Grace Spivey's religious mania been like a contagion? Had he picked up a mild case of end-of-the-world fever?

His laughter had a purging effect, and by the time it had run its course, he felt better than he had in weeks.

He used the blade of the shovel to push the dead dog and the canvas bag back into the grave. He threw the lid of the coffin on top of it, shoveled the hole full of dirt, tamped it down, wiped the shovel blade clean in the grass, and returned to his car.

He had not found what he expected, and perhaps he had not even found the truth, but he had more or less found what he had *hoped* to find — a way out, an acceptable answer, something he could live with, absolution.

Early May in Las Vegas was a pleasant time, with the fierce heat of summer still to come, but with the chill winter nights gone for another year. The warm dry air blew away whatever memories still lingered of the nightmare chase in the High Sierras.

On the first Wednesday morning of the month, Charlie and Christine were to be married in a gloriously gaudy, hilariously tasteless nonsectarian wedding chapel next door to a casino, which vastly amused both of them. They did not see their wedding as a solemn occasion, but as the beginning of a joyous adventure that was best begun with laughter, rather than with pomp and circumstance. Besides, once they made up their minds to marry, they were suddenly in a frenzy to get it done, and no place but Vegas, with its liberal marriage laws, could meet their timetable.

They came into Vegas the night before and took a small suite at Bally's Grand, and within a few hours the city seemed to be sending them omens that indicated a happy future together. On their way to dinner, Christine put four quarters into a slot machine, and although it was the first time she had ever played one, she pulled off a thousand dollar jackpot. Later, they played a little blackjack, and they won nearly another thousand apiece. In the morning, exiting the coffee shop after a superb breakfast, Joey found a silver dollar that someone had dropped, and as far as he was concerned his good fortune far exceeded that of his mother and Charlie: 'A whole *dollar*!'

They had brought Joey with them because Christine could not bear to leave him. Their recent ordeal, the near loss of the boy, still weighed heavily on her, and when he was out of her sight for more than a couple of hours, she grew nervous. 'In time,' she told Charlie, 'I'll be able to relax a bit more. But not yet. In time, we'll be able to go away together by ourselves, just the two of us, and leave Joey with Val. I promise. But not yet. Not quite yet. So if you want to marry me, you're going to have to take my son along on the honeymoon. How's *that* for romance?'

Charlie didn't mind. He liked the boy. Joey was a good companion, well-behaved, inquisitive, bright, and affectionate.

Joey served as best man at the ceremony and was delighted with his role. He guarded the ring with stern-faced solemnity and, at the proper moment, gave it to Charlie with a grin so wide and warm it threatened to melt the gold in which the diamond was set.

When it was official, when they had left the chapel to the recorded strains of Wayne Newton singing 'Joy to the World,' they decided to forgo the complimentary limousine and walk back to the hotel. The day was warm, blue, clear (but for a few scattered white clouds), and beautiful, even with the honky-tonk of Las Vegas Boulevard crowding close on both sides.

'What about the wedding lunch?' Joey demanded as they walked.

'You just had breakfast two hours ago,' Charlie said.

'I'm a growin' boy.'

'True.'

'What sounds like a good wedding lunch to you?' Christine asked.

Joey thought about that for a few steps, then said, 'Big Macs and Baskin-Robbins!'

'You know what happens to you when you eat too many Big Macs?' Christine said.

'What?' the boy asked.

'You grow up to look like Ronald McDonald.'

'That's right,' Charlie said. 'Big red nose, funny orange hair, and big red lips.'

Joey giggled. 'Gee, I wish Chewbacca was here.'

'I'm sure Val's taking good care of him, honey.'

'Yeah, but he's missing all the jokes.'

They strolled along the sidewalk, Joey between them, and even at this hour a few of the big signs and marquees were flashing.

'Will I grow up with big funny clown's feet, too?' Joey asked.

'Absolutely,' Charlie said. 'Size twenty-eight.'

'Which will make it impossible to drive a car,' Christine said.

'Or dance,' Charlie said.

'I don't want to dance,' Joey said. 'I don't like *girls*.'

'Oh, in a few years, you'll like them,' Christine said.

Joey frowned. 'That's what Chewbacca says, but I just don't believe it.'

'Oh, so Chewbacca talks, does he?' Christine teased.

'Well . . .'

'And he's an authority on girls, yet!'

'Well, okay, if you want to make a big deal of it,' Joey said, 'I gotta admit I just *pretend* he talks.'

Charlie laughed and winked at his new wife over their son's head.

Joey said, 'Hey, if I eat too many Big Macs, will I grow up with big funny clown *hands* too?'

'Yep,' Charlie said. 'So you won't be able to tie your own shoes.'

'Or pick your nose,' Christine said.

'I don't pick my nose anyway,' the boy said indignantly. 'You know what Val told me about picking my nose?'

'No. What did Val tell you?' Christine asked, and Charlie could see she was a little afraid of the answer because the boy was always learning the wrong kind of language from Val.

Joey squinted in the desert sun, as if struggling to remember exactly what Val had said. Then: 'She told me the only people who pick their noses are bums, Looney Tunes, IRS agents, and her ex-husband.'

Charlie and Christine glanced at each other and laughed. It was so good to laugh.

Joey said, 'Hey, if you guys wanta be, you know . . . ummm . . . alone . . . then you can leave me in the hotel playroom. I don't mind. It looks great in there. They got all kinds of neat games and stuff. Hey, maybe you guys want to play some more cards or them slot machines where Mom made money last night.'

'I think we'll probably quit gambling while we're ahead, honey.'

'Oh,' the boy said, 'I think you should play, Mom! You'll win, I bet. You'll win a lot more. Really. I know you will. I just *know* you will.'

The sun came out from behind one of the scattered white clouds, and its light fell full-strength across the pavement, sparkled on the chrome and glass of the passing cars, made the plush hotels and casinos look brighter and cleaner than they really were, and made the air itself shimmer fantastically.

It ended in sunshine, not on a dark and stormy night.

A selection of bestsellers from Headline

FICTION

BLOOD STOCK	John Francome & James MacGregor	£3.99 □
THE OLD SILENT	Martha Grimes	£4.50 □
ALL THAT GLITTERS	Katherine Stone	£4.50 □
A FAMILY MATTER	Nigel Rees	£4.50 □
EGYPT GREEN	Christopher Hyde	£4.50 □

NON-FICTION

MY MOUNTBATTEN YEARS	William Evans	£4.50 □
WICKED LADY Salvador Dali's Muse	Tim McGirk	£4.99 □
THE FOOD OF SPAIN AND PORTUGAL	Elisabeth Lambert Ortiz	£5.99 □

SCIENCE FICTION AND FANTASY

REVENGE OF THE FLUFFY BUNNIES Cineverse Cycle Book 3	Craig Shaw Gardner	£3.50 □
BROTHERS IN ARMS	Lois McMaster Bujold	£4.50 □
THE SEA SWORD	Adrienne Martine-Barnes	£3.50 □
NO HAVEN FOR THE GUILTY	Simon Green	£3.50 □
GREENBRIAR QUEEN	Sheila Gilluly	£4.50 □

All Headline books are available at your local bookshop or newsagent, or can be ordered direct from the publisher. Just tick the titles you want and fill in the form below. Prices and availability subject to change without notice.

Headline Book Publishing PLC, Cash Sales Department, PO Box 11, Falmouth, Cornwall, TR10 9EN, England.

Please enclose a cheque or postal order to the value of the cover price and allow the following for postage and packing:
UK: 80p for the first book and 20p for each additional book ordered up to a maximum charge of £2.00
BFPO: 80p for the first book and 20p for each additional book
OVERSEAS & EIRE: £1.50 for the first book, £1.00 for the second book and 30p for each subsequent book.

Name ....

Address ....

....

....